Flight
of the
Scions

Flight
of the
Scions

D. Moonfire

Broken Typewriter Press · Cedar Rapids

Cover art by D. Moonfire

All characters, events, and locations are fictitious. Any resemblance to persons, past, present, and future is coincidental and highly unlikely.

Some scenes and themes that appear in this book: animal injuries, birth control, death of named characters, drugs, forced mental intrusion, kidnapping, nudity, parental abandonment, questioning sexuality, racism, swearing, and verbal abuse. There is intimacy but no sex. There is no rape.

Broken Typewriter Press
5001 1st Ave SE
Ste 105 #243
Cedar Rapids, IA 52402

Broken Typewriter Press
https://broken.typewriter.press/

ISBN 978-1-940509-33-4

Version 1.0.3

To Mickey Zucker Reichert for the words I needed to hear.

To all the people who've inspired me at WisCon.

To Ms. Buczinksky, Ms. Palmer, Ms. Ross, and the rest of the Writing Works at Prospect High School in Mount Prospect, Illinois. Without them encouraging me to write while suffering through my teenage prose, I would have never kept writing.

Miwāfu

This novel has characters who come from the Mifuno Desert where the native language is Miwāfu. Names in this language are significantly different from English, so here is a short guide on pronunciation and usage.

The biggest difference is that every name is gendered, which is identified by the accent on the penultimate syllable. There are three types of accents:

- *Grave* (as in hèru for stallion) is a tiny tick that goes down to the right. The grave accent indicates a masculine aspect, either in physical gender, size, or power. Names with grave accents either end in a lower pitch or the entire word is spoken in a lower tone.
- *Macron* (for example, hēru for colt) is a bar over the vowel. This is a neuter term, used for many gender-free words or expressions within the language. It is also used for mechanical devices, abstract concepts, and children—both human and beast. Macrons are

spoken as a long vowel or drawing out the word just a beat longer than normal.

- *Acute* (héru for mare) is a tiny tick that goes to the upper right. The acute indicates feminine aspects of the word. It can represent control without power or precision. These words end on a high note or the entire word is spoken in a higher pitch.

The only instances where accents aren't used is adjectives or indication of ownership. So, if a valley is owned by the clan Shimusògo, it is known as Shimusogo Valley.

The names themselves are phonetic. A syllable is always from a consonant cluster to the vowel. For examples: Mi.wā.fu (IPA /mi.waː.ɸɰ̥/), Shi.mu.sò.go (/ɕi.mɯ.ˈso.go/), and De.sò.chu (/de.ˈso.tɕɰ̥/). The only exception is the letter "n" which is considered part of the syllable before it when not followed by a vowel. For example, ga.n.ré.ko (/ga.ŋˈre.ko/) and ka.né.ko (/ka.ˈne.ko/).

Miwāfu has no capital letters, they are added to satisfy English conventions.

Lorban

This novel is set in the Kormar countryside where the native language is Lorban. This is notionally translated into English, but there are certain quirks of the language that stand being called out.

- Lorban is roughly based on a casual form of Lojban.
- Names rarely start or end with vowels and native speakers have trouble with Miwāfu vowel endings.
- Lorban is accentless which causes trouble with Miwāfu array of tones.
- The letter "c" is soft and always pronounced as "sh" in "shape."

Lorban has no capital letters, they are added to satisfy English conventions.

------------------ Chapter 1 ------------------

The Letter

In ninety-five out of a hundred people, the first magical manifestation
of power happens by the age of thirteen.
—*Emerging Wizardry* (Volume 91, Issue 6)

Kanéko had seen the expression on the new postal carrier's
face before. It was the same look of surprise and disgust almost every stranger revealed in the seconds after first meeting her. When her father was present, adults would have
the civility to at least mask their expressions once they regained control of their senses. When it was just her, adults
rarely bothered hiding their true feelings.

Lowering her gaze, she hid her hand behind her back in
attempt to make herself smaller. She knew the gesture
wouldn't erase the sight of her dark skin or green eyes, but
there wasn't anything else she could do. Her mother said
Kanéko was the color of farming soil mixed with desert
rust. In a land of pale-skinned folk, there was no hiding
that heritage.

"Back off," snapped the courier. He clutched the bundle
of letters tight to his chest.

Kanéko glanced at the papers and envelopes in his arms. The top one held the seal of the Royal Academy of Knights. Her heart beat faster. She had been waiting weeks for it to arrive and she couldn't wait to read it. Despite the courier's expression, she decided to try again. "I-I can take them. It's okay. I'm Bartim Lurkuklan's daughter."

His lip curled further, and she could see his teeth. It reminded her of when one of her father's dog had gotten sick and snapped at everyone. He stepped back and lowered one hand to his sword.

Seeing it, a twinge ran down her back as she took a step back.

A few letters spilled out and fluttered to the ground. "Back off," he repeated before looking around.

Kanéko glanced over her shoulder to look for someone to prove her own legitimacy. The nearest building, Jinmel's smithy, was empty. Next to it, the village's only store was shut tight. The half-dozen houses lining the road leading up to the gate were also quiet. Everyone would be at lunch in the great hall. The gate itself had one of its two doors propped open with an old cart. Missing wheels and waist-high grass were both a silent statement of how long it had been since someone had last closed the heavy doors.

She gestured toward the keep. The copper embroidery on her sleeve matched her hair and sparkled in the sun. "Come on, I'll take you to my father."

The postal carrier stepped back. His sword inched out of its sheath. "I said back away, sandy! And go back to shit-hole of a desert you came from!"

Kanéko cringed at his words. She had learned years ago, it would be pointless to tell him she was only desert on her mother's side. He wouldn't believe that she had never left her father's lands, much less had never seen the vast Mifuno Desert. Nothing would change his mind; she could only hope he would listen if she remained polite.

"Please," she said as calmly as she could. "I'll take you to the others."

The carrier yanked his sword clear of the sheath with a scrape of metal. It was a short sword. Plain, but serviceable. On the hilt, she could see the crest of Kormar underneath his palm. He stepped back and waved the blade menacingly at her. "I said back!"

She cringed, worried that he would lunge forward and cut her.

"What is going on?" asked Jinmel as he came around from the back of his smithy.

At the sight of the older man with gray, frizzy hair, both Kanéko and the carrier let out sighs of relief.

"This thief," the postal carrier gestured at Kanéko with his sword tip, "tried to steal the mail."

Kanéko flinched again, her eyes locked on the tip of the weapon.

Jinmel smiled broadly at the courier. "You're new, aren't you?" His voice was tense. It didn't match his smile. His wrinkled hand tightened around the haft of a short hammer in his palm.

"Yes, so? Who are you?"

"Jinmel Sandor. That's my smithy right behind you." He pointed to the anvil which had his name embossed on it. Then, he held out his free hand for the mail.

The postal carrier chuckled as he handed the bundle of letters to Jinmel and then glared at Kanéko. "Sorry. I've never had someone try to rob me before."

Kanéko tore her eyes away from the sword and followed the topmost envelope as it passed between their hands. The man's insult stung, but she wanted the letter more.

"You haven't been robbed," muttered Jinmel. "She's an unarmed girl. You have a sword and ten stones over her. If you consider that a threat, then you need to seriously reconsider your life's choices."

The stranger froze before his mouth slowly dropped open.

Jinmel glared at him. "We have all known her since her father was changing her diapers in the great hall. You would be hard-pressed to find anyone who would believe a man like you was even remotely threatened by her presence."

He yanked the letters away from the carrier.

Kanéko turned to follow it and then reached up.

The carrier inhaled sharply and his hand inched toward his weapon.

Jinmel lifted it slightly and shook his head. "What do you say?"

"Please?" Kanéko whimpered as she imagined finally holding it. It was the acceptance letter. Everyone had been waiting weeks for it to arrive.

He chuckled and handed it to her. "Have the bartim read it for you. He's in the great hall."

Kanéko glanced at the carrier, then backed away from him to keep Jinmel between them. Then, as soon as she felt safer, she spun on her heels and hurried toward the hall while staring at the thin letter.

It was sealed with the imprint of the Royal Academy in Jinto Panzir, the same school where her father had learned combat magic. She hoped it would be addressed to her so she could open it, but it wasn't.

Her heart pounded. She would finally know what magical talent she had, and how powerful she would become. If she followed her father's heritage, she would be able to manipulate stone as easily as someone dipping their hand in

4

water, but a small part of her still dreamed that she would manifest one of the rarer talents such as folding space or healing.

With a giggle, she spun on her bare feet and rushed toward the gate.

"Kan!" Jinmel stopped her.

With a huff, she turned around.

He held out the rest of the mail. "What about the rest of this? Your father likes to dole it out, you know that. He says it makes him feel like he earned his title."

Next to Jinmel, the postal carrier blanched. "Y-You mean, she really is...?"

"The Bartim Lurkuklan's daughter? Yes."

"But... but, she's..."

"A girl? You're right." Jinmel's eyes sparkled as he grinned. "She's thirteen, actually. Almost not a girl. A little short on manners, but what do you expect? She's been waiting for that letter for months."

Kanéko blushed as she took the rest of the mail, tucking it underneath her arm but keeping the academy letter in her grip.

"No, she's sand... she is black." The man gestured to Kanéko with a curt wave. "The bartim is..."

Kanéko tensed as she waited for the insult.

Jinmel sighed, shook his head, and gestured for Kanéko to continue. Turning around, he spoke to the man. "Yes, and I'm glad you noticed that. Because if you insult her like that in front of her father, he's just going to beat you into the ground, and leave your corpse under a ton of rock. Her mother, who is from the desert, would use your intestines for her bow. In fact—"

Kanéko didn't want to hear the rest of the lecture. Spinning back, she ran through the gate and across the courtyard.

5

The bartim's keep consisted of a stone wall thrice her height and a four-story tower in its center. Around the inside of the wall were various buildings including stables with a well, but no horses, the armory, kitchens, and the great hall. Everything was made from stone slabs shaped by her father's magic. He had fitted each one with less than a fingernail's width gap between the edges.

She yanked open the great hall door and yelled over the sudden din. "Papa! Papa!"

The great hall was packed for the lunch crowd, a hundred people laughing and cheering and eating. Most of them listened to a story Kanéko's father was telling. She could hear him speak from the top of the table at the far end of the room.

Her father, Ronamar, held a turkey leg in one hand like a sword, and a stone mug in the other. Compared to the rest of the villagers, he was a mountain of a man, tall and broad. His short hair was brown with streaks of gray, and he had a few scars on his face and arms, but otherwise he was as fit as the day he retired from the army.

Heart pounding, she rushed through the crowds waving the letter. "It came!"

Ronamar crouched, looming over her. "What came? Oh!" He smiled. "Is it the bid for you? I'm going to sell you. I might even get a few dozen crowns."

Kanéko rolled her eyes and giggled. "No, Papa, the letter from the Academy. It came!"

A hush rolled through the great hall.

"Open it!" She shoved it into his chest.

"Fine, fine," grumbled her father as he dropped the turkey leg on his plate. It bounced off and fell to the floor. One of the dogs grabbed it and retreated back to the shadows.

Ronamar wiped his hand off and knelt to set the mug down with more grace. He took the letter from her, his tanned, thick fingers dwarfing her own, and tugged it free. With a grunt, he straightened before dramatically tearing off the end the envelope so he could pull out the letter.

Taking a deep breath, he began to read. "To Bartim Ronamar Lurkuklan, Fourth Circle Knight of Kormar, Hero of Dove's Peak, Mage-Knight of the..." He trailed off for a moment. "Hold on, I'm just getting through my accomplishments."

A snicker.

"There's a lot of them," he said with a chuckle, puffing out his chest.

Laughter bubbled up across the room.

Kanéko hopped as she watched him read silently.

Her father held up his finger. "Almost done."

"Papa."

The corner of his lip curled up. "Almost..."

"Papa!" Kanéko was smiling as she stamped her foot down.

"Fine," he rolled his eyes. "Thank you for... blah, blah, kissing my balls..."

From behind her, someone spoke up. "I hope she has fire magic."

"I'm voting for water."

"A round of stout says she has plant magic."

Laughter.

"You just don't want to farm anymore."

Ronamar looked out over the gathered people. "It's going to be earth or stone, so shut up." He winked at Kanéko.

She tapped the table impatiently. When he didn't immediately resume, she pulled out a bench to crawl up and get to the letter to read it herself.

Before she could, a hand pulled her back. She glanced down. At the sight of her mother's fingers, so brown they were almost black, she relaxed.

Mioráshi was shorter than her daughter by a full hand, but where Kanéko had the softness of a teenage girl, Mioráshi was compact, lithe, and scarred from years of battle. Her curly hair was cropped close to her head and she had intense green eyes that pinned Kanéko in place. "Slow down, *imapatsu* daughter." Her mother spoke two languages but often alternated between the two constantly. Kanéko knew Lorban, the language of the country, but only knew a few words of Miwáfu, the desert tongue. At least, a few words that weren't swears and insults.

Straining not to jump up and down, Kanéko rested her hand on her mother's. "I hope it's earth," she whispered.

Ronamar chuckled and returned to the letter. "Let's see... thank you for giving me the opportunity to examine your daughter..." He looked at her and winked again. "I think he means, thank you for giving us a huge amount of money to test your daughter because she's two years late manifesting her powers."

"Papa!" Kanéko blushed and shook with anticipation.

He returned to the letter. "Because of aberrations... verified with three separate..." A frown crossed his face. His lips worked silently for a moment.

The room grew even quieter.

His shoulders suddenly slumped and the smile dropped from his face. It was as if all the joy had been sucked out of him by the words on the page. Kanéko could almost feel the temperature lowering around her and the ground quivering under her bare feet.

Someone coughed.

Kanéko's skin crawled. "P-Papa?"

Ronamar snarled. He crushed the letter and dropped it on the table. When it hit, Kanéko jerked as if he struck her. He jumped off the table and strode past her and toward the door. "Everyone back to work," he announced.

No one moved as he stormed out.

Kanéko's lip trembled as she reached out for him. "P-Papa?"

The crinkle of paper startled her. She turned to see her mother unfolding the letter.

"What does it say?" asked someone in a quiet voice.

Mioráshi read the letter to the room, her voice shrill in the silence. "We regret to inform you that your daughter has no capability of manipulating magic. We therefore withdraw her application to the Royal Academy of Knights and will no longer consider her, or any of her offspring, for automatic acceptance."

An uncomfortable silence flooded the room, silencing everyone in an instant.

Her mother's face twisted into a scowl. "*Assholes,*" she said as she read it over again. Her eyes dragged over the page, as if reading it again would change the words.

Kanéko didn't know how to respond. It felt like something had just been carved out of her chest and left nothing but a bloody wound. She stared at her mother, silently praying to the Divine Couple that it was a mistake.

"That can't be right. You must have read it wrong. She's the bartim's daughter." It was the farmer. He stood up as to take the letter.

Mioráshi glared at him. "Listen, *you infested pile of maggot corpses,* I know how to read your language. So, if you want to keep walking without your *balls stuffed into your neck,* you shut it."

He shook his head and pulled his hand back.

The world stopped for one painful moment. Kanéko felt her heart skip a beat as tears burned in her eyes. "H-How? Everyone has magic. Everyone." Her voice sounded broken and afraid, tiny in the deathly still of the great hall.

She turned to look at the rest of the crowd. No one was looking at her.

"E-Everyone has magic. Everyone. Right? Everyone?"

No one looked at her. They were staring at the floor, packing up, or simply leaving. A sob rose in her throat and she turned back to her mother. "M-Mama?"

Mioráshi's eyes flashed as a growl rose in her throat. "*Gachímo* the bastards." Her mother continued to swear in Miwāfu as she pulled Kanéko into a tight hug.

Kanéko sobbed into her shoulder. "Why don't I have magic? It isn't possible, is it?"

Chapter 2

The Water Screw

In Miwāfu, those who cannot use magic are called *barichirōma*. Translated into Lorban, it means "cursed to be forever deaf."
—Dastor Malink, *Awakened Magic*

"**I** can't believe I'm going to miss your birthday." Jinmel said as he brought over a metal rod. "It's the first time you won't be here at the tower."

"I'm only turning seventeen. It isn't any special day."

"Hard to imagine it was only four years ago that you were dreaming of using magic instead of... this." He gestured to the metal contraption jammed at the end of the stable.

His words brought painful memories up, when she saw her father crumple the letter from the Academy in front of her. It was the last time he talked to her about magic; it was almost the last time he had spoken to her.

Wiping the sweat from her brow, she took the rod from Jinmel's hands and looked up at a metal bracket a few feet above her. In her mind, she could picture where it went but it looked like something wasn't lined up. She tried to force the end of a connecting rod into place with a jump. The rod scraped along the bracket but missed. She stretched up as far she could in an attempt to fit it.

No matter how much she tried, she couldn't get the holes for the cotter pin to line up through both the bracket and the rod at the same time. Annoyed, she planted one bare foot on a wooden brace, and then lifted herself for a better angle. Her nightgown rose up on her thigh, but she didn't have time to pull it down.

The rod slid further into the bracket with a clink, and she let out a satisfied chuckle. She lost her balance, but Jinmel caught her before she could tumble from her precarious position.

As he started to lower her, Kanéko shook her head. "Push me up... please? The holes aren't quite lined up."

She grabbed a nearby pipe. It was searing hot and her first reaction was to snatch her hand back, but she didn't want to lose her momentum. Forcing herself to tighten around the hot metal, she lifted herself until she could find a cooler grip. As soon as she could, she blew on her burned palm.

"Hurry up, my back can't take much of this." Jinmel spoke as he strained to hold her. "Not to mention, you are not properly dressed for this activity."

With both of them stretching, she managed to slide it into place. Elated, she yanked at the rod to test how well it sat in place. It was a perfect fit, despite taking a week to puzzle out its purpose and two days to forge.

"It isn't that important," she continued with a grunt. She grabbed the rod with both hands, threw all her weight on it, and then jerked violently. The bar scraped as it sank into place with a loud snap.

"Got it?" asked Jinmel. His voice was slightly muffled, he was looking away while he held her.

She nodded and braced herself again.

"Yes. Thank you." She pushed her long, copper hair from her face and behind her ear. Grease and oil from the night's work kept it limp and there was only a hint left of the sweeping curls at the end. The sticky strands clung to her stained fingertips, and she had to shake them free before she could inspect the rod and bracket. "Cotter pin?"

"In your apron, left side."

Kanéko glanced down to the apron covering her front. The grease-stained canvas had a dozen bulging pockets filled with tools, screws, and bits of wire. She glanced to the sleeve of her sleeping gown, where the silk had been frayed just a few hours earlier. Fresh burns and scratches covered older injuries along her dark skin. She balanced on the precarious perch and fumbled through her pockets until she found the pliers and a cotter pin. With a triumphant smile, she forced the pin into place and spread the ends to keep it from slipping out.

"There!" she announced as she hopped down. The hem of her gown caught an exposed screw and tore. She ignored it; one more rip wasn't going to be noticed among the other tears, burns, and stains.

She faced Jinmel. Like her, he had dark shadows under his eyes from working all night, but with his brown eyes, it made him look like he wore a mask.

"Remember," Jinmel said as he held up a finger, "you are going to bed as soon as it works... or doesn't, agreed?"

She glanced out the window of the stables. "It is almost morning. Probably too late."

"At least pretend to sleep. I've been up for five hours, and you never went to bed."

He gestured to a large boiler that towered over them, filling the entire end of the formerly-abandoned stable. A few feet to the side, in the corner, was a narrow well. A large

D. Moonfire

screw hung down into depths and a wooden channel led past the boiler and out the wall. "Ready?"

She looked through the shutters of the stable where the morning light was bright, "Papa is going to kill me if he catches me wearing this." She toyed with the charred end of her sleeve.

"He's going to kill you when you aren't in your bed. I distinctly remember hearing him tell you at dinner not to work on this before your trip."

"I know..."

"Bad enough you are ignoring his commands, but this trip is the law. You can't go against the Silver King's edict. Your father would be the one hunting you down and he won't grant you mercy just because you share blood."

Kanéko gave him a tired grin. "Then why do you encourage me? You caught me hours ago and didn't force me out."

Jinmel's shoulders slumped. "Because I know how important it is to you. And I want to see it working just as badly as you, though maybe for different reasons."

Neither said anything for a long moment. Kanéko toed the ground as she fought the urge to keep working. She couldn't leave the water screw unfinished, not with her father complaining about the mess every time he walked near the stable. She wasn't sure if it would still be standing when she came back a month later. She knew the reasons for the trip, but it didn't make it easier to abandon her project.

Reflexively, she glanced at the crumbled academy letter she'd received three years ago. She had rescued it from the trash and nailed it to a post to remind her why she had to finish. She remembered the look in his eyes when he got to those fateful words.

Jinmel sighed twice and rubbed his nose. "So, what's next?"

Kanéko sniffed and looked around. "What do we do now? Start the core? Compare it to the diagrams?" She gestured to the workbench and the plans for the water screw. The expensive plans she bought months ago from the back of an issue of *Emerging Wizardry*. It showed every part needed for the mechanism, but Kanéko and Jinmel couldn't get anything to work. On top of the diagram were their sprawled sketches of replacement parts, things they puzzled out, and random doodles.

"That thing is useless," he sighed.

"Then," she said hopefully, "just open the core?"

At Jinmel's shrug, hope rose inside Kanéko. She hurried over to the fire core, a foot-tall metal vase covered in runes. It was buried underneath a bag of moldy and scorched horse feed. She grunted as she shoved the bag aside. The vase was hot in her hand when she picked it up and carried it over to the boiler.

"Careful, Kan."

"I'm not going to drop it," she gasped, "again."

She pushed the core underneath the boiler and rested her hand on the lid. Four arms kept the lid clamped down, but as she touched the top, they released with a snick. The runes along the sides flickered brightly. "Ready?"

Jinmel grunted with a nod.

Kanéko pulled the lid off. Flames burst out of the vase and roared up. They hit the bottom of the boiler and splashed around the copper base. She scrambled back as the searing air choked her. Dropping the lid on the ground near the boiler, she backed up until she stood next to Jinmel.

He chuckled. "While we wait, go look for leaks. You check right. I'll check left?"

Together, they inspected the boiler as temperature and pressure rose.

Kanéko found herself glued to the largest gauge, watching it climb. She heard the first gear start to turn, a squeak and a creak that she tried fix weeks ago.

Moments later, the water screw began to rotate.

"It's working!"

"Kanéko! Get out here!" Her father's rough voice echoed across the courtyard.

She jumped and gave Jinmel a terrified look. "Papa!?" She rushed outside. When she saw water pouring into a horse trough, she slowed and smile broadly. In the second she stopped to look, her father cleared his throat loudly, making her resume her run to him.

Ronamar stood in the center of the courtyard, hands fisted at his side, scowling at the stables. He wore a simple shirt and trousers along with a rigid necklace of his royal title, a bartim. His brow was furrowed with anger. He cleared his throat before growling, "Why are you out here?"

"I got the pump working, Papa. Look—" Some of her excitement came back, but he crushed it by repeating his question.

"I said, why are you... out... here? In your sleeping gown? In the stables!? In the morning?"

Next to her, Jinmel excused himself and hurried back to the stables.

Kanéko wanted to follow him, but her father kept speaking.

"I allow this foolish hobby of yours—"

"It isn't foolish, Papa."

"Kanéko!" he roared and brandished his fist. "Stop messing with that thing! It is an abomination of nature. Just because you can't use... you can't do anything, doesn't mean —"

"I can do something, Papa! I'm—"

"You can't!" he roared, "You can't do anything. You are..." he shook his head, the pain and disappointment obviously in his face. "Do something that brings honor to our family. Stop messing with devices that explode in the middle of the night."

"It was only a ruptured pipe..."

"Enough!" He gestured to her ruined gown, "I'm tired of your mistakes. You should be in bed, not cavorting around like some sort of... of... I don't know what they call themselves!"

"Mechanic," she said sheepishly.

"Silence!" His roar echoed against the walls.

Around her, the ground rumbled as it responded to his anger. She could feel it bulging up and then lowering. Kanéko stared at the rock beneath her bare feet and held her breath. There would be more yelling in a second.

Instead of continuing, Ronamar took a long, deep breath and his voice calmed. "This is the last day you'll play with that..." He struggled with the word, "whatever that thing is!"

"It's a water screw, Papa."

"No, it's done. You're done. No more cores, no more designs, no more staying up late working in the smithy."

"But, Papa—"

"You are the daughter of a bartim, and it is time you acted like one. When you come back, I will—" He bellowed louder, "—have a daughter, not some greasy mech... mechanical... person!"

Silence filled the space between them. Kanéko struggled to find the words to convince him to change his mind. She peeked up at his face and watched as he worked his jaw in preparation for the next round of yelling.

Kanéko caught a high-pitched screech at the edge of her hearing. Turning her back on him, she cocked her head to listen to it.

Her father's voice grew deep and threatening. "Don't you dare turn your—"

The screech continued to rise in volume and pitch. It took her a heartbeat to recognize the sound of steam pouring out of a ruptured vent, but when it didn't die down, she knew that something else was about to give. She could picture it in her head: a crack in the boiler and a weld that blocked off a pipe's insides. A second whistle pierced the air, but that could only happen if Jinmel had turned the wrong valve.

Icy fear coursed through her veins. She took a running step toward the stables. "Jin!"

The top of the stable exploded in a cloud of timber, iron, and tiles. Shards of wood were blasted out of the way as the boiler lid shot straight up with a deafening bang. The concussion shattered windows and ripped the front wall off the stables.

The impact wave of the explosion slammed into her, peppering her face and body with rocks and chunks of wood. She flung her arms to protect her face as she staggered back. Between her fingers, she spotted a gear the size of her head ricochet off the ground and fly straight for her. She tried to move out of the way, but her body refused to budge.

Her father grabbed her shoulder, his fingers grinding into the soft spot between the bones. He yanked her back as he bellowed out a word her mind refused to comprehend. The spell gathered around his hands and his fingers glowed yellow from his bones. Without pause, he jammed his hands into the earth. The hard-packed ground flowed around his wrists as he yanked up. The earth formed a wall of soil and rock. He flung his arms open and the wall spread into a circular shield that blocked Kanéko's sight of the explosion.

Kanéko stumbled back and tripped. She barely felt the impact against her rear as she stared at the glowing wall of stone.

Tools and components slammed into Ronamar's shield. His feet sunk into the ground as she watched him focus on maintaining his spell. Above the wall of stone, more shrapnel flew into the air before it rained down. Ronamar lifted one palm and slashed it across the sky. The dirt shield spread out into a dome over them.

Debris hit her father's earthen protection and the ground shuddered from the impact. Wood and twisted metal bounced off the stone with muted thumps.

She staggered to her feet.

Her father counted aloud to three after the last of the impacts before he released the shield. Rock liquefied and sank back into the earth. Ronamar turned and glared at her. "You did this."

Tears in her eyes, Kanéko ran around him and sprinted for the stable.

A shadow crossed over her as something plummeted directly above her. She stumbled as she looked for cover. Her father's words rang out again and a stone shield formed over her head. The boiler lid bounced off the shield and slammed into the ground next to her. The earth underneath her buckled from the impact.

Kanéko gasped but continued her race to the wreckage. Dust and steam rushed out the door and she inhaled at the wrong time. Coughing violently, she reached for the door frame.

Two of the wooden beams slid into the stable and slammed into the water pump. A rolling boom rang out in all directions. The courtyard rumbled from the impact.

Kanéko stumbled from the tremors and lurched through the door. "Jin!"

Inside, the core rolled across the floor, and flames roared in all directions. She jumped over the jet of fire, and then grabbed the urn with both hands. The heat burned her palms. Staggering from the pain and weight, she crawled over the steaming wreckage of the boiler and threw the vase into the well. Flame and water met with a second explosion and a massive plume of steam rose into the air. Kanéko stumbled back, shielding her face.

As soon as she could, she resumed her search for Jinmel.

She found him pinned underneath one of the roof beams. Blood seeped from his trapped leg, and his face was black with soot. A cut crossed his face along the ridge of his nose.

Kanéko sobbed as she reached for him. "Jin?"

He groaned and muttered in a broken voice, "My head hurts."

Relieved, she hugged him tightly. "W-What happened?"

Jinmel's left eye opened. It took him a moment to focus on her. "I tried to adjust the pressure, but the valve slammed shut. I'm sorry. I opened it, but then—" He coughed violently, a rattling sound that frightened her.

Kanéko shook her head, "No, don't worry. Let me get you out of here."

She tried to pick up the beam, but it didn't even twitch. She looked around for something to use as a lever, calling out for help at the same time. In the back of her mind, she hoped to find something before her father answered, but she saw only useless metal and smoldering wood.

Ronamar crawled over the ruins and planted himself next to her. When he spoke, his voice was terrifying calm. "Kan, when I lift, you pull him out."

His tone allowed no question, no resistance, just like when he ordered his soldiers. She just nodded and wrapped her hands around Jinmel's shoulders. Her father braced himself over the beam, and then closed his eyes in concentration. Magic flowed from his hands and dripped into the ground. The hard-packed dirt responded. Rising up, it flowed under the end of the beam. Animated earth and stone pushed the timber toward the sky.

Jinmel let out a wail of pain.

Straining, Kanéko tugged at Jinmel until he slid free. Her father continued to lift the wood, his face reddened from the physical and mental effort, until Jinmel's feet cleared the shadow of the beam. When he let it go with a gasp, the magic stopped, and the wood crashed into the ground.

Behind them, in the well, the core let out a loud burp as the magical flames were extinguished.

Together, they carried Jinmel from the ruins of the stable. As soon as they were clear, Kanéko dropped to the ground and held him tightly. "I'm sorry, Jin, I'm so sorry."

Jinmel cracked open his eyes to look at her, and then his gaze slid to the stables. Kanéko peeked over. At the sight of the ruined boiler, now with two large beams of wood piercing its heart, Kanéko let out a devastated sob.

Her father followed her gaze. When he spoke, his angry voice prickled her skin. "When you come back, that thing will not be here. You will no longer talk about mechanical devices, and you are to never, ever, set foot inside Jinmel's forge again."

The rush of emotions slamming into her prevented any words from coming out. She clutched Jinmel and cried.

Chapter 3

A Simple Lie

Aye, healing magic be wonderful, if you can find it, but too many be dying if it weren't for the humble bone-setter.
　　　　　　　　　　—Ratmis Galador, *The Scarecrow Court* (Act 2)

Kanéko wiped the tears from her face as she limped down the tower stairs. The cut in her side still hurt, and she rested one hand on the bandage. Her bare feet slapped against the cool stone and dust rose up in front of the tall, narrow windows that let spears of light illuminate the wide curved stairs. Her only baggage was the canvas travel pack on her shoulder.

In two hours, she had to meet Garèo, a desert man who showed up five months ago. Her mother had hired him to teach Kanéko the ways of sand and horses. Kanéko disliked the dark-skinned man, not only because he insisted on speaking only Miwāfu, the desert tongue that Kanéko barely knew, but also because his methods for teaching involved chasing her around the tower until she threw up, forcing her to shoot arrows until her fingers bled, and berating her constantly. The only good thing he did was to never mention Kanéko's inability to use magic.

As much as she despised him, she couldn't stay home. She was required by law to go on the trip, to travel at least a hundred leagues from her birthplace. The Silver King's law didn't specify anywhere in specific, only that she and every other teenager needed to spend a month away from the place they had been born to experience the rest of the country. Not that she wanted to stay behind, with her father's fury still raw. When she had returned to her room to pack, her father's bellowing beat against her window as he ordered servants to clean up the rubble and to find the bonesetter for Jinmel. He interrupted her packing long enough to announce she would be paying for the healer, and then stormed off to have a drink in the great hall.

She reached the ground floor and padded through the dining room and into the vestibule. She stopped in front of the double doors, trepidation rising to claw at her heart. Beyond the wooden doors was the wreckage of her dreams. Her fingers trembled as she grabbed the handle. She choked back a sob.

Taking a deep breath, she opened the door and stepped outside. Her eyes rose automatically to the ruins of the boiler; it was the tallest thing still standing in the stables. She visually traced the pipes, looking for the valve that caused the explosion.

She couldn't find the source. Stepping closer to inspect it, she noticed that none of her tools were on the ground. Someone had picked them up while she was upstairs. Frowning, she trudged across the courtyard and peered into the wreckage.

She spotted footprints in the dust, ash, and mud. They were small, one of the many children that hung around the tower. One set of footprints trailed over to the imprint of her hammer, but the hammer itself was gone.

Kanéko sighed. Her father would have told the local children to gather up her supplies and put them in the storage barn. The next time a trader came visiting, they would pick what they wanted from the barn and make an offer in hopes of a profit.

The idea of her carefully collected tools being sold to some trader brought tears to her eyes. She had spent a year purchasing half of them with her allowances. Jinmel helped craft the remaining tools from blurry images and best guesses. She wished she could hide them until she got back. It would give her enough time to try again.

An idea came to her. She had a large chest in her bedroom that would be perfect for hiding everything. If she packed her tools away and then shoved the chest into a corner, no one would think to look inside for her missing tools and she would be able to rescue them when she returned.

Twenty minutes later, she finished wrapping the last of her tools in a shirt she never wore. She already knew where she would jam it into the heavily packed trunk. It fit perfectly and she closed the lid with a grin.

When she finished, she stepped back to admire her effort. It looked imposing and heavy; no one would even consider opening it.

With sweat dripping down her back, she looked for a good place to shove it. It needed to be buried, maybe under some canvas and ropes. Anything to

"Néko?"

Kanéko jumped at her mother's gravelly voice. She spun around and slapped her hand on the chest, in case it wasn't latched. Fear prickled the back of her neck as she turned to look at her mother.

Mioráshi perched on the edge of a hay bale just inside the door. She wore a blue dress, embroidered with the desert script. Her short bow, with its heavily carved handle and feathers at the ends, bobbed over her head like a snake's rattle.

"What are you doing, *foolish child?*" Her mother was calmer than normal, otherwise she would be swearing more in her native language, Miwāfu.

Kanéko thought furiously. "I-I was just making sure my chest wasn't too heavy."

Her mother raised an eyebrow and looked at the chest. "You had a *sands damned* bag you packed yesterday. It was small and light, *worthy* of travel. What is that *fupujyu chìdo?* Are you taking that instead?"

Sweat prickled Kanéko's brow as she realized she was trapped. While her parents fought frequently, her mother rarely disagreed with Ronamar's edicts. If she knew that Kanéko had hidden her tools, there was a good chance her mother would insist on telling her father or scream at her in two languages before telling her father.

Mioráshi cocked her head, the white strands in her curly hair almost glowing in the light streaking through the windows.

Kanéko fought the urge to look at the back of the barn as she thought furiously. There wasn't many options. She took a deep breath and tried to put on a casual face. "I couldn't get everything in it. In the bag."

"And that," her mother pointed at the chest, "is better, to carry something so heavy and *bulky?* Are you a *witless idiot who carries her bucket upside down on her head?*"

Kanéko nodded, cringing inside.

Mioráshi's eyes narrowed. Her knuckles tightened on her bow.

Kanéko squirmed under the look. She pictured her mother forcing her to open the chest and then the screaming would start.

"*A foolish child must learn through pain.*" Mioráshi straightened up and patted her bow. "Garèo won't be here for at least an hour. Come shoot arrows with me out back."

Her mother looked like she was struggling with words. It was the same expression that Kanéko saw whenever her mother tried to act like a parent and a source of authority. It rarely worked out for the two of them, her mother was fifteen years younger than her husband and only eighteen when Kanéko was born.

The only one of the three of them that had any family experience was Ronamar with his previous wife and boy.

Her mother tightened her grip on the bow. "It would be a good way to pass the time and... I'm going to miss you."

"I-I," stammered Kanéko. She felt trapped by the lie she started. "I was going to meet Garèo by the milestone."

Mioráshi's shoulders slumped. She gestured with her free hand to the chest. "How do you plan on bringing that *back-breaking* box with you? Drag it?"

"It isn't that heavy, Mama." When her mother didn't look convinced, Kanéko lifted the end and set it down, pretending she dropped it. With the tools inside, it was a lot heavier than she had thought, but she couldn't strain with her mother watching.

With a sigh, Mioráshi jumped off the bale. She rested a hand on Kanéko's shoulder. She didn't seem to notice when Kanéko flinched. "You're an *utter idiot with an empty vase for a skull.* Be safe."

She turned and strode out of the barn. There was no noise of her passing, no hint that she was even there except for the faint smells of bow oil and leather.

Kanéko stared in the direction of her mother and silently berated herself. She planned on hiding the chest, not bringing it with her. Now, if her mother found that she had left it behind, there would be questions and trouble.

27

Then she turned back. "Shit," she muttered. There was no way she could leave the chest in the barn. If her mother saw it again, she would ask questions that could result in the contents being confiscated again. The tools made it too heavy to drag back up to her room, not without taking everything out and carting the contents upstairs. She had to find a new place, somewhere safe that no one would look.

She mentally worked her way through all the surrounding buildings, looking for hiding spots but finding none. The few houses that gathered around the tower were all occupied and small. Jinmel's smithy would have been a good place but her father went there frequently. He knew the contents of her room and would notice her chest in a corner.

Beyond the buildings were fields that stretched out a mile in all directions. Officially, it was to ensure that any invader wouldn't have shelter or protection as they approached the tower.

The seconds passed by as she struggled with her options. The growing dread finally came to a peak. She was trapped. The only way to keep her tools a secret was to bring the chest beyond the milestones and into the surrounding forest. There, she could bury it among the roots and it would be safe. With all the padding inside, the moisture wouldn't reach the metal to rust it.

With her new plan, she strained to lift the end before dropping it with a loud thud. There were easily a seventy pounds of metal and wood inside.

"*Sands drown me*," she swore in frustration.

She stepped out into the road and looked at her destination. The milestone was exactly one mile from her father's tower. It was along a relatively flat road with a gentle hill at the end.

Returning to the chest, she opened it up and tossed her travel pack inside. She locked it and placed the key in her wallet, which contained around two hundred paper crowns —the currency of the realm—and an illustrated picture of herself with an official seal.

Kanéko steeled herself and then grabbed the handle. It would be a long mile.

───────────── Chapter 4 ─────────────

Waryoni Garèo

The chain is the basic unit of measurement at four rods or sixty-six feet. Ten chains make up a furlong and eighty make a mile. For shorter distances, there are one hundred links in a chain.
—Basic Children Education

Over an hour later, she was gasping for breath as she shoved the trunk the last few links over an exposed root. It bumped against the boulder and she slumped over the sunbaked wood. Sweat poured down her face as she stared at the rough, pitted surface. She was thankful it was in the shade instead of the sun that bore down on her back. Everything about her hurt: her arms, knees, and bare feet.

She struggled to pry her fingers off the handle. When she did, it took her a minute to get her digits to straighten without pain.

Still panting, she turned and leaned into the trunk. A mile didn't seem like a lot when she had walked it over the years. She knew most of the larger features, those weren't hard to miss, but it was different when she struggled to drag the chest even a foot. Every rut, rock, and swell of stone turned the heavy chest into an unbearable weight.

"Just... a few seconds." She looked around her as her body throbbed. There was no shallow embankment leading up into the woods around her, just the steep sides of a path carved into the earth by her father's magic. He had made a ditch on both sides to channel the water away from the center. The idea of trying to force the chest over the depression and up the side was more than she could handle.

Kanéko rolled to the side to look down the road. It looked like the sides were shallower a few hundred feet down the way.

The idea of dragging the heavy weight that far brought a moan of pain and despair. She lifted her head and peeled her hair from her face to look back at her father's tower.

"Sands!" she swore and slumped back. She didn't even fight the tears as she berated herself for not coming up with a better lie for her mother. Sliding down off the chest, she sat on the ground and rapped her head against the side of the trunk. "Sands! *Sands! Sands!*" The last two utterances were in Miwāfu. It always felt better to swear in her mother's language.

Kanéko stopped swearing after a few seconds. It wasn't helping. Slowly, she leaned back against the warm wood and considered her options: she could head back to the keep to get Jinmel's wagon or for her way down the road.

She gave herself a long count of ten before she forced herself up with a groan. She had to get moving.

As she peered around for a hiding spot, she heard a terrible noise. It was midway between a man being tortured and the wail of a drunk. She groaned. Only one person sang so poorly, her tutor Garèo. The desert man claimed he was one of the greatest singers in the world, but in the few months he had been around, Kanéko had yet to hear a single note in tune. She cringed as the volume grew louder.

Maybe "greatest singer" meant something different in the other language.

Remembering the chest, Kanéko looked around frantically for the fastest way to get hide the heavy box. She shoved it but the brief break had left her muscles aching and she could barely budge it.

The horrid singing grew louder. She turned as Garèo came into view.

He rode a bay mare but didn't bother with a saddle or bridle. Instead, he rode with one hand resting lightly on the horse's mane. To the side, a brown mare that Kanéko didn't recognize walked obediently with her head even with the bay's hindquarters. Like the bay, there was no rope holding the brown in place, but she paced as neatly as if there had been one.

Kanéko had read of desert clans with a close connection to horses. They communicated with their mind and hearts —telepathy—but Garèo never said he was one of those clans. Then again, he didn't talk about the desert or his clan, the Waryōni.

Garèo waved his hand in wide circles as he continued his song, moving every part of his body. He did the same thing when he was talking.

Despite the horrid tones emanating from his throat, both horses only flicked their ears in response.

He trailed off singing as he drew closer. His gaze dropped from her to the wooden trunk. His upper lip twisted for a moment, the black chevron mustache titling slightly. It matched the darkness of his hair and contrasted with the light green of his eyes.

Kanéko held her breath as he pulled his horse up to her travel chest.

Lifting his gaze, he slipped off his bay and crossed over to the gap to land on it. The wooden trunk shifted under his weight.

She heard a faint clink and winced at the sound.

The bay continued to walk past the chest, followed by the other horse. She wondered if they would turn away, but they stopped at a low bush and began to pick small fruits from the branches.

"*Kosobyo Kanéko.*" He used her formal desert name: Kanéko of the Kosòbyo clan.

It took her a while to distinguish the lack of accent on the name, it meant "member of". The complex rules of the language weren't second nature to her. She struggled with the response and couldn't remember the proper words. "Garèo."

His jaw tightened. "*Because I'm your elder, the proper way to address me is Great Waryoni Garèo. It is a sign of respect.*"

She felt a flicker of annoyance. Garèo demanded her respect, but she didn't understand why speaking formally was important to him. Her mother swore at him constantly and didn't even have a shred of respect for the dark-skinned man. She answered even though she knew it would only antagonize him. "What if I don't respect you?"

For a moment, she wondered if she went too far.

His eyes flashed, and a scowl crossed his face. "*Answer in Miwāfu, girl. Your mother hired me to teach you of the desert ways and that includes speaking in a proper language.*"

She struggled with a response. His insistence on formality was just one more thing that had gone wrong for her. One more thing that all started when she stopped to look at the water screw on the way to bed, knowing that once she saw it unfinished, she wouldn't be able to leave it alone. The events that followed were predictable but just as foolhardy as ever. Before she knew, she was reviewing her actions in an attempt to find the mistake she made that caused the explosion. It had to be something, some weld she had missed or a gear that broke. She needed to know.

"*Girl!*" Garèo snapped his fingers. "*Pay attention!*"

Kanéko jumped at his sharp tone. She looked at him as a wave of despair rose up. She made so many mistakes and ruined everything. She tried to answer, but only a choked sob rose out of her throat.

"*What happened, girl?*" He spoke in a sudden concerned voice, "*Are you injured? Are you unable to go on this trip? I was under the impression it was required, which is why I'm here to escort you.*"

She tried to answer him. "*I, um,*" she didn't know the right word, "broke it."

"*Broke what?*"

She fought her own emotions, reliving the explosion and seeing Jinmel's injuries. She took a deep breath. "*The... the...*" She gave up trying to speak Miwāfu, "water screw. I got it working, but then something burst on the boiler and it," she sniffed and realized she knew the next word, "*exploded.*"

His dark eyebrow lifted. "*Exploded?*"

"*Yes, took the roof off the stables, damaged the back keep wall, and shattered windows in the tower.*" Somehow, those words she knew.

Garèo whistled with surprise.

She took a deep breath, fighting against the sobs. "Papa is *tearing it down. I can fix it! I know I can! I can make it work.*"

He frowned again, then surprised her by responding in Lorban instead of Miwāfu. "I'm sure you'll find some new project when we get back."

Kanéko's tears burned her eyes. "He's banned me from working with Jinmel again. *I loved it. I love trying to figure out those designs. When I, I...*" She choked on the words, then

35

switched languages again to finish. "When I'm working out the design, it feels good. I got it pumping water and all those gears, they made me happy. And now... he's going to ruin everything! My life is over." She sobbed with her face buried in her hands.

"Did you die in the explosion?"

Kanéko looked up, confused. She shook her head.

"Did someone else die?"

She started to shake her head, and then stopped. *"Jinmel got hurt."*

Garèo stared at her with a look of disbelief and then sighed. *"I'd think that's a lot more important than a mere pump. Is he safe?"*

Feeling guilty, she looked away. "Papa says he'll be fine, but I have to pay for the healer. He broke his leg. And... probably the stables." Kanéko let out a fresh sob and covered her face. "It's over. It's all over."

"Are you dead?" He sounded impatient.

She looked up through her fingers. "No."

"Then it isn't over. Get up and move on."

Kanéko whimpered, *"I can't—"*

Raising his voice, Garèo snapped back, *"You can! You are Kosobyo Mioráshi's daughter and the heir of Ronamar Lurkuklan. You are intelligent and creative and stubborn. I'm sure your father gave also gave you some useful traits."*

"I-I—"

Garèo grabbed Kanéko's hands and held them tight. His skin was darker than hers, the color of freshly tilled earth and without her red tones. He squeezed her for a moment. *"Girl, your song only ends when the desert takes you."*

She had heard her mother use that saying more than once but she never understood it.

He released her and then held up his palm. *"You made a mistake, and then you were given a second chance. No one died and repairs will only take time and money. Both of which are available."*

She tensed to disagree, but he shook his hand.

"You need time. If anything, to clear both your father's and your head. Do you understand?"

Kanéko looked at him, her eyes searching his face. The tears slowed, and she took a long, deep breath. She thought about his words. They gave her a bit of hope, something she didn't expect from Garèo. She nodded.

"Good," chirped Garèo. He released her hands and stood up. He hopped back and jumped off the trunk. He gestured to it. *"And what is this?"*

"My clothes?" she lied with a blush.

"How did it get here?"

"I dragged it."

Garèo whistled as he looked down the path to the keep. His eyes scanned the fields. Then, before she could do anything, he reached down and picked up one end.

Kanéko inhaled sharply, then realized she couldn't give away her secret. She gulped and forced herself to calm down.

He dropped the chest and looked at her. There was a brief flash of confusion, then he reached down and picked it up again.

She almost whimpered.

He dropped it once more, then stood up and brushed his hands off. *"Well, too heavy for my horses to lug five miles to Rock River, in addition to the other stop we're making. Are you planning on dragging it?"*

Kanéko let out her held breath in a rush. She gasped and inhaled, flushing hotly when she realized she was about to reveal her secret.

Garèo didn't seem to notice. He pointed to her father's tower. *"I'm going to see if I can borrow a wagon from the keep. Do you want to come with me?"*

That was the last thing she wanted to do. "Can I stay here?"

Garèo looked over his shoulder and glared at her. He looked like he was waiting for something.

Desperate to placate him, she cleared her throat. *"No, Great Waryoni Garèo."*

Garèo jumped back on the trunk and balanced on the edge lithely. He gave her a sweeping bow. *"This is just one setback. Focus on the steps before you. You are going on a glorious adventure, far away. After eight weeks of visiting the ocean and lots of singing, you'll be back with new ideas and new adventures."*

Kanéko looked pained. "You're going to sing?"

He cocked his head. *"You mean, are you going to sing, Great Waryoni Garèo? And yes, of course. I'm one of the greatest singers in the desert."* He spoke with a confidence Kanéko knew could never be true.

As she tried to fight her growing despair, the bay walked up.

Garèo gracefully stepped back and landed on the horse. Without touching her mane or giving any sign of direction, the bay and the brown started off toward the keep as if he gave an order.

They had only gone a few hundred feet when a horse came around the tower and began to race toward them. It was Ojinkomàsu, a red roan stallion that ran wild near her father's tower. The enigmatic horse arrived a few days after Garèo first showed up, but Kanéko never saw anyone ride the horse or even tend to him. In fact, no one cared for Ojinkomàsu, but every time she saw him, he was freshly brushed and had no marks.

Ojinkomàsu covered the distance to Garèo rapidly. When he approached the rider and horses, he swung around and then pulled up even with Garèo's bay. The roan shook its head and slowed down, matching the speed of the other two horses smoothly.

Garèo glanced over at him, then back at Kanéko, and then returned his attention to the tower.

Together, the three horses and man continued along their way.

Kanéko sighed and smiled. She managed to keep her secret for a little longer. Turning around, she headed back to her chest and lifted the end of it. When she dropped it, she heard the clink of metal and groaned. If Garèo was a little more observant, she would have been forced to lie again.

"*Sands,*" she whispered angrily. Garèo might ask her mother about the chest and it would be suspicious if she got rid of it before he returned. She opened the chest to repack her tools to avoid them shifting and making more noises.

She was committed to bringing it with her, a heavy chest that no same person would bring along. All because she had to finish the water screw before she left.

Chapter 5

Lesson Plans

In the rural communities, most people never travel more than two leagues from their homes. This law is to improve that. I must blend my peo
ple together and make them strong.
—The Silver Monarch, *On the Young Journeys Mandate*

By the time Garèo returned with Jinmel's wagon, Kanéko
sat on the boulder pretending to read her book, *Ramus and
the Thrice-Blessed Rose*. Printed on cheap paper and filled
with unrealistic fight scenes and simple characters, the adventures made her smile every time she read it. Her copy
was well-worn, the edges curled up and the binding had
cracked repeatedly. Even though she had the words memorized, she couldn't focus on them. Every time she tried
to read, she started to fear someone would see through her
ruse and find her tools.

The horses came to a halt next to the boulder and chest.
There were only the two of them; Ojinkomàsu didn't return
with Garèo.

He stood up. *"Ready?"*

Kanéko redoubled her efforts to focus on the page, afraid
to say anything.

He hopped off and began to shove the chest on the wagon. While he lifted the trunk, she strained to hear a clink of metal. It hit the wagon with a thump, and she was relieved not to hear her tools.

Folding her book, she hopped off the boulder and onto the wagon. She sat down heavily on the bench, crossed her arms over her chest, and closed her eyes. She was tired, but mostly she didn't want him to ask her questions or insist she answer in Miwāfu.

To her surprise, Garèo continued to say nothing. He finished loading the wagon and got on next to her. The weathered wood creaked from his weight.

Without him making another sound, the two horses started forward and soon they were heading to Rock River, the nearby village.

Exhaustion gnawing at her, from the ache in her joints to the burning sensation behind her eyes. Her frustration and sorrow were a knife in her gut. Jinmel's injuries and the destruction of the water screw left her feeling helpless. She desperately wanted to go back home and fix the water screw.

Frustrated, she focused on the pump instead. She imagined in detail, remembering how it was drawn on the pages in the stable. When she couldn't puzzle it out, she imagined the gears coming off the page and arranged them in space inside her head.

"*Kanéko.*"

Kanéko didn't want to open her eyes. She minutely shifted her body to look more like she was sleeping.

Garèo chuckled dryly. "*I know you are awake. Sleeping people move differently with the wagon. They breathe in a rhythm and don't turn away.*"

Kanéko groaned and cracked open her eyes. She looked over at the dark-skinned man. "*Yes, Great Waryoni Garèo?*"

She poured her sardonic dislike for him in every word. She still didn't know why she had to call him *"great."*

"When I was at the keep, your father was looking for your tools. Apparently they were supposed to be somewhere. Do you know what happened to them?"

Kanéko's body tensed. She immediately thought about her cloth-wrapped tools hidden in her chest. A sick feeling pooled in her gut. She saw Garèo searching her face and she turned away. *"No."*

Garèo grunted. *"I was hoping to leave a message in Rock River. Oh well, if you remember, just tell me before we leave."*

Kanéko nodded her head quickly. *"Yes, Great Waryoni Ga-rèo."*

Another chuckle. *"Now that you are talking, we need to discuss my plans for this trip."*

Kanéko sneaked a look at Garèo, but the man's face was unreadable.

Garèo caught her looking and gave her a thin smile. *"We are to continue our lessons. This is a great time to improve your riding and archery. Your brawling and knife fighting also need improvement. So, every night, plan on spending an hour or two with me before you go to sleep."*

Kanéko's mouth opened in surprise. "But, this is supposed to be fun. A trip to see the country and learn more about the rest of Kormar."

Garèo narrowed his eyes and Kanéko realized she had switched to Lorban.

She cleared her throat but didn't repeat herself.

He held up his hand in a gesture of explanation. *"You are ignorant of your heritage. Your mother realized it, which is why she asked me to teach you. You speak like a toddler, and you have none of the social graces the desert demands."*

His jaw tightened while he paused for only a heartbeat. Then he said, *"No, you have been sheltered at your father's home for far too long. Not only are you going to travel beyond your comfortable little world, I will do everything to teach you how to be a woman of the desert and one of this sand-damned country, as well. You may not have pale skin, but at least you should be able to pretend to be one."*

The muscles in Kanéko's back and arms tightened, which also caused her various injuries to ache from the movement. She squirmed for a moment before folding her arms over her chest. "Mama is making you do this, isn't she?"

Garèo shook his head. *"No, not your mother or father. You."*

"What!?"

Garèo folded his hands in his lap and gave her a hard look. *"You spent your entire life within four leagues of the keep. Two bells travel at most. You have only dealt with a handful of small villages and your father's people. You've never lived in a world where you weren't known by everyone and respected by force because of who your father is. It's pretty obvious that you are completely unprepared for adulthood and taking over your father's legacy."*

Kanéko shot a dirty look at him and folded her arms tighter across her chest. *"I can take care of myself."*

Garèo grinned. *"Really? I'll have to test that. But, in the meantime, we will continue your lessons. And the first one will be to teach you how to survive with less luggage."* He gestured with his chin to her trunk. *"That is a shameful amount to carry with you."*

"Why?" She knew the answer, but she had committed herself.

"Because if feels like you have loaded the entire thing with those tools your father is looking for."

Kanéko blanched. A muscle in her arm began to throb in time with a headache.

Garèo shrugged. "Of course, only an idiot would carry so much heavy metal with her." He looked back at the chest.

Hatred replaced her annoyance and exhaustion. Kanéko clamped her mouth shut and turned away from Garèo. She had despised him since the day he had turned up begging her mother for a job. Her mother told Kanéko Garèo would teach her skills and language of the desert. His introduction had started with a brutal four-hour horseback ride to "test her skills" which had left her aching for days. When they weren't riding horses, he was beating her to the ground with brawling lessons or chasing her across the fields with a knife. And all the while, insisting on her answering every stupid question in Miwāfu, a language she would never need.

Neither said anything to each other, and soon Kanéko was bored. She let her mind drift, wishing the long hours would pass quickly.

Garèo cleared his throat once, and then burst into song.

Kanéko winced at the sound of it. Garèo's singing was just as bad as her mother's cooking. Maybe it was some desert trait that everyone had to be horrible at something that they desperately thought they were great at.

In Garèo's case, he took a popular song of a warrior defeating a dragon and brutalized it. He sang the wrong words to music that poorly spanned at least three octaves and had the rhythm of a chaotic storm. Groaning, Kanéko wished she could close her ears. Instead, she tilted her head to the best position to lessen the abuse and stared out into the forest.

She considered jumping off the wagon and running home, but her father would just send her back. She wanted to avoid Ronamar's rage as much as Garèo's lessons.

When Garèo continued to sing, she had to do something to distract herself. She let her mind drift and imagined different ways of escaping Garèo. There weren't many options, she hadn't been beyond her father's land, but eventually she settled on daydreams of running to Jinto Panzir, the largest town near the route they would be taking. Panzir also just gained a mechanics guild, the first in the area, and somewhere Kanéko dreamed of visiting.

She amused herself by imagining how she would run away to Jinto Panzir. With her skills, she knew that she could impress the mechanics there in a short time.

Garèo continued to sing.

They rode in torturous noise for a quarter bell. Then, Garèo turned the wagon off the main road to Rock River and headed down a rougher trail. Kanéko turned her head to read the sign as they passed. It said "Germudrir Sawmill" in thick, painted letters that had dripped.

"Where are we going?"

Garèo stopped singing, to Kanéko's relief, and pointed forward. *"To the mill. Maris, one of my students, is still there and we need to pick her up for the trip."*

When Garèo opened his mouth to sing, Kanéko rushed to prevent him. *"How many students do you have? You've arrived only five months ago."*

He cocked his head, as if thinking. *"Three, actually. You, Maris, and Ruben."*

Kanéko didn't know anything about the other students, but after Garèo's comment about her being unprepared for the world, she didn't want to point that out.

"We have about sixty littles coming with us on the trip. Some of them are from the outlying farm communities but mostly they come from the village. There are six chaperons, including myself. Even though I only teach a few, I'll be watching my fair share of the students, so you'll need to behave."

Her curiosity got the better of her. *"Only three students? Why so few?"*

Garèo smiled. *"I get the unwanted students. The ones who require a delicate hand or the patience of stones to deal with. You happen to be one of those."*

Kanéko prickled at the tone.

"Also, the ones that require more understanding or special training. My skills... were adept at handling you three."

She looked down at her hands. Blisters and burns covered her fingers and palm. Despite her dislike for him, she wanted to know more. After a few minutes of riding, she asked quietly, *"How do you survive on that? That doesn't pay much, does it?"*

Garèo chuckled. *"No, it doesn't. I also do odd jobs during my hours. Painting, hauling, repairing, and generally running messages around. I don't enjoy it, but at least I'm earning a warm bed at the school, and food in my belly."*

"Why don't you go back to the desert? Don't you have a clan who would take better care of you?"

Garèo looked haunted for a moment. He reached around and scratched his back, right below the two empty dagger sheathes he wore. He wore the scabbards upside down, so he could draw them out from underneath his arms, but Kanéko never saw a weapon in them. From their lessons, she knew he was adept at small blades, but he always borrowed them from her mother and never provided his own.

Kanéko prodded him when he didn't answer. *"Great Waryoni Garèo?"*

He looked at her and the expression faded. He gave her a grin that looked slightly forced. *"Did you know that Germudrir has a core-driven saw? It can cut through a tree in less than five minutes."*

Surprised, Kanéko gaped for a moment. She felt excitement quickening her pulse,. "Really? Can we see it? Do we have time?"

Garèo grinned. *"Since we are at the sixth bell, I thought we would join the mill for lunch. That way, you can look at the core and get some food."*

Kanéko's hatred of Garèo faded with sudden excitement. "When did they get it?"

"Three months ago."

She switched to Miwāfu in hope for more answers. *"Why didn't you tell me?"*

He shrugged. *"You never asked."*

"You knew I would want to know!"

Garèo grinned and held up his palm as if that was an answer.

Kanéko pressed for more information about the manufacturer of the saw, and how it was installed, but Garèo claimed not to know. After a few minutes, she realized he wasn't going to tell her anything else.

Sitting back down, she stared at the haze gathered above the trees. She didn't know there was anything else on her father's land that used mechanical devices. The idea that the mill, which she had never visited before, gave her hope to see a machine crafted by someone with the skill and knowledge that she didn't have. Maybe she could figure out what she and Jinmel had done wrong.

The fantasy of proving herself in Jinto Panzir became more of a reality. If she could solve her problem, then she would be able to find a master willing to teach her the rest of the trade. And then she could show her father she was still his daughter.

Chapter 6 ——

Germudrir Mill

Today is the day that all dalpre can look back and know they have a voice! We are no longer slaves!

—Tibrus Kalsain

As they approached the mill, Kanéko's excitement grew. She had never been there before. She knew her father visited every year to gather taxes, but she had never seen a reason to go with him. Likewise, he made little effort to include her in his duties ever since that fateful day with the letter. The mill paid the largest share of taxes in the bartim because of the profitable lumbering of old-growth forests to the south. The cut timber was shipped down the Logjam River to Jinto Panzir before being exported to the rest of the country.

When she saw a plume of smoke rise above the trees, her heart skipped a beat. *"Is that it? The core saw?"*

Garèo shook his head. *"No, the smoke comes from the other four chimneys. They are wood burning, using the scraps from the timber. The fifth one only produces steam, that's why it is white."*

"What kind of core saw? Is it a Silvers-Hasan? Or a Torp?"

Garèo shrugged. "*I don't know. You can ask Salcid Germudrir when you have a chance. He's the mill's alpha.*"

Kanéko wondered why Garèo said "alpha" instead of "leader" or "boss," but she didn't want to sound foolish.

"Gar! Gar! Gar!" A little girl's voice called out, interrupting her thoughts.

Kanéko looked around for the speaker until she saw a child run up to the wagon.

Garèo chuckled and the wagon slowed down.

"Gar! Gar!" The little girl ran up to the wagon and bounced up the side, her dress fluttering around her as she seemed to move in all directions. The wagon shifted with her weight as she scrambled to the top and then flung herself into Garèo's lap to hug him tightly. "I missed you so much!"

When Kanéko got a better look, she inhaled sharply. The girl wasn't human; no, she wasn't entirely human. She was covered in short brown fur with almost no bare skin visible. She had longer hair on her head, like any other human girl. It was the same color as her fur. Two ears, wedged and ending in tufts of fur, stuck out from the sides of her head.

Kanéko's breath came faster as she stared at the little girl. There wasn't one thing that made the girl look unnatural, but a combination: her ears were too high to be human, the eyes were large and reflective, and she had a tail. Every little detail scraped against everything Kanéko had seen before, and the only thing it left was a rapidly growing sense of unease. The girl sounded human, but there wasn't anything natural about her. She was a dalpre, a race of human/animal hybrids.

She looked away for a moment. On paper, the dalpre were written in sterile terms about their limited magical abilities or their natural tendencies to obey others. They were slaves, or had been until five years before Kanéko was born. She stole a glance. It was one thing to look at the precise, medical drawings, and quite another to see one moving in front of her.

As the little girl crawled over Garèo's arm, the muscles in Kanéko's jaw, neck, and shoulders tensed up. She knew that it was only a matter of moments before the girl focused on her and then they would be in close contact. She gripped the back of the bench, trying to figure out some way to avoid the child.

"Tivlin!" cried Garèo and hugged her back, "You've gotten so big!"

Tivlin wiggled around and planted her rear on Garèo's lap. A tail popped out from between Garèo and her and smacked against his arm. She panted with her long tongue sticking out the side of her mouth as she looked up at him. "Mar is almost ready. And she is getting pretty. And mommy is making lunch. And are you staying for food?"

Garèo chuckled, and Kanéko found it easier to focus on him instead of the unnatural girl in his lap. His green eyes sparkled as he squeezed Tivlin until she giggled. "Of course, Tiv. Have you met Kanéko?"

Tivlin peered at her under Garèo's arm. Her bright brown eyes widened along with her smile. Barking, she shoved Garèo's arm up and scrambled toward Kanéko.

Kanéko backed away, trying to avoid the girl's embrace. She forgot that the wagon bench didn't have an arm until she sat back into air. With a shriek, she fell off and slammed into the ground. Pain radiated from her tail bone and the cuts and burns along her palms. She looked around just in time to dodge out of the way of the wagon wheel rolling past her.

The girl's ears were flat against her head, and she whined. "Are you all right, Kan?"

Humiliated, Kanéko scurried to her feet. "Yes, I'm fine," she answered sharply.

"Kanéko, do you want to get back on?"

Kanéko peeked up at the girl watching her from the wagon. At the sight of the Tivlin's tail wagging back and forth, Kanéko shook her head sharply. "I'll walk."

Tivlin, who Kanéko guessed was only four or five, spun around. The girl's tail narrowly missed Kanéko's face. "Gar! Say that again!"

Garèo smirked. *"Kanéko, do you want to get back on?"*

The girl barked and clapped her hands. "And you talk funny!"

"You are a beautiful, adorable, little dog girl."

Tivlin barked again and launched herself at Garèo to hug him tightly around the neck. Her small body swung back and forth. "And I love you!"

Garèo looked over Tivlin's head at Kanéko. He gestured for Kanéko to catch up.

Kanéko brushed the dust off her rear and limped along the side of the wagon. As she drew even with the seat, the horses resumed walking. She followed, glancing at Tivlin when the little girl wasn't looking at her.

They came out from the trees, and Kanéko got her first look at the mill itself. It was a large barn, about a chain in height and five chains in length. There were large openings in one side. Inside, the machinery was shadowed but Kanéko could pick out furnaces and belts driving large saw blades. Four of the five chimneys belched out dark smoke, but the fifth only had a thin streamer of white steam rising up despite the loud buzzing erupting from the furthest door.

Tivlin hopped off the wagon and sprinted ahead.

Kanéko followed her with her eyes, then lifted her gaze to the rest of the mill grounds. Surrounding the barn were three long, flat buildings with dozens of numbered doors, dormitories. At the far end, a white, two-story house looked remarkably cozy compared to the rest of the industrial buildings.

In the yard in front of the house, there were womenfolk and children running around as they loaded food onto three long tables lined with benches. As far as she could tell, all of them were dalpre with ears sticking out and tails wagging. Most of them could have passed as human but a-bout a third of them were like Tivlin with fur covering their entire bodies and more bestial features.

Kanéko clenched her hand as she slowed to a stop. She didn't know where to look; everything she focused on se-emed surreal and unnatural. Her stomach rolled in discomfort as she tried to take in the shifting mass of furry huma-noids.

At least all of them were walking around like humans. They wore boots and simple, utilitarian clothes, much like others in her father's village. Even their colors were similar to what she had seen: browns, blacks, and streaks of white. Those with visible skin were heavily tanned, unlike the dark skin she, her mother, and Garèo shared.

There was just enough normality in the scene to make her even more uncomfortable.

Kanéko glanced around trying to find another human, something that she could focus on to quell her unease. There weren't any, unless she included Garèo. She tightened her jaw and turned back to him, clenching her fists and steeling herself to keep from fleeing the mill entirely; she wanted to see the saw before she left.

A bellowed command caught her attention and she reflexively looked toward it. A mostly human-looking dalpre stood in the center of the yard. He gestured and barked out commands that others rushed to obey. He had white-streaked black hair that blended into white ears and tail. He carried a writing board in his hand as he strode toward Kanéko and Garèo. Around him, a pack of children circled around as they squealed and barked. Non-humanoid dogs joined the mess as they intermixed with the children into a sea of movement and fur.

Kanéko stepped behind the wagon to shield herself. Her cheeks were burning but she didn't want to get too close.

As the older dalpre approached, the children peeled off to let him walk the last few steps alone. He held out his hand. "And well met, Garèo." He had a low, rumbling voice.

Garèo hopped off the wagon and took the hand, grabbing the dalpre right underneath the elbow. "Salcid, how are you? You look good. Finally got over that flu?"

"It took a while, but yes, and I've been working ever since." Salcid's hand caught Garèo at the elbow but it wasn't as confident as Garèo's movement. "We finally got ahead of schedule this year. And we have dry air. And good sun and a flowing river. And good news came in an hour ago."

Garèo smiled broadly and gestured toward Kanéko. "Have you met Kanéko, Ronamar's daughter?"

The dalpre held out his hand and Kanéko's skin crawled.

Salcid smiled broadly, his canines predominate in his expression. "No, I have never had the pleasure. And welcome to the Germudrir Sawmill, Lady Lurkuklan. Or do you prefer to use your mother's clan, Kosobyon?" He mispronounced her mother's clan name, just like most native Lorban speakers.

She hesitated before stepping out from behind the wagon. She held out her hand, mimicking Garèo. "I... I use... I mean, I'm Lurkuklan."

Salcid took it and held her firmly for a second. For an old man, he was very strong, and it startled her. "Well met, Lady Lurkuklan."

As soon as he relaxed his grip, she yanked back her hand. "Um, well met?"

"Garèo!" cheerfully screamed a female voice Kanéko didn't know. She saw a flash of a red outfit and black fur before another girl slammed into Garèo. To Kanéko's surprise, Garèo fell back and the girl landed on top of him.

The new girl crawled onto his chest, straddling his thighs, and sat down heavily. Her tail wagged back and forth, tugging at the small opening in her dress that let it move freely. Every time it snapped to one side, the girl's hips and buttocks shifted in the same direction. It gave the impression she was wagging her entire body.

Garèo gasped and struggled to escape. "Maris! Let me breathe!"

"Maris!" snapped Salcid.

Maris shoved herself away from Garèo and stood up. She tugged her shirt back over her exposed belly and hopped in front of Salcid. "Yes, Daddy?"

"Stop acting like a puppy," growled her father.

Maris was a little shorter than Kanéko, but where Kanéko was slender and lithe, Maris was plump and sturdy. She had curves, a heart-shaped face, and wide hips. She wore a flowing red skirt that kissed the ground and a matching top that strained over her large breasts. Her tail was still wagging which caused her entire body to rock back and forth, jiggling everything in short, distracting movements.

The more Kanéko looked at Maris, the more her stomach clenched. Maris was more human than most of the dalpre, with skin instead of fur covering most of her body, but Kanéko could see that her flesh had lighter patch over one eye. Her floppy ears matched Salcid's, sticking out except for a little flip at the end.

"Sorry, Daddy, I'll behave."

Garèo stood up. "I don't mind."

Maris looked back at him, her ears perking.

"I do," said Salcid.

"Then I mind just as much." Garèo grinned as he winked at Maris.

Maris stuck her tongue out at Garèo. It was longer than Kanéko expected, like a dog's tongue.

Kanéko gasped. She flushed when Maris glanced curiously at her.

Garèo held out his hand. "Maris, meet Kanéko, the bartim's daughter. She'll be joining us on the trip."

Maris's tail wagged, and the teenage dalpre smiled broadly. She rushed forward to hug Kanéko.

All Kanéko could think of was how much she didn't want the dog girl to touch her. Panicking, she staggered back. When Maris kept coming, she shoved at the dalpre as soon as Maris was in arms reach. "No! Don't touch me!"

Maris stepped back and dropped her hands down to her hips. She cocked her head. "What? And why?"

"Not right now, please? I don't want you to—" Kanéko tried to be placating, but she knew it was the wrong thing to say when Maris's ears flattened against her head and the corner of the dalpre's lip curled back. Kanéko looked at Garèo for help, but Garèo just held up his palms and shrugged. She thought she saw a smile on his lips.

"And what's wrong with me?" growled Maris.

"Maris..." Salcid growled.

Maris took a purposeful step closer. Her lip peeled back to reveal sharp teeth, and she balled her hands into fists. "What? Am I not good enough for you? And you can't stand to touch me? I can see that look on your face. And I disgust you, don't I?" With each word and emphasis on the "and" at the beginning of every sentence, her voice grew sharper and more pronounced.

Kanéko held up her hands and looked at Salcid and Garèo for help.

Salcid's ears were pressed against his head. His own lips pulled back in a snarl, but he was focusing on his daughter. He started to reach for Maris, but then Garèo stepped next to him and put a hand on his shoulder. Salcid stopped and looked at Garèo quizzically.

Kanéko opened her mouth to say something, but Maris interrupted her by covering the distance between them and shoving Kanéko back with surprising strength.

"And I said, I'm not good enough for you?"

Kanéko thought furiously for some answer that wouldn't further antagonize the dalpre. "No, I-I'm not comfortable with hugging."

"That isn't it, is it? It's because I'm a dalpre bitch, isn't it?" Maris's eyes blazed with fury.

Kanéko backpedaled. "Look, I'm sorry. Just... just leave me alone. Just go away."

Maris held up a fist. "I'll teach—"

"Mar!" Salcid rushed forward. He grabbed the teenage dalpre by the shoulders. Maris gave Kanéko a parting growl before her father spun her around and shoved her toward the house. "Get inside, girl!"

Garèo strolled forward with his hands in his pockets. *"Well, that was embarrassing."*

"What is wrong with her?" She glared at him. "She attacked me, Garèo!"

Garèo shrugged. *"Yes, but you started it. And made a fool of yourself in front of her and her pack. If you thought before you responded, you would have figured that out."*

"You did this on purpose."

"Yes, I did. You said you were able to take care of yourself, but you obviously failed. Later, Maris will help us—"

"Like hell I'll work with a damned dog! I'll be damned—"

"*Girl!*" Garèo's voice interrupted Kanéko's diatribe.

Kanéko stepped back but Garèo followed her. He leaned forward and whispered, "*More importantly, what would you say is the* dalpre's *most obvious feature?*"

Confused, she answered, "Their ears and tails, I guess."

"*And do you think they would have better hearing than normal?*"

A prickle formed in Kanéko's gut. "M-Maybe?"

"*Then you might want to duck.*" He stepped back rapidly.

Kanéko turned when she caught sight of Maris's swinging fist. Kanéko threw up her arm and caught the roundhouse with her left shoulder. The impact threw the surprised Kanéko to the side, and she dropped into a roll to escape. She came to her feet a short distance away. She remembered Garèo's lessons and held up her arms ready to defend herself.

Maris growled as she launched herself at Kanéko. Her dress flared behind her as she quickly covered the distance and reached for Kanéko's throat.

Kanéko caught Maris's hands and rolled back. When she hit the ground, she jammed her knee into Maris's gut and flung the dalpre over her head.

Maris hit the ground in a cloud of dust. She slumped and panted hard as her wide eyes blinked in confusion.

Kanéko turned to Garèo. "Do something!"

Garèo stepped forward. Then, he dug into his pants and pulled out some paper money. "Two, no, three, crowns on Maris!"

Kanéko gasped in shock but then her response quickly turned to outrage. "You, *horse-fucking, shit-eating bastard of a rotted cesspool!*"

In the corner of her eye, she saw movement and stepped back to avoid another of Maris's wild attacks. As the girl passed her, Kanéko kicked out her foot and tripped Maris.

The dalpre hit the ground again but surged to her feet quickly. Her dress fluttered as she spun around.

The other dalpre gathered around, calling out bets and holding money.

Maris charged.

Kanéko sidestepped to trip her again, but Maris's arm caught her in the throat. There was an explosion of light and agony. She collapsed to the ground clutching her neck.

"Rot in hell, you bitch!" screamed Maris. She grabbed Kanéko by the hair and yanked her to her feet.

Kanéko tried to regain her balance but couldn't with her hands covering her bruised throat.

Maris slammed a fist into her side.

Kanéko staggered from the blow. Dazed, she swung back but missed.

Maris grabbed her wrist and yanked Kanéko in a circle. It was a maneuver Kanéko remembered Garèo used once. Unbalanced, she couldn't get her feet on the ground to stop herself as Maris swung her in a wide arc before releasing her.

The crowd of dalpre melted away, and Kanéko stumbled toward the barn wall.

The impact with the red wall rang in Kanéko's ears. Her legs failed and she collapsed to the ground. Gasping for breath, she flipped over to see Maris stalking toward her. Shaking, she pushed herself up.

Behind Maris and on the edge of Kanéko's vision, Kanéko spotted an older, female dalpre step out of the crowd. She was entirely white, from ears to tail. She glared at the dalpre around her and then took a deep breath.

To Kanéko's surprise, the dalpre around the old woman suddenly dropped down and clapped their hands over their ears.

"STOP!"

It came out as a wall of sound, deafening and high-pitched. Kanéko covered her ears from the sharp pain that overwhelmed even the agony of her throat. She bit the tip of her tongue but kept her hands clamped tightly to her head until the echoes faded. Cracking open one eye, she noticed that only the old dalpre remained standing. In the distance, the woman's yell continued to rumble through the trees.

The woman regarded everyone through a tiny pair of glasses. She tugged her top over her waist before she spoke in a normal, motherly voice. "If you encourage Maris to ruin her dress, none of you are eating."

Maris got up from the ground, her ears flat on her head and her tail up between her legs. Her dress was tugged up between her thick thighs. "Sorry, Mommy."

The woman let out a huff and gestured to Maris and Kanéko. "You two, shake hands and stop acting like spoiled pups."

Humiliated that Maris won, Kanéko forced herself to hold out her hand as ordered. Her jaw muscles ached from the effort to keep from matching the snarl on the dog girl's face.

Maris glared at it until both of her parents growled at her. Reluctantly, Maris shook Kanéko's hand, holding below the elbow like adults. She squeezed down tightly, and Kanéko, feeling a challenge, did the same. It only took a second before Kanéko had to fight to avoid wincing.

Salcid growled. "Maris, come."

Maris snatched her hand away and stormed off, her dusty red skirt flowing behind her.

Kanéko used the back of her wrist to wipe the blood from her lip and glared daggers into Maris's back.

"*Yes,*" said Garèo walking up to her, "*you two are going to be good friends. Good thing that Mamgum stopped it.*"

"What did she do?"

"She's got a good voice to start with. Her magic just makes it impossible to ignore."

Kanéko stared at Garèo. *"Dalpre have magic too?"* Even as she said it, she knew dalpre had magical talents like everyone else. She read about it in *Emerging Wizardry* even though she never imagined she would experience it. She also read their talents were weak, but the Magnum's yell hit her with the same fury as her father's magic.

"Of course. Almost every living, competent person does."

She bristled at his comment. "I'm better than her."

"No, you're not. Just different." His voice was suddenly tense before he looked away.

Kanéko cringed at the sudden change of tone. She said the wrong thing again. Looking at his face, she could almost see his plans to make her miserable during the rest of the trip. A shiver of fear ran down her spine and she knew she had to make amends. She bowed in the manner he wanted and then spoke deferentially, *"I am sorry, Great Waryoni Garèo."*

Garèo turned back and smiled. He slipped an arm around Kanéko's shoulder and guided her toward one of the long tables. *"Forgiven, child. Now, you made two very useful mistakes here. First, you didn't take into account that the* dalpre *have better hearing than you. You shouldn't have insulted Maris when she could hear you."*

"And the other?"

"Always insult people in a language they don't know." Garèo grinned, *"That way, you can speak the worst of insults with a honeyed tongue and they will never know the difference. If you smile while doing it, they might even think you're being nice."*

As they approached the nearest table, the nearby dalpre got up and moved to other tables. Garèo set her down on the bench and sat down next to her.

Kanéko looked around her. There wasn't another dalpre within arm's length of her. Feeling embarrassed, she focused on the table in front of her. Piles of food filled the center of the table, mostly an assortment of meats and potatoes, more than she had ever seen at once. She reached out for a plate, but Garèo grabbed her wrist. *"Wait for Salcid,"* he whispered.

Kanéko spotted Salcid standing at the end of the middle table, Maris bounced on one side, smiling and waving to people. It was as if the girl had not just been in a fight. The bruise on the side of her cheek was obvious and Kanéko knew it had to hurt. Mamgum stood by his left arm. Salcid held up his hands and the noise quieted noticeably but didn't stop.

Mamgum looked around, and then she inhaled.

Maris and Salcid quickly took a step back behind her, a grin on both of their faces. The nearest dalpre looked up to see what she was doing and dropped their heads to the table and covered their ears.

Remembering the loud sound before, Kanéko clamped her hands over her head to protect her hearing.

Mamgum's bark tore through the noise. "Shut up!"

The volume of her voice punched Kanéko in the chest. Even with her hands over her ears, the sound brought tears to her eyes. When the ringing stopped, Kanéko was amazed —she heard no other noises but the sounds of the forest.

Salcid stepped forward. "Three pieces of news before we start eating. First, thanks to Garèo, Mar's suspension has been lifted. And she will be allowed on the trip even though she broke Pah's arm." He glared at his daughter.

Maris looked bashful and toed the ground, but there was a grin on her face.

"And she's very sorry for breaking his arm," he said firmly.

Maris's ears dropped and the smile erased from her face.

The dalpre barked once, raising their hands in the air as they did.

Salcid grinned and held up his hands. "Second, we just signed a contract for three hundred chains of heavy timber. It means a lot of work in the next month, but it also means that the Summer's Eve festival is going to be very good."

From the crowd, one of the workers yelled out. "But are we going to have more than a hogshead of ale this year?"

Salcid chuckled. "If we finish a week early, I'll purchase a tun from Panzir."

Another cheer, a single bark from all the dalpre.

Salcid waited for the noise to die down, and then held up his hands. "And, finally, I want to welcome the bartim's daughter, Kanéko Lurkuklan, into our midst."

Kanéko felt a blush rise on her cheeks. She looked around, not sure what to do.

The leader of the mill continued. "So, why don't we welcome her with open arms?"

Silence.

Kanéko's blush of embarrassment turned into one of discomfort. She glared at the dalpre at the tables and not a single one looked at her. Then three dalpre barked. Surprised, Kanéko looked around until she saw the source: Salcid, Mamgum, and Maris.

Maris looked genuinely happy with her arm in the air. After a few seconds, the other dalpre gave a single bark, but without the enthusiasm as the first two. No one raised their arm.

Salcid cleared his throat and the tables grew silent again. "Let us pray."

As one, the gathered dalpre bowed their heads. Kanéko looked around, still not sure what to do, and saw that Garèo also bowed his head. Not wanting to be the only one, she lowered her head and listened as Salcid spoke out one of the prayers of the Divine Marriage, one for blessing food.

Kanéko's father claimed to follow the Divine Marriage, but he didn't pray at dinner or anywhere else. Her mother and Garèo were bound to their clan spirits, just like the rest of the desert clans. In her mother's case, it was Kosòbyo; Garèo followed Waryōni.

Kanéko didn't feel a calling for any divine or spiritual power. She had read a few essays that suggested her inability to use magic was the reason.

Salcid's prayer ended with "And bless us all." As soon as the last word passed his lips, the dalpre attacked their food in a fury.

Next to her, Garèo dove into the food, hauling two plates in front of himself.

Kanéko reached out for a plate, but someone grabbed it before she could. She tried again, but it was also stolen.

Garèo came to her rescue by grabbing another plate, yanking it out of someone's hand and dropping it down in front of Kanéko. A dalpre went to grab it, but Garèo jammed a fork in the table between the furry paws and the plate.

Kanéko jumped at the viciousness of his attack, but the dalpre left her alone.

Gingerly, Kanéko ate in silence, peaking at the others around her, feeling very alone. Kanéko tried to follow the conversation, but it was too loud, too chaotic, and no one even made an effort to let her join. Everyone started their sentences with "And", "Or", or "But" and the conversations wove together in a confusing morass of words and topics.

After a few minutes of being ignored, Kanéko had enough. She snatched up her plate and held it for a moment to see if Garèo would notice. When he didn't, she slipped away from the table. She didn't know where to go, so she headed toward the mill and the core-driven saw.

Inside, the noise died down sharply and Kanéko let out a sigh of relief.

When she heard someone whispering, she froze for a moment. The sounds didn't get louder, so she sneaked for a closer look.

A pair of dalpre, a male and female, were on the walkway above one of the saws. A stack of plates rested on the grill next to them, but they were more interested in each other than their food or even the saw. When Kanéko saw that their limbs were intertwined and their clothes were pulled open, a flush grew on her cheeks and she ducked under a conveyor belt. She heard the rustle of clothes being pulled off behind her. Not wanting to see the naked creatures, she hurried faster along the lower aisles. When she got a better view of the mechanisms, she stopped caring about the dalpre.

Kanéko had read about mechanical devices before they found out she didn't have magic, but it wasn't until a few years ago that they seemed like a way of proving herself to her father. She only knew about most of them from newspapers and magazines. No one told her there were such things in her father's lands.

She admired the designs of the pump around the saw, from the wide aisles and the thick, sturdy pipes. Pressure gauges and vents were put in places she would have never expected, but it made perfect sense when she thought about it. Clumps of sawdust tickled her bare feet, and she breathed in the smell of freshly-cut wood.

Despite never seeing the machine before, Kanéko recognized some of the pipes and machinery from her blueprints and illustrations in *Emerging Wizardry*. It only took her a few minutes to find the fire chamber, the source of power that functioned like the core she used on the water screw.

Reverently setting down her plate, she padded closer. She could feel the heat rolling off the iron chamber. Inside, she knew there would be a foot-wide rune carved into the floor. Charged with power, it would burn for a year or more until the last of the magical energy faded. Like the urn, the chamber was rechargeable as long as the mage who created it was available to pour more energy into it. Above the heavy, sealed door, a small plaque held the name and lineage of the mage who created the rune along with the name of the mechanic who built it. Kanéko peered at it, her excitement rising. "It's a Farimon Chamber," she whispered reverently.

She had read about Farimon in *Emerging Wizardry*. He was one of the pioneers of rune magic and the inventor of the fire core and chambers. With his artifacts, those with a little or no measure of magic could use power indirectly. The saw at the mill and her water screw were just two applications of Farimon's inventions, and Kanéko couldn't help feeling more than a little respect for the man who had given her a chance to prove herself to her father.

Kanéko looked over the machine, and then traced the pipes and tubes that spread out from the core. They were similar to her designs, but the ones she worked with were based on gears, the saw blade used only a few large wheels attached to rods and bearings. The rest of it consisted of pressure pipes and gauges. It was simple and refined, far beyond what Kanéko had learned.

She smiled to herself as she sank to the ground, crossing her legs underneath her and peering up at the pipes and gauges. She followed each one, memorizing the network of pipes and struggling to learn from a man who lived on the opposite side of the continent.

When she hit the limits of what she could see, she got up and shifted to the other side of the saw blade. Sitting back down, she inspected the pattern of pipes and release valves. When the copper pipes stretched out of sight, she recalled the ones from the other side of the saw. It was relatively easy to imagine both sides at the same time. She could picture them in her head, a three-dimensional model of the entire mechanism that traced out every pipe, bolt, and joint.

As Kanéko puzzled through Farimon's designs, she wondered if she would ever get another chance to see a device like the saw again. She knew the itinerary planned for the trip: a long ride to the coast near the capitol, a few weeks of trips away from the beach, and then a return home. All of the stops along the route were cities highlighting the magical prowess and political might of Kormar. None of them interested Kanéko, she wanted to build machines not hear speeches.

She sighed. Only the nearest large city, Jinto Panzir, had anything resembling folks with mechanical skills. There was a growing community of engineers that she read about in *Emerging Wizardry*. They would understand her plight and maybe even accept her. She dreamed of heading there instead of the ocean.

"Lady Lurkuklan?" Salcid's voice carried through the machines.

Kanéko jumped at his voice. She looked up as the older dalpre walked toward her, his boots thumping on the wooden floor. He carried a plate and a mug. She felt a shiver of disgust at the half-human creature walking toward her, but she remembered Garèo's advice and forced herself to remain sitting on the ground.

Salcid stopped a few paces from her and set down his plate. Holding the mug in both hands, he leaned back into a cold water intake. "She isn't a bad girl, Lady Lurkuklan. My daughter, Maris."

He sighed before continuing, "And she can be hot-headed and impulsive, but she's a good girl. And she just..." He let out a soft growl. "She just has to prove so much to those in town. And she gets teased so much at school for being a dalpre. And she started school almost ten years after everyone else. But, it's been less than a year. And she doesn't think before she acts. But... I..." He grumbled in the back of his throat before he drank from his mug. "Could you give her a chance, please?"

Kanéko remained silent, a sullen anger burning inside her.

Salcid set down his mug next to his plate. "I've served your father loyally for my entire life just as my father served your grandfather. And Maris will serve you. And I don't want bad blood when that happens."

Kanéko looked up at the ceiling and she thought about Garèo's words. She had an idea of what to say, what to do, but she wasn't sure. She cleared her throat. "Salcid?"

"Yes, Lady Lurkuklan?"

"I-I'm..." It was hard to get the words out. "I'm sorry for insulting your daughter and your pack."

At his relieved expression, Kanéko felt a surge of relief. She only half meant it, but Garèo was right. She had to admit that it was her fault, even if only her initial words were offensive.

Salcid's tail tapped on the pipe and his ears perked up. "Thank you, Lady Lurkuklan. You'll find she is very loyal and friendly if you—"

He continued to speak, but Kanéko stopped paying attention. She realized that he expected her to follow in her father's footsteps. The only problem was her father made his name in multiple battles and becoming a Fourth Circle knight and a mage known throughout the lands. She could never fit in his footprints, not without magic.

Kanéko had to prove herself with the only skill she appeared to have: her mechanical skill. She needed to learn more and to find out how to create devices like the Farimon device above her instead of her fumbling efforts in the stable. She needed help and the only place she knew to find it was Jinto Panzir.

Garèo would never allow her to leave the rest of the students to go to Panzir. She suspected it also violated the Silver King's law that all teenagers must travel at least a hundred leagues before their twenties. But she could always do it later, once she proved herself to her father, and the world.

Inside her mind, she started to plan a way out of the trip so she could head for Panzir. Garèo would probably hunt her down, but she only needed a day or two to prove herself. Three, at the most.

She realized Salcid was still talking. She held up her hand to halt him.

When he stopped talking, she spoke. "I'm sure it will work out, and I look forward to that day."

It was a lie, but a good one.

Chapter 7

An Ally

The idea that teenagers need to see the world is a waste of money and time. They can learn everything they need in life by staying within a mile of home.

—Duke Mortir Galasnom

Kanéko knew that her plans for running away were a little girl's fantasy, but it didn't stop her from amusing herself with the idea. After her decision, though, the fantasies were more focused and precise. She focused on specifics: scenarios to avoid Garèo, how much food and water she needed for her trip, and even the best place to escape. She knew the route, at least roughly, and the trip would take them through Raisen before heading up north. Raisen was the closest point to Jinto Panzir and her best option.

Doubt plagued her, though. She knew that she would never escape Garèo, no matter what she did. But the fantasy helped her pass the time and not pay attention to her other troubles: Maris, the water screw, and her father.

As she daydreamed, reality seeped in through the cracks of her concentration. The aches and pains from her fight with Maris burrowed into her thoughts, reminding her of the dalpre behind her in the wagon. Kanéko gingerly pressed her lips together and felt the throb of her split lip.

Annoyed, she opened her eyes and stared out at the road between the horse's ears.

"Joining us again, child?" Garèo's voice was low but tinged with amusement.

She glared at him. She remembered how he humiliated her when he encouraged the fight and then bet against her. She knew it was a lesson, and she failed. The realization only sharpened her dislike of the darker-skinned man. *"Drown yourself in sands, old man."*

Garèo chuckled. *"Sometimes I wonder if being Great Kosobyo Mioráshi's daughter has infected you with her inability to communicate without swearing."*

"You are a rancid bucket of milk," Kanéko snapped.

"Naturally, you are without the magic that comes from her swearing, which makes you just a crow screeching at its own shadow."

"Rot in the seven—"

Garèo barked out a laugh, interrupting her.

The horse pulling the wagon shook his mane and snickered along.

Kanéko glanced at the equine then back to Garèo. She wasn't sure, but it seemed the horse also laughed at her.

He didn't need reins or a halter, only the harness to keep the horse attached to the wagon. She guessed he had some clan ability with horses, but he had refused to answer when she asked him earlier. She could only assume his powers by the way the horses responded without him touching them.

Kanéko turned away from Garèo and looked around. They were at the edge of Rock River, a town of two thousand on the edge of her father's bartim lands. She visited the town a few times, usually during festivals or tax season, but never just to explore. It was always as part of her father's entourage and he kept her close. She vaguely recognized many of the smaller houses on the edge of town, but she usually spent her time among the two-story buildings packed in neat lines along the main thoroughfares that crossed each other in the town center. The village illustrated the modern theories of civil planning, something Kanéko never thought about until she started reading *Emerging Wizardry*.

Unlike the small village at the keep, Rock River was a bustling town, and loud. Not quite the overwhelming noise of Germudrir Mill, but still far busier than Kanéko remembered. Visiting the village during somber occasions with her father, like Founder's Day, had left Kanéko unprepared for the village's everyday commotion. Her mouth opened with surprise as she watched the elegant women stroll down the street. They wore dresses she only saw in her serials. The illustrations on paper couldn't begin to describe the deep, rich colors or the flowing fabric. The cut of cloth accented narrow waists and moved beautifully to flared collars and sleeves. Kanéko felt a pang of jealousy at the women with curves, and she wondered how so many of them looked exactly like the pictures.

Like the women, the men strolling the street were dressed in their finest. They wore suits despite the dust rising up from the cobblestone roads and the heat of early summer. Kanéko gaped at their hats and canes, mostly worn for show but still a far cry from her father's plain outfits.

"Why do they dress up like that?" she asked in a whisper.

Garèo grunted. "They read about fashions from the ocean cities. And then they pay too much money to bring in fabric from other countries just so they can waste it on hiring a seamstress to make them a dress. To get some value in their useless outfits, they stroll up and down the streets, preening because they think they are someone because they bought an outfit."

Maris said, "But I think they're pretty."

Kanéko peered over at her shoulder at Maris. She didn't say it, but Kanéko felt the same way.

The dalpre sat on the far edge of Kanéko's trunk, her feet dangling over the back end of the wagon. She had her eyes closed and nose up in the air, sniffing loudly. Her tail thumped against the top of the trunk, a steady beat in time with her sniffing. Kanéko saw a smile on Maris's lips as the dog girl rocked her head back and forth.

"*Garèo?*" Kanéko whispered.

"*Yes?*"

"*What is the dog girl doing?*"

Garèo turned in the seat to look at her; the horse continued forward without his guidance. He smiled broadly when he saw Maris, and then turned to Kanéko. "*Smelling the air, even you should be able to figure that out.*"

"*I know that.*" She snapped at him, "*Why?*"

He shrugged and turned back in his seat. "*The same reason you remain awake at night working on your machine. The same reason we do anything. She is being herself.*"

Kanéko glared at Garèo but turned away before he caught her looking. She focused her attention on Maris, but then caught sight of Ojinkomàsu behind the wagon.

The desert horse walked along the side of the road, his shoeless hooves tapping on the cobblestones. Their eyes caught each other, and then he ducked his head behind a nearby barrel.

Kanéko stared in shock, wondering how the horse managed to find them.

Ojinkomàsu peeked up over the barrel and then ducked back down.

She chuckled at the sight of a stallion trying to hide beyond something a quarter his size. *"Great Waryoni Garèo, Ojinkomàsu is following after us."*

"I know," snarled Garèo but didn't look back, *"That sand-damned horse has been following us since outside of the mill."*

"How... how did you know? I never saw you look back."

"I can feel him in my head, no matter where I go."

Kanéko felt a chance to ask a question Garèo always avoided. *"Great Waryoni Garèo? Why do you refuse to ride Ojinkomàsu?"*

Garèo chuckled dryly. *"You are polite when you want something. What makes you think I won't ride him?"*

"You have a power with horses, but you never use them on Ojinkomàsu. My father said he is a beautiful horse and a worthy mount, but you make an effort to pointely ignore him."

He sighed and rubbed his shoulder, his fingertips stroking along the leather of his weapon belt. *"I don't deserve to ride Ojinkomàsu. Not now, not ever. But, I can't get rid of him either."*

She thought for a moment. *"You tried, right? But Mama wouldn't take him?"*

"Despite your inexperience, you are quite observant and intelligent. You would have been a credit to the sun." He sighed. *"I tried, but your mother knew that I didn't have the right. There is only one being who decides who rides Ojinkomàsu."*

"Who?"

She wasn't surprised when he didn't answer.

Kanéko focused on Ojinkomàsu. The horse walked behind an elegantly-dressed woman, keeping his head below her feathered hat. But, Kanéko could still see the horse's shoulders and tail around the woman's deep blue dress.

The woman looked up at Kanéko, slowed to a stop, and then turned around. When she saw Ojinkomàsu only inches away from her face, she let out a high-pitched scream.

The wagon slowed down and Garèo snapped his head a-round. *"You worthless, sun-burned spawn of a mule!"* He screamed in Miwāfu. Without waiting for the wagon to stop, Garèo vaulted off and ran back toward Ojinkomàsu, yelling at the top of his lungs.

Kanéko sat back to watch with a smirk on her lips. It was the first time she had seen him lose his temper.

Ojinkomàsu lifted his head, and then stepped back away. His rear slammed into another wagon and knocked it off course. The side of the wheel crashed into the boardwalk and a splintering noise filled the air.

The wagon driver fell off his wagon, and his two horses reared with panic. One ran straight as the other reared and the wagon threatened to tilt on its side.

"Gachímo!" Garèo belted out a word that Kanéko didn't know, and the two horses settled down instantly. Kanéko could see them strain to move, but something held them in place. Even their tails were still.

Garèo ran past the wagon and grabbed Ojinkomàsu's mane.

Kanéko settled into place to watch Garèo's struggle. She felt a fierce joy at his discomfort, and she knew she smiled, but didn't care. She watched as Garèo tried to interpose himself between the screaming woman and Ojinkomàsu, while grabbing for a horse with no reins.

Maris shifted in her seat as her ears perked up.

Kanéko tore her attention away to look at the dalpre.

Maris's tail thumped loudly thrice before it grew still. Her ears jerked, and the girl turned around to kneel on Kanéko's trunk.

Kanéko almost looked away, embarrassed to be staring at Maris, but Maris wasn't looking at her. Instead, she looked past Kanéko and down the street with a frown on her face and her ears against her head. Kanéko followed Maris's gaze, but didn't see anything besides people on the board-walks, wagons parked on the side of the road, and the normal life she expected in a village.

Then, faintly, she thought she heard a whistle.

"Ruben!" Maris's sudden bark hurt Kanéko's ears.

Kanéko twisted her body to identify what Maris was barking at.

The dalpre jumped past Kanéko, smacking her in the head with her tail. There was a brief flash of red fabric and a black hair before the girl landed heavily on the ground. With a growl, she staggered forward until she planted one hand on the cobblestones to halt her fall. Regaining her balance, she sprinted down the street. "Ruben!"

Kanéko watched her in confusion, and then called out over her shoulder. "Garèo? Who is Ruben?"

Garèo turned to look at her as he struggled with the crowds gathering around him and Ojinkomàsu, and then his eyes widened.

"Where is Maris—" he looked up the road ahead to the running girl, and then called out to Kanéko. "*Stop her!*"

For a moment, Kanéko considered actually obeying, but the aches and pains from her brawl with the dog girl stopped her. She shrugged. "Why?"

"*Girl! I said, stop her! Do it or she won't go on the trip.*"

The idea of Maris remaining behind seemed appealing. Kanéko shrugged again but said nothing more. She settled down with a smile on her lips.

Garèo's expression darkened. He pulled away from Ojinkomàsu, but the horse grabbed his sleeve and pulled back. Garèo struggled with Ojinkomàsu for a moment, and then snapped out sharply. "*If she hurts someone, you don't go!*"

"What!? Why? I'm not doing anything wrong!" Kanéko crossed her arms over her chest and glared back at Garèo.

"*I said stop her, Kosobyo Kanéko!*"

She saw the dark look in his eyes, a storm about to break. It was the same look as her mother's, right before she blew up. She spun to watch Maris race around a corner. Kanéko jumped out of the wagon. She managed to run almost a chain before she realized she would never catch up to the racing dalpre if she followed the same route.

Slowing down, Kanéko looked around for a shortcut through the block Maris ran down. It was a group of tall, two-story houses. Most of the brown stone buildings were built right next to each other, but Kanéko spotted a gap between two where the color of brick changed from a lighter brown to a darker shade.

She trotted over to the gap and peered down it. A six-foot brick wall separated two large gardens and she could see a larger, more ornate building on the block beyond the houses. A sign hung over the front gate of the building and she could read "—k River Sch—". It was the school where Kanéko, Garèo, and Maris would meet with the other students before heading out on the trip. No doubt, it was also where Maris headed.

Kanéko decided to take the shortcut. She ran to the brick wall and scaled it. Her bare toes caught on the deep gaps between the bricks. It only took her a few seconds to regain her balance on top before she sprinted toward the far side of the block. A moment later, she got her first clear look at the school.

There were over half a hundred teenagers milling around ten large wagons and five adults trying to manage the peace. Most of the students were laughing, rough-housing, and generally being bored. She saw two dice games on the corner of the block and a card game near the gate opening.

She spotted a number of teenage boys circling around a smaller child. The child had black hair and a black vest over a white shirt. The larger, older boys pushed the kid around. One of them, a blond boy with muscles of a farm worker, caught her attention because one of his arms was wrapped in bandages. She wondered how it happened, but then remembered Garèo's comment about Maris breaking a boy's arm; Pah was his name, or at least short for something.

"Ruben!" Maris screamed from the far end of the block.

Kanéko regarded the sprinting dalpre heading toward the front of the building. From the expression on Maris's face, Kanéko knew that the dalpre was about to hurt someone, but Kanéko didn't know who. She wanted to find out if Maris would get in trouble, but she also didn't want Garèo to make her life worse until she could escape for Jinto Panzir.

Kanéko quickly looked for some way to safely descend. Below her, she spotted a cart filled with painting supplies parked up against the wall. The back end of the cart provided a clear spot to land.

She backed up. Kanéko timed Maris's charge and her own plans. As soon as Maris came back into view, Kanéko sprinted forward and jumped from the wall to the cart. She intended to jump off the back and slam into Maris.

But, when her feet hit the wooden deck, she felt it lurch underneath her. The front of the cart snapped up, flinging painting supplies into the air. She tried to watch them but lost her balance again, and the ground introduced itself to her face.

Sprawled across the cobblestones, Kanéko heard a thick splashing noise.

The conversations near the school silenced.

She struggled to her feet and brushed her copper hair away to look at the results of her fall.

Maris stood in the center of the street with whitewash dripping off every part of her body. Rivulets of white rolled down her hair and soaked into her dress. More droplets clung to the tips of her ears before falling off with the girl's shakes. Maris looked down at her hands, covered in paint. She blinked twice, and then looked at Kanéko with a look of hurt surprise.

Kanéko felt a smile growing inside her but she forced it off her face before Maris noticed. Standing up, she brushed the dust off her shirt and returned Maris's hurt look with an impassive glare.

Maris's bottom lip trembled, and then she burst into tears. "I hate you!"

The dalpre spun around and shoved her way past the gathered students. Kanéko could hear her crying in the stunned silence. Kanéko sighed and glanced up at everyone staring at her.

Students whispered, but no one made a move to help her, or to walk away.

Finally, the silence was broken as the blond boy with the broken arm came out. "Are you all right, um, Lady Lurkuklan?"

She wasn't used to being called by anything besides her first name or the familiar "Kané." She cleared her throat and nodded. "Yes, I-I'm all right."

The blond boy was slenderer than she initially thought, but the lines of his muscles showed that he was also strong. Much like the men at the mill, he was obviously someone who did labor when he wasn't in school. He had an easy smile, which he focused on her. Kanéko didn't know what to say and had to fight the urge to look away.

"My name is Pahim dim Maldor, but you can call me Pahim." He bowed deeply. "And I'm at your service, Lady Lurkuklan."

"Um, it's Kanéko."

"Kanek-o." He struggled with the Miwāfu name.

Kanéko didn't know how to respond. She peeked around at the people surrounding her, wondering what they thought of the dark-skinned stranger in their midst. She realized she didn't want them to hate her like the dalpre did. She gazed at Pahim. "Kanek is good. Y-You can call me Kanek." Kanéko hated that she stammered, but with so many eyes on at her, she felt both humiliated and on a pedestal at the same time.

Pahim held out his good hand. Kanéko stared at it, and then grabbed him the way Garèo and her mother did, at the elbow. They both fumbled with the gesture since he obviously wanted to shake hands, but he grasped near her elbow with only the shortest of hesitations.

Kanéko blushed even hotter and looked everywhere besides Pahim. She focused on the bandage of his left arm. There were small runes written on the white fabric. As she watched, they crawled along the cloth and pulsed with power. The magical runes would keep the flesh and bone protected until the body could heal itself. She knew the creator of the bandage; the same old man had just rushed to the keep to heal Jinmel. He wasn't a full healer, but he was the only thing Rock River had.

The memory of Jinmel and the explosion choked her. She felt an intense wave of guilt, but Pahim still held her arm. She released her grip and pulled her hand back, still unable to look at his face.

Both teenagers stood in the center of the street. Kanéko didn't know what to do, and she toed the ground trying not to think about everyone staring at her. Then, rescue came from an unlikely source.

"Girl, where is Maris?"

She breathed a sigh of relief and peeked at Pahim.

The blond made a sour face at Garèo, one that Kanéko found funny. She resisted giggling. Pahim hurried away before Garèo could reach them.

Kanéko turned to watch as the desert man strode up.

Behind the desert man, Ojinkomàsu and the wagon horse followed quietly.

Garèo repeated his question.

Kanéko considered whether to answer in Lorban or Miwāfu, not sure which one would embarrass her more. She picked Miwāfu. "*She went into the building, Great Waryoni Garèo.*"

Garèo's gaze focused on the splatter of paint on the road. His voice was terse and angry. "*What happened?*"

Kanéko tried to find some way of explaining it in a way that would blame Maris. She lied, "*She was running down the street and tripped on the cart. The cans spilled and she got paint dumped on her.*"

Garèo's green eyes bore into her, and Kanéko fidgeted under the glare. She wondered if he would call her on her lie, but then Garèo gestured to the school with his chin. "*Go help her, girl.*"

"*Why? I didn't do anything.*"

"*Because you, she, and Ruben are going to be in the same wagon for the entire trip, and I want you to be at least civil. You don't leave anyone alone, not now, not ever.*"

"But—"

"*Listen, Brat! I said, go help Maris!*" His voice echoed against the buildings. The surrounding teenagers backed away at the fury in his tone. She watched as they hurried back to their games and groups, glancing over their shoulders at her and Garèo as they fled.

Kanéko experienced a flashback at the sight of their backs; it reminded her of the mill only a few hours before.

She focused her attention back on Garèo as she fought with the growing desire to lash out at him.

Garèo's attitude changed in an instant. He gave her the same dangerous look as at the mill.

Her lips tightened as she considered her options. Finding none, she spun on her bare feet and stormed toward the school. She would obey, at least until she had the chance to escape. A few students in the front split apart as she entered. None of them looked at her. She ignored them, lifted her chin slightly, and smacked open the front door before charging inside.

Since she was tutored in the keep, Kanéko had never entered the school before. She slowed down a rod's distance from the door and looked around in an attempt to orient herself. There was a wide hall that ran the entire length of the building. She spotted hallways at the front, middle, and back that branched off into what she assumed were classrooms.

Unsure where to go, she headed down the main hall while looking around curiously.

Like most rural schools, the Rock River School taught all students within an hour walk of the village. The pictures in the hallways ranged from the scrawled drawings of a young child to the slightly more refined landscape of an older child. One picture caught her attention when she recognized the Germudrir Mill. The scrawls looked like the work of a five-year old, but she saw Maris's name printed roughly on the bottom. Kanéko frowned because Maris seemed far older than she would have guessed from the picture.

She peered into classrooms, at the rough wooden benches and chalkboards covered with perpetual dust. She stopped at one door and wondered what it would be like to be in a class every day, learning with others instead of spending her days alone with tutors, Jinmel, and her books.

Kanéko continued to walk down the hallway. She reached the back of the school when she heard running water and Maris's humming echoing down the side hallway. Curious, Kanéko padded to the end of the hall, her callused bare feet scuffing on the wooden floor. At the end, she spotted an opening with a sign hanging on the right side of the arch. The sign said "Showers" with a droplet painted to the right of the words. Below the sign was a disc with "Girls" written on it along with a stylized image. Kanéko flipped the disc over so it said "Boys" with a corresponding picture. With a grin, she flipped it to "Girls" and went inside.

The water rained down in the shower area as Kanéko inched forward, pressing her hands along the wall to peek around the corner. She froze when she saw Maris sitting on a bench with her back to Kanéko. It took only a heartbeat for Kanéko to realize Maris was naked.

Maris's dark hair ran down her back, following the curves of her shoulders before ending near the middle of her back. Her ears were perked up, splashing water whenever she moved. The rivers of water continued down along Maris's tanned skin, along her curves, and over her wide hips.

A strange feeling crossed over her, as if she was thirsty without having a dry throat. Her stomach tingled and her skin to prickled with sweat, but it wasn't from a sudden wave of illness or nausea. Kanéko frowned as she turned away until the sensations subsided. Then, curiosity drew her and she peeked back.

Maris's tail continued from the end of her spine, dipping straight down but then curving up. It wagged back and forth slowly, water sluicing off it with every movement and droplets of water splattering in a line behind her. Even with the sluggish movements, Maris's entire body wagged with it.

Underneath Maris, a pool of water and paint reached out for a drain, circling around the grill in a white vortex before disappearing. Flecks of water splashed down into the puddle, thrown off Maris's wagging tail.

The dalpre hummed cheerfully as she cleaned her dress. Her hands worked steadily, rubbing the fabric together as she held it underneath the stream of water. Kanéko didn't see mist rising up from it and knew it was cold. To Kanéko's surprise, Maris didn't shiver, and her spirits seemed high for being recently doused in paint and now soaked.

Kanéko knew she should go in and apologize. Seeing Maris working in good cheer, even though the dalpre was crying moments before, she guessed that Maris had already forgiven or forgotten Kanéko. But, even with that, Kanéko couldn't find the courage to step into the shower. Her pride and humiliation stayed her feet. Not to mention, she was blushing and wasn't sure why. Her heart pounded in her chest as she fought with her guilt and other emotions.

Maris, not responding to Kanéko's presence, finished scrubbing her top. She spread it out flat on the wooden bench and bent over to grab her skirt bottom. Her large breasts hung in Kanéko's view, pale and large. The tips were darker than Kanéko expected.

Kanéko's blush grew hotter and she turned away, trying not to compare herself to the dalpre. She concentrated on sneaking away and came up with a story of how she couldn't find Maris but stopped when she saw someone standing in front of her.

It was the black-haired child Pahim tormented. He didn't make a sound as he stared at her.

She started to say something but then she did a double take. His face looked too old for a youth. Instead, he looked similar to the other students outside. She took another look, forcing herself to take in the details.

He was short, maybe slightly over a yard in height, but his head looked large for his arms and legs. His body was proportional to his limbs and she realized he was probably her age, just much shorter.

Kanéko gulped and, for the second time in the day, she faced something utterly foreign to her upbringing. Then, she caught sight of his eyes. Unlike most of the country, he didn't have the browns of the Kormar folk or even the green eyes of the desert. Instead, he possessed a piercing blue gaze that bore directly into Kanéko.

She trembled, unable to tear her eyes away from him. Her hand still clutched the edge of the wall leading into the showers, but she didn't know where or how to move. His eyes had her trapped. A whimper rose in her throat, and her breath grew shallower the longer their gazes matched.

Then, in the back of her head, she felt a strange itching sensation, like something tickling the back of her thoughts. She frowned and tried to step in any direction besides the blue-eyed boy. He didn't even blink as he stared at her, which frightened her almost as much.

As soon as she thought about his blinking, the boy blinked once, slowly and deliberately.

Kanéko wondered if he could somehow read her mind.

The boy cocked his head for a moment. His expression didn't change. Then he stepped to the side and gestured with one hand for her to pass.

Kanéko pushed herself off the wall and hurried past him. She looked over her shoulder, and he stared back at her. Embarrassment and humiliation burned inside her; they were two feelings she had grown accustomed to that day. She ran down the hall, slowing down only near the center of the school. She stopped and peeked over her shoulder, but the boy was gone.

She breathed a sigh of relief, and then winced when she heard Maris cry out, "Ruben!" A moment later, barking laughter.

Kanéko needed to escape. She turned down the side hallway and ran toward the door she saw at the far end. She would exit at the side of the school, but hopefully away from Garèo and the others. She didn't know what to do or where to go. The door banged open as she ran out. Coming to a stop, she spun around and slammed the door shut behind her.

"You look—"

Kanéko shrieked with surprise when Pahim started to speak. She fell back against the door and a strong hand grabbed her to prevent her from falling. She looked up at the blond teenage boy, her mouth working silently as she struggled with fear and her pounding heart.

Pahim chuckled and set her against the wall before releasing her. "You look like you were chased by a monster."

Seeing his smile, Kanéko gave him a hesitant grin. "No, just Maris and... and... the short boy."

Pahim rolled his eyes. "Garèo's other little freak, Ruben. He's a vomen."

Vomen, the short people from the Isle of Vo, a forbidden place of secrecy and corruption. The isle was known for many things, including powerful magic where everyone worked in perfect unison and silence. In her books, nothing good ever came out of the isle, and she suppressed a shiver at the thought.

Pahim continued, "You don't want to be around them. They are outcasts and monsters."

"But, Garèo—"

"Garèo isn't much better," he grumbled. "The only reason Maris and Ruben are assigned to him is because the bartim told the school to give him a job and none of the other teachers want the bitch and short one. Monsters." He finished by leaning on the wall next to Kanéko. His eyes drew down her body slowly.

The look made her uncomfortable, like he was staring too much.

"You're too pretty to be a monster though," he finally said.

She twisted at his words. She didn't know how to respond.

He slowly looked away and gestured with a lazy wave toward the edge of town. "Some days, I can't wait to get out of here."

"The school?" she asked.

"No, Rock River. As soon as I hit seventeen, I'm going to see if I can join my father's airship."

All the discomfort and fears burned away in the sudden excitement. Kanéko gasped and smiled. "Your father owns an airship? A real ship?"

Pahim grinned but shook his head. "Not quite. He's on the deck crew. The *Burning Cloud Queen* is run by Captain Sinmak Bilmour. It flies out of Jinto Panzir."

Kanéko sighed as her dream of running away came back. "I heard Panzir has the largest air dock in a thousand leagues."

Leaning his side on the wall to keep looking at her, Pahim said, "It does. There are these four buildings with decks between them, at least ten stories tall. Airships of all sizes, from the small boats to the frigates, come in and dock. And the town itself... well, I don't think I've seen more—"

Kanéko couldn't help but interrupt him. "They have engineering? Machines? Cores?"

Pahim's brown eyes stared into hers and he smiled broadly. "They have everything. There is a crafting quarter where they design and build machines. There are even three workshops off the main road that make steam cars. Just last year, the city council allowed them on the streets without resonance permits."

"Really? What about the laws? I thought most towns still arrest the drivers for using artifacts in city limits."

"Not Panzir. They have three builders on the council and have proven that driving a steam vehicle won't cause every artifact in town to explode. And no one has gotten even a headache in the presence of a machine."

"Wow," she sighed, "I wish I could see it."

He didn't answer.

Kanéko leaned back on the wall and stared out into the school yard as she listened to the noise. She liked Pahim, but she wasn't sure why. He was the only person she'd met that wasn't upset with her. Or it could be the first time she ever met a teenage boy alone. She smiled, wondering if her dreams would eventually include him.

"Come with me," Pahim said.

Kanéko gasped and looked at him, a flush growing on her cheeks.

Pahim's smile broadened but he held up his hands. "No, no, not like that. I mean, on my wagon to the first campground. I'm the driver."

"Oh," Kanéko said in an embarrassed tone, "I thought... what about Garèo?"

Pahim shrugged and leaned his head on the wall. His blond hair caught on the bricks. "Garèo's going to stick you with Ruben and Maris in wagon ten. I think he's planning on driving that one since he hasn't assigned one of the older students to it. Ruben is older but he can't handle horses at all with those tiny arms. So..." He turned to her. "Come with me."

Kanéko's heart skipped a beat. She thought about Garèo's threat to train her every night, Maris attacking her, and even Ruben's unblinking eyes. It didn't take long to make a decision.

"I will."

He pushed himself off the wall. Reaching down, he plucked something off the ground.

Kanéko watched as he separated the dirt from around a seed. With a grin, Pahim closed his hands. A moment later, green leaves peeked out of his palm. A dandelion pushed up between two fingers and blossomed in a few seconds. He held out his hand. "For you."

Kanéko looked down at the flower, stunned and flush with the offering. She took it and stroked her fingers on the warm petals. She saw movement and looked over to see Pahim holding out his hands for hers.

She transferred the dandelion to her other hand and then rested hers on his palm. Her darker skin contrasted with his tanned grip, but he was gentle as he drew her from the wall. Kanéko blushed as Pahim guided her to the front wagon.

There were already six other students in the wagon. They were all older than Kanéko by a year or so, much like Pahim. She tried to remember the names of the three boys and the three girls, but by the time Pahim finished introducing her, she had already forgotten. It didn't help that they showed no interest in her. As soon as Pahim introduced them, they returned to their private conversations.

Pahim crawled up on the wagon and sat down on the bench. He patted the seat next to him, an obvious request for Kanéko.

She continued to blush hotly as she crawled up on the wagon next to Pahim, settling down on the thin cushion. She was excited and terrified at the same time.

He grabbed the reins and snapped them. The two horses started forward and the wagon jerked as it began to move.

Kanéko froze as she saw Garèo on the far side of the road, trying to wrangle a bunch of younger teenagers into a wagon.

He caught her gaze and stood up, a quizzical look on his face. Without her saying anything, she saw his green eyes darken and a frown cross his face.

She held her breath, waiting for him to call her.

After a few tense seconds, he shook his head and returned to his job.

Breathing a sigh of relief, Kanéko settled down on the bench. She smiled, enjoying the first taste of freedom she had felt since the stables exploded. It was finally going to be a good trip.

Chapter 8

Camping Partners

Kosòbyo's venom fills the veins of his clan members. He grants them endurance to survive the desert and an endless will to fight against all odds.

—Waryoni Tesúma, *The Feathered Serpent* (Stanza 8)

Kanéko's rear ached from a long day's travel. She groaned and adjusted the cushion underneath her in a hopeless attempt to reduce her discomfort. Her hair, braided to keep it bound from the wind, smacked the back of her elbow. She was tired of pulling it out of her face, the hard-board of a wagon bench, and everything else on the trip.

Next to her, Pahim snapped the whip against the horses' flanks. One of the horses threw his head, but neither the horse nor the wagon moved any faster over the rutted path. He seemed to do it to relieve his own boredom.

"About how much longer, Pah?"

Pahim smiled. He rubbed his nose with his arm and peered down the road. "I'd say about another ten minutes or so. The campground is on the northern side of that group of trees."

"Good, because I need a break."

D. Moonfire gment>

"Soon, Kanek."

She glanced at the others in the wagon. There were eight of them. Most of them passed the hours by sleeping on the benches and the floor. The travel bags were all used as pillows and cushions.

The only two awake were a dark-haired girl and a boy with a farmer's tan. They huddled in the far corner of the wagon, limbs intertwined as they touched and kissed.

Kanéko looked away quickly, uncomfortable with their intimate moment but drawn to it at the same time. She peeked over her shoulder until one caught her looking and glared. She snapped her head forward in embarrassment.

Desperate to keep her eyes away, she watched the wagon in front of her, pulled by a horse without a driver. It was Garèo's but only Maris and Ruben rode it. Garèo was currently riding in a different wagon out of sight. He knew that Kanéko was in the wagon with Pahim, but when he changed the order of wagons only a bell ago, he said nothing to either of them.

A bark drew her attention. Kanéko looked to the wagon in front of her where Maris crouched on the edge of Kanéko's trunk. Her eyes were closed, and her tail wagged violently. The sloppy smile on her face looked innocent, but comical.

Behind her, Ruben reached out with his tiny arm and snatched her tail.

Maris yelped and rolled forward, plummeting off the wagon with a thump.

Kanéko gasped and held her breath. She didn't think the dalpre could move before Pahim's wagon struck her.

Maris recovered quickly, scrambling back on the wagon and then jumping over the chest to land on Ruben. She pinned him to the back of the front bench before purposefully licking his face.

94

Kanéko smirked as Ruben's tiny arms flailed for a moment then they tumbled to the wagon floor and out of sight.

A heartbeat later, Maris's tail popped up, snapping back and forth. Kanéko could imagine her entire body moving in time with the swishing limb.

Pahim pointed toward the two and muttered. "Like children. They shouldn't even be here."

"Why are they?"

"Well, Maris's father probably bribed the town elders to get her in the school. If I had my way, she would be locked up with the rest of the dalpre."

"You mean at the sawmill?"

"No, I mean as slaves like the Blessed Father intended." His voice grew tense and angry, "Dalpre don't belong in schools and they sure don't deserve to run businesses like the mill. A human could do a better job with that place than a bunch of dogs. In fact, when they forced us to allow Maris to school, she couldn't even add two numbers or write her name."

Kanéko squirmed in her seat, not comfortable with Pahim's sharp tone. To distract him, she asked a different question, "How long ago was that?" She amended her question to make sure he didn't misunderstand. "When Maris arrived?"

"Two, maybe three years ago."

"Thirteen, and she couldn't read?"

He scoffed, "None of them can. I think only her father actually knows numbers. That was supposed to be the reason he sent her. Shouldn't have bothered, I say."

"How... how could they not? I mean, everyone knows their numbers and letters."

"They don't have the ability to learn. They're animals. It's part of their breeding. Maris still can't even read a book.

95

That is why Garèo is Maris's keeper, to keep them from the rest of the students. Ruben reads, and Maris fumbles through her tests."

Kanéko thought back to the mill. She could see humanity in the dalpre's actions. As much as she was uncomfortable near them, they weren't much different from other people. There was something about Pahim's words that felt wrong, but she didn't want to say anything to upset him.

She watched Ruben and Maris wrestle in the wagon.

Maris caught Ruben and tossed him into the air.

He landed on the edge of the chest and bounced off, windmilling his tiny arms silently as he plummeted to the ground.

Kanéko's heart skipped a beat, but Maris just hopped out of the wagon and grabbed him before he hit the ground. She tossed Ruben into the back and jumped in after him.

Ruben rolled over and made a grab at her tail again.

Maris barked and sat down on the smaller teenager's head.

Kanéko gestured toward the two. "What about Ruben?"

"The dwarf? He and his father are the only ones around home. His father isn't much taller than him. Garèo tells us to call them 'little people' but I consider that a joke. They aren't little, they're deformed. Huge heads and tiny arms. Twisted by the Isle of Vo. Heard of it?"

Kanéko thought back to her adventure novels. The dark isle featured in many of her novels as a place of terrible curses and monsters. Very few of the heroes in that book came out unscathed from the terrible place. She shuddered at the thought. "Yes, they were in my Nash novels."

"They say Vo changes people. I think it just shrinks their dicks and makes their heads too big."

Kanéko smirked at the thought and focused on Ruben.

The dwarf stood on Maris's chest, miming his dominance until the dog girl's foot snapped out and tripped him.

"Can he... is he stupid like Maris?"

Pahim remained silent for a moment, then he shook his head. "No, Ruben might be weak and tiny, but he's usually has the best scores in class. He also uses big words when he speaks, and only the teachers understand him. Garèo paired him with the bitch as a tutor, probably hoping they would average out to a single person, and they've been together ever since."

"Oh."

Kanéko let her eyes drift past the wagon in front of her to the entrance of the campsite as it came into view. Though the sun still burned brightly a few fingers above the tree line, someone had set up a line of torches to mark the opening. Three wagons had already stopped at the entrance. She watched teachers try to herd the teenagers further into the camp. She smirked as the boys and girls spread out instead, grabbing their bags and disregarding the clearly marked signs.

"I bet there will be singing," said Pahim.

She gestured toward Garèo, who had come to a halt at the campsite. Unlike the other teachers, when he bellowed out a command, the teenagers obeyed. "Garèo will insist on it."

They both shuddered at the thought. Pahim shook his head, "He keeps claiming he's a great singer, but every time he opens his mouth, I want to bury my head underground."

Kanéko grinned. "Every time I hear him, I just want to cut off my ears. Mama says he has talent also, but I've heard dogs howling that sounded better."

Pahim's eyes sparkled, and he favored her with a mischievous grin. Then he pointed to a hill with a large copse of trees on it. It stood on the opposite side of a road and well over a dozen chains before the campsite entrance. "Want to avoid song night?"

She looked at her keeper then over to Pahim. She answered with a smile and a nod.

Pahim grinned broadly and snapped out his whip, turning the horses and leading the wagon off road.

Behind them, in the wagon, the others sat up with curiosity.

Pahim announced cheerfully, "Finding a better spot without the kids. You all game?"

No one argued.

He stopped a few chains from the road, close enough to hear the faint sounds of the other teenagers but far enough that only a hint of movement was visible through the trees. They grabbed their supplies and headed to a low spot near a pond.

Kanéko helped Pahim set up his tent. She clutched the mallet and pounded stakes into the ground. She noticed Pahim watching her, and she fumbled with the mallet, dropping it with a blush.

Pahim knelt next to her, and she felt a brief skip of her heart. He wrapped the rope around the stake, his fingers brushing hers.

She sat back and watched as Pahim finished pitching his tent. It didn't take him long to get the musty canvas set up and catching the light breeze that coursed through their makeshift campsite.

Pahim's friends began setting up their tents, pairing off as they prepared to share. One of the tents was obviously meant for the couple kissing earlier, but the other two were paired along gender lines.

With a start, Kanéko realized there was only one tent with room for her: Pahim's. She gasped as she stared up at

Pahim, unfamiliar anticipation burning through her veins. She was afraid to say anything.

Pahim smiled at her. "Don't worry, Kanek, I'll take care of you." He returned to the wagon and grabbed another bundled tent from underneath the bench. He flapped it open right next to his with a grin. "It would be unseemly for a future bartim to be found sleeping with common men."

Kanéko giggled to hide her discomfort and relief. She snatched the mallet from the ground and helped him set up her own tent.

Garèo walked up before Kanéko finished pounding in the first stake. He looked unhappy as he peered at the tents around him. His hands remained in his pocket, but when he focused his green gaze on her, she felt a shiver down her spine. Around him, the other teenagers stopped pitching their tents and waited with guilty looks on their faces.

"Planning on staying here tonight?" He asked all of them, but his eyes remained locked on Kanéko.

No one answered until Kanéko spoke up. "Yes."

"I am not happy with you."

Kanéko could see that none of the others understood Miwāfu, but they responded to the sharp tone by backing away. She swallowed before she responded. *"I want to stay here, Great Waryoni Garèo."*

He thought for a second before answering. *"I won't stop you, Kanéko, you are supposed to grow up. But this is not the way I would expect one of Kosòbyo's to act."*

She said nothing, waiting for him to continue.

He didn't say anything at first. Instead, he turned around and started to walk away.

She waited impatiently for him to leave.

He stopped at the edge of the clearing and her stomach tensed. Without looking back, he spoke curtly. *"Kosòbyo Kanéko, you will present yourself for archery lessons in twenty min-*

utes. You'll bring back food and drinks here for your new friends. You all can skip out on the activities, but you will attend my lessons."

Relief flooded through her. She let out her breath in a long exhale, unable to take her eyes away from the desert man calmly walking through the trees.

"Um," Pahim sidled closer, "what did he say?"

Kanéko smiled at him. "He says we can stay."

Around her, the others cheered and then went back to their activities.

Pahim frowned. "That sounded very serious."

"Well, I need to be at archery practice in twenty minutes. But, I get to bring back food."

"Great! Mind if I come along?"

She blushed at his request and found herself unable to look into his brown eyes. Staring at the ground, she shook her head and tried to fight down the burning of her cheeks. "No, I'd like that."

"Well," he said in a sly voice, "we better hurry and finish pitching your tent."

Chapter 9

Archery Lessons

How can you be a warrior without a horse underneath you and a bow in your hands?

—Kyōti proverb

They left their tents after a half hour of stalling. Pahim beside her, the back of his hand occasionally touching hers as they walked down the road.

Garèo sat on one of the wagons, a large bundle of arrows at his feet and two bows, a desert horse bow and a Lorban war bow, resting against his thigh.

"You're late," he grumbled.

"Sorry, Great Waryoni Garèo."

"We'll start you with the war bow, then the horse bow. Fifty, fifty, and fifty arrows."

"What will the last fifty be for?"

He grinned, "On horseback. The campsite owner has a mount he is particularly proud of but wants to sell it to me. I want to see how well he rides. I won't buy it, but these pale-skinned people think that if a desert folk likes a horse, it's worth more than its weight in meat. I found that Kormar horses have no voices, so it should be right for a beginning rider."

She flushed at the insult, balling her hands into fists. Garèo watched her, and she knew he waited for her to snap back. Instead, she set her jaw tightly and held out her hand. *"Please, Great Waryoni Garèo, the bow?"*

Garèo held out the heavy bow.

Bending over, she picked up the first bundle with narrow tips and long feathers. She looked over to Pahim who gave her an encouraging smile. Kanéko took a step toward him, but Garèo's voice shot out.

"Now, Girl! I'm hungry."

Turning on her heels, she walked over to the first line on the ground. Away from her, she could see an impromptu target set up between two trees. A measuring chain lay coiled next to her, no doubt used to determine the distance. Beyond the target, she could see a smaller target another chain away and finally a third one an equal distance beyond the second.

Behind her, Garèo spoke up curtly, *"Fire on the beat, one additional arrow tomorrow for each miss today."*

Kanéko held the heavy bow in her hand and snapped the string that bundled the arrows. Setting them down at her feet, she picked up two. Putting one in her mouth, she fitted the first. Her world grew dark as she focused on her target. She felt her heart pounding and willed it to slow. Focusing on her breath, she watched how her entire body pulsed with each beat, a twitch that could be the difference between a hit or miss.

Garèo slapped his hand on his thigh. Between one breath and the next, she released the arrow. It shot through the air, slamming into the nearest target along the second ring. Snatching the arrow from her mouth, she fitted it before Garèo slapped his hand again. When he smacked his hand, she let the second arrow fly through the air. It punched into the rim of the furthest target. She grabbed the next one from the ground but was barely able to aim before he clapped.

Shaft after shaft flew through the air. She could easily hit the nearest target. She focused on the second and third and missed more often.

Garèo kept up with his pace, slapping or clapping his hands together in a rhythm. Fortunately, he didn't say anything. When he increased his pace, she struggled to keep up, barely getting an arrow on the bowstring before releasing it.

She missed the last eight shots and felt a flush burning on her cheeks from the humiliation. When the last arrow clattered on the ground beyond the first target, she hung her head.

Someone applauded.

She froze.

At first, she thought it was Garèo, but immediately dismissed it. Peeking up, she saw Maris standing next to Ruben, clapping her hands as she bounced up and down. Kanéko started to smile from the attention but stopped when she caught sight of Pahim. She turned away, trying to fight the rush from the unexpected applause.

Garèo cleared his throat and brusquely jammed the horse bow in front of her. "*That was terrible, Girl. You missed seventeen times and barely hit the target on twelve more. Tomorrow, we'll add twenty-three to your fifty.*"

"I hit more than that!"

"*I'm adding an extra arrow for every two that you barely hit. Maybe then you'll learn how to fire with more skill than a child. I can only hope you'll get better with this sooner than I run out of arrows for you to break.*"

Kanéko stared down at the Kyōti horse bow he held out to her. Unlike the Lorban war bow, which stood as tall as herself, the horse bow barely touched her hip when set on the ground. The aged wood felt warm in her palm and the feathers at the top shook with her heartbeat. She ran fingers along the curved surface and took a long breath. Somehow, just holding the bow gave her comfort.

He released the bow and spoke harshly, *"Hopefully, you won't be as pathetic with your own heritage."*

Her improving mood soured instantly, leaving only humiliation and anger in its wake. Kanéko stormed over to the arrows and grabbed the second bundle. Unlike the first set, the horse bow used shorter shafts with wider feathers and a broad tip. She dug her fingers around the rope binding them together and hauled them to her firing line. Using one arrowhead to cut the rope, she propped the arrows and prepared to fire the second bow.

Garèo barely gave her a chance to aim when he clapped his hands.

Reflexively, Kanéko fired, and the arrow missed the first target by a few links. The second missed by almost a chain. She flushed hotter and forced herself to ignore the next clap, taking the time to aim carefully. When the fourth signal came, she fired smoothly and the arrow arched through the air, punching into the center of the third target.

Pahim and Maris cheered her on.

Kanéko hit the third target again, this time on the rim. Encouraged, she fired in time with Garèo's clapping.

Before she knew it, she was done. Her fingers clutched the empty air at her feet before she glanced down to see only an empty string on the ground at her bare feet. She only missed seven times. A broad smile stretched across her face, and she set the tip of the bow on her foot and stood up straight.

"You're amazing!" yelled Pahim, which only widened her smile.

Surrounding the archery range, other students had gathered to watch with curiosity. Maris and Ruben were in the front, and the dog girl clapped happily while bouncing energetically. Next to her, Ruben tapped fingers into his palm in a slow, measured rate. A smattering of other clapping and cheers rose from the others.

Kanéko stared at the gathered teenagers and felt some of her mood evaporating. She could feel their gazes on her and didn't know if she could meet up to their expectations. She saw curiosity in those eyes and felt distinctly different than the others with her green eyes and dark skin.

"*Better,*" grumbled Garèo as he walked up, "*but your aim is still terrible.*"

Behind him, a horse with bridle and reins followed his footsteps.

Kanéko tore her gaze away from the students and gestured to the target. She used Miwāfu to avoid the others understanding her words. "*I hit almost every time.*"

Garèo's green eyes glowed in the dusk and he shook his head curtly. "*What you didn't miss, I barely consider a hit. I'd expect Miorāshi's daughter to hit the center fifty out of fifty. Not some rim or edge.*"

Kanéko's mouth dropped open in shock. She gestured to the target and snapped sharply, "*I hit the furthest target!*"

He looked down the shooting line, then shook his head. "*No, you hit the third one.*"

"*There isn't a fourth...*" Her voice trailed off as she finally noticed the fourth target: a single circle painted on a tree two chains beyond the furthest target. A torch burned near the tree, giving enough light to reveal the target. "*You have to be kidding!*"

Garèo shrugged. "*Miorāshi's could hit it every time.*"

"*I bet you can't,*" she replied sullenly.

He answered by snatching the bow from her hand. Reaching up, he pulled an arrow from the bundle strapped to the horse's saddle. He didn't even pause to aim but released the string as soon as he pointed the bow in the right direction. The arrow shot out with a crack and plunged into the edge of the furthest circle.

Kanéko stared with shock, her mouth open. Around her, the students cheered louder for him than Kanéko.

Garèo jammed the bow back into her hand. *"I'm adding ten tomorrow for that demonstration."*

She squeezed the shaft of the bow, her lips pressed into a thin, tight line. *"You almost missed."*

"You are the daughter of a talented archer and a Kosòbyo. The bow is your clan's weapon. You should able to beat me every time. And twenty more arrows tomorrow."

Kanéko pressed her lips together tight to avoid more punishments.

He held out the reins to her.

She looked over the dappled brown stallion. With a deep breath, she grabbed them. The leather hung loosely in his hand, but the horse had made no effort to step away.

Then, as Garèo turned away, she felt the strength of the stallion yanking the reins from her fingers.

She dropped the bow to grab with both hands, bearing down on the mount. Garèo's disapproving grunt only made her more flustered and she took a long time to calm down the horse enough to pick her bow back up.

"Children of Tachìra don't let their bows ever touch the sand."

She snapped back, *"We aren't in the desert, so it hasn't!"*

As she struggled to get on the equine, she distinctly felt Pahim's and the others attention on her back. She wanted to impress everyone, but the reins kept slipping from her fingers. Glancing over her shoulder, she saw Pahim grinning. She snatched the reins and clamped her fingers tightly over them. Looking away, she glanced across the horse and saw Garèo on the other side. He wore a glare of disapproval which only fanned the storm of emotions inside her.

Swearing under her breath, she managed to settle properly on the horse. Unlike Ojinkomàsu, who refused anything but a blanket, the horse beneath her wore a poor-quality saddle with a broken pommel and frayed stitching. She made a face while running her fingers on the cracked leather edges.

Garèo grunted impatiently. *"I'd like to eat my dinner before dark. You may not be joining us, but I plan on enjoying some singing."*

Kanéko glared at him and tugged the reins to spin the horse around. The stallion resisted at first, but she dug her heels in and manhandled her mount around. Kicking, she set the stallion into a gallop a furlong down the road. Turning around, she pulled up her bow and kicked the horse into action with a little more force than she intended.

The horse started to buck but then quieted. It trotted forward.

She fired five arrows at the largest target, hitting once. Without looking at Garèo, she spun the mount around and took a second pass. This time, she hit the rim of the target.

Garèo called out as she passed, *"Faster, girl!"*

Accelerating into a gallop, she continued to shoot at the target, missing far more often than she hit. She felt the burn of humiliation but couldn't focus enough to hit. After the sixth pass, the horse stumbled on the turn. She started to kick it into a gallop, but Garèo stopped her with a barked command.

Coming to a halt, she panted and stared at the target. Arrows littered the ground and she hated the sight of them. Only four arrows stuck on the target, none of them even close to the center.

Garèo approached. "Hold on."

She watched him warily.

He knelt down just behind the horse's right front hoof.

Underneath her, the horse grow still and hold its breath. The stallion lifted one foot obediently and set it in Garèo's hands.

He inspected the horse for damage. When he stood up, he motioned for her to dismount.

Kanéko did, then staggered as sore muscles reported themselves. The tips of her fingers burned from firing the bow.

Garèo held out his hand, but she leaned away from him.

She spoke gingerly, "Is the horse okay?"

"Yes, but it is getting dark," he said in Miwāfu.

Kanéko leaned against the panting horse and took a deep breath herself.

He shook his head and held out his hand for the bow. *"We're done for tonight. Hopefully tomorrow, you won't be as terrible."*

She glared at him.

Garèo stepped closer and spoke in a quieter, but much angrier, voice. *"Girl, you are acting like a spoiled child with no concept of the hard realities of—"*

He paused and took a deep breath. When he spoke again, his voice was less angry. *"The path you are racing down is lined with dangers. Whatever your plans are, I hope that you don't burn the sands by making an irreversible decision."*

She frowned, then shook her head. "What... *what do you mean?*"

"Your father's culture honors virginity, or at least the appearance of innocence, in girls such as yourself–"

Kanéko blushed hotly.

Garèo leaned closer. *"—and you seem to be quickly running to Pahim's bedroll."*

Kanéko couldn't match the burning eyes that bore into her. She stared at the ground and clutched the bow tightly.

Garèo continued. *"Mioráshi would skin me, you, and Pahim alive if you come home with child."*

"I won't—"

"The correct answer is 'Yes, Great Waryoni Garèo.' And then go feed your false friends."

Anger and humiliation warred inside Kanéko. She hated Garèo for pushing her the second they left her father's lands. The threats of practice every night and knowing that she would be the center of attention during it, smoldered her throat. She also felt humiliated that he spoke frankly of the questions she asked herself. She didn't know if she would do anything with Pahim, but having it laid bare by his scathing words only fueled the anger inside her. *"Yes, Great Waryoni Garèo."*

Garèo turned his back on her and tended to the horse.

After a second, Kanéko limped away to gather up the arrows that didn't break. When she did, she bound them in string and set them down next to the bow and headed back to the camp.

Pahim joined her. "You were amazing!"

Embarrassed, she smiled bashfully. "Thank you."

"No, I mean really amazing. I've never seen someone hit a target that far away!"

"Quiet," she said with false modesty but enjoying every word he said. She looked down to see Pahim's hand held out for her. She thought back to Garèo's words and reached down. Their fingers touched before they slid their palms together.

He glanced at her and she blushed even hotter.

Pahim slid his fingers between hers, and they walked into the camp holding hands. "Kanek?"

"Yeah?"

"Why do Garèo and you keep speaking that language?"

"What, Miwāfu?"

"Yeah, I guess. It sounds barbaric."

She sighed, secretly enjoying the feel of their hands together and how it made her heart beat faster. "My mother hired him to teach me about the desert. Culture and language. We've been doing it for about five months. Mama says it is his price to stay in Rock River, but neither will explain what that means."

"I just think he's a terrible teacher and singer."

"Yeah, there is that. But, besides Mama, he is the only person from Kyōti around here."

Pahim grinned, then spoke slyly, "Aren't you from the desert?"

She shook her head. She started to lift one hand, then realized she didn't want to release his hand. She held up her other hand to show off her light brown skin. "I've never been there. I grew up in Papa's keep, but Mama wants me to at least pretend to know the desert ways. Garèo keeps telling me I have to be better, but I'm good enough."

"You're more than 'good enough,' you're fantastic. Incredible. And..." she looked at him as he paused. He finished with "I think you are beautiful too."

She blushed once again and squeezed his hand tightly. She didn't have to listen to Garèo, she knew what she was doing.

Chapter 10

Boar Hunt Inn

The Boar Hunt Inn is famed across all of Kormar as a provincial stop in the rural areas. It offers many opportunities for hunting, both of game and for discrete encounters by Kormar nobility.
　　　　　—Rastin Kadromith, *History of Kormar*

With every passing mile, Kanéko felt further from the small, comfortable world she grew up in. Instead of rolling hills and trees, the earth ended in jagged peaks of bare rock. The densely packed forests, the lifeblood of her father's land and the mill, grew sparser until only patches of trees dotted the tapestry of wind-blown grass. Even the road, a dirty reddish color, was different from the dark earth surrounding her father's keep.

They were on the tenth day of travel. Kanéko was tired of waking up to a line for the latrines and another line to get bowls of oatmeal and dried fruits. Every night, Garèo dragged her through brutal lessons for archery, brawling, survival, and fitness. The only thing that made the days passable was Pahim's presence and the occasional bottle of stolen lager or wine.

Kanéko rested on Pahim, her cheek on his muscular arm. She could feel the tiny shifts of his body as he balanced on the wagon. He used his left hand to snap the whip, if only to keep his right arm slipped around her waist.

She rested her gaze on her hand to inspect the bruises and scratches on her knuckles. The most recent came from when Garèo flipped her to the ground. She landed but not before a rock gashed her hand. She flexed and the scab reopened. Impassively, she watched blood well up before wiping it on her pants.

Maris's barking caught her attention.

Kanéko peeled her face off Pahim's bare arm and peered over his shoulder.

Three wagons back, she could see the dalpre playing with Ruben. Maris barked as she jumped off the empty bench on the wagon and plowed into the small boy who was standing in front of Kanéko's trunk. He went down in flailing arms and legs. A moment later, Maris heaved him up, and he went flying.

Kanéko's heart beat faster as she watched him soaring toward the back of the wagon.

Ruben landed heavily on the trunk with a loud thud.

Kanéko flinched, both for his impact and concern for the tools secreted inside. Gulping, she turned to Pahim. "Pah?"

"Yes, Kanek?"

"Maybe we should bring my trunk on this wagon? Maris and Ruben are rough-housing on it. I don't want it to spill or crack."

"Why? Let them carry it. We don't have enough room in here." His tone was sharp.

Kanéko didn't want to press the issue. She leaned back to look at the other students in the wagon. After weeks of travel, she still didn't know any of their names. A few of them mumbled theirs when Pahim introduced them, but her hesitant attempts to encourage conversation ended with turned backs and stony faces. It became evident that they were Pahim's friends, not hers.

With her thoughts darkening, she turned to rest her cheek on Pahim's shoulder.

"Kanek? What's wrong?"

"Nothing," she said without any energy, "I'm just tired of traveling."

"We live in a big world. It takes a long time to travel."

"If I had an airship, we would be there already."

"We can always continue on to Jinto Panzir, Kanek. Just you and me?"

Kanéko smiled at the thought, her dream of fleeing to the city burning brightly in her mind. It was only a few days south from where they rode. She didn't know if she could do it, but the fantasy gave her an addictive thrill.

Her daydreams kept away the growing dread for that night. She missed so many arrows the prior night that Garèo simply added three hundred more to the next lesson. It would be a long and painful lesson. She turned her hand and looked at the callouses forming on her fingers and palm. The scars from her work on the water screw were finally fading, hiding underneath the fresher scars from bow, knife, and horse.

"Hey, look up ahead."

She lifted her gaze as the wagon came up over a hill. When they slowed at the top, she looked down into the valley where two rivers merged into one. At the junction, a village spread out in all directions. From her vantage point, she could see the single story houses radiating out from the center like a wheel. It reminded her of her hand-carved gears.

On the far side, stood a large building with two long wings. It was pressed up against the tree line. It was larger than her father's keep. In front of the building, four lines of stables looked like tic marks on the edge of a fenced-in yard.

"That's huge!"

"Yep, Kanek, that is Boar Hunt Inn. The larger caravans stop here because of the services and the lack of room taxes. It is also the mid-point between our home and the ocean."

"Are there bathing?"

Pahim chuckled and squeezed her hip. "Yes, hot baths, showers, soft beds, and doors that close... and lock."

Kanéko longed to be comfortable again. She stopped, thinking about Pahim's words. "You've been here before?"

"A few times. My father used to take me here when he guarded merchants like those," he pointed to a line of wagons rolling into the yard. "I love coming here."

Kanéko smiled coyly. "Does that mean you'll be my tour guide?"

Pahim nodded his head gracefully, "I'll show you all the sights this good inn has to offer: the stables, the well, and this nice little path to the waterfalls." His voice grew deeper and his eyes twinkled.

Kanéko felt a flutter in her stomach. A blush crept up on her cheeks and she looked away to avoid embarrassing herself. She spotted Garèo sitting on a wagon behind her.

He was talking to a teacher and two students.

She felt a surge of anger toward him and her smile faded. "Once I get past my keeper."

Pahim grunted for a moment. "I have an idea about that..."

"What?"

"It's a surprise, bartim."

Chapter 11

Stonewait's Gallery

Favors can open doors no gold or silver can unlock.

—Proverb

The Boar Hunt Inn impressed Kanéko. There were about sixty windows on each wing, arranged half to a floor. Two sets of doors led into the main hall where a steady stream of merchants, teenagers, and workers filed through in a cacophony.

Kanéko's discomfort grew. She had never been around so many people. It felt like hundreds of people crammed into the yard, all talking and yelling. It reminded her of the dalpre mill. The sound hurt her ears and she squirmed closer to Pahim for protection. "Is it always this loud?"

"Yes," said Pahim, "but only in evenings and mornings. Everyone comes in late and leaves early. The rest of the day is just quiet cleaning and preparing for the next night."

Her brown hands clutched his arm, trying not to hamper his attempts to drive the wagon into the yard. Near the door, she saw the other school wagons already stopped to the right. Students spread out despite the efforts of the exhausted teachers to corral them.

Garèo stood on the first step of the inn, yelling at the top of his lungs. After a week, even his commands were ignored more than obeyed.

She ducked down and watched him through the crowds as Pahim continued to lead the wagon. Instead of stopping at the front, he wound his way past two merchant caravans. Guards fingered their swords as they watched Kanéko and Pahim. None of them said anything to the two teenagers.

Coming out the far end of the caravan, Pahim stopped the wagon. "Kanek, why don't you get off here? I'm going to bring this around in front."

She held him tighter, her breath quickening. "What do I do?"

"Keep away from Garèo. I'll find you in a few minutes." He gave her a sly grin.

Kanéko felt uncomfortable with the idea of being alone. She held him tightly as she sat up. "Okay, just a few minutes, right?"

"I promise."

Kanéko slid off the wagon. The earth felt like rock beneath her, no doubt pounded solid by years of traffic. She trailed her fingers on the wagon side before stepping away.

Pahim circled around the yard and headed for the front door.

A pair of caravan guards glared at her. Wrapping her arms over her chest, she turned around slowly. She spotted a smaller yard to the side and headed over there to get away from the noise.

Near the center of the side yard, she spotted a crowd gathering. There was all variety of people staring at something, from well-dressed merchants to inn staff. The ones in the back lifted themselves on their toes to peer over the shoulders of the people in front of them. Others were crawling up on nearby wagons to look.

Curious, she headed over.

A liquid sloshing noise drifted over the whispered voices and jostling people. It sounded tinny, like water poured into something metal. She recognized the sound when Jinmel filled the boiler at home.

Kanéko stopped and cocked her head. Her curiosity was rising. Judging from how quickly the water sounds raised in pitched, she guessed that it was a smaller tank than she used. She guessed about a dozen gallons.

There was a ripple of surprise. She looked up just in time for a ruddy light to flash through the crowds. Everyone stepped back from a wave of heat that radiated from the center. She spotted a flash of flames as a fire core was being shoved into place underneath a boiler.

"Oh," she said and stepped through the crowds as it broke apart in surprise. The heat didn't bother her, she had burned herself on a fire core enough times in the last few months.

It only took Kanéko a moment to clear the crowd. When she spotted a large iron device with wheels, her sound of surprise ended in a gasp. It was a steam-powered vehicle, an automobile. The large boiler in the back and tall chimney was almost exactly like the one she saw in *Emerging Wizardry*, though much smaller than she expected. Instead of being able to hold six, it would be a challenge to seat even two people on the narrow seat.

The driver was a portly man who was making a big deal of snapping the fire core into place. He had a bowler hat perched on his head and a pair of heavy goggles dangling from his neck. Sweat dripped down his face and soaked the front of his button-down shirt. He was also all smiles as he pointed to needles in the gauges that slowly tilted to indicate growing pressure.

The magical vase that heated the boiler was not visible. It had been buried in a nest of bent pipes and junctions that created a nest of metal. According to *Emerging Wizardry*, the metal was needed to prevent the vase from interacting with the surrounding crowd's magical talents. If it wasn't there, then a powerful mage could cause the core to explode.

She smiled and inched closer. It would be a few minutes before it was fully pressurized and ready to drive. She wondered if she would be allowed to ride it, if she asked nicely.

Beyond two seats, the boiler, and the core's shield, there was very little to the automobile. The tall wheels at the corners and the rectangular chest mounted on the front to counterbalance the weight of the shield told her it was a Ramnis-Cubrick vehicle, one of the first designs native to Kormar.

Kanéko stepped closer, peering down into the cage to get a better look at how it was mounted.

The driver looked at her and then his eyes widened.

She smiled at him as she tried to impress that she knew about his pride and joy. "This is a Ramnis-Cubrick, right? A Perpetual Momentum Mark—"

His gaze twisted in a scowl and he shook his hand at her. "Get away, you sand-blooded whore!"

Stunned, she stepped back. "No, I just wanted—"

The driver launched himself from the vehicle and covered the distance between them in a heartbeat. With one heavy gloved hand, he pulled back and slapped her hard across the cheek.

The force of the blow spun her around. She managed to keep standing as she reoriented herself to her attacker.

He chased after her. "Away, you desert bitch!"

Frightened, Kanéko staggered back. She expected to collide with someone, but the crowd split apart on each side of her until she was forced to stumbled to a halt on her own.

The driver continued after her; his face twisted in a sneer as he bellowed incomprehensibly.

She held out her hands, palms up to show she had nothing in them. "I just wanted to look at who made it!"

"Like you can read, you damn thief. You just want to steal it. Get away from my car! Guards!"

Kanéko didn't know why he called her a thief. She looked around and then realized she was the only dark-skinned person in the yard. She continued to back up, trying to avoid the driver who stormed after her.

Her back smacked against the side of a wagon. She let out a shriek and spun around, losing her balance. Her arms flailed out and she tumbled into the man accusing her.

He grabbed her shoulders and dug his fingers into her skin. With a growl, he shoved her forward.

Kanéko stumbled. When her bare foot caught on a leather shoe, she crashed to the ground. She managed to plant her palms before she hit her face, but the impact briefly drove her wits from her.

"She attacked me!" yelled the driver right before his kick caught her in the ribs.

Kanéko cried sharply and curled up to protect herself.

Another kick caught her back. Dust peppered her face.

"Thief!"

"Sandy!"

Men loomed over her with masks of rage on their faces. Their boots and shoes flashed as they struck her.

"I-I didn't mean to," she cried as she looked up at them through her fingers, "I just wanted to look!"

"Stop!" A man's voice cut through the crowd.

To her relief, the kicking stopped.

A heartbeat later, an older man with slicked-back gray hair and a neat suit pushed his way from the press of people. He was short, maybe five feet tall, but had an easy face. He ignored everyone else to stop next to her.

Trembling, she looked up at him.

He held out his hand for her.

Kanéko, unsure of herself, took it and pulled herself to her feet. Her sides and ribs ached from the kicks. She felt the glares of all the men on her. They were muttering quietly but she didn't need to hear to know what they were thinking.

The driver spoke to the older man. "Come on, Falkin, I don't want some sandy idiot breaking off something important. This is expensive, it took two years of savings to commission it."

Another man spoke up. "We don't need her kind around here."

"Kick her out."

"Run her out of town!"

"You don't need her at the inn."

Falkin ignored the calls as his brown eyes searched Kanéko's face.

She wrapped her arms around her and stared at the ground. Except for the man in the suit, all of them were angry.

"I've seen you before," said Falkin. "You are in Stonewait's, aren't you?"

Every year, Stonewait's Gallery sent an artist to illustrate her family. The artist came right at the beginning of spring and would leave behind last year's gallery. Ronamar's entry was two pages long and listed all his battles, granted titles and accomplishments, and a record of his first family and their assassination. The second page was for his accomplishments of magic, up to and including the title of Fourth Circle Earth Knight of Kormar.

Kanéko's own illustration was a tiny square in the entry to his second marriage. The artist had reversed the image, so her face was almost completely black on a white background. In the entire book, there were only two darker-skinned illustrations done that way, and one of those was her mother.

There were thousands of illustrations in each of the Stonewait's Gallery volumes that documented over five thousand nobles and their families. She didn't think it was possible anyone could have recognized her among them.

"Yes, sir." She spoke as politely as she could, "On page 773 of last year's volume eight."

In the brief pause that followed, she looked at the faces that had been twisted in disgust and anger. They had attacked her suddenly and gave her no chance to defend herself. Clearing her throat, she spoke louder, "I'm the daughter of Bartim Ronamar Lurkuklan, Fourth Circle Knight of Kormar."

The mood of the gathered men changed instantly. The man who slapped Kanéko blanched. The others started to back away, pretending that they had never been involved.

She expected to feel joy at seeing them cowed, but the expected feeling never came. Instead, her throat burned, and she was disgusted at herself. She had never used her own father's fame to avoid conflict before. She never had to. Everyone had already known who she was.

Falkin cocked his head. He seemed unimpressed by her declaration. "Do you have proof?"

Kanéko nodded. She fished into her trousers and pulled out a leather wallet. On the front was her father's shield, the symbol of his land with the bartim crest underneath it. She flipped it open. On one side was a color illustration of herself and a golden seal from the Stonewait's artist. Unlike the printed version, hers matched her skin and hair color.

On the other was a description of her family along with her physical appearance. She handed it to Falkin.

He took the wallet and inspected the contents. He handed it back. He spoke with a wry smile, "Please forgive Master Mardas Devinsir." He gestured to the man who first slapped Kanéko. "He didn't realize you were a bartim's daughter."

Mardas sputtered, "I-I—"

Falkin interrupted the merchant. "And I'm sure Mardas will offer his sincere apologies by giving up the Royal Suite for the night." Falkin turned to Mardas pointedly.

Mardas gaped at Falkin but when Falkin nodded, Mardas gave a dramatic sigh. He turned to Kanéko. "Lady Lur-Lurkuklan, I insist you take my... the best suite in the inn."

At Falkin's nod, she agreed. "Thank you, Master Mardas Devinsir."

Falkin stepped forward to whisper in Kanéko's ear. "Give me a second to talk to Mardas. I will have your luggage moved up to the room."

Kanéko was terrified Falkin made an assumption about her ability to pay. "Um, Falkin?"

The older man stepped closer. It was close but not intimate. "Yes?" he asked in a quiet voice.

"Is he really going to pay for it? I-I can't afford a new room. I have less than two hundred crowns in my wallet."

His eyes flashed up for a moment before he made a soft grunting noise. "Don't worry about money, Lady Lurkuklan. Mardas will cover your room. I will make sure the rest of your night is well taken care of." At Kanéko's blank look, he explained himself, "Any and all other services you wish from the Boar Hunt Inn for this visit. Don't hesitate to ask. No charge."

"Why, Falkin?"

"Mardas trades with Rock River twice a year in iron and brass. He makes about a third of his—"

"No, no," interrupted Kanéko, "why are you," she pointed at Falkin's chest, "doing this?"

Falkin smiled and gave a short bow. "You are as astute as your grandfather." He chuckled. "Your family has enjoyed the famed hospitality of the inn many, many times. Your father has been very good for my business and a loyal patron of my inn. One could say his crowds have made an excellent investment in my inn. I wish to extend that same hospitality to you in hopes that you will grace the inn frequently during your, no doubt in my mind, illustrious life." He held out his hands in apology. "Though, Lady Lurkuklan, my offer of gratis will not be a frequent occurrence. You have to understand, I do run a business and nobles such as yourself will be expensive when someone is paying the bill."

"So," Kanéko said warily, "you are giving me a taste of the good life in hopes I spend my father's money here later?"

Falkin cocked his head and smiled. "Very blunt, but yes. Later, I hope you spend your money here for many years."

"And Madras?"

"It is never too early to learn the art of politics. Madras is a good person to practice on since he is eager to please you. He also needs to be a bit more aware of those with influence around him. He should have known or met you long before this point. I always told him to memorize Stonewait's."

"And you are getting us together because…?"

"Because, Lady Lurkuklan, if your land prospers, both you and Madras have more money to spend here. You will remember him when you take your father's place, and he will remember me when he succeeds his mother."

Kanéko smiled. "Who is being blunt now?"

Falkin held out his hands in apology. "I've been working with the nobility of Kormar for most of my life, as did my father before me and his mother before him. You are young, you need blunt. Later? We'll see what you need from me."

She found herself smiling in kind. "Thank you, Falkin."

"No, thank you. If there is something I can do, don't hesitate to ask any of my staff. They will be made aware of my offer."

Kanéko watched as he walked away, and then realized she could ask something. "Falkin?"

He turned. "Yes?"

"There is a desert man with the school, goes by the name of Garèo. He won't approve of me being moved to a better room."

"Then, I'll do my best to make sure he never finds you," Falkin said with a bow.

Kanéko relished the rush of excitement at his words.

He strolled toward Madras with open arms and an easy smile.

She watched him, her heart skipping with excitement, even as she wondered if Falkin had some other scheme in mind.

"Kanek!"

Kanéko turned toward Pahim as he ran up.

He stopped in front of her. Gulping, he wiped his hands on his pants and patted his pocket. "Sorry, I lost track of you. And then Garèo pinned me in a corner asking about you."

Kanéko worried her lip. "You didn't tell him?"

"No, of course not," he said with a smile. He reached out and ran his hand along Kanéko's arm. "I would never betray you. But, I don't know if I can save you from his evil plans."

"What plans?"

"I saw him pulling out a pair of tents and setting them next to a horse. He also asked for dinner and breakfast food for two. I think he's going to drag you away tonight." Pahim looked sad, "I'm sorry, Kanek, I tried."

Kanéko sighed, feeling her emotions burning on the edge of her thoughts. For all the joy she felt when Falkin offered the inn's services, the idea of Garèo forcing her to leave the inn left her with an icy heart and growing rage. "Like the divine hell I'm going to let him."

"Kanek? What are you—"

Kanéko froze as an idea came to her. If Garèo spent the night running around, he couldn't drag her away. A grin crossed her face while she signaled for a nearby serving girl.

The girl finished delivering three large mugs of ale to a merchant before she came over. "How may I help you, Lady Lurkuklan?"

Kanéko was relieved that Falkin's orders had already been communicated. She hoped that he wouldn't mind if she took advantage of his offer to cover her entertainment. "You know the students from Rock River?" At the girl's nod, Kanéko grinned. "Could you scare up a couple bottles of cheap wine and lager? And deliver a few to each of the rooms?"

The girl looked nervous for a moment, and Kanéko wasn't sure if she just overstepped her bounds. But then the girl bowed. "Yes, my lady."

When Kanéko didn't ask for anything else, the girl ran back to the great hall of the inn. Kanéko watched with a self-satisfied smirk, and then turned to Pahim. "Let him try to find me with sixty drunk students."

Pahim laughed. "By the Divine Couple, I think I love you."

She felt a strange twisting in her gut and cleared her throat to distract herself. "Want to check out the Royal Suite?"

He gaped in surprise. "How!?"

Kanéko turned her body and arched her back. She gave a wry smile. "I'm just lucky, I guess."

Pahim stepped back and regarded her. After a moment, he gave her a dramatic bow. "I'm afraid, Lady Lurkuklan, that the evil bandit Garèo is inflicting me with lessons on 'respect' for not telling him where you were. As soon as I finish, I'll find you and show you that I have not learned a single thing."

Kanéko giggled and waved good-bye to Pahim. She jammed her hands in her pocket and headed inside to find the Royal Suite.

Chapter 12

Virsian

There are many ways of gathering information and only one is the blade of a torturer.

—Gamastorn Fluk, *A Prince and His Men* (Act 2)

Kanéko let out a satisfied sigh as she stepped out of the steamy bathroom wearing naught but a robe. Water clung to her brown skin, coursing down the various scars, burns, and bruises. Her copper hair stuck to her back, cooling faster than the rest of her body. She pulled it off her skin and wrung it free of water. Droplets splashed down on the thick carpet beneath her feet.

The rest of the room, including the carpet, was trimmed in red and dark greens. Every wall was carved in relief, filled with grand scenes of hunting and battle. A four-poster bed with posts thicker than Kanéko's thigh dominated one wall of the room and thick curtains hung from the canopy. A large window looked out into the back of the inn. The suite was on the third floor with a view of the dense forest behind the inn. It reminded Kanéko of home.

She returned to her trunk, leaving moist footprints behind her. She traced the lock with one finger before opening it with a key from her wallet. Hastily gathered clothes remained on top. She plucked out the first bundle, a shirt she hadn't worn in years, and unwrapped her hammer. She smiled to herself and ran her fingers over the "K" carved into the handle.

A knock at the door interrupted her thoughts.

Kanéko gasped and jammed the tool back in the trunk and slammed the lid shut. Tightening the robe around her waist, she cautiously padded up to the door of the royal suite. She wondered if Garèo had caught her already. She cracked the door open and peeked outside.

On the far side of the door was a feline dalpre, a cat woman. But, where Maris was short and curvy, the woman before Kanéko was tall, thin, and elegant. Her entire body was covered in short fur, a light cream color with chocolate tips on the edge of her pert ears and nose. Her face looked angular, almost gaunt, but her rich brown eyes drew Kanéko's attention.

To Kanéko's surprise, she didn't feel the same revulsion she felt when she first saw the dog people. Instead, she felt awe as she stared at the woman. Except for the ears and fur, the cat woman was as beautiful as the women in her magazine illustrations. Kanéko trailed her gaze down, admiring the light blue dress wrapped around her hourglass figure. The dalpre's tail waved lazily behind her; she had a ribbon that matched her dress tied to the tip.

Kanéko was blushing and she didn't know why. She gulped and cinched her robe tighter around her waist. "Um, hello?"

The dalpre gave a bow, much like the other serving folk at the inn. "Master Falkin requested I come up and see if Lady Lurkuklan would like one of my services. I'm skilled in massage, manicures and pedicures," she held up a small leather satchel, "and healing."

Kanéko's grip tightened on the door. "Magical healing?"

The dalpre hesitated but then said, "It is a service only provided to a select few at this inn. I am but a minor talent."

"All healing magic is rare." Kanéko felt a pang of jealousy, she wished she had even a small measure of healing magic. It would have been better than having no power.

The dalpre smiled, her top teeth peeking past her lips. "Yes, and a valuable and discrete service to the Boar's Hunt Inn."

Kanéko hesitated for a moment. She had never experienced magical healing before. She found herself staring at the dalpre.

"Do you wish me to leave?"

Kanéko didn't want her to leave. "Y-Yes, I'd like that. No, I mean, please stay."

"Yes," purred the woman, "My name is Virsian, and I'm your servant tonight."

"I-I guess that's okay," Kanéko backed away from the door and left it open.

Virsian followed, looking at the closed trunk curiously before taking in the room. She focused on Kanéko's dirty clothes strewn across the bed and pressed her lips into a disappointed frown. Slowly, her gaze returned to Kanéko.

Kanéko stood in the middle of the room, unsure what to do.

The cat woman padded over to a heavily carved wooden desk. The slight sway of her movements brought her tail in a graceful arc. She returned to Kanéko and stopped in front of her.

Kanéko gulped and shivered. She looked up into Virsian's brown eyes, afraid to ask about what came next.

"Relax, Lady Lurkuklan."

"Y-You can call me Kanéko."

"Kanéko," Virsian said the name as if she tasted it. "Call me Virsian, Vir, or anything else you wish."

It took a moment to realize that Virsian pronounced Kanéko's name correctly. Her shoulders tensed with anticipation. "I don't know what to do."

Virsian stepped closer, until they were inches away. "Then let me." She slipped her hands in Kanéko's and drew the teenager to the bed.

Kanéko's heart beat faster.

With delicate fingers, she plucked the clothes off the quilt and set them aside. A moment later, she motioned for Kanéko to lie face-down on the bed.

Heart pounding, Kanéko obeyed, and then held her breath as Virsian slipped Kanéko's robe off.

"For the massage."

Kanéko rested face-down on the bed. She was nervous until she felt Virsian's hand caressing her back, and then all her nervousness slipped away as the warm hands began to massage her.

"My, are you a warrior?"

Kanéko shook her head. The dalpre traced the scars from one of Kanéko's accidents with the water screw. "No, no, that was when I fell off a ladder."

"And this?" A finger traced a burn on Kanéko's hip.

"Bumped into a fire core when I was trying to tighten a bolt."

Warmth flooded from Virsian's fingers, delicate and sweet and tingling at the same time. It was the first time Kanéko had experienced healing magic. It felt like a tickle of fur and the rough rasp of a cat's tongue. It seeped into Kanéko's skin and eased away the aches of the travel.

"This is a nasty bruise," murmured the dalpre.

"From Maris, a bit—" Kanéko felt uncomfortable and changed her phrasing. "—dalpre at the mill."

"A brawl? I can feel knuckle prints in this, she is very strong. From nine... no, ten days ago?" Kanéko's shoulder tensed and Virsian silenced immediately, her hands working at the knotted muscles. Kanéko melted with the relaxing sensation.

"And now it is gone."

She still felt a few aches from the fight at the mill, but Garèo's lessons left their brand on her body: a scab on her lip, a soreness on her hip, and even an occasional twinge in her chest.

As Virsian worked her hands across Kanéko's body, the magic soothed everything away. "Tell me, Kanéko, why so many injuries on such a young girl?"

Kanéko, eyes closed, started to explain Garèo's lessons. As Virsian massaged her, Kanéko continued to work backwards, telling Virsian about the brawl at the mill and the ruined water screw. Every time her story caused her body to tense up, the dalpre worked at the sore muscles. Virsian didn't ask for more, but Kanéko kept on speaking, pouring out her heart and frustrations to the strange woman. The only secret she kept to herself was her half-planned fantasies of running away.

By the time Virsian finished with her massage, Kanéko felt like a puddle of mud, relieved and relaxed. Her mind was at peace, just like her relaxed body. She let out a contented sigh as her body tingled with healing energy. It flowed through every vein, and she felt as refreshed as waking up at home.

Virsian helped her back in her robe before sitting Kanéko up. "There you go, as beautiful as a princess."

Kanéko blushed from the flattery.

"Oh, missed a spot." Virsian ran a thumb along Kanéko's lower lip. It tingled as the healing magic faded the last remains of Kanéko's fight with Maris. "Perfect."

"Thank you, Vir." Kanéko felt liquid inside, relaxed and heated at the same time.

"I'm not done. I must get you even more beautiful for your dinner with Falkin and Mardas. We still have time to do your nails."

Kanéko bit her lip, but Virsian stopped her with her thumb. The touch was warm, and Kanéko shivered at the closeness.

"Don't do that, your body can't take any more healing magic for at least for half a week. Fortunately, you don't have any broken bones or serious injuries."

Kanéko rubbed her flawless finger, remembering when it bled before her trip. "I know the body can only take so much healing. I'll try not to get in any more fights."

Virsian's ear perked up and she grinned. "Come on, I have this beautiful color for your nails."

"I don't have a dress."

Virsian looked at the trunk. "All that and no dress?"

Kanéko blushed, thinking about how she had just grabbed random clothes from her wardrobe. "No."

"No matter," Virsian purred cheerful, "let's see what you have."

"I-I—" Kanéko reached out to stop Virsian but the dalpre slid over to the trunk and opened it up. Kanéko felt a blush rising in her cheeks as she got up to stop her. When she saw Virsian pull out her hammer, she froze.

Virsian peered over her shoulder.

Kanéko cringed and stepped back.

"Don't tense, please. It will ruin the massage." Her ear perked up, and she set it aside. She pulled out Kanéko's clothes, picking and sorting through them until she made three piles: clothes to use, clothes to return to the trunk, and a stack of tools.

Stunned, Kanéko watched with her mouth open.

When she turned around, her smile had two teeth peeking out from her lips again. "Now, let's make you look stunning."

"What about the...?"

"Your chest? It's a secret, yes?"

She nodded.

"I will never speak of what happens in this room. I promise you that, on the honor of this inn and our reputation."

When Kanéko didn't response, she took a handful of clothes to the bed. It took her surprisingly little time to turn a random selection of Kanéko's clothes into a dress using nothing but a pair of scissors, a few threads, and a handful of pins. When she finished, she helped Kanéko don her new outfit. Afterwards, she brushed Kanéko's hair and braided it. She painted Kanéko's nails and dabbed perfume on the teenager's throat. When she finished, she stepped back with a purr and a smile.

Kanéko looked in the mirror and felt like a queen. She didn't recognize the face and body she grew up with. "I'm beautiful."

"Yes, you are," breathed the dalpre, "But, it is almost time for your dinner."

"Vir?"

"Yes?"

"Is Falkin really just doing this for more business? The hair, massage, the room?"

A nod.

"He seems so kind and generous."

Virsian shrugged. "Falkin and his family have always considered themselves teachers for the titled youth. I think most of the bartims, covins, and even some ducolins have visited the inn during their younger years. The Silver King spent a summer here, in this room, but that was when he was still a prince and the Puzzle King reigned."

Kanéko had trouble picturing a world when the Puzzle King—the Silver King's and Golden Queen's father—was still alive. It was before the civil war that almost tore Kormar in half over a century before. "Really? I never realized that the inn was so old."

"Thirteen generations in Falkin's family."

Kanéko looked down at her fingernails, admiring the blue color tipped with white. It matched with the dress Virsian had pieced together and set off her darker skin. She smiled and shifted her body so the fabric would slide along her legs. "Thank you, Vir."

"I am your servant," came the purred reply.

Kanéko carefully replaced her tools, wrapping each one in fabric, before locking the trunk. She bashfully explained her actions. "I don't want anyone to know."

"I will never tell. However, but we have about ten minutes before the ninth bell and your dinner."

Kanéko finished up, took one more admiring look of herself in the mirror. She reached up to tug on the hair that Virsian coiled up on her head, but one look from the dalpre and Kanéko let her hand drop.

"Okay," Kanéko sighed dramatically, "I'm ready."

They managed to get halfway down the hall when Pahim and his friends came around the corner. Pahim walked in front, a bottle of lager in his hand, and laughing loudly. When he spotted Kanéko, he came to a halt and his jaw opened.

"Kanek?"

Blushing, Kanéko turned around for him, loving the rapt looks he and his friends gave her. "You like?"

"Y-Yes, but why are you so beautiful? I mean, why are you dressed up like that?"

"I have a dinner."

A strange look ghosted across Pahim's face. "Dinner with who?"

Kanéko felt a sudden need to explain herself. "Falkin, the owner of the inn, and a merchant. It's, um, why I got the room."

"Oh." There was something darker in Pahim's voice. He lowered the bottle to his side. His eyes flicked back and forth with his thoughts. She watched as his eyes lifted up to look at Virsian and his face darkened again.

Kanéko felt a prickle of annoyance at the sudden change in his attitude. "It's going to be a couple hours."

"Um, can we use the room?"

Her initial response was to say no, but Kanéko nodded after a second.

Pahim turned and headed straight for the doors.

Kanéko waited for him to give thanks, but he quickly became focused on inviting the others into her room. Her heart stung from his behavior. She worked her jaw and glared at him, but he didn't look back.

When Virsian tugged her arm, Kanéko reluctantly turned away and followed the cat woman.

Chapter 13

The High Life

Life doesn't change with a flash and a boom. It changes with a chance
encounter in an alley, an unexpected smile, or a turned back.
                            —*The Queen of Beggars* (Act 1, Scene 2)

Kanéko buzzed with excitement as she floated down the
hallway. The dinner with Mardas and Falkin went far better
than what she expected. She was too nervous to say anything until Falkin encouraged Mardas to talk about his new
steam-powered car. Kanéko suspected that Falkin knew of
her interests, but it broke the ice and the two of them
talked long into the night about engineering, mechanics,
and materials. Mardas traded in brass and iron and knew
far more than she could ever imagine about how metal
handled pressure and heat. She knew more about how the
gears and mechanisms worked.

Lost in thought, she pulled up her dress to her knees and
started up the stairs. Her bare soles scuffed on the wooden
slats. She decided she needed to wear shoes more; everyone
she met at dinner looked surprised at her calloused feet
and she heard a few whispers about her dark skin. The attention made her feel self-conscious. They saw her as coun-

try nobility, quaint but backwards. Kanéko made a note to ask Virsian about shoes before she left in the morning.

She yawned and tried to remember the last time she heard a bell. After a moment, she recalled the first bell some time ago but not the second; it was very early in the morning. Trailing her fingers along the wall, she headed along the hall of the second floor.

Footsteps on the stairs behind her stopped her. She peered over her shoulder, blinking to clear her fuzzy vision.

A moment later, Maris padded up the stairs. The dalpre's ears were pressed against her head, and she looked sad. The sight of Maris's dark fur brought an instant dislike surging through Kanéko's tired mind. Her smile dropped as she waited for Maris to go away.

Maris wore a heavily patched white shift. Kanéko could see faded stains overlapping each other. The fabric clung to Maris's curves, reminding Kanéko of her own slender body. Without thinking about it, her eyes drifted down before she forced them up. She noticed something in Maris's hand and focused on it instead. It was a small leather envelope with bright stitching on the front.

"Good morning," the dalpre spoke gingerly, "Kanéko."

"Aren't you on the first floor? Why are you here?"

"I heard you," Maris's ears perked up, "when you came out of the dining room. And I wanted to talk to you." She toyed with the envelope.

A prickle of fear and danger rushed through Kanéko. She slipped one foot back, ready for Maris to attack her.

"No, not to fight. I just..." Her tail drooped and she ducked her head. "I'm sorry you don't like me, Kanéko. And I didn't mean to get upset at the mill. But, they always tease me about being fat. And stupid. And a bitch. And, I thought you were doing the same."

Kanéko's stomach twisted with guilt and shame.

The dalpre continued as she toed the ground. "And I know you don't like me. But I was looking forward to sharing a room with you tonight. But I can't. And I wanted to give you this." She hurried over to Kanéko and held out the envelope.

Kanéko took it, surprised that her fingers shook as she clasped the warm leather. "What is it?"

"It's Maiden Root. You take one a day. And you put them in hot water, like tea. And it prevents you from having puppies."

Kanéko bristled at Maris calling her a dog. She forced herself to relax and looked down at the envelope. Someone had stitched "Maris" on the front in many colors and she could see where someone had removed the threads of an older name. She ran a thumb along the holes, her gaze picking out "Mamgum."

Maris stepped back quickly. "And I know you like Pahim. And he wants you. And he won't think about puppies, boys like that won't. But you have to take it every day for at least a week before it starts to work, so you might want to wait if you can."

Kanéko couldn't comprehend the guilt storming through her, eroding the anger she felt for the dalpre. She looked up with tear-filled eyes. "Why?"

"I don't hate you."

Before Kanéko could respond, Maris spun on her heels and raced down the stairs. Her feet slapped loudly down the hall and her tail smacked against the wall.

Kanéko stood alone in the silent hall, holding the surprise gift in her hand. A tear ran down her cheek, and she sniffed. She wiped it from her face before anyone noticed. Then, she turned and headed back to her room. As she did, she ran her thumb along the envelope, tracing the name as she struggled with unfamiliar emotions.

The door was unlocked. Inside, she was surprised to see Pahim's friends sprawled on couches and chairs. Dozens of empty bottles and empty plates littered the floor. The smell of alcohol, food, and sex hung in the air.

Kanéko stepped in the room and closed the door behind her. Her eyes scanned the room as she tried to control the storm brewing in her chest.

Two of the teenagers, the ones always making out, were on the couch. Motes of colored light hovered over their bodies—it was the girl's magical ability—and she realized they were moving against each other in a lazy rhythm. Only a sheet covered their bodies, but there was no question what they were doing. Neither looked up at her.

Another two were sleeping in the chairs. One of the guys still held a bottle in his fingers as he snored loudly. Kanéko stepped further into the room, looking for Pahim. She found him on the bed, sprawled out but still dressed. Setting down Maris's gift on the end table, she circled the room and stood next to him.

He was handsome, with his muscular body, blond hair, and pale lips. She loved being with him. She remembered the walks they enjoyed around the campground, out of sight of others and just standing next to each other. She wondered if he would kiss her, and when he did, what it would feel like?

She scanned the room, picking out more bottles of wine on the floor and platters on the tables. She didn't know what she wanted. Part of her wanted to crawl into the bed with him and let her fantasies take place. Another part of her wanted to beat him and chase everyone out of the room. It felt wrong that they had a party without her in her room. She sighed.

Pahim's eyes fluttered open. He looked at her, and a broad smile stretched across his face. "Kanek," he whispered, "sorry, I was waiting up for you and dozed off."

Kanéko looked around for a place to talk. She rejected the bathroom, and then remembered a balcony hanging off the back of the room. She pointed to it and cocked her head.

Pahim nodded and sat up. He grabbed a bottle of wine and followed after her.

She closed the doors behind them and breathed in the cooler night air. It was dark, but the small sliver of moonlight lit up the forest behind the inn. The smell of rain washed over her with a breeze and she took a breath to clear her head.

"How was, um, the dinner?" He stood next to her and she felt a tiny bit of excitement creeping back.

"It was fun. We talked about iron and brass and steam cars."

"Sounds... exciting," Pahim muttered. He pulled the cork out of his bottle and took a swig. He held it out to her.

She looked down at it. She had only had a glass during her dinner and Falkin encouraged her to drink slowly. But, now that she wasn't in a tense situation, she wondered if she should drink.

"Go on, you deserve it."

Kanéko nodded and took the wine. She took a tentative swig. As the burn coursed down her throat, she pulled a face. It was far stronger than the wine Falkin offered that night. She coughed, and then blushed when she saw Pahim smirking at her. "That's strong, Pah."

"They have good stuff here."

She looked down at the bottle, knowing that Pahim's "good stuff" was probably the cheapest wine in the inn. She took another pull and found it didn't burn as much the second time.

He pried the bottle from her grip and took a gulp.

Kanéko worried her lip as she thought about her next words. "Pah?"

"Yes?"

"Could... you not invite your friends next time?"

He looked surprised, and then grinned broadly. "Just you and me?"

She almost said "alone" but nodded instead. "I'm supposed to be representing my father." That sounded right to her. "What if I was paying for all that wine?"

"You can cover it, can't you?"

"I only have a couple hundred crowns in my wallet. In there," she nodded with her chin, "is probably twice that in bottles and food."

"Oh," his eyes flashed with guilt, "I'm sorry. I didn't know." Then he smirked, "But, you have a couple hundred more crowns than me. I have twenty-one crowns, eight rings to my name."

There was a brief but uncomfortable silence. To fill it, she spoke softly, "I can take care of you."

Pahim stepped closer so their hips were touching. "Then, my bartim, those freeloaders will be gone before you wake in the morning."

"Good," said Kanéko. She felt Pahim's closeness like a brand, the heat rolling off him searing her senses. She leaned into him, her skin tingling.

Pahim handed her the bottle. When she took it, he slipped his arm around her waist to hold her closer. "Think tonight could get any better?"

Kanéko fixed her eyes on him as she drank from the bottle. The wine slid down her throat and pooled in her stomach. She set it aside. When she released it, it slipped off the edge. Kanéko grabbed for it, but the bottle slipped from her fingers and plummeted to the ground. It hit with a wet smack and shattered glass.

Pahim chuckled. "I'll get some more from inside."

As he returned to the room, Kanéko leaned over the railing and looked down. A large garden filled the space behind the inn. It was a couple chains long, going from the wall of the inn and reaching into the woods. From her vantage point, she could see dozens of little paths leading to dead ends filled with benches and quiet places to talk. She amused herself by tracing them with her mind.

"It is a lovely night."

Kanéko gasped as she heard Garèo's voice from below. She ducked down and leaned on the railing to peer over the edge, her heart beating faster as she waited for him to call out to her.

Garèo and Virsian walked with arms intertwined as they headed into the gardens. The cat woman's tail swayed lazily as she spoke, the tip of it occasional tapping against the back of Garèo's leg.

Virsian batted him with the hand that wasn't intertwined in his fingers. "Don't try to impress me. I don't know that much of the desert tongue."

He chuckled as he looked at her, his dark skin almost black in the dim light. "Then how will you know if I sing the right words?"

Kanéko shook her head and whispered. "No, don't let him sing. Whatever you do, don't sing."

Virsian purred and rested her head on Garèo's shoulder. "You just spent hours trying to get your wards to sleep. Do you really want to wake them up this close to the inn?"

He smiled broadly. "I have a beautiful voice, you know."

Kanéko pulled a face.

143

Virsian's tail snapped violently a few times before quivering to a stop. She looked at him with shimmering eyes before leaning closer. "Why don't you show me back in my cabin?"

"Of course, my lady."

To Kanéko's surprise, they didn't head back to the inn but instead continued into the garden trails. Frowning, she lifted herself to peer over the railing and watched them walk among the shadowed leaves. In her mind, she traced their position but where she expected a dead-end only resulted in them slipping into a gap between two bushes and out of sight.

Kanéko wished for more light as she raised on her toes, trying to figure out where she mapped the trails wrong in her head and also where the couple went. Well beyond the line of trees, she saw a brief flash of a door opening and warm light coming out before it went dark.

"Oh," she whispered to herself, "there are cabins back there."

It made sense the staff would have a private place outside of the inn. She didn't expect it to be so far away. With a smile, she leaned against the railing and updated her mental image of the garden paths to include the new information, including what she expected the cabins to look like.

The door creaked as Pahim returned with two bottles. Handing one to her, he leaned against the railing. "Better than being stuck in a room with that bitch girl, huh? I heard she and Ruben were sharing a room with Garèo."

"I just saw him. I think he's going to spend the night with Virsian back there, where they have cabins."

Pahim pulled a face. "That cat whore?" He made a gagging noise. "No accounting for taste. Figures he'd get the hots for a non-human. Probably why he is always around Maris. He is trying to get into her skirt too."

She listened to his words with an uneasy feeling. But, he focused his smile on her, and she felt the warmth of his attention again. Pushing aside her concerns, she took a large swallow of the wine. It burned down her throat. It was far stronger than the last bottle. With another breath, she took a gulp before letting out a tiny gasp and lowering it to her chest.

"To tomorrow," she said.

Pahim's eyes sparkled. He lifted his own bottle, but instead of clinking it, he slipped into her arms until his chest pressed against hers. He looked down and whispered deeply. "How about tonight?"

Her heart beat loudly with his closeness. She could smell his body, a now familiar scent that made her cheeks flush. She thought about Maris's gift on the night table. "Not tonight."

He sighed. "I'm not good enough?"

"I'm just not ready to do that." She gestured in the room where the motes of light danced along the ceiling.

"How about a kiss?"

Kanéko peeked up at him. She could see his brown eyes searching for her face, and his lips parted with anticipation. Her hands trembled as she considered his request.

To answer, she lifted her chin and closed her eyes. Her heart pounded as she waited for him to kiss her back. The touch of his lips against her own sent an electrical current coursing through her body. It was her first kiss with someone besides family, and she drowned in the excitement. Her heart pounded even louder, a steady thump that shook the air around them, deafening her with the intensity of unstoppable machinery. She held her breath as they kissed, unwilling to forget a single moment of it.

From above, a sudden light shone on her face. Kanéko opened her eyes as the light faded and she caught sight of something moving along the sky. Surprised, she broke the kiss.

An airship flew above the inn. It was a retrofitted sea ship hanging below a rigid shell. Lanterns lit up the entire hull. The shell had been painted bright orange, like flaming clouds in the sky. The powerful beat she felt wasn't her own heart, but the steady pounding of a steam engine. Two banks of oars stroked through the air, the canvas between the poles billowing in waves.

"Kanek?" Pahim was frustrated.

Kanéko couldn't look away. "It's beautiful," she whispered. Her eyes sought the exhaust of the ship, where heat rippled the air around the lanterns. Below the vents, thick pipes plunged back into the ship and along the sides, no doubt to drive the oars. She could almost picture the mechanism in her head, using ideas from the mill, her dinner with Mardas, and the magazines she had read over the last few months.

"That's the *Burning Cloud Queen*, my father's ship."

Kanéko gasp and tore her eyes away. "Really? How do you know?"

He pointed to the rigid shell. "It's the only orange and yellow airship in the area. You can't see the name in the dark, but Captain Bilmour had a painted queen on a cloud throne on the bow."

"Do you think I could see it? Will it be back?"

"We'd have to go to Panzir."

She considered her fantasies. The lure of the airship was strong, but her dinner with Mardas showed her a different path she could take. She felt herself on a crux of choices. She sighed and closed her eyes. "I don't know right now. Let me think about it."

"How about another kiss?"

He didn't steal her breath the second time, but she smiled anyways. Not because he was kissing her, but because she might see an airship in the morning.

Chapter 14

Changing Plans

The reputation of virginity speaks volumes about the character of a young noble. Those unable to manage their basic instincts are unworthy of their titles.

—Jascon Komdies, *The Price of Title*

Kanéko woke up slowly, with a smile. The soft sheets clung to her body and she didn't want to ever leave the bed's comfort. At the idea of spending the night in the campground, she screwed up her face and wished that she could stay at the inn until the end of their trip.

Nature and her bladder, on the other hand, had other ideas. Groaning, she forced her eyes open. When the searing light blinded her, she draped her arm over her face and moaned. "Oh, damn the sands, just make the sun go away!"

Pahim chuckled from the far side of the room.

Kanéko rolled toward his voice and risked opening her other eye. The first sight was his naked back, lined with muscles, as he dug through his own bag. He pulled out a shirt and stretched it out. He turned around. "Morning, Bartim."

They had done nothing more than kiss on the balcony, but it was a sign of their deepening relationship and the potential for something far more intimate later. She enjoyed the warm feeling of anticipation that spread throughout her body. She glanced down and she noticed she wore nothing but her underwear. Surprised, she sat up and pulled the blanket to shield herself from his eyes. "Good morning. What time is it?"

"Half past the fifth bell."

"Fifth? Don't we usually leave at the fourth?"

"Yes," he said with a smirk, "but apparently the class went on without you."

"How did you convince Garèo to leave without me?"

"Oh," he patted his pocket for a moment, "The others took the wagon ahead. He thinks you left early."

Her eyes scanned the room. True to his word, his other friends were gone. They left the debris of their party behind: empty bottles and platters on every surface she could see. The formerly stately room was a complete mess. She clicked her tongue with annoyance and then returned her gaze to Pahim.

He finished pulling on his shirt and tugged it down. While he ran a hand through his blond hair, he chuckled again. "And as soon as the bartim is ready, we can leave any time."

"Are all the wagons gone?"

"Yes, but I got another. If we are lucky, we'll show up after Garèo has already gone to sleep."

Kanéko smiled wistfully. "That would be nice." Her eyes rose up as she said, "But Garèo's going to kill me when he catches me."

Pahim walked across the room to the bed, his boots tapping on the thick carpet. He leaned to kiss her, and Kanéko lifted her chin so their lips met. He was forceful and tried to wrap his arm around her.

She didn't feel the same passion from the night before and twisted out of his grip.

He hesitated before pulling back. "Why worry about Garèo? You are Ronamar's daughter. He isn't going to do anything."

Kanéko yawned, still clutching the blanket to her chest. "I'm too tired to figure it out right now. All I want to do is crawl back in bed." She almost said, "without you," but didn't.

"You can sleep on the wagon," suggested Pahim. He dug his hands in his pockets and backed away from her. He returned to his bag to button it up. She watched him gather up his bathroom supplies and jam them into his pack. When he finished, he set it down by the door.

Kanéko clutched the blanket tighter to her chest. "Pah? What's wrong?"

"Nothing," he muttered. Standing up, he turned around and sat on the edge of a dark desk. "I'm just kind of uncomfortable here." He gestured to the room. "I half expect that Falkin guy to burst in and demand you pay for all this."

Kanéko groaned. "I don't want to think about that. I don't know what he's going to do because I don't have enough..." her eyes focused on her open wallet next to the Maris's gift. She reached out and snatched it up to look at the contents. She flipped through the ten crown notes and came up three bills short. "Why am I missing thirty crowns?"

Pahim shrugged and gave her a bashful smile. "I had to get a wagon."

Her mouth opened with surprise and a surge of annoyance. She closed it tightly before she managed to calm herself. "Ask me, next time."

"Yes, my lady."

An uncomfortable silence filled the room. Kanéko clutched the blanket tighter as she considered her options. When she couldn't wrap her mind around the hangover, she sighed. "I need to get cleaned up."

When Pahim didn't respond, she made a turnaround gesture with her finger.

Pahim frowned. "I saw everything—"

"Not when I'm sober, and you didn't see everything. Now, turn around, Pah."

With a dramatic sigh, he obeyed.

Kanéko slipped out of the bed. She kept the blanket wrapped around her body until she fished out clothes from the trunk. She locked it and headed toward the bathroom. Closing the door behind her, she let her head hit it and sighed. *"Why can't life be easy?"*

She busied herself with cleaning as she dreamed about the *Burning Cloud Queen*. She scrubbed herself down with hot water, and then braided her hair into a tight line down her back; she used the wire to tie it off at the end. The feeling of her hair on her smooth fingers left a tiny thrill and she smiled at the memory of Virsian healing her. She dressed in a light blue blouse with embroidered flowers on the sleeves and tan trousers that ended mid-shin.

A half hour later, Kanéko came out prepared to take on the world. Pahim wasn't in the room and neither was her trunk. She looked around at the mess and winced inwardly. "I hope Falkin doesn't mind."

She felt guilty for what Pahim and his friends did. Her lips tightened when she realized she had done the same thing by sending the wine and beer to the various rooms. She grabbed her wallet and Maris's gift from the side table. Opening her wallet, she looked at the remaining bills. He had just taken her money without asking. He had also taken her chest without letting her know.

His friends made no effort to talk to her but they were willing to take advantage of her windfall with Falkin's gift.

As much as she didn't want to admit Garèo might be correct when he said "false friends."

Maybe she needed a bit of time away from Pahim.

After one last look to the ruined luxury of the room, she headed downstairs to the great hall. In the late morning, the hall was nearly empty of anyone but the staff of the inn. She felt exposed and circled around the room toward the front door to avoid attention.

"Lady Lurkuklan, a word?"

Kanéko stopped, her heart beating fast at Falkin's words.

The older man came through a door on the opposite side of the hall. He looked just as neat as before, with a dark gray suit and a tie around his neck.

Caught, Kanéko turned on her heels and headed to the center of the room.

Falkin shook his head as he approached. "I knew you were going to cost me some money last night, but that was... inspired. I almost wasn't ready to trust my talent."

Kanéko felt sick to her stomach for a moment, and then realized what he said. "What?"

Falkin tapped his head. "My talent. I know how much you will cost me in the next few days. I see it as a number floating over your head." Kanéko cringed but Falkin smiled warmly. "And... I also know how much I'll gain from your continued patronage over the years. Don't worry, young lady, you will be a positive balance in my books soon e-nough."

"Y-You mean, last night was all right?" A cautious relief rose in her throat.

"Well..." he drawled. He hooked Kanéko's arm and pulled her to an empty table. A swarm of servants rushed past him, wiping down the table and pulling out the bench for Kanéko.

She sat at his gesture.

"Let's say, I wouldn't suggest you have many of those type of surprises in the future. The staff will be working all day to clean the rooms and I'll probably have to clean out the outhouses before the end of the week. And I heard the Royal Suite is a considerable mess."

Kanéko's cheeks burned.

"Did you enjoy your dinner last night? I hoped it was educational."

She smiled at the change of topic. "Thank you, Falkin."

"I do my small part to further the titled youth of Kormar. I look forward to seeing you again." He bowed and headed out of the great room toward the kitchen.

A few minutes later, food was delivered, and she dived into it.

Pahim entered the room with a serious look on his face. He peered around and headed to her. "Kanek."

"Pah, need some breakfast?" She held up a plate of eggs and fried goat.

"Um, no," he muttered in a distracted tone, "I already ate." He stood between Kanéko and the door but didn't make any move to sit down. He clenched his hand into a fist for a long moment before relaxing it.

"Are we in a hurry?"

"Yeah, I don't want to be around when Falkin catches us."

She grinned. "I already talked to him. He already knows about the mess."

"Oh, that's a relief," but Pahim didn't relax. He looked over his shoulder and rubbed his fingers on his trousers.

Kanéko frowned as she watched him, a prickle of unease teasing her senses. "Pah?" she whispered.

He glanced over his shoulder, and then muttered darkly.

Kanéko used the opportunity to lean to the side and peer past him.

Three men stood right inside the door to the inn. They wore the same uniform, black with maroon trim on the cuffs. All three also wore a bright red armband on their left arm. The leader was bald and tanned; his face was almost as dark as the desert folk. His brown eyes were small and i-nset. He looked like he had a scowl permanently etched into his face which the scruff of a beard did nothing to hide.

Kanéko shivered and ducked back behind Pahim. "Who are they?"

"Not sure," Pahim said quickly in a low, tense voice.

"What do we do?"

"Keep your head down, Kanek, and get to the north yard. I have the wagon ready to go."

"Where's my trunk?"

"It's on Ruben and Maris's wagon. They also left late."

Kanéko lowered her head and watched the men heading toward the notice board. Spotting an opportunity, she got up from her seat and headed for the side door. She reached the door just as Falkin stepped through.

He opened his mouth to talk to her. She saw his eyes flicker above her head for a moment, and then a frown crossed his face. He closed his mouth with a snap.

Kanéko gave him a strained smile, pointed to the three men with her thumb, and then slipped around him. As soon as she could, she ran for the end of the hall and out the side door. It took her long, stressful seconds to find Pahim's wagon.

It was a small thing, large enough for a few bales of hay and a bench wide enough for two. Pahim's bags were jammed in the back but nothing of hers. Pahim sat on the front, sweating nervously, as he peered around.

She slipped up on the wagon when he wasn't looking. The wagon settled down from her weight, but Pahim didn't notice until he turned around.

When he finally noticed her, he jumped. "Oh, the Divine Couple! Kanek!"

"Ready to go?" She asked with false bravado and a bit of smugness for surprising him.

Pahim answered by flicking the reins and starting the single chestnut mare moving. He guided the wagon out the side gate and to the road.

Kanéko smiled to herself. Maybe he wasn't so bad. Shifting her body around, she scooted up to him and rested her head on his shoulder. "You take care of me too, don't you?"

"Yeah... I do."

She yawned, the brief stint of excitement emphasizing her exhaustion.

"You can sleep, Kanek, if you want. We have three bells before we get to the camp."

"I can stay awake, if you want."

"Sleep, Bartim, and this servant will serve you."

Kanéko struggled to stay awake, but the gentle rock of the wagon and the rhythmic squeak of one wheel pushed her into the world of dreams.

Chapter 15

Reward Money

Trust and faith are powerful. She built her army on those two rocks.
—Padraim Solture, *Riddle of Stone* (Act 2, Scene 6)

Kanéko started awake when a murder of crows cawed nearby. Groaning, she cracked open her eyes and stared out at the burning red sky. While she slept, she had turned so her back was flat against the hard wood and her head rested on Pahim's lap. Her feet dangled over the edge of the bench. She could feel the muscles moving in time with the shaking wagon. With a yawn, she blinked to clear her eyes and peered up to him.

The young man stared forward, the reins in his hands lightly resting along his wide palms.

"Pah?"

He jumped at her voice. Looking down, he licked his lips and there was a brief moment of some unknown emotion before he smiled broadly. "Kanek, I didn't know when you'd wake up."

She yawned and sat up. Her mouth felt like chalk and a headache throbbed. "How long was I sleeping?"

To either side of the road, she didn't recognized the trees or her surroundings. It would make sense if they had been riding for a while, but she still tried to picture where they would be on a mental map. She realized she didn't know the area at all and wished she had seen a map of the inn's surroundings before she had left.

"About three and a half bells, seven hours."

It took a moment before his words sank into her thoughts. Kanéko gasped and looked up sharply. "Three bells?"

"You were up during lunch for a while, don't you remember that?"

She frowned as she tried to remember. A vague memory of him offering her a skin of water came up but nothing else. She shook her head and groaned from the headache. "Pah? Didn't you say we would be at the campsite in three bells? Garèo is going to kill both of us."

"Well, I took a wrong turn." At her frown, he continued, "Oh, it's not that far. We'll probably get there by the ninth bell... about two hours from here..." His voice trailed off as he looked down the road.

Kanéko waited for him to say more. When he didn't, she shifted away from him as she remembered her thoughts earlier. She didn't feel in danger, but her discomfort at the situation grew with every passing moment. As she tried to think about what bothered her, her thoughts grew fuzzier and she let them drift.

As they rode, she watched the trees on both sides of the road stretching as far as she could see. Curious, she turned her head and looked back the way they came, seeing more trees lining the dirt road. Her eyes rose up to the light that baked the right side of her face. A memory from one of Garèo's lessons pricked her thoughts. She looked at the sun as it kissed the top of the trees.

"Pah?"

"Yes?" He spoke in a terse, distracted voice.

Kanéko gestured to the sun. "Why are we going south?"

His body tensed. He twisted and rolled his neck.

A prickle of concern ran down her back, an icy finger traced her spine. A beat pulsed in her ears as she looked up at his concerned face, trying to read his expression. As casually as she could, she rested a hand on the back of the wagon bench. "Pah?"

"I said I missed the fork."

Kanéko shifted away from Pahim. "Pah, we are going straight south, aren't we? Isn't the campground northwest of the Boar Hunt Inn?"

The muscle clenching in his neck told her everything. Kanéko sat up away from him and turned to face him. "What is going on?"

Pahim sighed. "I... I just thought you wouldn't mind."

"Wouldn't mind what?" pressed Kanéko. "Where are we going?"

"Panzir."

She clamped a hand on the back of the wagon, the tension in her body squeezing her chest. She gasped and tried to force out words, but only a grunt came out. She closed her mouth and tried again. This time, the words came out screaming, "Jinto Panzir!?"

"Look—"

For all of her fantasies, Kanéko never thought she would actually go to the city. There were too many unknowns that were left behind in the fantasy. Where would she sleep? How would she get food? He had already taken some of her money and she didn't think a hundred crowns would last long. Even if she could manage to fend for herself, she didn't have her tools. "No, no, we can't go there. Not now!"

"Why not? You were talking about it and Garèo was—"

"Because I'm not ready!" Kanéko screamed.

"We have everything we need—"

Kanéko spun on the bench and gestured at the empty wagon. "We have everything? Where!? I need my tools in my trunk. I need clothes. I need something besides the stuff on my back and my wallet. How are we going to survive on a hundred and seventy crowns for a month?"

"You said—"

"I also said I wanted to kiss you!" She stood up on the wagon, still screaming. "Obviously, that was also one of my stupider ideas!"

Pahim looked up guiltily. "I thought with your title—"

She snapped shrilly at his tone. "You didn't think!" She punched him in the shoulder. Stepping to the side, she jumped off the wagon and winced when her ankle rolled beneath her. A stabbing pain raced up her leg. Unwilling to show weakness, she limped to the side of the road.

Pahim scrambled to stop the wagon. "Come on, Kanek, it won't be that bad!"

"You!" She took a step toward him and pointed. "are never to call me that! Just... I—," she ground her jaw together, "I need to clear my head before I kill you."

Limping, Kanéko stalked off the road and headed to the tree line. She reached it and plunged into the trees, desperate to get out of sight. As she passed branches, she slapped at their leaves.

"Sand-bleached bastard!"

Her bare feet sank in the moist soil until she broke free of the underbrush. She couldn't hear Pahim, but his voice wouldn't carry far through the surrounding bushes and trees.

"Castrated son of a snake!"

Tears burned in her eyes as she continued to storm forward, shoving bushes and branches aside. The ground grew rocky as she approached a ridge running parallel to the road. She stomped hard as she headed up toward the top. When the sharp pains in her twisted ankle increased, she forced herself to plod through it.

"Brains of curdled milk!"

By the time she reached the top of the hill, she regretted twisting her ankle. A burning ache ran up her thigh and she had to hobble the last few feet before she could stop at a large tree. Looking around, she spotted a rotted stump and she limped over to it.

She wanted to keep swearing at Pahim, that is what her mother would do, but the words wouldn't come. Yelling didn't make her feel better, and it didn't solve anything. She sighed and kept her mouth shut as she reached the stump and sat down heavily on it.

The perch shuddered but held her weight.

Kanéko took a deep breath and lifted her throbbing foot slightly to relieve the ache. When it faded, she cringed and set it down. Instead of the sharp pain she expected, it was only a dull ache. Letting out her breath in a rush, she increased the weight on the ankle and rolled it slightly, exploring her injury.

She remembered reading a similar scene in her Nash novels. Her favorite hero had broken his leg while fighting a ginorak, a fire-breathing lizard. Thankfully, she didn't feel the grinding of bones or the sharp pain that the author had written about. It was just a burning ache from strained muscles or maybe a forming bruise. Relieved, she tugged up her pant leg and looked at her mud-streaked ankle and heel. The skin was tender and discolored, a bruise but nothing compared to the injuries she had acquired in the last year.

Her mind spun furiously for a moment as she tried to come up with alternative. She would be safe at the Boar

Hunt Inn until Garèo came back for her. She glanced at the woods, back the way she came. She could walk back, but it would be better if she had the wagon. Kanéko pondered for a moment. She had some money in her wallet. Maybe she could pay Pahim to take her back. Once she was there, she would avoid him, but it was the best way to return to safety.

Her thoughts went to Jinto Panzir. She had only read about the city in her magazines and heard about it in rumors, but it would have been the perfect place to prove herself. She let herself dream for a moment before she pushed herself back to her feet. It was time to stop and face her life.

With a sad sigh, she limped back down the ridge and followed the imprints of her feet back to the road. She smiled to herself as she did; if she wasn't stomping in anger, she would have been lost. She shook her head. "I can't believe I was considering *fucking* him."

It took her longer than she remembered to return to the road. Just as she saw it through the wavering curtain of leaves, she heard hooves pounding against the hard-packed earth. They slowed as they approached.

Kanéko inched forward, holding the branches against her as she peered out from the tree line. The horses were to her right, circling Pahim's wagon. A prickle of fear ran down her spine, adding to her anger.

For the briefest of moments, she considered calling out to them for help, but then she recognized the leader: the bald man from the inn. He did not smile and something about his dark gaze silenced the words in her throat. Heavy scars scoring his tanned skin and were easily visible from the distance.

As the man circled the wagon, he kept one hand on the hilt of his sword. It was a curved blade, about two feet long with a thick wooden sheath that glinted in the fading sunlight. His other hand rested on the reins of his horse, keeping the mount walking in a small circle around the wagon. He wore a small travel pack on his back that looked like the same one Kanéko originally had prepared. It was a desert-style travel pack with well-worn leather.

Finally, he came to a halt next to the wagon and peered into the back of the wagon and then up to the front. "You were at the inn, weren't you? Did you see a girl? Dark skin, brownish or reddish hair. A sand blood, a foreigner? Probably has some money, doesn't show a talent with magic?"

Kanéko pressed her hand to her mouth to mute her panting. She had expected the stranger to ask about the road or gossip, not to ask for her. The magical talent question proved the point. There were very few dark-skinned people in the local area and most of them would have some sort of clan magic.

She glanced at Pahim, silently begging him not to speak up.

Pahim grunted and looked down. "Yeah, I know her."

Kanéko shook her head, desperately trying to silence him with nothing but a glare. Her heart pounded as she stared at him, terrified of what the stranger would say next.

"Really?" The bald man sat up straighter and looked around.

Kanéko pulled back as his gaze approached her. The pounding in her ribs moved to her ears, drowning out the sound. She had to take deep breaths before it calmed down enough for her to hear his response.

"Where is she? Do you know?"

The blond teenager crossed his arms over his chest and inhaled sharply, causing it to puff out. "I saw the poster."

The bald man threw back his head and laughed. It was a deep, booming laugh that made Kanéko's stomach churn. "Oh, that is what this is about? Money?"

In the pause that followed, Kanéko bit her lip and clutched the branches. The leaves shook violently as she tried to hold herself still to hear his response.

Tears burned in her eyes and blurred her vision. She shook her head silently, wishing that Pahim was looking out for her and not some reward.

Pahim pulled a piece of paper from his pocket. He unfolded and handed it to the man. "Ten thousand is a lot of money."

"N-No..." whispered Kanéko. One of the branches cracked in her palm and she froze, staring at it in shock and then up in fear that they heard her.

None of the men even flinched.

Pahim shrugged. "I want it. You get the girl and I want the money and a job on the *Burning Cloud Queen*."

She stepped back slightly but couldn't go any further. She wanted to keep watching despite the sour boil in her stomach and the beating under her ribs.

The bald man turned it around to read it, and then handed it back. "You saw us in the inn, why didn't you just deliver her there?"

"I saw the *Queen* heading back to Panzir, I was hoping to catch Captain Sinmak Bilmour there."

The bald man chuckled and patted his wallet. "I would have given you the reward money right at the inn."

Pahim turned and looked down the road they were riding along. It must have been toward Jinto Panzir. "My dad is on the *Queen*." He sighed and looked down, "I wanted to present her to him first."

"Your dad? Who's he?"

"Torvis Maldor, he's an engineer. He joined, um, three years ago."

The man's face tensed for a moment. "I knew Torvis, but you better talk to Captain Bilmour."

Kanéko noticed that the stranger's grip on his sword tightened.

"What's your name, boy?"

"Pahim. Pahim Maldor, but most people call me Pah." Pahim held out his hand.

The stranger took it. "I'm Cobin Starisen. I'm the ground commander for *Burning Cloud Queen*. I can pay you here, if that is what you want."

"Yes, sir. That would be nice."

Cobin looked around.

Kanéko ducked down to avoid his gaze.

"Then where is she? I have a black bitch to deliver if either of us want to get paid."

When Pahim looked toward the trees, Kanéko backed further into the woods. She snarled silently at him, cursing him underneath her breath.

He gestured to the woods in Kanéko's direction. "She ran off less than twenty minutes ago. I was expecting her back soon. She twisted her leg, and there isn't anyone else out here. It's either me or a long walk to Jinto or back to the inn."

Cobin looked along the tree line, scanning it as he scowled.

Kanéko continued to step back until she lost sight of the man but still heard his voice. She held her breath as she strained to listen.

"We have a quarter bell at most before it grows too dark, and I want that sandy in ropes before that happens. Tom, provide light. Bin, to my left and start sounding. Pah?"

"Y-Yes, sir?"

"Do you want to stay here or help us hunt? I'll throw an extra thousand crowns if you capture her."

A low rumble shook the ground but quickly faded. Around her, the trees swayed from the sudden movement.

Kanéko gulped. She couldn't stop the trembling that shook her body. More tears threatened to fall, but she wiped them clear and glanced back, memorizing the route back into the depths. In her mind, she could picture where she needed to put her feet and hands when she finally had to run. Curiosity, however, kept her from running.

"Truth be honest, I'd rather not remain on the road. Garèo will be coming back—"

"Garèo!? Waryoni Garèo!? You know him? Where is he!?"

Kanéko flinched at Cobin's sudden yell.

"H-He's," Pahim's voice cracked, "on the road to Two Firs. But, he'll be back when Kanek doesn't show up."

Cobin's voice grew hard. "Boy, if you catch her tonight, I will personally give you twenty thousand on the spot. The same goes to the rest of you. Twenty thousand crowns bonus to each of you if we catch that sandy bitch now!"

There was nothing else Kanéko needed to hear, she had to flee. She turned and sprinted into the woods. Her bare feet sank into the soft earth, and she stumbled on the rocks underneath, but she already had her route planned for almost fifty feet. She ran blindly as she trusted her memory. Every time her aching ankle took her weight, though, she winced from the sharp pain. She held one hand over her face and charged forward, protecting her eyes as she fled blindly.

"Found her!" cried out a voice. "Two chains down, on the left! Hai!"

She ran faster, plunging into the woods racing as fast as she could. Her bare feet smacked against the ground as she came to the ridge and scrambled up it, using her hands for balance.

Behind her, pursuers crashed into branches and bushes, swearing loudly as they tore into the woods. Two of them were on horseback, she could tell from the cries of the animal, but they were easily covering the distance.

She pushed herself, but sharp pains ran up her ankle and she had to limp forward. Every time her feet pounded against the ground, it felt as if she was running in mud. Sharp rocks tore at her bare feet, thorns scraped against her arms, face, and shoulder. She gasped for breath as she looked around for a clear route but couldn't find it.

"*Sands!*" she snapped.

"I heard her! This way!" yelled Pahim dangerously close to her. More branches snapped as he charged after her.

She clamped a hand over her mouth when she realized she had revealed her location with her swearing. Panting into her palm, she ran as fast as she could. Every part of her body ached from fear and terror. Her bare feet bled from the numerous cuts and the sharp pain of her ankle hobbled her attempts to sprint.

Kanéko tried to push herself but she couldn't move any faster. Her feet refused to push past the pain. Her lungs couldn't get enough air. The struggle she had with keeping up with Garèo's lesson was nothing compared to her desperation to escape.

Pahim came up behind her. He was bigger than her, fast, and he was wearing boots. She felt the wind when he tried to grab her.

She let out a cry and tried dodging out of the way, but she slipped and bounced off a tree instead. There was a flash of Pahim's scowl and his outstretched hands before she spun to the side.

Pahim grabbed at her hair and he yanked her back. He grunted loudly.

Kanéko's back slammed into his chest, and her scream echoed through the woods.

Pahim wrapped one arm around her, obviously trying to pin her arms to her chest. The strength she admired before turned dangerous and terrifying.

She knew her chance for escape would dwindle if he pinned her. Thinking desperately, she threw her head back but almost lost her balance. Trying again, she planted her feet and then slammed backward with all of her might.

The back of her skull impacted with his nose. There was a satisfying crunch as cartilage shattered from the impact.

A burst of pain blinded her briefly.

Swearing, Pahim fell back. His grip tugged at her but slipped away.

For the briefest of moments, she considered running, but then she realized that the boy who had betrayed her was only feet away. With a growl, she spun around on her good foot.

He had staggered a few feet. Blood poured down his face and neck. It splashed down his shirt.

Enraged, she swung at him but missed. "Rot in hell," she yelled at the top of her lungs, "you *sand-cursed bastard!*"

"Shut up, you stupid sandy!" Pahim lashed out at her but also missed. He wiped his face with his other hand and shook it clear. Blood splattered against the leaves below them, leaving long trails of crimson against the ground.

She spotted a rotted branch. The top of it was thick, but large enough for her to grab with both hands. It looked like it was only partially in the ground as it wavered back and forth from their swinging.

Kanéko memorized where it was and then attacked, swinging furiously but not trying to hit.

Pahim dodged out of the way and attacked her, but she avoided his blows easily.

When the opportunity came, she spun around and grabbed the branch. Yanking it hard, she was relieved when it broke free. Without looking for him, she brought it in a low arc around her body and then up as soon as she saw him.

The tip of the weapon bounced against Pahim's inner thigh before the thick wood crunched into his testicles. The wood shattered from the impact and shards of wood exploded in all directions.

Kanéko staggered forward from the unexpected loss of weight. Her shoulder smacked into him, and she cringed, waiting for him to grab her. She kept a grip on the remains of her stick. Less than a foot of wood remained but it was enough to defend herself.

When Pahim didn't attack her, she looked into his face. They were only inches away. Pahim's eyes were wide enough they were almost white. He shook violently and bubbles of blood popped from his destroyed nose. A long gasp escaped his lips, splattering her face with his blood.

She pulled back and followed the trail of blood down his neck and chest.

Pahim clutched his groin with both hands. A large hunk of wood stuck out from between his fingers. It had punched into the side of his leg, into the meaty part of his thigh. Blood poured down his leg as he clutched his testicles and the bloody shard at the same time.

The gasp continued to escape his lips, the sound growing higher pitched with every passing second.

Kanéko glared at him, panting. Sweat prickled her brow as she regarded the boy who had tried to sell her for ten thousand crowns. It was more money than most people made, but that didn't matter. She had kissed him.

Anger burning through her, she swung the remains of her stick at the side of his head. The remaining wood cracked with the impact against his skull, but she squeezed down with her fist and followed through the punch. Her knuckles popped against his bone and the force threw him to the side.

She considered attacking again, but a snapping branch told her there were more coming for her. She looked up wildly, trying to orient herself. She didn't recognize the trees, but she pictured the area around in her head and quickly replayed the chaotic fight between her and her betrayer. Finding a different direction, she abandoned Pahim and hobbled away as fast as she could.

It was darker than she remembered. She could barely see in front of her, but the dim light gave her enough to slip between the trees. Unable to see the ground, she tripped frequently and cut her hands as much as her feet.

Behind her, a glowing light flickered against the trees. It was a bright blue, and unnatural, to say the least. She remembered how Cobin had told one of his men to use their light which meant they were behind her.

Panting, she struggled to keep her back to the light and well away from its shine. The flicker gave her a few hints but that didn't stop her from cracking her head against low-hanging branches or walking into spiderwebs. Each time, she had to fight crying out and revealing her location. Not swearing was even harder.

One moment, she was hobbling along the ground and the next there was nothing. Unwittingly, she let out a shriek as she plummeted forward, slamming into a steep embankment before bouncing off rocks. Blind, she clutched in all directions to stop herself from falling, but she only managed to pull a few roots loose before her back smacked into water.

River water flooded into her mouth and nose as she dunked below the surface. Panic surged through her, and she scrambled helplessly in all directions, kicking out as she tried to regain her feet.

Time seemed to slow as she choked; it burned her lungs and seared the inside of her nostrils.

She flailed, clutching her hand to grab something, anything. Her knuckles scraped on rocks. She tried to grab them again, but she failed to get a solid grip. She spun around with her effort, but she couldn't figure out which way was up.

Her throat seized up. She managed to jam her toes into the ground. The nerves in her foot screamed out in agony, but she used it to push herself up to the surface and flail for something to grab.

Her hands caught on a root, but it slipped through her fingers.

She bobbed underneath, water flooding into her mouth.

Choking on the icy liquid, she surged up and grabbed the root with both hands. Her knuckles cracked from the effort as she held tight, gasping for breath as she regained her senses. Her breath came out in ragged gasps, washing her hand in warmth.

Kanéko looked around, but she was blind. With a groan, she pulled herself up the riverbank and then crouched in a knot of bushes. Peering through the leaves, she dreaded seeing the light of the men chasing her.

When she saw them in a distance, she had to fight back a sob.

They were still far away but approaching quickly.

She gulped, but a cough rose up. She planted her face into the water to muffle the noise and coughed violently. Before she had to inhale, she lifted her face from the water and breathed in deep. Water trickled down her aching throat, but it was nothing compared to the water already there.

"Quiet!" snapped Cobin. "Where is she?"

Kanéko held her breath, her eyes tearing up from the effort not to cough.

"She isn't running, I can't feel the vibrations through the river noise, sir."

"Keep at it, Bin. The stupid cow will run soon enough."

"Yes, sir."

Kanéko thought furiously for a moment. She had read about earth powers that could feel movement along the ground. The water around her must have muted the man's ability to detect her.

Even though she could barely swim, Kanéko pushed herself away from the shore and headed downriver. She could come out later, when she was far enough away from her pursuers.

---------- Chapter 16 ----------

The River

In the desert, the drink you take may be your last. The rock you pass
may be the final shelter. And you may never see the sun again.
—Tesominona Bikaróchi, *Seven Winds* (Act 2, Scene 1)

Kanéko woke with a start, terrified by her nightmares and
the strange noises that surrounded her. She sat up quickly
and slammed her head into a rocky outcropping. Stars exploded across her vision as she fell back down, hit a muddy
puddle, and splattered muck in all directions.

In her dazed confusion, she couldn't remember how she
had gotten underneath the rock, but soon the memories
came flooding back. She let out a shuddering breath and
squeezed her throbbing skull even tighter.

"That bastard," she whispered in a broken voice, "That
sand-cursed bastard."

She groaned and thought back to the night before. Her
idea to dive in a river had seemed like a good idea, but the
fantasy novels she'd read had never said how hard it was to
keep her head above water when her strength was flagging,
or how to navigate in the dark. The mercenaries were able
to track her by sound and vibrations, so she remained in

the cold water, cowering in a clump of rocks until her hunters finally went away.

Somehow, she had managed to crawl on shore and found the outcropping where she now was for protection. Kanéko vaguely remembered sliding into a shallow pool. Lifting her head, she realized that her shelter only hid her body behind a thin screen of marsh grasses. Beyond, she could see the sparkling waters of the river. She scanned the shores for her abductors but didn't spot anyone.

Moving with care, she braced herself in the mud and pushed herself to a sitting position. She leaned on the earthen bank. Her hair felt heavy and swollen with the mud she had slept in. The formerly pristine outfit she put on the day before was now covered in a uniform, brown sludge. She morbidly tested her injuries, wincing from the sparks of pain from touching her cuts and scrapes. A large bruise ached between her shoulder blades and shallow cuts along the soles of her bare feet burned with every movement. Her twisted ankle added to her misery, but at least it wasn't broken.

Kanéko didn't know what to do. For a moment, she considered crawling back into the pool and waiting for Garèo, but he would never find her in the mud.

One of his lessons from the desert came back to her: just keep moving.

Kanéko struggled to get on her knees and crawled up the shore. After a few chains of slow, painful movement, she felt weak and pathetic. She pressed her face into a bed of leaves for a moment, and then groaned as she pushed herself to her feet.

"Damn them." She hated both Garèo and Pahim, but their imagined taunts kept her moving.

Completely lost, she turned in a circle to scan the forest around her. Two Firs and Garèo should be to the northeast, but she didn't know how to figure out a direction. Tears burned her eyes as she spun around again with a feeling of helplessness rising to squeeze her chest.

She slumped against the tree and started to cry. Hot tears poured down her cheek, and she slid back to the ground, giving up. She prayed that Garèo would find her. A month of his torments would be worth being rescued.

No one came.

Kanéko's tears stopped flowing and the dry heaves ended moments later. In the silence that followed, she remembered something. The sun rose in the east and set in the west. Guessing it was morning, she headed toward the sun and hoped she would find a road soon. She didn't have a path to follow and had to force her way through the brush, vines, and branches. Fresh scratches scored her body, leaving tiny brands of blood and pain behind.

"Damn both of them to having sand shoved up their asses until it pours out of their mouths."

Chapter 17

Directions

The tradition of marking every mile of every road throughout Kormar has continued to prove itself as a waste of time, money, and effort with modern maps and high-speed vehicles.
—Scorin Rekusar, *Modernization of Kormar's Bureaucratic Infrastructure*

Kanéko peeked out from the tree line with trepidation and scanned the road. Her body trembled from exhaustion. She barely saw through the piercing headache and hunger that growled in her gut.

Seeing the heavy brush on both sides did little to help her mood. The plants had already left their mark on her, and the scratches still oozed blood through the dried mud. She took a hesitant step from the trees, ready to dive back at the first sound of a horse or rider.

Walking for hours barefoot had done nothing to dull the ache that burned her inner thighs and sapped her strength. At the feel of the hard-packed dirt against her bruised and bloodied feet, Kanéko whimpered. She looked up into the sun, which only reminded her that hours had passed since she had found a small pool of clear water to drink from.

Wiping the sweat from her brow, Kanéko looked back and forth along the road. She wasn't even sure which way was north or south. After a few seconds of looking, she gave up and picked a random direction. She limped down the road.

It didn't take long before she came to a milestone. The bright white marker gave her hope and she limped the last few chains before kneeling down in front of it. She had to brush the dirt off it to read it. Once cleared, the marker read "JP 29 mi". On the other side of the road, a second marker read "RS 25 mi". It took her a moment to decipher that "JP" meant Jinto Panzir and "RS" would be Raisen, the small village around the Boar Hunt Inn.

Kanéko looked to the south, toward Jinto Panzir. A shudder coursed up her spine, and she turned her back to the city. Pahim waited for her there, along with Cobin and whoever had posted a reward for her. She regarded the road to the north.

"Twenty-five miles? I can do that." she said without confidence. The very idea of walking that far on bare feet left her feeling cold and alone, but Garèo's words came back to her.

"Just keep moving."

Chapter 18

Nobody

Honor, like all virtues, has many requirements. It is meaningless outside of the context of family, wealth, and title.
—Tintin Tavoli, *The Self-Made Storekeeper*

Two miles and an exhausted hour later, Kanéko could
barely keep her head up as she trudged along the road.
Every part of her body hurt; every breath came in shuddering gasps. The sun beat down on her left side, and her
sweat kept her muddy clothes sticking uncomfortably to
her body. Her feet slapped down on the road, one after the
other. It took all her energy to just keep walking.

A faint smell tickled her throat. She looked up blearily
and sniffed the air. Among the scents of leaves and grass
and earth, she caught something else. Sniffing again, she
took in a deep breath of wood smoke and felt a glimmer of
hope.

Kanéko looked around for some sign of fire. She didn't
see anything, but a fresh breeze from the north brought a
stronger scent of wood smoke. A moment later, she thought
she smelled meat cooking, and her stomach rumbled.

She started down the road with a flush of a second wind. She made it almost a half mile before she finally saw a hazy tendril rising above the trees.

The sun was just starting to touch the tops of the trees when she came to her destination. Panting from her last-minute surge, she leaned against the sign announcing the village: Lassidin. Her eyes scanned the rest of the sign and she recognized Count Zantir's seal but not the local bartim's. Below, someone had painted the population of the village: 82.

The breeze brought more scents of cooking to her and Kanéko turned toward the village. Only a dozen houses clustered in the center. Even from the sign, she could see a single public house shingle—a crossed knife and fork over a plate—hanging in front of one door.

She headed toward it.

As she walked down the dirt lane, she kept her eyes glued on the restaurant's front. She hesitated only when she realized that the villagers watched her with curiosity and poorly-veiled distaste. A small boy pointed at her with one outstretched but steady hand. For a moment, it looked like Ruben.

Kanéko frowned and felt her thoughts focusing on Ruben with an intensity that surprised her. She could almost feel the short teenager's eyes on her. Just as quickly as she started thinking of Ruben, her thoughts returned to food and shelter.

She stopped at the door and peered into the pub. Like many public houses, the place sported a few tables scattered about a small room. Someone had set up two more outside, but neither were occupied. Inside, people sat at all the tables, chatting, smoking, and playing card games. Most of the patrons looked to be in the latter half of their years, but she saw a few men in their twenties.

The conversations slowed as she felt their attention focus on her. One of the men in the far back leaned into an open door and yelled out.

"'ey, Sarom! There be a black girl begging!"

Kanéko blushed and stepped up to the door as a thin man wearing an apron stepped out from the far side of the room. Black hair framed his slender face and his smile looked almost peaceful, but as soon as he focused on her, it dropped.

Sarom shook his hand at her as he strode across the room. "What do you want, sandy?"

Kanéko stammered, "I-I'm hungry, could I please get some food?"

"No!" came the harsh response and some of the patrons laughed. Sarom stood in the door, shooing her away. "Now, git, I don't have your food here."

"Please," Kanéko almost sobbed, "I-I'm lost, and I just need—"

Sarom reached behind one of the chairs and grabbed a large stick. His face stretched into an angry mask. "I said git!"

"Please! I don't have a lot, but my father is Bartim Ronamar Lurkuklan. He isn't from around here, but all I want is a bit of food."

He raised an eyebrow before grunting. Crossing his arms over his chest, he spoke sharply, "You saying you are a bartim's girl?"

She nodded hopefully. "Yes, my father is—"

"Prove it," Sarom interrupted sharply.

Kanéko dug into her pocket and pulled out her wallet. Mud dripped from the edge, and she fumbled to peel it open. She inspected her portrait with growing despair. The colors were washed out and smeared across the paper, leaving only the Stonewait's gold seal. On the other side, water blurred the words leaving an unintelligible mess behind.

"You call that proof?" sneered Sarom. "You think some desert scum's forgery is going to fool me?"

Kanéko looked up helplessly. "No, this is mine. I swear. I just fell in the river—"

Sarom swung the stick at Kanéko's head.

She ducked under it. "I didn't do anything!" she screamed.

He swung again, almost hitting Kanéko. Her foot caught the rut in the road and her leg gave out. With a groan, she tried to retain her balance but a third swing from Sarom caught her in the arm.

She collapsed to the ground.

Sarom raised his stick to strike again.

Kanéko held out her hand to protect herself. Fear burned brightly inside her. She was helpless.

"Junior!"

Sarom winced.

The voice came from an older man who looked like Sarom, but with decades of age weathering his face. The older man stopped next to Kanéko as he addressed Sarom. "What do you think you are doing?"

Sarom finally lowered the stick. "Getting rid of some sand trash, dad. She tried to pass herself off as a bartim's girl. Desert scum." He spat at her.

Kanéko flinched from the spit but couldn't avoid it. It splattered against her arm before rolling down through the dried muck.

The senior interrupted him. "And how did she try to prove it?"

"Some bad picture."

The older man turned to look at Kanéko. Without saying a word, he held out his hand.

Kanéko fumbled as she picked it off the ground. Unfolding it, she handed it to him.

The older man inspected it, clicking his tongue. "Can't see much, um...?"

Kanéko felt a strange prickling on the back of her neck. She cleared her throat and tried to look helpless while sprawled out on the ground. "My name is Kanéko Lurkuklan."

"Hard to read, but I've seen that seal before." The older man held out his hand for her. Kanéko took it, and he pulled her to her feet. "I'm Sarom Senior and the foolish boy here—"

"Foolish! You damn well know—"

Sarom Senior reached out and grabbed his son's shoulder. Kanéko saw him squeeze tightly, and the words died in the younger man's throat. Then, the father turned back to her. "I'm sorry for my son, he can be rather rash. We don't have desert folk here often."

Someone muttered from the restaurant. "We never have those scum here. Stay in the desert, I say."

Sarom Senior glared inside the restaurant. Then, he favored Kanéko with a gap-toothed smile. "Come, the least I can do is get you some food. You look like you've been rolled in mud and baked over a flame."

Kanéko ran a hand through her hair and a shower of dust poured between her fingers. She looked at the dirt clinging to her hand and sighed. "I've had a bad day."

"I can imagine. Come on, Junior will feed you."

"Dad—" Junior's protest stopped when his father glared at him.

Sarom Senior returned his attention to Kanéko. "Go on in. I need to talk to Junior here for a moment about his manners."

"Thank you, sir."

Kanéko ducked her head and limped into the restaurant. Inside, nine men glared at her. Then, silently, the two at the nearest table picked up their plates and moved to join the others. Not a single word was said as she stumbled into one of the abandoned chairs and sat down with her back to the door.

A few minutes later, Junior came back in and stood stiffly in front of her. "I am sorry for hurting you," he said in a monotone.

Kanéko thought through a number of responses she could use. She went with politeness and bowed her head. "Thank you."

Junior pointed to the kitchen. "I will make you food."

From behind her, Kanéko heard Senior speaking. "Goslin, your wife is calling."

"My wife? She isn't... oh, sure."

Sarom Senior came around the table and sat down across from Kanéko.

She looked up at him thankfully, and then got a strange double-image of Ruben again. He wore a black vest and a bowler hat, but she never saw him wearing a bowler before. She blinked to clear her vision and caught only the tail end of Sarom's question.

"... happened to you?"

Kanéko cleared her throat. "I... I..." The words were difficult to get out. She felt tears burning her eyes.

"Tell me about it?"

She began to start explaining her plight, but something stopped her. She closed her mouth and sighed. "I probably shouldn't. I don't know if they are still around."

"Who?"

"Some uniformed guys, dark with a red armband."

Sarom pulled a face. "I've seen their kind around here in the last few days. They are looking for someone and offering a lot of money, I hear."

Kanéko's mouth closed with a snap. She glanced over her shoulder toward the door. To her surprise, the rest of the patrons in the room had disappeared in a matter of moments, leaving her completely alone with Sarom Senior.

Concern and worry rose up at the change. Her eyes flicked to the door, and she spotted unexpected shadows across the threshold. Afraid of staring too long, she turned her head back and then brought up the details of her arrival in her head. Like the pump, she could picture the size of the entrance and how the light would shine to create the shadows.

It didn't take her long to come to a conclusion, there had to be people waiting right outside of the door.

The prickling in the back of her neck redoubled. She turned her gaze to Sarom Senior and spotted the reflection of his son right inside the kitchen, holding a knife.

Kanéko's heart beat faster as she focused on Sarom Senior while trying to listen for her attackers. She surprised herself by speaking smoothly. "A lot of money?"

He cocked his head in a nod. "Yes, ten thousand crowns is more than most of us make in a lifetime."

Dividing her senses, she concentrated on keeping her face calm while she listened to the sounds. There was a creak of the boards moving and a rhythmic scrape of something rough; she guessed it was rope being uncoiled. Her eyes flickered to the walls, and then across the older man. She cleared her throat. "Are you going to take it?"

He hesitated for a moment, his brown eyes flicking back and forth as he looked into her gaze. Then, without a word, he nodded.

"W-Why?" she choked.

He folded his hands on the table in front of him. "My village needs the money. We need tools to fix houses that need repairs. We all have taxes to pay, and Junior's wife is sick. With ten thousand... well, we can take care of our own."

Kanéko took a long breath, her legs tensing for a fight. "Have you no honor?"

"I can live with myself for this. I'm sorry, but we need that money more than a life of a desert stranger."

"Damn you," she whispered angrily. Rage flared up inside her. Kanéko's hand snapped out, grabbing a serrated knife from the table.

Sarom Senior pushed back from the table before she could slash him.

Kanéko sprinted for the door as she saw men stepping in front of it. She spotted an opening between their legs and threw herself into a somersault that brought her past them.

A hand grabbed her hair.

She yanked it free and surged to her feet on the road. Her ankle hurt but her veins sung with fear and she felt the discomfort fade away.

A dozen men spread out from the restaurant in a circle. Most of them held ropes and chains in their hands, but she saw a few clubs bobbing on shoulders. None of them wielded sharp weapons, no doubt in an effort to capture her alive.

"You greedy, *shit-filled bastards*!" She waved the knife at the nearest of the villagers, backing away as quickly as she could. She furtively looked around her, but the men surrounded her.

Sarom Senior came up, holding out his hands. "Come on, girl, just set down the knife. We won't hurt you."

"You're kidnapping me!"

Junior snapped back, "We need that money."

"*Drown in sands!*" she snarled.

186

Junior lunged forward, his stick coming in an overhead blow.

Kanéko watched it arcing toward her and dodged at the last moment. She whipped her knife around and brought it up, catching him in the chest. The cut parted his shirt and left a bloody line from rib to shoulder.

Junior fell back with a scream.

Someone grabbed her shoulder.

Kanéko spun around to slash again. She saw the frightened look in Senior's eyes, and she froze. Her blade stopped with the sharp point nearly touching his skin. She couldn't bring herself to kill him.

Hands grabbed her and pulled her back. Someone twisted her wrist until she dropped the knife, and another person wrapped a rope around her neck.

She screamed and kicked out with all her strength, but the exhaustion and trials weakened her and efforts to defend herself were futile. She managed to slip her head out from the rope.

"She cut me!" screamed Junior as he towered over her and brandished a bloody palm.

Kanéko tried to lash out, but hands pinned her down to the hard-packed ground. The smells of sweat and violence suffocated her. Then she saw Junior holding a knife in his hand and a mask of rage on his face.

His father stopped him by grabbing his wrist. "Junior! She's worth ten thousand alive, but nothing dead."

"They won't notice another cut, Dad! An eye for an eye, you said those desert scum follow those rules."

Kanéko tried to break free again, but they held her down too tightly. Pinned to the earth, she felt vibrations coming through the ground. At first, she thought it came from Senior's yelling, but then she recognized it as the pounding of a horse. She pictured Ruben coming to save her, but she didn't know why she would ever consider the tiny teenager in the middle of a fight.

She threw everything she had to break free. It was a one in a million chance, but the adrenaline gave her the strength to free one arm and leg.

Hands fumbled to pin her down again.

She punched and kicked them away.

Sarom Senior bellowed. "Stop her!" The older man leaned over her. "Look, stop struggling! You won't get..." his voice trailed off as he looked up.

Kanéko watched his face hopefully.

Senior peered out from the side of her vision, and then his eyes grew wide

One of her attackers yelled, "Look out!"

Hands dropped her as everyone fled.

Kanéko looked up to see one of the school's horse-drawn wagons racing toward her. Maris's ears peeked above the horse and she realized that the image of Ruben was disturbingly accurate; she had pictured him exactly as he sat at the reins.

The horse swerved at the last minute, and the wheel caught her hair, yanking her down and clipping her head. Kanéko jerked away before the second wheel struck her.

"Kanéko!" Maris barked. She jumped off the back of the wagon. The girl wore a black dress with white trim and looked out of place next to Kanéko's muddy outfit. Her tail wagged as she raced to Kanéko. Maris grabbed her arm and pulled Kanéko to her feet. "Come on, stupid. And we need to go!"

Over Maris's shoulder, Kanéko saw Junior run toward her. He held a knife over his head. She gripped Maris and cried out.

Maris dropped Kanéko and spun around. Her lip curled back, and she took two steps toward Junior and kicked forward. The bottom of her foot caught Junior in the stomach, and he folded over. Maris shoved him back, and he hit the ground.

Kanéko gasped and grabbed the wheel of the wagon. Shuddering with exhaustion, she pulled herself up.

A small hand presented itself and she looked up to see Ruben holding it out. His bright blue eyes burned in her mind and she somehow knew that there was no anger in his sapphire gaze.

She took the offered hand and he helped her up with surprising strength.

"We need to flee, Kanéko Lurkuklan, and we do not have time for hesitation." His voice was soft, a whisper of sound, but she could hear it as clear as day.

Kanéko flipped over the edge of the wagon and landed heavily in the space between the bench and her trunk. She pushed herself up to look back over the edge.

Maris stood between the wagon and the village men. She snarled loudly, a remarkably canine sound that resonated with the growl from her chest.

Ruben snapped the reins and the horse pulled on the wagon. As soon as the wagon started to move, he whistled three sharp blasts.

Maris's ears perked up. She dropped her stance and spun on the balls of her feet. She sprinted after the wagon, her black skirt fluttering in the wind. The horse continued to accelerate, but the dalpre caught up and jumped smoothly into the back.

Ruben brought the wagon around the center of town and aimed it north.

Kanéko gasped and stared at the two teenagers in shock. "What are you doing?"

"You need assistance. Maris and I are providing it."

Kanéko focused on the dalpre. Maris crouched on the trunk, her lips still curled back and a glare burning in her eyes. She sniffed the air and a growl vibrated in her chest. "Rub, they're chasing us."

In the village, four of the villagers had retrieved their horses. They chased after them, quickly eating up the distance to the wagon. Sarom Senior whipped his horse frantically at the front of the group.

Maris sat down heavily on the trunk. "Well, at least we just made them angry."

Kanéko stared at her. "W-Why did you save me?"

"Rub heard you. And you needed help. And you are hard to find," she grumbled, "And I'm tired. And we've been riding all night. And I want food."

Rub spoke calmly, "I said you could slumber while I navigated. Maris Germudrir. We need to lose weight, or we won't be able to outrun our pursuers."

"How about this? You want me to dump it?" Maris patted the trunk.

Kanéko remembered something Sarom Senior had said about needing tools. "The trunk!"

"But I just said that," muttered Maris.

Kanéko leaned on it as she got to her feet. She dug through her wallet until she found the key to the trunk. Fumbling, she shoved Maris away and managed to unlock it.

"And what are you doing now? Changing?"

"Shut up," snapped Kanéko.

Maris's mouth dropped open and her ears flattened on the side of her head. Her lip pulled back.

The wagon jerked as it drove over a rut.

Kanéko dug into her clothes and felt around. When the steel of her chisel fit in her hand, she let out a gasp of relief. "There!"

Looking up, she saw Sarom less than a chain behind them. She pulled out the chisel and held it up. "Here's your damn tools!"

Sarom Senior looked confused and Kanéko tossed the chisel at his chest. It missed and hit the ground. Before it finished rolling, the horse raced past it.

Kanéko realized he wouldn't stop for one tool. She decided to give him all of them. She crawled over the trunk to the back of the wagon. Her hands, bruised and aching, fumbled to the bolts holding the back of the wagon together. She managed to pull one pin. She reached for the other, but Maris was already there, pulling the pin free. The wagon gate fell off and clattered to the ground.

Sarom's horse jumped over it as it spun on the dirt. The other horses easily avoided the tailgate.

Maris, a confused look on her face, asked, "What are we doing?"

"Pushing the trunk off. It has my tools. It's heavy and big."

"Okay."

Both girls crawled back over the trunk and into the space between the trunk and the front of the wagon. Kanéko planted her feet on the trunk and her back on the side of the wagon. With her flagging strength, she pushed with all her might.

Maris joined her. When the dalpre shoved with her feet, the trunk slid toward the edge of the wagon. With a final surge, it plummeted off the end of the wagon. It hit the ground and cracked in half. Tools and clothes spilled out into the mud.

Sarom saw the trunk in front of him and yanked on his reins. The horse tried to jump over it but couldn't get its back legs high enough. A loud snapping noise and a high-pitch squeal cut through the air.

Kanéko winced. In agonizing slowness, she watched the horse collapse to the ground with Sarom underneath.

Maris turned on her. "And why did you hurt the horse? She didn't do anything!"

"I didn't mean to!" snapped Kanéko.

Behind them, the other horses slowed before turning back toward Sarom and the shattered chest.

"Like what you did to my dress?"

"Yes, exactly like your dress! I'm not perfect!"

"And I don't like you now," Maris snarled at her, stood up, and then crawled over the back of the bench, leaving Kanéko alone in the back of the wagon.

Kanéko waited until Maris's tail disappeared before letting out a long sob of relief and anguish. She buried her face in her hands and started to cry.

Chapter 19

Lessons Learned

The greatest of Tachìra's gifts come not with silver or jade, but blood of horses flowing in the veins of men. They are the *herutonùfi*, horse kings, and the greatest of his champions.

—Kimáni Ryoshìko, *Death of the Horse Thief*

"I'm thinking of something green."

At first, Kanéko couldn't identify the girl's voice through the exhaustion blurring her thoughts. She didn't remember falling asleep. She started to sit up, but then recalled slamming her head on a rock and stopped. She forced herself to relax, to become aware of her environment before moving again.

She almost missed the response to the girl, a boy's soft whisper right on the edge of Kanéko's hearing. "That deciduous tree by the boulder."

"What?"

"The tree with the wedge-shaped leaves that fall at the end of summer. Right there, by the granite boulder you think resembles a cat cleaning itself."

"Oh. Yeah." Maris giggled, and Kanéko heard a thumping noise.

Kanéko opened her eyes slowly, staring into the orange-streaked clouds high above her and a much closer black tail wagging back and forth. She focused on Maris's rear until the last of the fog dissipated. Next to Maris, Ruben sat on the left side of the wagon bench, his short form barely visible from where Kanéko laid on the floor of the wagon.

Maris's tail rapped on the back of the bench for a moment. Then, she spoke up excitedly. "Oh, I'm thinking about something red!"

Ruben turned to look at the dalpre. He had a slight smile that didn't reflect in his eyes or the rest of his expression. "That red rubber ball hidden underneath your cot."

The dalpre playfully smacked Ruben on the head. "Don't cheat, Rub!"

"I'm not!" even speaking loudly, Ruben's voice never rose above a whisper. "You are always thinking of that ball, Maris Germudrir. It's like saying you like playing with the cats when no one is looking."

Maris grunted. "I don't like you. And I don't like cats that much."

Ruben chuckled dryly. "Do not lie. You love chasing them."

"No, I don't," she said sharply, but Kanéko could hear a hint of amusement in her voice.

A brief pause. Then Ruben spoke. "Is that a squirrel?"

"Where!?" Maris launched herself off the wagon.

Kanéko closed her eyes in fear that Maris would see her looking.

"No need to pretend anymore, Kanéko Lurkuklan. You have two minutes, four seconds before she returns."

She froze. Embarrassment burned her cheeks. She didn't realize Ruben knew she was awake. When she opened her eyes, she saw him leaning over the back of the bench. In his hands, he held the reins and the horse continued to walk along the trail, but teenager didn't even look over his shoulder to guide the equine. His blue eyes bored into hers. He didn't seem to blink enough and Kanéko felt uncomfortable looking up at the smaller, but older, boy.

Clearing her throat, she sat up. "How long was I... out?"

"Approximately one hour, thirty-three minutes. We are not being followed at this point."

"Does Garèo know?"

"He does not."

She yawned, feeling more comfortable than the last time she woke up. "Where are we?"

Ruben sat back in the bench and pointed down the road. Kanéko peered in the same direction, spotting a plume of smoke rising up from above the trees. "Approaching Dalashon Village. After that, about five hours, twenty minutes until we return to the Boar Hunt Inn."

Kanéko's eyes widened as she stared at the plume of smoke. The events of the last village still burned brightly in her thoughts. She shook her head. "No, I-I don't think that is a good idea. They'll be waiting."

"The mercenaries?"

"Yes," sighed Kanéko, "Have you seen them?"

Ruben nodded slowly, and then turned around to sit down. He tugged on the reins. The horse slowed down and Maris jumped on the wagon with a thump that shook Kanéko.

Leaves clinging to Maris's hair, she stepped over Kanéko. Maris's dress brushed on Kanéko's head before the dalpre sat down heavily next to Ruben. She grabbed a leaf and tossed it aside. "That wasn't fair, Rub, and it wasn't a squirrel. It was a coon."

She spoke with mock anger, but Kanéko could tell from her tail that the dog girl felt some excitement from her brief run. Up close, she noticed that the girl's skirt had a slit in it so her tail could wag freely. The seam showed signs of being frequently repaired, judging from the three different colors of thread. Without moving, Kanéko inspected the rest of Maris's dress, noticing the frayed edges and faded colors along the hem. Unlike Kanéko's clothes—before she swam across a river—Maris obviously wore hand-me-downs.

Ruben spoke in his quiet voice. "Kanéko Lurkuklan required a moment of silence to join the conversation. Distracting you provided a much needed quiet to allow social entry without embarrassment."

Maris peeked over her shoulder at Kanéko, her eyes widened, and her inhuman ears perked up.

Kanéko glared up at her, but then couldn't remember why she would be angry at the girl who just rescued her. She saw a dark emotion rising in Maris's expression and quickly forced herself to smile. She rolled on her knees before leaning back on her heels. "How did you find me?"

Ruben pointed to the north. "We were driving to Three Firs and stopped for a meal one hour past midday. If you remember, we usually ride alone because—"

"And no one likes me," pouted Maris, "and they say I'm stupid. And a bitch."

"That is the correct term—"

Maris growled and he stopped before finishing his sentence.

Kanéko said nothing, but she felt uncomfortable at Maris's words because Pahim had said the same things. More importantly, she hadn't disagreed with him.

Ruben cocked his head and paused. A heartbeat later, he continued. "We were passed by a trio of mercenaries on horseback. Maris identified them as coming from the Boar Hunt Inn."

"And they smell like grease. And old water."

"One hour, nineteen minutes later, they returned going the opposite direction. They were racing. I discerned they were searching for you."

Kanéko shook her head in confusion. "How did you know that? Did they say anything? And why are you so precise about numbers?"

Ruben cleared his throat. "Yeah, something like—"

Maris interrupted him with a wide smile and a wagging tail. "And he feels them in his head."

Ruben shot Maris an angry glare, and then his eyes caught hers. As fast as his anger showed, it faded behind an expressionless mask. He looked away.

"In his head?" asked Kanéko.

Maris's ears rose up, and she bounced in her seat. "Yes! And he can tell when they are obsessed with someone. And they were..."

Ruben glared at her, and her voice trailed off. Maris whimpered and held her hands over her mouth to silence herself.

Kanéko looked back and forth between the two teenagers, confused by their half-sentences.

Ruben cocked his head. "Well, from the evidence, I assumed you were in trouble and concluded that since you didn't pass us, you were either at the Boar Hunt Inn or took an alternative route. When we backtracked, Maris caught your scent along this road, so we turned toward it. We spent the night north of this approaching village, Dalashon, and then resumed searching at first sunlight."

Kanéko worried her lip. "Why?"

"You were in need."

Maris's ears drooped and she looked sad. "And Ruben said you were in trouble. And Pahim smelled like he wanted to fuck you. But he was also not in the wagons. And he's mean. And I don't think he liked you. And I don't hate you."

Kanéko opened her mouth and then closed it. She found herself unable to look into Maris's wide eyes and looked away.

Ruben responded softly, "It was also the morally correct action, regardless of flighty canine reasons."

"Bah," pouted Maris.

"And," Ruben grinned, "she knows I'd tell her progenitors."

"And if you tell my daddy, I'll hit you again."

Ruben gave Kanéko a sly grin but said nothing.

Maris grumbled and sat on her hands.

Kanéko leaned on the bench, watching the road as she tried to think of where to go. She thought about Falkin and the comforts of the inn, and then realized that the men from the *Burning Cloud Queen* would be looking for her there. She considered running to the ocean, but she couldn't figure out how to escape the mercenaries. Finally, she thought about fleeing for home, but ten days on wagon seemed like an eternity. Not to mention she didn't know how to hide from seekers.

Ruben broke the silence. "How do we secret you through Dalashon Village without detection? The road goes through it, and there are no trails around the village that can handle the wagon and horse."

Kanéko looked at the contents of the wagon. She spotted a threadbare blanket and two travel packs. "I could hide under the blanket?"

Ruben shook his head. "That would not be sufficient. One of those uniformed mercenaries stopped us this morning and insisted on upturning the wagon's contents. They didn't recognize your travel trunk or your father's seal, which I feel demonstrates a poor education on their part, but I think they'll catch you if we try to simply hide you."

"Why were they looking for me?"

"There is a reward for a significant amount of money but lacking in details beyond the more obvious physical ones. I have not seen the poster but it was clear in their thoughts. I suspect they are aware you are a bartim's daughter but we are significant far away for them to be familiar with your family's symbols."

Kanéko swore in Miwāfu and slumped. The bench creaked with her movement and she tensed, fearing it would crack. She struggled with her thoughts as she made a show of balancing herself, but she knew he was looking at her for an answer. She looked up, hating the words about to come out. "I could walk around the village."

Ruben glanced at her, his eyebrow rising with a question. "Are you skilled at traveling without markers?"

She thought back to the hours of wandering the woods. Her shoulders slumped. "No."

"Probably not safe then. I cannot leave you alone without sufficient skills."

Kanéko sighed and leaned back, another Mifúno curse on her lips.

Maris glared at her. "And stop swearing!"

Kanéko snapped back, *"And why don't you drown in sands?"*

"Stop it!"

"No, I won't, you empty-headed cow."

"Stop it!"

"I'm sure they'll find us faster with you two yelling at each other." Ruben spoke softly but with a voice that cut through their raised voices. His eyes remained riveted on the road.

Kanéko's mouth closed with a snap.

Maris grumbled. "Just let her walk around. I'm sure she'll get lost, and then you won't have to tell daddy."

Without thinking, Kanéko reached up and smacked Maris on the top of her head.

The dalpre grabbed her head and whimpered. "Ow!" Her tail curled up under the bench of the wagon, pressing tight against the wood.

Maris looked at Ruben with wide eyes. "Aren't you going to say something smart?"

Ruben said, "You deserved it. Stop pushing her."

Maris whimpered loudly. "She is saying mean things about me!"

He sighed, "And you are both presenting yourselves as spoiled brats. Now, please be quiet, I am trying to route a path through the area."

Kanéko felt a blush rising in her cheeks. Her shoulders slumped and she sighed. "*Sorry.*"

As they rode in silence, Kanéko thought about her options. It didn't take her long to realize the inn was the safest place. She spoke up. "I think the Boar Hunt Inn is the best place to go."

Ruben flicked the reins. "What if they are there? It would be reasonable to assume they are going to use the inn as a coordination point until they locate you."

"I can hide or something, maybe in the woods around it. Maybe in the garden behind it. You can stay in the inn and wait for Garèo. Assuming he will come back."

"He will," Maris announced. "He would never abandon his pack."

Ruben thought for a moment, and then nodded. "Better than nothing. Waryoni Garèo would come back as soon as he discovered that four of us are missing, presuming Pahim dim Maldor doesn't return."

Kanéko felt a surge of anger at Pahim's name. Her lips pressed into a tight line, and she scraped her ragged nails on the deck of the wagon, pretending it was his face.

She felt an itch in the back of her mind. Looking up, she saw Ruben watching her with his concerned blue eyes.

Ruben turned away. "I am regretful that I was unable to identify your danger from Pahim dim Maldor earlier. His mind is... cloudy to me. More so than usual. Teenage males lose much of their cognitive abilities while in the presence of females they wish to mate with."

It took only a moment for Kanéko to comprehend Ruben's complex response. She blushed hotly.

Maris made a high-pitched whine and stood up sharply, sniffing the air. Her tail snapped out and smacked Kanéko in the face.

Kanéko started to rise up but she stopped when she saw Maris poised on her toes to reach higher.

The dalpre sniffed loudly. She cocked her head and did it again.

Kanéko stared up in confusion, and then took a hesitant sniff of her own. She could only smell earth and plants. She tapped Ruben on the shoulder, and then pointed to Maris. "Ruben?"

Ruben's eyes came into focus, the blue somehow sharpening in a heartbeat. "I know."

Kanéko looked back and forth. "Know what?"

Ruben turned to her. "The mercenaries are looking for you again. They are on this road."

"I know that already."

He turned toward her and spoke seriously. "No, they are approaching now."

Maris pointed to her nose. "And we are downwind of their horses. There is at least four of them. Maybe... twenty minutes away. A quarter bell at most."

Kanéko stared at her, trying to comprehend how anyone could smell something so far away. As she thought, a light breeze washed over her face and she had to resist the urge to sniff like Maris.

The dalpre sat down, and the bench creaked from the impact. To her surprise, Kanéko felt a small measure of jealousy and the sharp blade of humility as the two teenagers seemed to perceive things so far away. She stared between Maris and Ruben and tried to come up with a plan. "Look, can you stop? If they are coming, I need to get off the road now."

Ruben pulled to the side. He set down the reins. "Come on, Maris, gather up the travel supplies."

"And we are all going?" Maris bounced hard on the wagon, shaking it, before hopping off.

"It would be remiss to leave Kanéko Lurkuklan alone in the woods. I can extrapolate the terrain while traveling. I suspect that knowledge would make it easier to keep her safe."

"I could go with her," said Maris.

"In terms of brutality and defense, you excel. However, you are unskilled in the woods."

Maris looked like she would argue, and then she sighed. "I trust you, Rub."

Kanéko slid off the wagon. As her aching feet hit the ground, she groaned. Even if walking was a good idea, she couldn't handle more miles on her bare soles. Before leaving home, she spent her entire life without shoes, but she had never walked so many miles over rough ground. She needed something for protection. Glancing around, she found a blanket and pulled it out of the wagon. With her teeth, she tore into the edge and then ripped off a long strip.

"What are you doing?" asked Maris.

"Wrapping my feet," announced Kanéko. She continued to tear the blanket into long strips before bringing the ruined remains of the fabric to the edge of the wagon and dangled her feet over it. One strip at a time, she wrapped the cloth around her feet. She tried to move as fast as she could, but she almost ripped the fabric the wrong way. More straps circled around her calves and she tied it off. Cautiously, she slipped off the back of the wagon and landed on her feet.

The fabric padded her feet and she let out a sigh of relief. She turned to see Maris watching her curiously. The dalpre carried three bags and next to her, Ruben carried a smaller one.

Kanéko took a hesitant step, and then a second. After a moment to balance on the balls of her feet, she leaned back.

Ruben came around the wagon, his short legs giving him a sway to his step. "Is that sufficient comfort and protection?"

Kanéko nodded.

Maris whimpered. "Ruben, they are getting closer. And moving really fast. And their horses are sweating. And they're hurting those poor creatures."

Ruben pointed toward a bank of trees. "If we head in that direction, we will avoid the roads entirely. We'll come up from the south of the inn and maybe have a chance to find a safe route. It will take longer, but they probably won't find us."

Kanéko looked around and the horse's movement drew her attention. She thought about the one she injured a few hours before and felt her chest tightening from the sorrow. She wasn't sure where the sympathy came from, but she thought the hours of her mother and Garèo driving the desert lore into her head. Maybe their lessons had finally started to affect her.

Standing by the wagon, she could see a trail leading in the direction Ruben pointed. She returned her gaze to the wagon and saw it in a different light, a large sign pointing to where they fled the road.

She turned back to Ruben. "We have to do something about that."

"Let me." Ruben hurried in front of the wagon. He reached up for the bridle and the horse obediently lowered its head. He stared into its eyes but said nothing. Kanéko thought she saw his eyes glowing for a moment.

Ruben released the horse. "Completed."

The horse pulled away from them and accelerated into a trot. The wagon bounced after it as the horse ran down the road.

Maris whimpered softly. "Why did you do that?"

"How," Kanéko asked, "did you do that?"

Ruben cocked his head for a moment. "That will increase the difficulty of tracking us. Come, we need to depart from the road."

Kanéko knew that Ruben didn't answer her question, but she could feel the sands of time hanging over her.

"Oh. I..." the dalpre sighed to Ruben's response, "And I didn't think of that."

Kanéko started to give her a sardonic reply when Ruben patted her on the arm.

"I know," he said, "but there are many things you do not think of. That is why I'm here, remember?" He took the lead and headed straight for the trees. He moved easily through the tall grasses despite his short legs. Kanéko could only see his hat, a black bowler, above the frayed ends of the grasses.

Maris grinned and stared after him. "Because you need me to defend you, right, Rub?"

Kanéko watched the two teenagers walking into the tree line. She turned and looked down both directions of the road. From the point when Maris had sniffed out her pursuers, to when they were standing on the road was only a few minutes, but it felt like a year had passed. She returned her gaze to Maris just as the dalpre disappeared behind an oak tree.

Swearing softly to herself, Kanéko hurried up the bank of grass to the trees. She didn't know what would happen, but she felt a lot safer having Ruben and Maris beside her.

Chapter 20

Travel Partners

... no dalpre shall ever be provided public schooling without written consent from a count.

—*Unified Codex of Kormar Law* (Volume 4)

"**W**orst trip ever," muttered Kanéko under her breath. In front of her, Maris's ears perked up and Kanéko tensed with the realization that even the smallest of sounds caught the dalpre's attention.

Maris started to turn around but stopped when a butterfly flew past her. Her ears flattened and she lunged for the insect. The butterfly escaped, and Maris squealed as she jumped off the animal trail to chase it.

Kanéko let out a sigh of relief. The anger she felt at Maris from their first encounter still colored her thoughts. But the dalpre fought to save her, and she still remembered when Maris gave her the Maiden Root at the inn. Kanéko didn't understand the dalpre at all, and she was afraid of insulting or upsetting the girl.

Maris came back to the trail, and Kanéko averted her eyes to look at Ruben instead. To Kanéko, Ruben was as alien as Maris, but he surprised Kanéko by steadily leading them around the village. Even with short legs, he seemed inexhaustible in stamina and adept at moving smoothly along the rough terrain. His movements seemed more in tune with nature than Kanéko had imagined possible. She never saw him slap at insects buzzing around them or struggling with the roots that buckled the ground. He managed to slip through the brush and vines without even a scratch, whereas Kanéko tore her clothes every time they switched game trails.

She rubbed her cuts and glared at the boy, wishing he would trip or even just get a cut somewhere. At least then he would look like Maris and herself.

Ruben stopped and turned to her. His bright blue eyes stared directly at her and she blushed without realizing why.

Between them, Maris came to a halt. She followed Ruben's gaze and her ears twisted. "What?"

Ruben smirked then turned to look at Maris. He spoke in a soft whisper. "Nothing, just thought I heard someone muttering something bitter."

"There is a bunch of boars in the next valley over," Maris supplied helpfully and pointed to the east. "But I think they are fighting."

Kanéko scanned the hills, trying to find sign of the boars or anything Maris claimed she saw. On the very edge of her hearing, she thought she heard grunting, but it faded after a second. "How... I mean, how do you know that?"

Maris beamed and pointed to her nose. "I can smell them around here." She then pointed to her ears. "And I can hear the grunting."

The desert girl glanced back to the rocky ridge. "How are you sure it is boars?"

"Because we are near the Boar Hunt Inn." Maris giggled. "And they had a map in the great hall that said there were sounders around here."

Kanéko frowned. "Sounders?"

"Packs of boars."

"I didn't know—" Kanéko found she didn't like Maris knowing more than herself. More and more, she felt helpless around the two others.

"It was written on the map."

Kanéko gave her a hard look before grunting. "Should have stopped before you told me that. I would have thought you were smart or something."

A hurt look plastered itself on Maris's face. "But I am smart!"

"What, because you can read a map?"

Maris balled her hands into fists. "Yes, I can read. And it isn't like all dalpre are il... illi... illiterate. At least I," she spat out the word, "don't get lost in the woods like a pup! Wandering around because some boy tried to kidnap you!"

Kanéko opened her mouth to snap back. But, Maris's words struck deep and she closed her mouth. Her anger quickly faded. Instead of speaking, she shrugged in sheepish agreement.

Ruben walked up to Maris and put a hand on the dog girl's hip. Maris's tail stopped moving and she turned toward Ruben. For a heartbeat, she looked back up at Kanéko with her hurt look before talking to the other teenager. "I'm smart, right?"

Ruben grinned. "There are different types of smarts. From reputation, I would wager that if we find a mechanical device, Kanéko Lurkuklan would be able to discern its function long before you could figure out how to remove it from its container."

Kanéko smirked, but Ruben wasn't done.

"But in the woods, I think you are far more capable of surviving than her..."

It was Maris's turn to give Kanéko a self-righteous grin.

"... but then again, my knowledge exceeds both of yours combined."

Both Kanéko's and Maris's faces fell. They looked at each other, and then at the smiling boy. Ruben shrugged, and then pointed to the rocky ridge. "Please remain at this location for four minutes, twelve seconds. This trail is curving east, the terrain has changed since my memories, and I require a bearing."

Kanéko found a rock to sit on. Fingers of blue-green moss covered the top and she used it as a pad for her aching rear. As she settled down, the delicate smells of flowers and dirt drifted to her. She watched as Ruben turned off the trail and started to climb the side of the valley.

Across from her, Maris sat down heavily and pouted. "And I don't like you."

Kanéko focused on the dog girl. Maris's anger was mercurial, and it didn't seem worth the effort to get upset. "Okay."

"And you are mean and rude, and you insult me."

"When?"

"I heard you calling me *bitch, idiot,* and *moron* when you were talking to me."

Kanéko's mouth opened. She had changed languages when she was insulting Maris less than an hour before, somehow the dalpre knew the words. "And you understand those? Those are Miwāfu words."

Maris nodded, but continued to glare at her.

"Where? Um, how?"

Maris scratched her nose. "Ruben is teaching me. I don't know everything, but Garèo always said if you don't understand something, learn it before you hit it. Because just hitting things gets you in more trouble." Her ears came down. "At least that is what Garèo keeps telling me when I get in trouble. And I get in trouble a lot."

Kanéko stared at her in shock. Besides her mother and Garèo, no one else spoke the desert language. "You started learning Miwāfu on this trip? In the last few days?"

Maris's ears pressed to her skull, and she flinched at Kanéko's sharp tone, but she nodded again. "I'm trying."

Kanéko worried her lip for a moment. *"How much do you know?"*

Maris perked up. She struggled for a moment before she carefully said, *"o i noshìma a kīchi midòni."*

Kanéko giggled. She could understand Maris's words, but just like Kanéko only a few months ago, Maris missed some accents. With Miwāfu, a missing tone changed the word entirely. "The words understands the smell?"

"What?" Maris whimpered, "I didn't say that."

"You probably meant *'a hichi midòni'* which means 'some words.'"

"And, that's the part I don't get. And why all the funny sounding letters. You have four words for horse that all sound the same."

Kanéko grinned and leaned back. "There is only one word for horse, heru. The rest tell you what type of horse. We use *'héru'* for mare and *'hèru'* for stall—"

"And," Maris interrupted her, "I get that. But, they are really close to each other. I get confused if you mean mare or stallion. And then you add all those words together. I know that 'king' is *'tonùfì'* and 'horse king' is *'heru tonùfì'*. But I don't know what a horse king is, but it's important to Garèo because I hear him talking about it. Well, if it was a male because the word hangs down like balls."

Kanéko hesitated because she saw Maris in a slightly different light. For someone who didn't know any words of

Miwāfu a week before, she had picked up some of the complexities quickly.

Maris spoke up, "Kanéko?"

"Sorry," Kanéko drew her thoughts back, "You're right. Females have rising or mountain accents, males have falling or valley. Children accents rise and fall, a ridge accent, because they act like both at different times."

Maris smiled, and her tail wagged happily. "Thank you. That makes more sense. Ruben knows the words, but he can't really explain them. He memorizes. But he doesn't understand what he knows. And he's like a talking book."

Kanéko struggled with a response. She wanted to thank Maris for saving her, but her pride refused to let the words come out. She decided to change topics. "Why did you start coming to class?"

Maris bounced on her rock for a moment. "Your father said I could."

"Why not, um, why not everyone else?"

"You mean at the mill? Or the rest of the pack?"

Kanéko said, "You're the only one at the mill who comes to school, right?"

Maris toyed with her skirt. "You remember that drought four years ago?"

"Yes...?"

"Well, the people in the bartim were having trouble paying your daddy's taxes so he could pay taxes to the count. And my daddy had a really good year since we got rights to this hardwood grove that sold well up in the north... Well, my daddy had some extra money so he offered to pay your daddy extra taxes for a few years to make sure your daddy could pay the count his money. And naturally, your daddy said he had to do something for my daddy, so your daddy gave my daddy a, um, a boon."

It took a moment for Kanéko to parse Maris's sentences. She frowned as she thought back to the drought. She remembered her father struggling with the taxes; actually she recalled the screaming fights about money. When he stopped yelling, Kanéko had forgotten about it. She never even thought that the Salcid or the mill would factor into that silence.

"So that is why you started school?"

"Yep!" beamed the dalpre, "I'm the first at the mill to ever go to school. And I'm the only other one who understands numbers like daddy. But, that was before the school."

"Salcid never went?"

"No, my daddy taught himself. And he has trouble with bigger numbers, like over a thousand. That was because he grew up a slave and they didn't teach dalpre numbers."

Kanéko continued to struggle with the concept. "But, if your papa paid that much in taxes, couldn't he ask for a lot more than just sending you to school?"

Maris nodded. "I think so. But, if my daddy asked for too much, and then he would be hurting your daddy. So, he asked for the one thing he thought was important... me being smarter. And your daddy had to ask the count for permission too, so that ended up being really expensive, but not with money."

She frowned, "And I don't really understand that. And, the count said only one of us could go because he don't like us." Her ears pressed against her head again, "Everyone was so smart when I got there. And they pushed me around and were mean and nasty and rude. And they called me an idiot. And I don't like them."

"This was before Ruben?"

Maris's tail began to wag again. "I met Ruben a long time ago, when I was six and he was, um, eight. Right after they moved into the area, and his daddy started working for

213

your daddy. When Tagon, that's Ruben's daddy, found out I was going to school, he asked Ruben to tutor me because I was... not smart."

"Because you never went to school before that?"

"Yeah," pouted Maris, "so I had to work really hard to catch up to the others at school. Daddy let me skip cutting days and Mommy said I didn't have to cook so I could study with Rub. Bor didn't like it, but daddy told he had to stop grumbling. And, I still don't get everything, but I try so hard."

"You—" Ruben whispered suddenly from Kanéko's side.

Kanéko jumped and flailed in surprise.

He leaned to the side, and she missed. There was a sly look on her face. "—have acceptable progress in adapting quickly."

Blushing, Kanéko lowered her hand even though she missed him. She looked away as she sat back down on the rock. A sharp edge dug into her backside and she shifted slightly to find a more comfortable spot.

Maris grinned. "Thank you, Rub."

Ruben studied Kanéko's face for a moment. Then he grinned broadly. "You resemble someone who has realized a lot more happens in the world than you see from your bedroom window."

She blushed. With one finger, she scraped at the dirt-stained bandages over her palms.

Maris spoke up in the silence that followed. Her tail thumped against the ground. "I'm hungry. Are we leaving now?"

Ruben grunted and pointed to the west side of the valley. "I think we should climb that ridge. If we cut through the next valley, we can use the following ridge to walk almost the entire way to our destination."

Kanéko looked at the rough rocks and steep cliffs. "That looks like a hard climb."

"The next one is difficult, but there are trails along the peak that will alleviate much of the further discomfort. I can get us to the easier places to climb, but it will still be strenuous."

Kanéko looked at the gently sloping valley they sat in. "How much longer is the long way?"

"A day, maybe two. The route puts us through the region of some territorial boars. Unfortunately, there are no optimal ways to avoid climbing and still make reasonable time while maintaining safety. I also doubt my ability to find enough food to feed all three of us for long. I'm... not good at acquiring meat, and we'll lose a lot of time if I have to forage."

Maris said, "Rub and his daddy won't kill animals. Because it hurts them in the head."

"Oh," sighed Kanéko. She looked down at her lacerated palms and felt the aches and pains in her body. Lifting her gaze up, she regarded the rocky edge of the hill.

Ruben said in his soft whisper, "I don't know how to avoid your discomfort. I'm sorry, Kanéko Lurkuklan, I tried to find a better way."

Kanéko grunted as she stood up. "Better get it over with."

Maris whimpered. "What about your hands? Don't they hurt? Won't you fall?"

Kanéko really didn't want to climb, but she didn't have much of a choice. She favored Maris with a smile she didn't quite feel. "I'll heal."

Chapter 21

Landslide

The valleys around the Boar Hunt Inn are famed not only for hunting but also for rockslides and sinkholes.

—*Kormar Hunting Guide*

"I'm tired of walking," wailed Maris.

Kanéko rolled her eyes. She leaned on the ragged rock wall in front of her and tried not to think about the sweat prickling her skin or the baking sun that made it difficult to breathe. She was twenty feet off the ground and perched on a small ridge of rocks.

A swarm of bugs crowded her, tickling her ears and face.

Careful not to fall, she waved her hand to disperse them. In the brief respite, she drew in a long breath that tasted of dust to calm herself. Then she made sure she had a good grip before looking down to where Maris paced back and forth at the foot of the cliff. "I know, Maris."

The dalpre was about ten feet below her. The bare skin of Maris's face was red from the sun; Kanéko wondered if Maris burned underneath the fur on her ears and tail. Maris pouted. "My feet hurt. And my tail is knotted. And it is really hot! And I'm tired of climbing. And I don't like Ruben!" The last bit came out in a high-pitched scream aimed straight up the cliff.

Kanéko winced, peeking to see Ruben's response.

The short teenager was near the top of the cliff, about twenty feet above Kanéko.

The boy shrugged without looking back. He reached up and grabbed the next rock. He smoothly pulled himself up over the top of the cliff, his short stature looking more like an animal than human.

Kanéko shook her head. Turning on her heels, she peered down. "Come on, Maris, the faster we climb this thing, the faster you get to sleep in a real bed."

Maris stopped her pacing and pouted at Kanéko. Her ears flattened to her skull. "But you won't get to sleep in a bed. If they catch you, we won't be able to help you."

Kanéko crouched down on the edge of her rock. "I'll rest after all this. In my own bed at my papa's tower."

Maris's ears perked up, and her tail wagged faster. Dust from the trail scattered off her skirt with her rear shaking. She made a hesitant reach for the rocks before pulling back.

Kanéko gazed to the rocky face above her. She reached up for the next ridge, and then winced as the raw rocks scraped her lacerated palms. She pulled back her hands, frowning at the cuts and scratches. Gloves would have been useful.

Getting an idea, she tore off a length of the stained fabric from her calves and wrapped them around her hands like fingerless gloves. Every movement threatened to pull her away from the cliff face, but she had gotten used to working around burning metal and her movements were precise and efficient as she tied them tight around her aching palms.

Protected, she grabbed the ridge. The wrappings caught the edge of the rock, and she took a deep breath before pulling herself up. Her makeshift protection held, and she crawled up the rock face with less pain.

Twenty feet looked like a short distance. By the time she reached the top of the rocky ridge, she had to stop and gasp for breath. She focused on Ruben, balanced on the cliff edge like a gargoyle.

He looked back at her and smiled. There wasn't even a droplet of sweat on his forehead.

Kanéko glared back. "And I don't like you," she announced, trying to match Maris's tone.

He smirked.

After a second, Kanéko grinned. She started to laugh, and Ruben joined her, chuckling quietly with his shoulders shaking.

She leaned on a ragged tree to catch her breath.

Ruben pointed, and Kanéko turned to look in the same direction. In the far distance, she could see plumes of smoke rising up above the tree line.

"Our destination."

She sighed. "It's so far away."

"One league, four chains," came Ruben's quiet response, "At this rate, about three hours, twenty-two minutes. The elevation changes slow us down significantly."

Kanéko groaned.

Ruben shrugged again. "Otherwise, our rate is relatively predictable."

She waved in his general direction. "I know, I know. Just seems overwhelming at this point."

"Just take it one step at a time," supplied Ruben.

Kanéko chuckled. "Mother always said, archery starts with one arrow. And Garèo said just keep moving."

"Same inspiration expressed with idioms from different cultures."

From below, Maris's voice rose up. "Um, help?"

Kanéko shoved herself from the tree and ran to the edge. She leaned over to peer down.

Maris had managed to scale almost the entire distance, but she had slipped from a rocky outcropping about five feet from the top. Half of her body hung off as she clung to rock with white knuckles. Her large breasts were crushed against the cliff, spilling over another edge. A high-pitched whine filled the air. "H-Help?"

Kanéko didn't have time to panic. She dropped to the ground to reach down for her.

With a whimper, Maris grabbed her wrist with her free hand and pulled, her weight almost dragging Kanéko off the edge.

Kanéko grunted as she braced herself. Then she focused on pulling the dalpre to the top.

Maris whined as she crawled over the edge and then collapsed. Her tail draped over her rear as she laid face-down on the rocks.

Ruben padded up to her. "Are you injured?"

Maris looked humiliated, her ears and tail flat against her body. She rubbed the bottom of her breast. "My tits hurt."

Kanéko watched her with concern. "What happened?"

"I thought you left me. And then I crawled up as fast as I could. And then I slipped. And then I started to fall. And... I called for help," Maris's voice ended with a whine.

Kanéko sighed and fought the urge to pat Maris on the head. "Why?"

"Because you were talking about how long it would take. And walking. And then you both were on top. And you were laughing. And I didn't see you, and then... I got lonely."

A fly landed on Maris's ear, and she flicked it to chase it away.

"L-Lonely?" Kanéko fought the smirk.

Maris whimpered, "Yes."

Ruben shrugged. "Pack members are rarely out of sight of someone they trust. We were remiss in having our conversation out of line of sight but within range of hearing. Even if Maris Germudrir could have seen our movements, it would have resulted in her taking fewer risks."

Maris stared at him with a blank look.

He sighed. "I should always sit on the cliff while discussing options with Kanéko Lurkuklan."

"Yes! And you should have stayed where I could see you! You weren't suppose to leave me, Rub!"

Kanéko patted her on the shoulder. "I'm not going to abandon you, Maris. I'm lost without you and Ruben."

Maris watched her, a confused look on her face.

Kanéko sighed and leaned back on the tree. "I've never really been outside the sight of my father's tower. And in the first trip, I made a complete weed of myself, treated you and Ruben like hell, and ended up falling for a blond snake who just wanted me for the reward money."

Maris cocked her head, and her ears perked up. "Who's the snake?"

"Pahim," snapped Kanéko, "That horrible bastard. I mean... We slept together, and what does he do?" Kanéko's voice rose up as rage filled her. "He kidnaps me and tries to sell me off like some slave!"

Maris gaped. "You fucked Pahim?"

Kanéko blushed hotly. "No! Not like that. I mean, we were in the same bed but we... didn't do anything. I swear!"

Maris snickered. "Right. I won't tell anyone."

"I didn't!"

"Are you sure—"

"Maris," interrupted Ruben, "cease teasing."

Maris closed her mouth but didn't stop smirking.

Kanéko let out a sigh of relief. She never knew anyone her age who teased her. It felt strange but good.

Ruben hopped off his rock and pointed to the northeast. "If we follow this ridge that way, we can meet up with the next one, and then over to there," he swept his finger as he spoke, "and then there. That way, we only will have to climb down at the end. However, it will increase the travel time by thirty-three minutes."

"Good," said Kanéko and Maris at the same time. The two girls looked at each other before Kanéko looked away with a smile. Ruben walked past them and Kanéko gestured for Maris to follow. The dog girl hopped after Ruben, her tail wagging and a skip to her movement.

Twenty minutes later, their cheer faded, and Kanéko struggled to put one foot in front of the other. Exhaustion sapped her strength, and she couldn't stop panting for breath.

In front of her, Maris struggled, stumbling occasionally as she followed Ruben.

The path dipped into a tiny ragged ditch only a few feet deep.

Ruben ran down the middle and up the other side. He casually stepped off the game trail and perched on a rock. When he stopped moving, he looked like a statue atop the fancy buildings in her magazines.

Maris tripped and lurched down into the depression. Kanéko rushed forward. She grabbed Maris by her tail and the back of her shirt before Maris hit the ground. Together, they came to a halt at the bottom of the dip.

"Are you all right?"

Maris tugged her tail and shirt from Kanéko's grip and turned toward her. "I think I'm..." Her voice trailed off as her ears perked up. She glanced around her before return-ing her attention back to Kanéko. Her ears were flat against her head and she looked sad. "I think I broke the cliff."

"Broke what? I don't—" Kanéko never finished the word as a loud crack shook the air. The rock lurched underneath her, dropping a foot. She let out a scream and crouched down, looking around frantically for the source of the movement.

Fissures spread out underneath Maris and her, spreading out up along both edges of the ditch.

"*Sands!*" Kanéko spun around, looking for a safe spot. In a few heartbeats, she saw the path separate from the cliff as the rock began to slide down. Scrambling, she pulled her-self up to the steadier side and turned around to give Maris a hand.

Maris hadn't followed her. She remained in the center of the buckling rock, ears against her head and tail between her legs. She stared at Kanéko with wide, tear-filled eyes.

"Maris!" called out Kanéko. She stepped on the unsteady rock, but it crumbled underneath her. She braced herself and held out her hand. "Come on, damn it!"

"I'm sorry," whimpered the dalpre.

The cliff around Maris collapsed, and she was swallowed by a cloud of dust that billowed up. The rumble was deafe-ning, and it shook the ground and air.

Kanéko screamed as she dropped to her knees. The im-pact left pain rocketing up her legs, but she pushed past it to reach into the cloud of dust. "Mar!? Maris!" The cloud choked her, coating her face as she tried to find anything besides sharp rocks and sheared off roots. She touched something slick and pulled back her hand. It looked like thick, black oil but it burned her skin. Whimpering, she wiped her palm off and shoved her hand back in the cloud.

An acidic, fishy scent of whatever she had on her hand swirled around her. She wrinkled her nose and concentrated on reaching back into the boiling cloud.

The rock underneath her knees shuddered. She gasped and peered over her shoulder. A fissure ran behind her, and she felt her perch separating from the cliff. Swearing, she scrambled back and launched herself to safer ground.

Her former spot broke off the cliff, and a boulder the size of a wagon plummeted out of sight into the dust.

"Maris Germudrir!"

Kanéko jumped at Ruben's surprisingly deep and loud voice. As she clutched her handhold and kicked the cliff to find footing, she looked up at him. She couldn't see him at first but then caught sight of his eyes. Their brilliant blue glow reflected an azure halo in the swirling dust, highlighting his body and drawing her attention to his intense look.

His voice echoed in the valley, but she heard it as if he was yelling directly into her ears. It seemed to be inside her head, bouncing around her skull. She tried to push her thoughts away, but they drew her back in, replying the two words endlessly with startling clarity.

She closed her eyes as the image of Maris being crushed to death slammed into her thoughts. Intensely detailed and graphic, the horror of it choked her, and she clutched a thick root until her knuckles turned white. It was too much for her and dizziness grabbed at her.

A blast of air slammed into her face and chest, pushing her back from the edge. She barely caught herself before she fell.

Movement caught her attention. Cringing, she looked up to see something large and dark shooting straight up. A plume of dust trailed after it, marking its path as it sailed hundreds of chains into the sky.

Kanéko frowned. She couldn't identify what flew above her. It didn't look like a creature of any sort, it spun but otherwise had no movement other than straight up.

The object slowed and seemed to hover in the air.

She gasped and realized it was the rock that had just fallen into the ravine, her former perch. Somehow, it had been launched high into the air. She glanced at the boiling dust cloud below her and then back to the rock.

It began to plummet. The dust behind it marked the curve of its path. She could see how it would fall on the far side of the ravine.

Kanéko lurched forward. "Mar!"

The boulder punched into the opposing cliff. An explosion of rocks turned the cliff into a smoking crater. Large hunks of stone rained down into the cloud, disappearing out of sight. It took seconds for the clattering to fade.

She screamed out. "Maris! Mar!"

Kanéko scanned the settling dust for any sign of Maris. When she didn't spot any, she focused on the rocks instead. Spotting a steady-looking outcropping, she tested it with her toe before dropping down on it. She landed on all fours and crawled over the edge. "Maris?"

From her vantage point, she could see where the side of the cliff had crumbled and filled a rock-filled gorge. The bottom was about a chain below her. Dust stung her nose and the back of her throat while she waited impatiently for the last of it to settle.

The long seconds passed with the rapid beating of her heart. She clutched the edge of the rock until the sharp edges dug into her palms. Only the cloth over her hand protected her from bleeding.

Finally, the air cleared enough. She spotted Maris immediately. The dalpre was on her back in the middle of a crater. She looked untouched by the avalanche that fell around her, but there was a thick trickle of blood coming from the corner of her mouth.

"Maris!" screamed Kanéko. She spotted another rock to jump on. Before she could jump, she did a double take on the crater. Even with her meager experience, there was something wrong about it. The desperation to get down to Maris fought with her curiosity and concern. Biting her lip, she took a longer look.

She wasn't expecting to see even radial lines spreading out from Maris's impact. The rock beneath her was blasted clean with waves of dirt, rocks, and dust forming a halo around the unmoving dalpre. A few weeds were straightened out, as if someone had pulled each one away from Maris at the point of impact.

It didn't look like a crater from the rocks hitting the ground but more like the many explosions she had seen while struggling to create the water screw in the stall.

The sense of wrongness rose, but she couldn't identify why the impact crater looked like it had been formed by an explosion instead of Maris's body crashing into the ground. She glanced over her shoulder toward the top of the cliff and called out to Ruben. "I-I'm going down, she's hurt."

Without waiting for a response, Kanéko climbed down the side of the rock. Her cloth-wrapped feet and palms protected her from the worst of the sharp rocks, but she still scraped herself before she hit the ground. She ignored the pains as she raced over to Maris and knelt next to her.

The dog girl didn't move and Kanéko felt a sob catching her throat. She brushed off the dust that had settled on Maris's body.

The girl groaned and clutched her head with both hands. "Owwie..."

"Maris!" Kanéko grabbed the girl in a tight hug.

Maris whimpered and Kanéko froze, unsure what to do.

Maris opened one eye, and then the other. Her tail wagged weakly. "I hurt my head."

Kanéko started, and then smirked. "Your hard head broke the cliff."

"Sorry."

"Can you sit up?"

"And I... no. Help me?"

Kanéko grunted and slipped one arm underneath Maris, using their combined strength to slowly ease her into a sitting position.

Maris leaned into her, panting.

"Maris, are you all right? Do you feel any sharp pains?"

"Only my tail."

"Is it broken?"

"No," croaked the girl. "You're kneeling on it."

"Oh!" Kanéko blushed as she shifted position.

Maris grabbed her tail and cradled it in her palms.

Kanéko looked her over, surprised to see only superficial damage, and most of it to Maris's dress. Dust clung to Maris's furry ears but otherwise the dalpre appeared unharmed from falling so far.

"Um, we should check for broken bones." An uncomfortable feeling fluttered in her stomach. "Could you, um, do that? I don't want to touch anything... painful."

Maris started to feel her arms and legs, testing each limb. After a few minutes of anticipation, the dog girl shook her head. She licked the blood from the corner of her mouth with a surprisingly long tongue before she spoke. "Nothing really hurts."

"Good. Can you stand?"

The dalpre strained for a second and then sighed. "Help me up?"

Kanéko crawled over and helped Maris stand up. The weight was almost too much for her, but she was able to get to her feet while still holding the dalpre.

The dog girl swayed, and Kanéko kept her arms around Maris's waist, holding her tight until the girl regained her balance. The torn dress ripped further with Kanéko's effort.

Maris swayed before slumping against Kanéko.

Kanéko muttered under her breath, "Worst trip ever."

Maris giggled then winced. "But, you're with me, so it isn't bad. And I'm having fun."

Kanéko stopped, the dalpre's words in her head. She sighed. "You know, I never read about this part in the Nash stories. He loses, rips off his shirt, then picks himself up and goes into the next adventure."

Maris's ears perked up. She regained her balance but didn't move her head from resting against Kanéko's shoulder. "Nash the Dragon Slayer? I have that book."

Kanéko smiled. "Really?"

"Yes, the pack likes it when I read out loud to the puppies. We've gone through that book so many times that," Maris coughed, "the binding broke. We use string to hold it together."

"Did you like Nash and the Turtle Shrine? I think that was the best one."

Maris whimpered and looked at Kanéko with confusion. "Turtle... Shrine? There isn't a turtle in that book. I know that much."

"There are close to fifty Nash stories."

"F-Fifty? We only have the one," she paused, "I guess the first one?"

"Yeah, I..." Kanéko's words trailed off as she stared into the brown eyes of the dalpre. She wanted Maris to like her and she didn't know what she was supposed to say to make that happen. She worried her bottom lip, and then took a chance. She reached up and brushed the dust from the girl's hair. "I have a lot of them. When we get back, I'll give you the ones... I'll give you all of them. I don't read them anymore."

Maris's tail started to wag.

Inside, Kanéko felt a bit of relief at her response. It was the right thing to say and, to her surprise, she realized she meant it. Somehow, the dalpre was growing on her. She liked how she knew exactly what Maris thought about her, unlike the snake Pahim and his lies.

As if reading her mind, Maris said, "And I like you."

Kanéko replied, "I think I like you too."

Maris squealed and grabbed Kanéko, hugging her tightly. Then she groaned. "Um, owwie. No more hugging today."

"Deal," grinned Kanéko.

Maris turned around, "Hey, Rub, guess... um, Rub? Where are you?"

Kanéko looked back up the cliff. "I don't think he came down."

She pointed to the side of the collapsed area of the cliff. It had rough outcroppings and ridges compared to the sheered-off part that had collapsed. "I think that is the best place to climb back up."

"And, knowing Rub, he'll be making a rope. After telling the woods how each strand should be perfectly aligned."

At Ruben's name, Kanéko's mind brought up that deep voice that rumbled across the valley and the disturbing image of his glowing eyes. "Um, Maris?"

"Yes?"

"Did Ruben's eyes ever... glow?"

Maris smiled cheerfully. Her fall and injuries appeared not to bother her. "Oh yeah, they do that."

"Really?"

"When he thinks really hard, his eyes get sparkly. And then his daddy gets really upset at him. Ruben is not supposed to think hard or speak loudly. But, when his daddy isn't around, that is how he finds me." Maris started hobbling toward the spot on the cliff. "He can find people from really far away, but they have to be really scared or angry or happy. Or fucking. And then he whistles, and I hear him. That is how he knew I got into town... back at Rock River." Maris rubbed her ribs again.

Kanéko followed after Maris. At the foot of the cliff, she pointed to the spots for climbing before she asked another question. "Before I dumped paint on you?"

"Yes, I knew he was in trouble because of the whistle. Three quick and then one long means come fast. And he uses that when Pahim corners him or someone else is picking on him."

"Does Garèo know that?"

Maris looked at Kanéko guiltily. "Um, actually, none of our parents know the whistling or thinking. We'd both get in trouble. I'm not supposed to fight, and he's not supposed to think, so we kept it secret. Last time was when I broke Pah's arm. He was beating Rub in the corner, and I had to stop it. So I broke his arm so he wouldn't hurt Rub. I was afraid Daddy would get upset, so I said I just punched him instead of throwing one of the tables at his head. Would you... please don't tell?"

Kanéko felt overwhelmed. "I won't tell anyone, I promise." She turned to the rock and to the closest ridge. "Look, if I boost you up, you should be able to pull me up, if you are up to it."

Maris sighed, and then she looked around. "Better get started?"

Kanéko nodded. She knelt on the ground and intertwined her fingers together to give Maris a foot-hold. Maris lifted one foot and put it into her palms. Her movements brought the smell of Maris's fur and dust past Kanéko. It also caused her skirt to ride up.

Kanéko looked away. "On three. One."

Maris crouched down; her brow furrowed in concentration.

"Two."

Kanéko felt Maris tensing with anticipation.

"Three."

Maris surged up and something slammed into Kanéko's face.

Kanéko saw a flash of Maris's foot before the back of her head cracked into the rocks behind her. Her vision exploded with white light. Blinded and dazed, she slid to the ground.

It was only a few seconds before Kanéko could see again. She groaned and held the back of her head, feeling for blood, but her hand came away clean. Relieved, she staggered to her feet. Looking around for blood, she spoke blindly, "Maris, are..."

She was inside another blast crater. Like the first one, there were radial lines spreading out from where she had been bracing herself for Maris to jump. Dust hung in the air, swirling in eddies and vortexes around her.

Looking up, she saw a distinct wake of dust being pulled up into the air to form a line that reached the top of the cliff. Frowning, she looked down again. Even the weeds were uprooted by the force of whatever hit her.

"That wasn't her foot," muttered Kanéko. Still holding her head, she limped away from the cliff face and looked up.

She didn't see Maris. "Maris? Where are you?"

At the top of the cliff, Maris's head peeked out.

Kanéko's eyes widened. It was too far for anyone to jump much less cover the distance in a second.

Her heart pounded faster, and she felt a sour taste in the back of her mouth as she realized there was only one way to explain what was happening: magic. She took a hesitant sniff of the air, this time looking for the telltale scent of energy. It was there, a sharp scent like when lightning struck near her father's tower one morning when a visiting air knight had a nightmare. She took another breath.

Kanéko scanned the center of the crater, seeing only the results of an explosion, not a fall. After the number of times the water screw's boiler had blown up, she had learned the difference between an explosion and something falling apart. And now, she stood in the center of something that had burst.

There were no shattered artifacts on the ground and she was sure it was just the three of them. That meant the source had to come from Maris when the dalpre used magic to jump to the top of the cliff. She probably also reflexively used it to prevent injury when she fell.

Kanéko wasn't sure what type of power Maris was manifesting. If she could do only one thing, jumping and buffering a landing were both the same skill, then she would be a talent. If she could create more effects, then she would be known as a mage.

Most teenagers manifested power in moments of crisis.

Maris just gained her power.

A surge of jealousy rose inside her throat, choking her as she imagined she had just been granted power.

"Kan? Kan!?"

Kanéko's head snapped up and she groaned at the pain from her neck.

Maris stuck her head over the cliff. "Ruben is lying down!"

"And?" Kanéko had to claw her way out of the ruined fantasies playing her head.

"He's just shaking around and twitching. And I can't wake him. And he's drooling. And it's all foamy."

Memories rose up in the back of Kanéko's head. She had read of seizures in her books. They were dangerous. Shoving her emotions aside, she stepped closer to the cliff and peered at the top. She raised her voice and yelled back, "Can he talk?"

"No! He's just mumbling. The... the words don't make sense. But, I mean he doesn't usually—"

Kanéko's mind spun furiously. "I think he's having a seizure, I read about them. Just... keep him comfortable, I'll be right up there!"

Maris's head disappeared. Kanéko looked around, her lips tightening into a thin line. "Worst trip ever."

She took a few steps back and regarded the cliff. Her eyes scanned the ragged rocks, gouges, and exposed roots. She picked out a path up the cliff: spotting places she could climb, where she had to jump, and even places to avoid. To her surprise, it was like the designs of the water screw and the core-driven saw, just instead of pipes and gears, it was rocks larger than her head and life-threatening falls. Except for the first step which required a running leap, she could easily scale the cliff. As she planned her route, Kanéko rewrapped the bandages on her hands.

Taking a deep breath, she took a running leap up the cliff. She grabbed the first ledge with her fingertips. Panting, she pulled herself up. Dust clung to her sweat-soaked, dark skin. Kanéko didn't stop, following the map that she had built in her head and jumping blindly to the next ridge. She almost missed it, but she caught it at the last second. She found the next ledge and continued to climb.

It only took a few minutes to scale the cliff. By the time she reached the top, she panted heavily. Her arms and legs shook with the effort of standing. As soon as she saw Ruben on the ground, shaking violently, spittle dripping from his mouth, adrenaline flowed through her once again.

She dropped next to him. Maris tried to hold him still as he shook. Kanéko started to do the same, but then she stopped. Ruben's eyes glowed from behind his closed eyelids. The color seeped through the sparkling tears that ran down his cheeks.

His eyes cracked open and she saw only pure sapphire. She felt his attention focusing on her. As their eyes met, the world spun and she clutched the ground. In her thoughts, images blasted through her, dredging up long-forgotten lessons and books: pouring over *Emerging Wizardry* in her bedroom, walking around her father's lands, gazing across the forests on their wagon trip, and then a blur of more images of her travels. It felt like she was reviewing her life, looking for something, but with an intense clarity and purpose.

Kanéko gripped Ruben tightly, panting as her memories rushed through her head. Each one came rapidly, dredged out of forgotten places in her mind before being plastered across her consciousness.

It stopped as quickly as it started. She was ten and sitting underneath her father's dinner table while reading her new book on herbs. One page had a hand-drawn illustration of a white-petaled flower. She didn't know the words at the time, but the intensity of the memory allowed her to recall the plant's medicinal properties. Jonahas root could ease aches and the petals were able to dull the mind against mental intrusion.

Kanéko gasped and gulped. She stumbled forward to push Maris's hands away. The dalpre resisted, but Kanéko yanked her away. "Don't stop him from shaking. Just make him comfortable and be sure he doesn't hit anything."

"But, he's shaking. I think he's hurt."

"Yes, but I need to find..." Kanéko worked through the fresh memories and remembered the lessons associated with them. Then, she remembered the flower. It grew in the area. "I need to find Jonahas root."

"I know that one. And it smells like sweet, stale beer. There is a patch near the back of the barn. And some of the kids would eat it when they drank—"

"Can you smell it here?"

"It will help Rub?"

"Yes, it dulls the senses. I'm—" she struggled with understanding, "—I think Ruben needs it."

Maris stood up. "I'll find it." She sniffed the air twice.

Kanéko paused as she felt a breeze kick up, sending the smells of dust and plants to her. The wind circled her, first blowing from the west, but then from the northwest, north, and around to the northeast. Maris's skirt waved across her vision as the breeze rotated around her.

The jealousy returned. The changing wind was too deliberate; it came from precisely the direction the dalpre had pointed her nose. She was already demonstrating a second, distinct trick with magic which meant she had more than a simple talent. Maris was an air mage. With Kanéko's luck, she could be as powerful as her father with training.

Tears burned in Kanéko's eyes. She struggled to contain the rage and sadness that flooded through her. She was supposed to be the one who had powers like that.

"Found it!" cried Maris. She ran to the south and climbed over the ridge of the hill before diving out of sight.

Kanéko watched her for a moment then shifted her attention to Ruben. She sniffed and wiped the tears from her face. She shifted her position underneath Ruben's head, cupping him with her thighs.

Her thoughts turned to the wind that responded to Maris and even to the explosion that had thrown her back. She sniffed the air, tasting ozone again. There was no doubt a-bout it, there was magic in the air.

She fought more tears. Shaking her head, she gazed into Ruben's glowing eyes. "It isn't fair. I spent my entire child-hood praying for the day I would manifest a talent. I re-member almost drowning myself in the river because most people find their magic in times of stress. Then," she tensed at the memory, "I found out I can never use magic. So, what happens? Your *sand-damned* girlfriend ends up finding wind magic. She has a strong talent, at least." She gave a bitter snort, "And with my luck, she'll be a mage and have all wind magic."

Kanéko barked out a bitter laugh. "Damn it. I'm never leaving home again." She looked down. "And look at you. Your eyes are glowing. *Damn the sands to the darkness and fire*, why are you two so special when I'm not? Why do you have such strong powers?"

Ruben continued to shake and shiver. One arm came close to a rock, and Kanéko reached over to push the ob-struction aside, making sure he could move without injury. His eyes cracked open and spears of blue light leaked out from the opening.

Kanéko stared for a moment, and then reached down to steady his head with both hands. His twitching was stro-nger than she expected. She leaned over his tiny form to re-gain her balance. When she looked back, she accidentally looked into the bluest light she had ever seen.

Another blast of images crashed into her. This time, she half expected them and found some way of cramming them into one corner of her mind, channeling them to project on a mental wall instead of consuming her own thoughts. The scenes were familiar, as if they were her memories being pulled from her subconscious.

The first ones were disjointed images and scenes of her childhood. None of them made sense but they were intense in their detail and clarity, despite being long forgotten.

Memories of the inn and the road flashed through her mind. They retraced their trip to the edge of the village. Kanéko recalled seeing a small, wilted Jonahas plant right outside of the Boar Hunt Inn. She didn't even remember seeing it. A transition and she was six years old again, paging through an illustrated book. She concentrated as she recalled the entry on Jonahas Root. It could be dangerous to telepaths—fatal to Ruben—but it was used to defend against psychic intrusions.

Then the memories became more recent, replaying the world as they entered the valley, then fast forwarding to the cliff before slowing down to show the details of the cliff collapsing underneath Maris. Her eyes blurred as she relived the experience.

Then she realized the images were being distorted by whatever caused her to relive her memories. She tried to concentrate on the foreign directions, but the images grew hazy and broke up. When she relaxed, they slipped away. It took her precious seconds to find a mental state where she let the images flash across her thoughts but maintained her focus enough to pay attention to the details.

She knew it was Ruben directing her thoughts. He was trying to tell her something with his body unable to function. She forced herself to relax to let his thoughts guide her.

Ruben focused her attention on the opposing cliff of the ravine, near where the boulder exploded. With a gentle guidance for him, she opened her eyes and stared at the spot.

Between the earthquake and the boulder, a deep fissure had formed down the side. It was too dark to see into it but small whorls of dust continued to swirl in the opening. A few rocks bounced down both sides where the stone had buckled.

Her memories welled up again, directed by Ruben. He was trying to tell her something about the fissure but no intense images came. Instead, it was just a general sense of foreboding driven by memories of when she was a little girl reading about the arcane horrors in her books. They were vague, formless terrors but the sense of danger was palatable.

Kanéko's heart beat faster and sweat prickled on her brow. She gulped against her dry throat. The details grew more focused to when she tried to rescue a cat out of a tree. She remembered how it scratched her, but it was only the beginning as a rapid series of flashes of animals biting, scratching, and hissing at her came blasting across her mind.

A large rock fell from the cliff. She stared at it even as Ruben guided her to look away. She couldn't help but stare at the rocks buckled even further. Streams of gravel poured off the cliff as more cracks broke open in both directions from the first one.

The fishy smell grew more powerful, wafting across the ravine. It mixed with the scent of rock dust, sweat, and blood.

A prickle of fear ran down her spine.

She sniffed again, but the blood smell was more powerful. She frowned and looked around for a moment before the scent drew her attention down.

There was blood leaking out from the corner of Ruben's glowing eyes. His entire body was tense, the muscles standing out as he shuddered. More spit foamed at his mouth, but it was bloody.

Swearing in Miwāfu, she scooped Ruben off the ground. Staggering under his weight, she found her balance and stood up. She stumbled up the trail and away from the fissure.

Then she realized the ever-present buzz of insects had died between one heartbeat and another. A horsefly fell from the air, rolling on the bare rocks at her feet. Somehow, she knew it was dead before it hit the ground.

The compulsion to turn around slammed into her, powerful and overwhelming. She tried to resist, but a pressure bore down on her, squeezing her chest as she even considered disobeying. Shaking with the effort, she twisted her hip and peered across the ravine to the largest fissure.

This time, there was something in the darkness, a crimson light the size of a door or wagon.

Panting, she found the urge to look directly into the light rising up inside her. Like the command to turn around, it pummeled against her thoughts like fists against her chest. She fought it, clutching Ruben tightly as tears ran down her cheeks.

But for all her hopes, she couldn't stop herself from opening her eyes wide and staring directly into the blood-red light. As she focused, she realized they were eyes of some massive beast. She saw a terrible intelligence behind light.

Then, the creature's thoughts thrust into her brain with a bright light and stabbing pain.

Unlike Ruben's flash of memories, the demands came as a punch to her gut. Kanéko heard herself screaming as she felt a tidal wave of imperative force crush her will. Blood dripped from her nose as parts of her mind burned from the intensity of the images that crashed into her.

She couldn't move. She tried, but her body didn't respond.

Kanéko sobbed as the creature's mind burned at her own consciousness. She only got brief glimpses of wars and battles. Unlike Ruben, the new images came from memories she had never experienced. They were being carved directly into her mind, not recalled from her past.

Then, darkness and silence. Kanéko blinked with the severed connection. She struggled to make sense of whatever saved her but then her vision came into sharp focus. She was staring at the dalpre's chest.

"Maris!"

"Kan? Your nose is bleeding. And did Ruben hit you? And why is he still foaming? And why is he bleeding?"

Kanéko lifted her hand to her nose. When she touched sticky heat, she pulled it back and looked at the bright crimson on her fingertips. "N-No, he didn't."

She focused on a large handful of flowers Maris held out to her. They were exactly the type she had pictured. They weren't for Ruben; it was for the two girls. It would shield her and Maris from whatever horror was inside the cliff. She grabbed one and squeezed it like her book suggested. The thick sap coated her fingers. Dredging through the memories, she remembered the best way to take it and lapped at her fingertips.

Tentatively, she lapped at her fingertips. It tasted sour and bitter. Within seconds, it pushed back the burn of the creature's thoughts from her skull.

"Kan! I thought they were for Rub."

"They're for us," she said. Standing up, she shook her head. It would take too long to explain and there wasn't time if the creature got out. She held out her sticky fingers. "Lick."

"W-What?"

"Lick!" Kanéko yelled.

Maris shrugged and leaned over. With her long tongue, she licked at Kanéko's fingers. The movement was fast, but Kanéko felt a strange heat flutter in her stomach.

Clearing her throat, Kanéko hefted Ruben. "We need to run!"

"What?"

Kanéko shoved Ruben over to Maris who easily took him. Then Kanéko grabbed the rest of the flowers from the dalpre's hand.

The mental pressure returned. She felt the urge to turn around and look back at the fissure. With concentration, and the Jonahas in her blood, she could resist only with supreme effort.

The dalpre's eyes grew glassy and she started to turn toward the far side of the valley, no doubt to look around, and Kanéko screamed out shrilly. "Don't look!"

"Why—?"

Kanéko slapped her. "Just run!"

She wrapped her hand around Maris's free wrist and pulled her along the path away from the cliff. With every step, she could feel the creature's mind casting out for her, ordering her to stop and turn around.

Maris finally stopped resisting and ran next to Kanéko. "What are we running from?" she gasped.

"The worst damn trip ever!"

Chapter 22

Flight

The most common use of Jonahas, a small flowering plant, is to dull the
pain of over-imbibing alcohol.

—*An Introduction to the Wild, A Survival Guide*

"**I**... can't... breathe," Maris panted.

Sweat pouring down her face, Kanéko slumped. She
said, "If you can say that, you can breathe."

Maris looked up with her ears flat on her head. "And I
don't like you."

Kanéko tried to chuckle and decided it wasn't worth the
effort. She crawled over to Maris and sat down next to her.

Maris looked at her, and then at the shivering teenager
in her arms. "Is Rub going to wake up?"

Kanéko grunted, "Yes, I think he's stronger than we, um,
I thought. We just need to get him to the Boar Hunt Inn.
Virsian should be able to heal him enough to recover."

Scrambling to her feet, Maris hefted Ruben. "Then I
want to go now."

Kanéko stood up and brushed the dust from her thighs.
She couldn't get the glowing red eyes out of her head. She
watched Maris walking ahead.

The dalpre had stopped a distance away and turned to her, panting heavily.

Kanéko gave a false smile and hurried after the girl. "Come on, let's save Ruben."

Together, they walked along a series of animal trails. In the sweeping hills, their desperate flight turned into a heat-baked trudge. With Maris's sense of smell, they easily headed toward the Boar Hunt Inn, but exhaustion took its toll on them.

They reached a ridge that stretched out in both directions as far as they could see. Without a word, Kanéko held out her hands for Ruben.

Maris looked at her, and then shook her head curtly before she turned back to the hill. A stubborn look crossed the dalpre's face and she mounted the hill.

"Maris," said Kanéko.

"You're the hurt one, Kan. You need your strength."

Kanéko followed after Maris. "Come on, let me help. You were also hurt."

Maris turned around, swaying for a moment before she glared at Kanéko. "I'll sleep later."

Kanéko stared in shock, remembering when she used the same words.

Maris's tail curled. She set her jaw before she said, "Don't worry, Kan. And I can carry Ruben as long as I have to. All day, all night, all year. He's my friend and I will not abandon my pack."

Kanéko didn't try again. She just walked after the dalpre, trying not to the think of the summer heat bearing down on her. She prayed for a wind, anything to relieve the sweat pouring down her face and chest.

A rushing noise rose up behind her. She looked to see a breeze rippling toward her.

She almost let out a sob of anticipation. "Maris, hold on."

Maris continued over the hill to a boulder just under the ridge. She leaned her shoulder against the rock and cradled Ruben against her chest. Her tongue flapped as she panted. Turning her head, she looked up at Kanéko and rested her head on Ruben's head. There was pain in her eyes, and Kanéko felt it tugging on her heart.

Kanéko gazed longingly at the smoke in the distance. Only an hour at most. She turned back to the breeze, closing her eyes in anticipation.

Maris called out from below. "Kan?"

"Just a second," said Kanéko, desperate for the wind.

"Ruben is shaking again."

Kanéko lurched around, her heart almost skipping a beat.

Ruben shook in Maris's arms, a line of drool dripping down the corner of his mouth. To her surprise, blue light leaked through his eyelids.

Kanéko rushed over and dropped to her knees in front of him. "Ruben!?"

His eyes cracked open, just the smallest sparkle of blue. Remembering how looking in his glowing eyes brought up memories, Kanéko lowered herself to match gazes with the nearly unconscious boy.

A juxtaposition of memories crashed into her. The red eyes were rising out of her father's stables, expanding with terrible force. Then, a shadowy image of her father yanking his hand out of the ground brought a wall of Jonahas plants to shield her. They curled up and over, protecting her as the eyes slammed in with brutal force.

It took her a moment to interpret the images. The sap from the root was wearing off and the presence was coming back. She needed more to protect Maris and herself.

Kanéko's eyes snapped open, breaking the mental communication between her and Ruben. She turned around and forced herself to pay attention to her surroundings with new knowledge. The approaching wind longer held a promise of air to cool her sweat but was now the herald of dread for whatever chased them.

"Maris," she said, standing up, but it was too late.

The wind kicked her in the chest and alien thoughts punched into her mind once again. Memories burned into her mind, filled with fresh rage, anger, and pain. This time, they were more focused. Words came flooding into her mind, written across her thoughts as much as bellowed into her memories. «We are Damagar.»

The creature had somehow named itself, not dredging up memories like Ruben, but carving its identity directly into her.

She screamed, barely aware of her knees hitting the ground.

Damagar picked through her being, forcing her consciousness until she could only think of one person: Ruben.

Images of herself and Maris standing on the ridge came into her mind, forced in by the foreign thoughts. The details were incredible, down to the pulse in her neck and the sweat under her shirt. She could sense every bit of mud dried on her skin and the sweat under Maris's armpits. Every detail seared her mind except for a gap where Ruben would have been.

Disjointed memories played through her mind, tracing back and forth as they walked forward talking, then they would rewind and she would experience them again.

In each case, Ruben wasn't there. They spoke to empty air and looked into spaces that pushed her thoughts away. Even his name was somehow blurred and intelligible.

Finally, the image froze with her on her knees, bent over space as she cried out a word the beast could not remember.

Damagar couldn't see Ruben, even though the boy lay right next to her. Its mind tried to follow her thoughts but somehow slid around the very memory of Ruben himself. No matter how much the creature tried to direct Kanéko's mind, it couldn't force her to picture the telepath. «The Broken Thought must die, Kosobyo Kanéko, Kanéko Lurkuklan. We will find him and destroy him as a threat he will become.»

Kanéko couldn't stop crying as its presence pummeled her. She grabbed the ground and scraped her nails through the dirt. She felt violated from the alien ripping through her consciousness. All she could imagine was his burning red eyes and its search for Ruben. Shuddering with the effort to breathe, Kanéko tried to regain control of herself and her mind.

She dredged up memories of her own life, tugging on the good and bad. It didn't work. Her efforts to remember were sluggish, and the images refused to come up; instead, the image of Damagar's eyes replaced any thought she had.

In desperation, she tried to find anything to push back the eyes of Damagar. Memory after memory refused to come up, until, with a flash, a single image appeared: the water screw. Weeks, even months, of obsession brought the designs into perfect clarity. The thoughts of Damagar dimmed as Kanéko focused on pulling apart the water screw in her mind and assembling it mentally. She traced through the gears and pistons, mapping out every pipe and joint.

When his thoughts slammed into her, the images blurred. She concentrated harder, forcing months of thinking and dreaming about the screw to shield her from Damagar's mind.

She ground her teeth together and focused harder, detailing every cut of every screw and gear. The more she concentrated, the more the alien thoughts faded. Suddenly she sank completely into her designs, exploding the individual parts in her mind and rebuilding them.

Damagar's mind ripped away from her with an audible pop.

When she opened her eyes, she could feel the tears streaming down her face. Holding herself still, she waited for Damagar, but its presence was no longer in her mind. She had evicted it from her mind and felt a rush of excitement at her accomplishment. She stared down at her ragged fingernails and wondered if it was pain or obsession shielding the terrible creature from her consciousness.

Her thoughts were interrupted when Maris whimpered next to her. The dalpre laid on the ground next to Ruben, curled up in a tight ball. Maris's shoulders shook with her tears and she whimpered, "Make it stop, make it stop, make..."

Kanéko raced over to her, unwrapping the cloth around her hand. When she found the sap soaking the loop of fabric, she squeezed out a few drops on her fingertips. Crouching down, she ran her sticky digit along Maris's lips.

The dog girl jerked away, but then turned back to lick her fingers.

Kanéko squirmed at the strange heat inside her as the dalpre licked her fingers clean. After a few seconds, she leaned back and re-wrapped the cloth around her hand. She spotted a few droplets on one finger and licked them herself, she wasn't sure if her obsession would be able to keep out Damagar without help.

Like before, the sap worked quickly on both of them. Maris stopped whimpering, and her gaze slowly came into sharp focus.

Kanéko smiled with encouragement, whispering to Maris. *"Come on, bitch. Come on, we need to go now. We need to go."*

Maris whined pitifully. "Kan?"

"Yes?"

"I don't like Damagar. And he wants to hurt Ruben."

Kanéko held out her hand. Maris took it. Grunting, Kanéko pulled Maris to her feet, and together they picked up Ruben. The smaller teenager had calmed down once Damagar's thoughts moved on, but he still had a line of drool in the corner of his mouth. Kanéko wiped it with her hand, and then pressed a palm against his heated forehead.

Maris held Ruben tightly, hoisting him up. Her ears flattened against her head as she glared at Kanéko. "And I won't let it have him. He's mine. Mine."

D. Moonfire

Chapter 23

Shelter

The Crystal Spheres Techniques are for training mages. Organized aro-
und the ten spheres of skill, they teach control and power for all levels
of talent.

—Primer on Crystal Sphere Techniques

Night came quickly, but Kanéko and Maris didn't stop until
they reached the Boar Hunt Inn. Coming from the south,
they avoided the roads and crept through trees behind the
building. Every few minutes, Kanéko froze and listened for
the wind, but she couldn't hear it rising up behind her. She
only dreaded that Damagar would find them in a different
way, one that she couldn't plan for.

Maris, with her better sense of smell, led the way while
Kanéko held Ruben tightly. Their approach was masked by
the sound of insects buzzing in the air. When she first
heard a mosquito, Kanéko almost gasped for joy. Somehow
hearing the smallest of creatures alive gave her hope that
Damagar wasn't near.

In her arms, Ruben moaned softly.

Kanéko held his head. "Hush."

Then, a whisper in Kanéko's ear startled her. "I'm not a newborn infant, if you recall."

Kanéko stopped. Kneeling down, she lowered Ruben while whispering for Maris.

Ruben smacked his lips together a few times, and Maris spun around. Gasping, she ran over and tackled Ruben, hugging him tightly. "Rub! I thought you—"

"Quiet!" hissed Kanéko.

Maris continued in a loud whisper, "—wouldn't ever wake up."

Ruben rubbed his hair and smiled. "Sorry, I tried to contain myself and it caused my mind to..." The pause went on longer than Kanéko ever heard Ruben hesitate. He shook his head. "Forgive me, I believe I have reinforced that which Damagar is afraid of. I should be able to avoid seizures in the future."

Kanéko felt a sense of relief. "Are you sure? Do you know if he is close?"

"No, but I'll find out when Damagar comes within two leagues." Ruben gave her a sudden smile. "You know, Kanéko, you are competent at telepathic reception. You possess a sizable foundation of memories, an analytic view of the world, a highly adaptable mind, and a remarkable acceptances to new experiences."

Kanéko blushed then gave him a mock glare. "Just keep your thoughts to yourself... except for emergencies, all right?"

"Acknowledged. I regret being a burden. To both of you."

Kanéko cleared her throat. "Ruben." They both looked at her. She spoke softly to avoid attracting attention. "Do you know where we are?"

His eyes glittered, and then he looked around him impassively.

With his height, Kanéko didn't think he could see anything. He had been unconscious for the last hour.

"Approximately eleven chains, one rod south of the Boar Hunt Inn."

Kanéko stopped, startled by the specificity of his response. "H-How did you know?"

He gave a slight smile and pointed to the trees above them. "That was planted ninety-three years ago. And that," he pointed in the opposite direction, "was planted a year later. There are twelve cabins," he pointed into the shadows, "three rods, two feet in that direction."

Kanéko gestured to the darkness. "Have you been here before?"

Maris giggled and held Ruben tightly. "Rub remembers things. He knows it from before he was born. And he knows history. And lessons. And everything."

Kanéko looked at Ruben who glared back at Maris.

Ruben spoke sharply, "I told you that, canine, because you promised you wouldn't speak about it to anyone."

Maris bowed her head. "Sorry."

Ruben sighed and dragged his fingers through the shadowed grass. "She would figure it out sooner or later." He looked up and his blue eyes glittered in the dim light. "Kanéko Lurkuklan is quite astute. In fact, I suspect she might already know why."

Kanéko started to shake her head, and then stopped. Her mind spun for a second, and then she cocked her head. "It has to do with you being a telepath, right? You read someone's mind before you answered?"

Ruben shrugged. "Partially correct. But, the mind was my own. Children of Vo have access to a shared memory; it is called the *votim*. But, my access to the *votim*, and therefore my memories, ceased eighteen years, four months, and twenty-one days ago."

"What happened then?"

"I was born."

Kanéko had no way to respond to his answer. She stared at the blue eyes for a moment, and then looked away. She turned toward the cabins that Ruben identified, and she remembered the night on the balcony. "I have an idea. Virsian has a cabin there. I could hide there, and you could send food if it's safe?"

Ruben shrugged. "That seems a reasonable plan."

"Any idea which cabin is Virsian's? I knew they came this way, but didn't know about the cabins."

"I cannot. That decision was made after I lost access to my memories."

Maris spoke up from where she tugged petals from a flower. "She's in the furthest cabin from the inn."

Kanéko stared at her. "How do you know?"

Maris smiled bashfully. "Garèo was late this morning. And I sniffed him out."

"Oh," Kanéko said, "that makes sense."

"And he was fucking Virsian at the time."

Kanéko gaped at Maris as the dalpre bounced and grinned. "Maris!"

"Well, they did. At least three times. They were both really loud. And I tried to wait but they just kept going."

Maris didn't seem shocked at all, but Kanéko didn't want to know about Garèo having sex with anyone. She held up her hands. She felt a blush burning on her cheeks and was glad for the darkness, "Look, point me toward the right cabin. I hope Virsian is with us and not looking for a quick crown."

Together, the three teenagers sneaked their way to the cabins. Maris led them to the far one. When Kanéko tried the door, she found it locked.

"*Sands.*" She turned to Ruben. "Any chance you know how to unlock it?"

Ruben shrugged. "Procure a key?"

Kanéko rolled her eyes and looked down at the lock. She remembered a part in one of her Nash novels where he picked it, but after the fiasco trying to escape in the river, Kanéko's trust in stories had plummeted. She also didn't have tools to use. "Maris, how about—"

She couldn't see Maris. Turning around, she peered in the darkness around them. "Where is she?"

On the far side of the cabin, the sound of breaking glass echoed out from the darkness. Kanéko winced, covering her ears as if it would stop anyone else from hearing it. She saw Ruben smirking at her and pulled her hands back, her cheeks burning with embarrassment.

"Maris is breaking a window in the back," supplied Ruben.

Kanéko turned away to hide her blush. "Thanks, I figured that out on my own."

"You do possess an incredible sense of perception."

The door shuddered then creaked open. Maris stood inside, her ears flat on her head and her tail down between her legs. "I, um, opened the door."

Kanéko stared in shock, and then started to laugh. "That is one way of getting through the lock. I'm sure Virsian will forgive us... I hope."

"And you aren't angry?"

Kanéko shook her head.

Maris squealed and hugged her tightly. "And I like you!"

Kanéko hurriedly quieted her. "All right, I know. Now, go find out if Falkin or Virsian is trying to get the reward or if they will help us. Here..." She pulled her wallet out of her pocket and handed it to Maris. "It was ruined in the river, but Falkin might recognize it and give you credit."

Maris nodded confidently. "Don't worry, Rub will know if they are lying. He knows things like that."

Kanéko's stomach rumbled. "And, get me some food, please?"

Maris giggled and stepped out of cabin. She grabbed Ruben by the arm and dragged him toward the light of the inn.

Kanéko entered the cabin and locked the door behind her. She found a candle and lit it using a bit of flint. The flickering light almost blinded to her dark-adjusted eyes. She quickly drew the curtains to hide her presence.

Virsian's cabin was not what Kanéko had expected. She thought it would look like the Royal Suite, but it looked closer to her parent's bedroom. Mismatched furniture lined the walls; some of it was bleached wood while other had the same dark tones as the stuff from the Royal suite. The entire one-room cabin smelled of incense and perfume, but it was a light scent that permeated everything.

She amused herself for a few minutes peeking through Virsian's possessions, but she didn't want to pry too much. Kanéko sat on the bed and felt a brief shiver of revulsion knowing that Garèo and Virsian had sex on it. But, the trip left her exhausted and the mattress was warm and smooth underneath her hands. With a yawn, Kanéko laid down and promised that she would just close her eyes to rest.

---------- Chapter 24 ----------

Midnight

Mages train from an early age, building discipline and skill. Training teaches how to control the surges of power that always come at the beginning.

—Primer on Crystal Sphere Techniques

"**Y**ou know—" Virsian's voice broke Kanéko from her dream.

Kanéko's body crawled with fear, and she forced her eyes to open slowly to find the feline dalpre leaning over her.

Virsian's brown eyes stared down at her. She continued with a purr, "—the last time there was a teenager in my bed, it was me, sixteen years ago."

Kanéko did a quick bit of math, but kept her mouth shut. She looked around, half expecting to see mercenaries from the *Burning Cloud Queen,* but they were alone in the cabin.

"Don't worry, I'm alone."

"I'm sorry," Kanéko sat up, "I didn't mean to sleep."

Virsian rested a hand on Kanéko's shoulder. "You needed it. I can see it in your aura. You haven't slept or eaten enough for a girl your age."

Kanéko focused on Virsian's hand, wondering if there was a trap gathering for her. "What about my friends?"

"Maris and Ruben are currently enjoying Falkin's hospitality, but I don't think it will last."

"Why? Does he need money?"

"No, Falkin is helping. Captain Sinmak's men occupy the entire east wing. The captain is currently out, but his commander, a man name Cobin—"

Kanéko shivered at the memory of the bald man.

"—is making all of our lives impossible. He's chased away most of our customers and has taken over the great hall for his personal workshop."

Kanéko realized she didn't know where Virsian stood concerning her reward. "Um, do you know what they were looking for?"

Virsian's eyes slid over to her and she smiled, her fangs peeking out from her lips. "You, actually."

Looking around for escape routes, Kanéko gripped the blankets on the bed.

Virsian chuckled and leaned over to tap Kanéko on the nose. "Neither Falkin nor I have the intent of cashing you in for a mere ten thousand crowns."

"Really?" Kanéko remembered Falkin's talent of prescience. "How much does Falkin think I'm worth?"

"Oh," Virsian spoke dramatically with a grin, "A lot more than ten thousand. The future is always changing. But, safe to say neither of us will betray you. Falkin always follows his long-term investments, and I have no love for men looking to steal women."

Kanéko let out a long, shuddering sigh. She looked over to Virsian and gave a tired chuckle. "This hasn't been the best of trips."

"I can imagine." Virsian's dress rustled as she shifted position. She held up her hands. "Mind if I work on those injuries?"

Kanéko rolled over and stretched out on the bed. At the first touch of Virsian's fingers, she tensed up, but then she felt the dalpre's healing magic soaking into her skin. It felt intense and soothing after the last few days of misery. Virsian eased the aches and pains of Kanéko's journey with her hands and magic.

"Your friend, Maris..."

"Yes?"

"Did she manifest? I don't remember her producing feedback but when she first arrived, I could feel her approaching even before she walked inside."

A spike of jealousy drove into Kanéko's heart. She closed her eyes and let out a deep breath. Even as she prepared to speak, tears burned her eyes. "Air powers. She is also more than a talent; I saw her do at least two distinct powers. She has to be a mage."

She sniffed and wiped her face.

"Oh, my." Virsian's hands dug into a knot in Kanéko's shoulder. The healing energy soaked into her muscles and she felt her skin crawling as scratches and bruises faded. A rush of warmth filled her, and she squirmed slightly under the touch.

"Dalpre mages are very rare, you know. Because of our breeding and how we were created. Our former masters didn't want their slaves rising up against them."

Kanéko groaned from the pain of the massage and then moaned from the release the healing magic gave her. "One in twelve thousand officially, but *Emerging Wizardry* said..." Her voice trailed off as she thought back to her fight with Maris in the mill. She groaned as she thought about Maris and her new talent with magic.

"You just tensed up. Why?" The hands never stopped.

Kanéko sighed and stretched out against the warm blankets. She rested her cheek on the pillow to look at Virsian. She focused on the perked-up ears. "This trip is nothing like what I expected. I got in a fight with Maris, got kidnapped by a boy I thought I liked, and then—"

She remembered Sarom Senior's injured horse. "Oh, god, I forgot." She pushed herself up in a sitting position. "Can you heal horses?"

Virsian frowned and her ears perked up. "Yes, why?"

"I... accidentally hurt Sarom Senior's horse, in the Village of..."

"Lassidin. I know him. Was the horse hurt badly?"

"I think," Kanéko felt her lower lip trembling, "I think I broke its leg. I didn't mean to; I was just trying to stop him." Fresh tears ran down her cheeks. "It was an accident, I swear."

Virsian pulled her into a hug. "It's all right. I'll send a note to Sarom tonight. If he hasn't put the horse down, I can heal it."

All the pain and frustration of the last few days, from Pahim's attempt to abduct Kanéko to her flight through the woods at night, poured out. She clutched to Virsian as sudden sobs wracked her body. As the tears slowed, she felt the tingling of Virsian's magic still filling her body as the dalpre held her tight. She looked up, inches from the cat woman's face. "You did that, didn't you?"

Virsian's body vibrated with soft purrs. "Healing the body is only one part of the process."

Kanéko sat back. She felt better, a weight had been removed from her shoulders. "Th-Thank you." She wiped the tears from her eyes. "I needed that, didn't I?"

"Yes, you—" Virsian sat back sharply, shock on her face. "You don't have resonance. None at all."

Kanéko took a deep breath. It was hard to admit it, but the cat dalpre stated it as a surprised fact. "No. I'm inert. I have no ability to use or feel it, except when it," she gestured to her back, "affects my body."

"But, you seem to know a lot more than most. *Emerging Wizardry* isn't for the lay person. I found it too complicated to understand even a quarter of the articles."

Kanéko felt an old wound opening. "I only found out years ago. Before then, I was going to inherit Papa's power. Or least dreamed I would. I spent so much time reading the books and trying to find some way to follow in my father's footsteps. I probably have a few years worth of articles memorized."

Virsian gave Kanéko's arm a squeeze. "Do you think you could help Maris?"

"How?"

"Since she's a dalpre, they won't let her at the schools in Jinto Panzir or anywhere else. Maybe you could... teach her the basics?"

Kanéko grinned. "The first sphere of Crystal Techniques? I can do that, I have it memorized. Including the exercises for control and strength."

Virsian smiled and let out a sigh of relief. "Thank you. There aren't many of dalpre mages, and I really want to get her training before she makes too many mistakes or acquires habits that will hurt someone."

With a start, Kanéko looked at Virsian in a different light. "Who taught you?"

"My mother. She was the bone-setter for the inn. She was human but my father was dalpre. And, as you know, the child of any dalpre is always a dalpre."

It was one of the facts of life. A nature of the dalpre breeding. The wizards who created them a thousand years before bred them to be slaves and wanted to ensure there would be no questions about illegitimate breeding.

Kanéko nodded. "I will. I promise."

Virsian stood up and hugged Kanéko tightly. The fur of her face tickled Kanéko's cheek and Kanéko wrapped her arms around Virsian, holding the slender woman tightly. "Thank you, Lady Lurkuklan."

"Call me Kan?" Kanéko felt foolish for asking.

Virsian pulled back. She smiled and her ears quivered. "Thank you, Kan."

Kanéko didn't know how to respond. She stretched her arm out in front of her and looked at the smooth, unblemished skin. "Looks like I didn't spend the night in the woods."

"You need food." Virsian smoothly stood up and walked to the door. She picked up a tray of covered food and brought it back.

At the first smell of roasted meat and vegetables, Kanéko realized she was famished. She scooted over to the edge of the bed and took a bowl from the tray. She dove in.

Virsian sat down next to her. "Do you know what you'll do? Where you'll hide?"

Unsure, Kanéko peeked over at her. She thought about hiding at the inn but knowing that Cobin was only a few chains away made her nervous. She wondered if she could make the journey home, using back roads and Ruben's knowledge, but Lurkuklan Tower was so many days away. She pushed the childish idea to the back of her mind and answered Virsian with a shake of her head.

Virsian smiled and gestured to Kanéko's bowl. "Eat, Kan. If you don't have plans, Falkin and I think you should spend the night here. Tomorrow night, we'll send you and your friends to one of the hunting lodges in the woods. He says your father used to spend weeks out there with one of his friends."

Kanéko froze at the idea of leaving the cabin and being caught. She gripped the blankets underneath her until her knuckles ached.

Apparently unaware of Kanéko's thoughts, Virsian gestured to the south. "The inn has a number of them. They are private and well-stocked. Suitable to royalty. Those men," she hissed, "will never find you out there. And, we can send Garèo there when he comes back." She smiled. She rested a hand on Kanéko's shoulder. "Now, eat and rest. I'll be back in a few hours."

Chapter 25

Fight or Flight

Information is the lifeblood of battle. Without it, a fight is nothing but a brawl.

—Ryontsu Sugéto

A door slammed against the wall and Kanéko woke up with a start. She snapped her eyes opened and listened, holding her breath to hear details.

A rustling at the door and the clink of metal told her that someone fumbled with the latch. One of the pictures near the door scraped against the wall and Virsian let out a muttered curse.

Kanéko sat up and wiped the sleep from her eyes. "Vir?"

Virsian spun around and hurried to the bed. "Get up." There was a rushed, panicked tone in the dalpre's voice.

Fear raced through Kanéko's veins. She fumbled with her blankets. "What happened?"

"Maris saw some boy—Pahim was his name, he works for Cobin. He was in the great hall. She attacked him, and now both she and Ruben are in trouble. I must get you out before they search the cabins. Disguise yourself," she pointed to the wardrobe, "with clothes from there."

Heart beating rapidly, Kanéko fell out of bed and snatched a plain cream top from Virsian's wardrobe. She also grabbed a black belt with a bird buckle and a warm brown jacket made of doeskin. The dalpre's pants didn't fit so she was forced to use her own stained trousers. Her feet were also too big for the shoes she found. Kanéko quickly wrapped her feet and hands in the fresh strips of fabric; it worked well enough, and she didn't have an alternative or time to find something better.

As she pulled on her clothes, she spoke quickly. "Vir? Where are we going?"

"I don't know, but hurry." Virsian tugged on her tail and glanced out the window.

Kanéko buttoned down her shirt and leaned on the bed. "What about Maris and Ruben? We can't leave them."

Virsian gave her a helpless look. "I'm sorry."

Ice ran through Kanéko's veins. She gripped the side of the bed as the world spun around her. She could feel the soft blankets crumpling in her grip as she stared at Virsian. "W-What is going to happen to them?"

"I don't know, but if you don't hurry, you'll find out." Virsian grabbed Kanéko and pulled her toward the back door of the cabin. "They'll probably kill me for helping—"

Kanéko felt sick at the idea of leaving the other two. She knew that Virsian was right but hated it. She had to flee, even if it meant abandoning Maris and Ruben. "It's dark. We'll get lost."

Virsian sighed and wrung her hands together. "I can see in the dark, but... I'm not exactly sure where the hunting lodges are."

She hissed, and her body shook as she furtively peered at the window. "I've never been that far in the woods, not since I was a little girl. I-I grew up here. But, Kan, we really don't have time."

"I don't have much choice, do I?"

"I'm sorry, I really am."

Kanéko wasn't sure if Virsian was sorry more for leaving Maris and Ruben, or that the cat woman obviously wasn't prepared to travel for miles in the night, with nothing but vague directions. "Let's go, we'll figure it out on the way."

"Oh, thank the Divine." Virsian jumped and hurried across the cabin. She threw open the back door and stuck her head out to look.

Kanéko peered over the cat woman's shoulder into the inky darkness of the woods. On the far side of the inn, not even a single spear of light lit up the dense underbrush or the animal trail they followed to the inn. She cleared her throat, "Vir?"

"What!" Virsian whispered loudly, her voice cracking.

"I can't see out there. It's too dark."

"Oh... oh!" Virsian held out her hand. "Just step outside. Then get the door."

Kanéko set her palm in the warm, furry hand of the older woman. She let herself be dragged out into the darkness. With her free hand, Kanéko shut the door behind her, blinding herself with the night. She whispered, "Vir?"

"Hush," came the returned whisper, "just get a rod away. Trust me, please?"

She stumbled on the rough ground beneath her feet. Her wrapped feet were padded, but she could feel every bump and ridge. Her breath came hard and fast, the excitement and fear rising.

Virsian stopped. "Put your hands over mine."

"Why—?" Kanéko clamped her mouth shut as she felt Virsian's warm palm press over her eyes. Kanéko shivered at the touch; in the darkness, Virsian was more intimate than Pahim ever was. She reached up to spread her fingers over Virsian's furry hands and held her breath.

Holding her face, Virsian began to whisper. The words that meant nothing to Kanéko, but there was a structure, a rhythm, like a song that Kanéko didn't know. It was a spell.

White sparks danced across Kanéko's vision. The light moved in waves, like the surface of the river in the moonlight. She tried to focus on them but couldn't.

"Okay," Virsian pulled back her hands, "open your eyes."

Kanéko trembled as she cracked open her eyes. The world was bright but cast in shades of gray. There was a muted, spectral quality to her vision. Kanéko's lips parted as she looked up at a sky shot with pastel blues and greens.

"It's a dark vision spell." Virsian sounded tired as she stepped away. "I never used it on someone else before. Did it work?"

Kanéko turned and looked back at the inn. Mercenaries marched along the outside of the building, holding lanterns and sticks in their hands. The light was blinding, like looking into the sun.

A muffled boom shook the ground and dust poured out of the kitchen door and up through the chimney of the great hall. A scream of rage rose up followed by a loud thump. It was Maris.

Gulping, Kanéko cringed at the noise. "I can see."

Virsian smiled broadly. In the spell-fueled vision, her eyes glowed with an intense brightness. She held out her hand for Kanéko. "Come on."

Kanéko glanced back with misgivings of abandoning the others stabbing her in the gut. She shook her head and wiped a sudden tear.

Another boom shook the ground beneath their feet. Kanéko glanced back at the inn, a couple chains away at least, and was surprised that she could feel the impact through the ground.

Maris's voice cut through the night. "I'll kill you all!"

Virsian gasped. "If she doesn't stop resisting, they'll kill —" She clapped her hand over her mouth. She whispered through her fingers, "I'm sorry, I didn't mean... I'm sure they won't..."

Kanéko turned back, guilt tearing at her. She heard Maris howl shrilly and every window burst out from the back of the inn. A cloud of smoke and glittering dust flew out of every opening, puffing out and obscuring the inn. She felt the impact in her chest.

A deafening hiss filled the air, and something shot up on the far side of the inn. Kanéko followed it with her eyes.

It ignited into brilliant light and Kanéko's eyes blurred with the brightness before the spell compensated. A second flare of light ignited next to the first, leaving two lines stretching high into the air. A pounding heartbeat later, a third, and then a fourth line of lights stretched up into the air, higher than she could imagine. It almost looked like it scraped the clouds before the rocket exploded in an ear-piercing crack of noise.

Kanéko shuddered as the rocket's explosion rolled off in the distance. She lowered her gaze to the dust surrounding the inn. She didn't have a choice anymore, she had to go back. She took a step toward it.

Virsian grabbed her hand with both of hers. "Kan, no!"

Kanéko looked back at Virsian, and then returned her fretful gaze to the building. "They need me."

"You'll be caught!"

Knowing the dalpre was right, her mind spun furiously. She couldn't wait for Garèo or anyone else. She thought back to her idea before she slept. Home. If they could, they would go home. She pulled her hand free from Virsian. "I can't. I have to."

"Please, don't go." begged Virsian, "I have to take care of you. I'm responsible for your safety."

Kanéko turned to Virsian but took a step back. "I know, but this is the right thing. Look, if you find Garèo, tell him I'm going—" She wondered if she could trust Virsian, and then she realized that Cobin might force her to reveal Kanéko's destination. Then she thought about her lessons. She smiled, no one else should know the desert tongue. "Do you...do you know Miwāfu?"

"No, I—"

"Tell him I'm going *dòtsu.*"

"I—," Virsian shook her head, "I don't know that word. I can't speak that language. Dot...sun?"

"He will know what it means. Just repeat it to him, and he'll understand. If you don't know it, then you can't tell others."

Virsian stood there, a frown on her face, as she mouthed the Miwāfu word.

Kanéko turned on her heels and started toward the inn.

"Kanéko," said Virsian suddenly.

She slowed down. "Vir, I have—"

"No, one second."

Kanéko stopped and turned around. She looked at Virsian and saw something else, fear and determination in her eyes. Her father's stories about combat healers, how dangerous they were, drifted through her mind and she backed away slowly. Virsian could prevent her from helping the others.

Virsian caught up with her. "Please, trust me?"

Kanéko didn't know how much Virsian would force her. The look in the dalpre's eyes scared her, and she wanted to run.

The dalpre whispered softer. "You can save them, just let me help, please?"

Kanéko's back bumped against a rough tree. She inhaled sharply but didn't move as Virsian pressed a warm hand on her chest, right between Kanéko's breasts. Her heart pounded loudly as she tensed for whatever Virsian had in mind.

Virsian closed her eyes and began to whisper a different spell. It was long, a discordant sound as the dalpre struggled with the words. Tiny sparks of yellow rose from her hands, plucking at the fur of her arm. The light burned Kanéko's eyes and she followed it up in the canopy, trying not to think of the hand on her chest or how her breath quickened with the tingle of magic coming from the furry paw.

The spell filled her from the inside. It left an acidic taste in her mouth and a tightness in her chest. Her heart pounded in her ears, and she felt her senses growing sharper. The darkness pulled back even further, and she could see as clear as day. Her pulse slowed, a steady beat that shook her bones with every thud. She looked down from the trees to Virsian, her body moving sluggishly.

Virsian's head was only a few inches away. The soft whispers of the spell pummeled Kanéko's cheek; she could feel the woman's breath for each word and syllable.

Kanéko inhaled slowly. Over Virsian's shoulder, an insect swam through the air, too slow to be flying. It buzzed lazily as it slowed down until Kanéko could pick out the wings beating the air, punching down with a rhythm that she could never have seen before.

Memories rose, of her father talking about the battles he fought in. There was one where he defended a temple of healers. He told her about a spell used to boost the perceptions and strength of a warrior to inhuman levels. It was illegal outside times of war, and a capital crime to even know without being a knight like her father. But, Kanéko stood there, watching a fly crawl across the air as the forbidden magic flowed through her. A joy filled her, and she felt her heart skip a beat with excitement. She only dreamed of magic like this, a dream denied her when she failed the tests.

Virsian pulled back her hand, a sluggish movement. Her mouth moved, and the slow words came out. "You... have... ten minutes... be safe."

Kanéko reached over and kissed her on the lips. It was brief and short, but Kanéko could never thank Virsian e-nough. She pulled back and felt the blush oozing up to her face. With a grin, she ducked her head under the slow arm of Virsian and headed to the inn.

She stumbled when the magic boosted her stride. She moved too fast, too strong, and she almost slammed into a tree. Her father never mentioned how hard it was to move under the influence of such magic. Kanéko stopped for a heartbeat and tried again, moving forward with tiny jumps until she determined her new limits. By the time she reached the back door, she was comfortable enough to ac-celerate into a sprint for the main hall.

In the great room, Maris and Ruben were in the middle of two dozen men on a floor covered with sparkling dust. She had heard of warriors using crystal to disrupt telepathy and mental powers.

Maris held her arm where blood flowed from between her fingers. Steady vibrations shook the entire girl's body. Her lips were pulled back in a snarl; her teeth shockingly white as she glared at the men surrounding her.

Ruben stood with his back to her, a knife in his hand, blood dripping from its blade. His eyes were an intense blue—glowing—and his face twisted in concentration.

To her right, Kanéko spotted a man on the ground as he crawled behind the bar clutching his side. In front of the bar, Pahim stood with a sword out, brandishing it between himself and Maris. The bastard still had bandages on his face from where Kanéko had attacked him.

She started to glare at him but then noticed Cobin on the far side of the hall as he pointed into the room and slowly bellowed commands. He wore a pair of goggles with almost black lenses that hid his eyes. He had his sword out, a slightly curved blade that looked like a desert weapon without a name carved along the dull edge like every other Kyōti blade she had ever seen.

Kanéko couldn't find a clear route to her friends. She felt the seconds passing dangerously fast. The world sped up minutely as if to remind her.

Then she found an improbable route her enhanced speed and strength could make. A place on the bar, perfectly dry between a bottle of red wine and a rag. Another spot on the back of the bar led to a place she could use for balance on the top shelf. She didn't know if she would make it, but with the spell fueling her movement, Kanéko took the risk.

Sprinting forward, she dropped down and slid between the legs of a mercenary. She kicked him in the back of the knee. Before he fell, her slide brought her underneath a table. Her feet smacked on the leg of the table and the entire thing shifted a foot to the side. Grabbing a bench, she shoved with all her might. The bench knocked over two men and the movement brought her right up to Pahim.

He slashed down with surprise, his body moving sluggishly.

She lashed out and caught him between the legs. It had worked the first time, but now her foot hit a solid cup protecting his manhood. Kanéko flipped back and yanked a stick from a slow-moving mercenary. Grabbing it with both hands, she swung it in a high arc before she brought it down on his wrists. The impact shocked her hands. She felt a crunch that vibrated through the wood.

Pahim lurched forward. He tried to catch himself, but his hands failed him, and he hit the ground with a slow-motion collapse.

As he fell back with a sluggish scream, she jumped on the bar. Her left foot hit the exact spot she aimed for. With a surge of strength, she leaped up. She overshot her next landing point and shot up into the rafters. Coming down, she grabbed a thick beam above the bar, swung under it, and then launched herself up into the air. As she came down, she planted her feet on the thick, coarse wood and kicked out.

She flew over the fight and landed heavily on the floor between Maris and Ruben. Stretching, she planted her left hand on Ruben's shoulder.

The world stopped.

New information about the great hall flooded her mind. The dimensions and weights of every item in the room burned across her vision. She could identify everything from the sizes of the individual crystals in the air to the exact amount of force needed to move the heavy table next to her. Inferred histories of weapons, both their manufacture and their use in war, floated over each blade and club. Even scratches and cuts on the flagons were expanded into probable motions that caused every ding and dent. The memories were Ruben's, forced into her mind, but she saw them the same way she saw the designs she obsessed over.

After a stunned second, she grasped onto the new memories and thought about her options. As she did, probabilities and chances flew through her mind. She knew instantly her odds of pulling a weapon from someone's grip and the difficulty of tugging both of Maris and Ruben out of the room.

Elation burning bright, she used Ruben's analytic skills to find some way of getting her, him, and Maris out of the danger. She ran through her options, picturing how the fight would take place. As soon as she started to imagine it, Ruben would fill in the gaps and probabilities of responses. The information was overwhelming, but she managed to keep it in check as she worked through a series of rapid-fire scenarios.

It felt like an hour before she realized she couldn't come up with a plan using only Ruben's memories. There wasn't enough to save all three of them. She only wished Maris's magic manifested earlier, or that the dalpre was trained.

Her train of thought brought new memories to the fore, of her father and grandfather drinking and laughing over their own combat training. They were trying to scare her, but she listened with breathless excitement as they ranted about how their masters pushed and pushed them, driving them to irrational rage and forcing them to respond with magic instead of fists.

Kanéko grinned. She had a new plan: Maris. She would teach the volatile dalpre how to use combat magic in the middle of a fight. Her own memories welled up, solidified by Ruben's knowledge, and she imagined exactly what they needed to do to awaken the volatile dog girl's magic. She sent the plan over to Ruben who flashed an acknowledgment.

She released Ruben and the world accelerated.

A mercenary rushed her, trying to club her with the flat side of his sword.

Kanéko swung her stick to block him. As the impact of the sword hit her weapon, she turned and kicked out with all her might.

He flew back, and she stumbled.

Her back slammed against Maris. Kanéko turned to see Maris punching another man, her fist driving into the man's shoulder. Kanéko prayed for forgiveness and grabbed Maris.

The dalpre spun around, a confused look on her face.

Kanéko slapped her as hard as she could.

Maris took the hit without moving. A hurt look crossed her face. With Kanéko's accelerated senses, her response came out slowly. "K-a-n, why—?"

Kanéko needed Maris to lose her temper. She only had a few stories from her family that gave her the idea, but she didn't have any choice. She slapped Maris again before stepping sideways to crack her stick against a man's head.

Maris gaped, and then jumped. Spinning around, she grabbed her ass and screamed down at Ruben who had pinched her. "Rub!"

Kanéko leaned back and smacked Maris in the back of the head. She ducked under a wild swing from the dalpre and jammed the stick into another man's stomach. He bent over in time to catch Maris's back-swing.

The spell fueling her movements slowed down. Kanéko only had a few moments before she was once again a mundane girl with no powers. The realization saddened her, but she pushed it aside to focus on her plans. She dove back to Maris to yank the dalpre's ear.

On the far side, Ruben parried a sword attack and jabbed Maris in the thigh.

Together, they defended Maris and attacked her at the same time. Kanéko felt dizzy as she bounced back and forth, trying to keep them away from the dalpre even as she tried to provoke Maris. Every movement, she watched for the signs her father and grandfather warned her about the instinctive response with violence and magic, the smell of acid in the air, and a beating against her skin.

"Stop it!" Maris tried to dodge Kanéko's smack and ran right into another of Ruben's pinches. She spun around and the air swirled around her. "Stop!" she yelled in a higher pitch scream.

The air grew violent around them. Crystal dust rose up in a circle around them, curling around like a slow tornado. Kanéko smacked Maris harder. "Come on, idiot! *Bitch!*"

Maris's eyes widened with shock. Kanéko pulled back to block an attack, and then saw the shock turn into instant rage. Maris screamed shrilly. "I'll hate you!"

Around Maris's fist, the wind gathered. Crystal and sawdust spun around her hand as the air grew hot. Kanéko felt the wind being pulled from her lungs and the whirls gathering around the dalpre's hand.

Maris drew back to punch Kanéko, a mask of rage on her face. The dalpre no longer saw anything but fury. As Maris lashed out at her, Kanéko grabbed her shoulders and spun her toward the front of the hall.

Standing in the front door, Cobin blanched and stumbled back. A ball of air burst out from Maris's hand and slammed into him. The front wall shattered and blew out, shards of woods and glass flinging beyond the end of the horse yard and into the darkness of the night.

Kanéko took a second to plan her next move. Grabbing Maris's arm, she tugged the dalpre through the gaping opening.

Maris resisted until Ruben grabbed her tail and pulled just as insistently. She stumbled forward. Her face was pale and Kanéko could feel her trembling from the effort.

As she raced out the opening of the inn, Kanéko spotted a travel bag lodged against one of the shattered timbers holding up the porch. She snatched it and threw it over her shoulder. She only hoped there were supplies inside.

Out in the yard, there was more room to move. Kanéko spun around, looking for a horse to flee on. She spotted one, but it was racing into the darkness. She turned around again, still yanking Maris behind her. She tried to find some faster form of travel. Part of her hoped that there was one of the steam cars in the yard, but she found nothing. Despair clutched her heart as she tried to figure out some way of outrunning the mercenaries.

Maris whimpered. "Kan!"

"Not now," snapped Kanéko. She hefted the bag on her shoulder. "I'm working on getting us out of here."

"Then why were you hitting me?" Maris whimpered and pouted.

Kanéko saw the men recovering inside the inn. She spun on Maris and stomped the dalpre's foot with all her might.

Air rushed up as Maris screamed out. "Ow!" A blast of air caught Kanéko in the chest.

Half-expecting the girl's fury, Kanéko planted her feet on the ground and forced herself back, fighting the wind that howled around Maris.

Maris slapped Kanéko. Sparks flew across Kanéko's vision, but she managed to hold her ground. "Stop that!"

Kanéko, her face grim with concentration, ignored the pain radiating from her cheek. "No." She spotted a bow on the ground a rod away; a few feet beyond it there was a quiver with arrows spilling out of it. She looked at the men through the cloud of dust swirling around them. They were staggering out of the great hall, weapons in hand. "Rub, ideas?"

"Negative," came the strained whisper.

Kanéko looked around again as Cobin stepped forward from the darkness. Blood dripped from his face and his sword glinted in the light from spilled lanterns. "*Pretty impressive, little girl. He taught you well.*"

Kanéko hesitated, startled by Cobin speaking Miwāfu fluently. She just told Virsian she was going home in hopes that no one would know the language. A sick feeling twisted in her stomach, but she couldn't change her plans.

Cobin continued, speaking loudly over the wind that surrounded the three. *"I'm more interested in finding Great Waryoni Garèo."*

A brief plan from earlier gave her an idea. Kanéko stepped around Maris to Ruben and rested her hand on his shoulder. As soon as she felt their mental rapport, she forced herself to speak as calmly as she could. *"What do you want him for?"*

As she spoke, she pictured the *Primer on Crystal Sphere Techniques* on her workbench. Thanks to Ruben, the memory came up as clear as every day she pored over it.

Cobin chuckled and continued to walk closer. *"I'm going to kill him."*

His comment almost broke Kanéko's attention. She stared into the goggled man's face, seeing hatred and anger in the tight-set jaw. She wondered what Garèo had done to provoke Cobin.

Behind him, she could see the mercenaries picking themselves out of the destruction. They leaned against each other and looked around in confusion. Only a few looked in her direction, but they didn't seem inclined to follow their leader.

Ruben touched her hip and Kanéko started. Remembering her plan, she snapped at Cobin, *"Drown in sands, bastard."*

As she waited for his response, she found the page she remembered. It was one of her favorites since it talked about how air witches could fly.

"Someday I may, but not today. Give up, Great Kosobyo Kanéko, and accept that you are surrounded. If you do, I promise you won't be harmed."

279

Ruben radiated confusion. She recalled the game when she woke up in the wagon, when Maris was talking about a ball. As soon as she thought about it, she could picture it. A bright red ball hidden behind the corner of a bed. Kanéko imagined herself flinging it up in the air. When Ruben didn't respond, she superimposed Maris with the ball, showing the dalpre chasing after it.

Realization dawned on Ruben's face. He ducked around Kanéko and grabbed Maris to pull her down and whisper in her ear.

Around them, the circle of wind died down. Kanéko remembered the bow and raced for it. Cobin chased after her, but Kanéko beat him and snatched up the bow and arrows. She dodged his outstretched hand and used her other elbow to jab him in the stomach.

It was like hitting a solid wall.

He grabbed at her. His fingernails scratched her back, but his other hand caught her hair.

Kanéko spun around and kicked him in the side of his knee. The strike sent shooting pain up her leg, but it was enough to break his grip. She yanked her hair free, losing some strands, and sprinted back. She cried out as soon as she was within arm's reach. "Rub, now!"

Ruben grabbed Maris's face with both hands. His eyes flared a brilliant blue as he dragged the dog girl's gaze into his own. A wall of wind blasted between Kanéko and Cobin and threw him back.

The dalpre spoke in a soft, distant voice. Her tail was down between her legs as she concentrated. "And I see the ball, Rub. Now what?"

The air grew tense and tight, a pressure building around them. Kanéko grabbed her stolen pack and her bow. She clutched to Maris tightly from behind and closed her eyes. She screamed, "Throw it up!"

Nothing.

Kanéko let out a sob, wondering if she had failed. She had tried so hard to save them.

The world exploded in sound and pain as something grabbed her entire body and yanked up. Kanéko choked at the air whipping across her face and clung on with all her strength. She couldn't hear anything but howling wind and her own screaming. Her feet kicked out but there was no ground underneath her.

The grip pulling her down slowed and then reversed. Wind blew up from below, buoying her against Maris's body. Shaking, Kanéko opened one eye and saw nothing but darkness. Gasping, she peered over Maris's shoulder and looked down at the tiny pool of light that was the Boar Hunt Inn. They were chains above the ground and Kanéko knew that she would never survive a fall from that height.

Kanéko grabbed Maris tighter.

The air sputtered around them and Maris groaned with effort. They fell a short distance before fresh wind surged around them.

"I'm tired," whimpered Maris.

Kanéko clutched tighter. "Just a little more power, just keep it moving. We—" she looked down and gulped at their height, "we need to get down before you run out of energy."

Kanéko tried to reach out for Ruben, but she couldn't move without losing her grip on Maris. "R-Rub? Mar? We have to get down. South, east, and down."

The wind intensified and the pool of light beneath them began to slide away. Seconds later, they were over darkness. Kanéko's enhanced vision could see far enough down, but she couldn't spot anything except for the tops of trees sailing by.

As soon as it had started, the wind stopped. As they began to fall, Kanéko snapped, "Rub! Keep her up!"

Magic crackled the air, and the wind came back, hard and brutal. It threw them up before it died. Before they fell a rod, the air slammed into the tree and bounced them higher into the sky. They skipped across the sky like a rock, each time falling lower as Maris's power faded.

Kanéko cried out. "Stay awake! You're going into spell shock. Come on, Mar, stay with us!"

The ground came up, and Kanéko could see it in terrifying detail. She yelled directions, trying to bring them down on the ground.

They were only ten feet above the ground, skimming above the plains when Maris passed out. The energy dissipated and the wind stopped in a heartbeat.

The silence suffocated Kanéko.

They fell in a short arc.

Kanéko, terrified, pulled Maris and Ruben into a tight hug, cradling both of them as they plummeted. She hit the surface of a pond with the flat of her back. Agony crashed into her, blinding her with pain. Water engulfed them, and she choked as it flowed into her mouth and nostrils.

She panicked and flailed around. Her feet hit the soft, spongy bottom and she reoriented herself. Kicking up, she slashed and clawed at the water until she surfaced. Gasping, she spun around until she saw Maris and Ruben floating next to her. She grabbed both of them and dragged them to the shore. With her fading might, she pushed them out of the water. She tried to crawl out herself, but her body refused to move. As a choking darkness yanked her into oblivion, her last thought was to keep her head out of water. She managed to grab on to Maris's tail as she slipped into unconsciousness.

Chapter 26

Revelations

Telepathy is neither a one-way street nor a walkway. One side needs to have the magical talent to communicate, and the other must be willing.

—*Exploring the Depths of the Mind*

Kanéko stared at a massive gear looming above her. It was metal, but she had never seen anything so large made out of steel. She knew it would take a powerful mage to shape it, but part of her wished someone without magic could mold metal at that scale. The thought saddened her but then her focus drifted to the purpose of the gear.

As she concentrated, she saw other gears and pistons attached to the large one. It was a device of some sort, complicated and massive. A smile graced her lips as she started to work her way through the linkages and ratios in an effort to find the power or the purpose of the machine.

When she gave up, she had lost track of time while the device remained unsolved. It was a wall of mechanical devices that had no purpose or reason. For all appearances, a shifting mechanism for the sake of being there.

She was dreaming, she could think of no other explanation.

Kanéko relaxed almost immediately and let herself enjoy the pointless designs. It was peaceful tracing through the mechanisms, seeing how her efforts with the water screw and what she learned about the mill had integrated into her dreams.

With a smile, she reached out and pressed her hand to a massive piston larger than a house. Impractical but beautiful, she imagined it having beautiful scroll work and designs along the ends.

The piston blurred. Metal rose up underneath her palm as elegant designs spread out like a plant, caressing the metal sleeve. The more she focused on it; the details grew sharper.

Kanéko pulled back and admired her work with an approving nod. She could finally interact with the designs in her head. Sweeping her hand back, she summoned gears and pistons. It only took a moment to rebuild the water screw and boiler from scratch, then pull it apart to reassemble it. She could see where one of the joints was weak and where it probably ruptured. That was what had destroyed the stable. Next time, she wouldn't make the same mistake.

She sighed and let the screw crumble. Turning around, she looked at what her mind had created. The rest of her dream was a field of boilers, smokestacks, and every combination of machine she could imagine. It stretched as far as she could see and disappeared in a haze of oily smoke and steam.

A page fluttered across her vision. She reached out and snatched it before it blew away. It was part of the water screw's design, just as she pictured it in her head. A bit of color bled through the page and she flipped it over. When she saw a little girl's scrawl of herself doing magic, she dropped the page in surprise. It fluttered away, dancing between two mechanized grape presses.

The surface below her consisted of writings and pictures she had created as a child, the dreams she had while sitting at her father's feet, the lessons she learned when she was obsessed with magic. Her world of mechanical perfection was built on her childhood fantasies of magic.

Her surroundings clicked from countless gears meshing, ticked from clockwork devices counting down seconds, and even the faint thud of pistons driving home. The world around her pulsed and beat in time to some ethereal metronome.

Joy filled her as she walked along a trail of magic books and oil pans.

She spotted a hill in the distance and headed toward it. Her bare feet slapped on the paper ground as she ducked underneath a boiler larger than her father's tower. She stopped abruptly when she came to the edge of a chasm, a cliff plunging straight into the darkness of oblivion. The cliff wall beneath her bare feet was made from fantastical devices that shook the ground.

As she admired the world around her, a new smell intruded on her thoughts. It wasn't the sharpness of burning oil or the scent of paper. Instead, it was sour and tangy, fishy. She frowned as she tried to remember the familiar smell. She licked her lips and took a deeper breath. It took her a moment, but then she recalled the black substance on her hand during the cliff collapse.

Kanéko realized she was wiping her hand on her hip. She lifted her hand and stared at the blackness that coated her palm. Thick rivulets ran down her wrist. Where the liquid touched, her skin tingled. She brought her hand closer and sniffed, the fishy smell was coming from the oil.

Frowning, she looked up while still trying to scrape it free on her trousers.

A pair of glowing red eyes stared at her.

She gasped and jerked back.

The eyes were on the far side of the ravine, hovering beyond the cloud of oil smoke and dust rising between them. Unhidden by the rock, they loomed over her in a palpable aura of menace. Each eye was massive, larger than a horse. It had no pupils. It was just a glowing red orb that somehow gave the impression that it was staring straight at her.

Kanéko took a step back.

«We are Damagar.» The words slammed into her mind, twisting her own thoughts to form the concepts instead of dredging up memories like Ruben had done. She felt helpless and vulnerable, as if the creature was somehow growing deep inside her.

It took a step forward, reaching out with one massive paw. Large claws curved out of three distinct toes, and she spotted webbing between each one. She couldn't focus on the rest of the creature's shape through the haze of the ravine, but the foot was clear. When it smacked down on the ravine, it crushed the countless devices into a spray of oil and debris.

«We know you, Kosobyo Kanéko, Kanéko Lurkuklan.» The words pummeled her as the creature stepped further into the ravine. «We are in your head.»

Her concern twisted in fear. She stepped back again, stumbling over a pile of childhood drawings. She flailed out and grabbed the nearest pipe. The metal sizzled underneath her hand only a moment before sharp agony raced up her limb. It was searing hot. Knowing that she would fall if she let go, she forced her fingers to remain wrapped around the burning metal just long enough to regain her feet.

The ground shook beneath her. She looked up with surprise as ripples raced through the countless devices around her. Axles and pistons snapped as the ground buckled in expanding waves. Spurts of oil and smoke followed.

Kanéko got back to her feet and peeled her hand away from the pipe. Strips of flesh were left behind to sizzle and cook away, filling the air with the smell of burning flesh that quickly mixed in with the oil. Blinking past her tears, she clutched her hand to her chest.

She had burned herself repeatedly while working on the water screw. It wouldn't take long for the initial agonies to fade. Tensing, she counted up as she waited for her body to remember.

As the sharpness of her pain faded, so did the quakes. Panting, she waited for the throbbing to subside.

When she looked up, the glowing red eyes were still staring at her. Damagar had continued to approach, but it moved slowly. Its bulbous shape was just coming down into the ravine, crushing acres of the pointless mechanisms. Oily smoke swirled around it, revealing a heavily textured surface over an obsidian body. «We communicate, nothing more.»

Kanéko stared in shock, her pain forgotten. Damagar's shape teased her memory, it was familiar, but she couldn't quite place it. She frowned and peered at it closer, wishing the oily smoke would clear to give her a better view.

Responding to her thoughts, a wind blew across the ravine. It tugged at the haze of smoke and dust, drawing it into streamers that rolled through the pipes and around Damagar's body. She could see thick ridges and wart-like knots on its dark skin. The large bumps disturbed the streamers of smoke that raced around its body.

With a final surge, the haze was clear, and she could focus clearly on Damagar.

It was a toad. A massive obsidian toad with glowing red eyes that looked like cracked rubies. From the size of the ravine and its feet, she thought it was about eighty or ninety feet across and about a hundred long, excluding its feet. Each paw was easily a rod across. The maw of the creature slowly opened, and a tongue ran along the ridge before it snapped its jaw closed again.

She shuddered at the sight. The tongue was thicker than her torso.

Damagar took another step toward her, crushing countless gears into scraps of metal and spurts of oil.

Fear rose inside her. She didn't want the creature to get any closer.

The far side of the cliff pulled away from her, stretching the bottom of the ravine along with it.

The disruption pulled Damagar away from her, but that didn't stop it from taking slow, measured steps that crushed new machinery. Its eyes never left hers and she could feel the pressure of its thoughts approaching her, terrifying and overwhelming.

Kanéko tensed with anticipation.

Despite the growing presence, it didn't speak again. No powerful thoughts slammed into her consciousness; no memories were forcibly dredged up from her subconscious.

Her fear ebbed. She watched it continue to pace toward her, the cliff still drawing away out of sight, but the creature continued to stalk her wordlessly. She clenched her hands into fists. Agony blossomed on her injured palm, but she pushed it aside.

Time continued to inch forward. Around them, the broken gears squealed against each other, and a rapid clicking noise rose up. The smell of machine and fish oil filled the air, both burned in the back of Kanéko's throat.

Finally, she couldn't wait any longer. "Well? What do you want?"

Damagar blinked one eye and then the other. It took another step.

"If you don't want anything, get out of my dreams! Out of my head!"

It finally responded. A pressure built up inside her head and she heard the whisper of a dozen different voices crashing into her mind. Concepts and thoughts were burned into her thoughts, drowning out the squeaks, hisses, and scrapes of metal that surrounded her. «... must kill the Broken Thought ... before it kill us.»

She closed her mouth with a snap. When Damagar didn't follow up, she said, "W-What? What are you talking about?"

«Kill the Void Child, the Broken Thought.» It seemed as if Damagar had tried to frame a description but failed. She knew what it was talking about though, there was only one other person with her. Like before, it was as if it couldn't picture or even name Ruben directly.

Kanéko remembered how Ruben plucked the memories out of her mind. She knew that Damagar could do the same, to find the perfect words, but the idea of the creature inside her head left Kanéko feeling cold. She turned her head away from Damagar, looking down at the ground to avoid looking into its eyes.

A small black frog was at her feet. It looked up with tiny crimson eyes. «We're already here, Kanéko Lurkuklan, Kosòbyo Kanéko. You cannot escape.»

She caught movement in the corner of her eye. Looking over, she saw another small frog.

«We only communicate.»

When Damagar used a plural to describe itself, she didn't get an image of the giant toad. Instead, it was a group of figures projecting in unison, a choir of distinct personalities that combined together spoke as Damagar. None of them were human nor were they even the natural creatures she had read about. Instead, they looked like the monsters and nightmares twisted out of animals. There were bipedal cats, bird-like creatures with wings for arms but human-like faces, and even one beast that looked like a bear without hair.

Curious and with her anger dissipating, she concentrated on the swirl of individuals that popped in her head. With her focus, words and descriptions welled up into her consciousness: the leaders were Strategy, Preparation, and Observation. There were others, dozens with more specific titles related to the body like Right Leg, Heart, and Breath. The names were surprising. They were all names for abstract concepts or functions, not arbitrary labels.

It only took her a moment to realize their names and functions were the same. Damagar needed all of them to even move. The creature was too big and powerful for a single mind to control its form. It needed all of them.

As his connection to her grew deeper, she felt hundreds of other personalities still sleeping in its mind. The ones that responded to her were the only ones awake. They spoke to her, but she could imagine the noise if they were all aware of her.

Cold fear rippled through her dreams, and the ravine spread further apart. She shook her head and held up her hands. The storm of thoughts was already too much, she couldn't take more. "Out! Out of me!"

«We will leave, but we need you to extinguish—» She felt Damagar reaching into her mind. His thoughts were jumbled and powerful, surging around in her thoughts as he forced her memories to rise up to the fore. «We cannot see it. We cannot name it beyond a label, the Void Child, the Broken Thought.»

As Damagar responded, Kanéko concentrated on its powerful thoughts. She could almost pick out the individual personalities that pummeled her. Each one had different motivations and desire. Damagar's Right Leg only wanted to move; Strategy was trying to keep her mind away by shifting her attention to Damagar's Heart. She lost herself in feeling the beat of a powerful heart even as she realized she had been misdirected.

With all her effort, she forced her attention back on Damagar's Strategy. "Why me?"

Damagar responded by driving its memories into her mind, burning away everything but the intense images she was forced to experience.

She saw herself on the cliff, but as Damagar perceived her. Her thoughts leaked out from her mind, exposing her jealousy and growing friendship like a cloud of pollen. Her thoughts were ordered and neat but, at the same time, fluid.

Next to her, Maris was a chaotic storm of rapidly shifting emotion and ideas. They moved from happiness to sadness, from affection toward Kanéko to the itch on her butt.

Ruben was not in Damagar's thoughts at all. His voice, his presence, even his footsteps didn't register to the creature. Like before, the two girls spoke to empty space.

Damagar knew that the cliff would collapse before even Maris registered the shift of stone and the loosening of soil. Its blood had seeped into the ground and weakened it.

She tried to focus on why the creature's black blood was in the ground, but Strategy managed to redirect her thoughts to the moment when the cliff collapsed.

Kanéko watched as Maris plummeted to the ground. Feet above, her air magic manifested and caught her, softening the blow so she landed gently on the ground instead of being smashed into the rocks.

A sudden explosion startled Kanéko. It came form the top of the cliff as a howling storm of brilliant blue blossomed into existence and then collapsed into a tear into reality itself.

She had never felt or heard the explosion that Damagar experienced.

Curious, she forced her own memories to superimpose on top of Damagar's. The explosion happened at the same moment Ruben yelled for Maris. The only difference was she heard a booming voice echoing in her head. Damagar never heard Ruben's voice, only heard the blast.

The physic creature's experience became starkly different than Kanéko's. While she was trying to pick her way down to Maris, it was fighting a powerful pull from the fissure.

The suction clawed at its mind. It left jagged rips that burned away Damagar's memories and yanked at the distinct personalities that made up its thoughts. The invisible storm attacked Damagar as Kanéko blissfully inspected the crater her friend had created.

In the psychic world, Damagar's personalities panicked as they were assaulted by the inescapable pull of Ruben's presence. Most of the personalities were unable to respond, they were focused on moving body parts or preparing long-term strategies, not defending against a void that threatened to destroy them.

However, one of Damagar's personalities rose up to fight. Stubbornness was a humanoid frog armed with a ragged spear. It had been crafted from one of Damagar's earliest experiences and represented the drive to keep going even through mortal injuries inflicted centuries before.

Stubbornness never slept and it was ready to fight. Before any of the other personalities could be ripped from Damagar's mind and destroyed, the humanoid frog tore itself free of Damagar and flung itself into the psychic storm that threatened them all.

Kanéko's heart pounded in her chest as she was forced to experience the sorrow of watching a fragment of Damagar's personality sacrifice itself. Every sense of hers had been pulled it to feel, hear, and even smell as Stubbornness was swallowed up by the all-consuming void that Ruben had become.

Then, just as more personalities were about to be ripped free and destroyed, Stubbornness's claws reached out of the void to grab the edges of the fissure. It yanked the tear closed before it was lost forever.

Just as quickly as the physic void had formed, it was gone and Damagar could no longer perceive Ruben.

Sorrow and despair rose up from Damagar as the realization that it had lost its drive in an instant. Without Stubbornness, a sense of loss flooded through the other personalities. They had no direction beyond surviving through spite.

Strategy responded by waking up another fragment of Damagar's mind, Self-Preservation and then Anger. The former would wake quickly, but not too fast as to awaken—

Damagar's thoughts were interrupted sharply as Strategy severed the link with Kanéko. Even her world of machines and fantasies disappeared in an instant, leaving in her in a darkness where sleep would quickly swallow her.

In the moments before she lost consciousness, she thought about what she had experienced. It was clear now why Ruben wasn't supposed to "think hard" as Maris said; he was a threat to psychic creatures but those who had no ability to sense those powers would be untouched by his presence.

No wonder Strategy tapped Self-Preservation. It needed to survive. She guessed it also meant that Damagar was set on destroying Ruben before he could destroy it.

Any other plan faded away as she fell into a dreamless slumber.

Chapter 27

Waking Nightmares

Telepathy leaves fragments in other minds. For non-telepaths, this in-
flicts night terrors as the host rejects the foreign thoughts.
—Gaston Bermes, *Legal Ramifications of Telepathy*

"Kan! Kan!"

Kanéko's eyes snapped open.

Maris crouched over her, holding her hands on Kanéko's
chest.

Kanéko's heart continued to beat rapidly against her ribs,
painfully thudding despite the fading memory of Damagar's agony.

"Kan?" Maris leaned over. "Your eyes are open. And does
that mean you are awake?"

Panting, Kanéko waved her hand. "I-I'm all right."

Maris sat back with an expression of relief. Her tail
waved back and forth. Looking over her shoulder to the
left, she called out. "Kan's good!"

Ruben chuckled dryly. "I determined that when she
stopped crying out in her dreams."

Kanéko blushed and sat up. "Where am I?"

Maris pointed to her right. "We landed by a pond. And it smells like wet plants. And dead fish. And that green stuff on the top doesn't taste good. But it is good to clean up. And then Ruben found some food. And he made a fire and he's cooking."

Kanéko followed Maris's gestures, first to a pond of water with insects lazily buzzing above it, and then to where Ruben roasted tubers and onions over a small fire.

A rumble came from the sky above where gray clouds boiled. Kanéko could see darker clouds to the west, moving toward them. A gray haze below the storm indicated rain.

Maris interrupted her thoughts with a hurt tone, "And I don't like you."

Kanéko returned her attention to Maris. "Why not?"

"You hit my foot. And then you slapped me. And you kept on hitting me."

As Maris spoke, a breeze rose up around her. The grasses waved back and forth, and her black hair danced in the breeze. Kanéko caught the scent of ozone in the air, the acidic smell of magic.

Kanéko blushed. "Well, I was, um, improvising."

Maris looked confused. "Impro... vising?"

Ruben, his voice a whisper again, called out from the fire. "Defined as: to compose and perform or deliver without previous preparation."

The dalpre's ears perked up. "Making up stuff? That's what happens when daddy and Bor get into a fight and Bor keeps trying to come up with new reasons why he shouldn't be in trouble. And Daddy calls that lying, Rub, not 'imping.'"

Kanéko crawled to her feet and looked over to the pond, trying to find a private spot. "Something like that, um, is there a place I can get cleaned up?"

Maris pointed to the near edge of the pond. Kanéko's eyes looked down and traced a damp trail to Maris, who still dripped water on the ground. The wet fur underneath her dress caused droplets to roll down the black fabric. The material stuck to the dalpre's breasts and hips. It reminded Kanéko of when Maris was naked in the shower.

Kanéko felt a blush rising. "Somewhere private?"

Maris cocked her head. "Private? Why do you need private? Do you have to shit? I did that over—"

"No, to clean up."

The dog girl cocked her head. "But, I don't understand."

Ruben stood up and circled around the fire to put his back to Kanéko. "Bring your attention here, Maris Germudrir, and help me finish cooking this food."

The dalpre bounded over to Ruben and sat down heavily on the ground.

Kanéko stared at their backs for a moment, expecting Ruben to peek over. When neither did, she walked over to the pond. At the water's edge, she spotted a ragged square of fabric still dripping wet. Picking it up, she flipped it over in her hand before she recognized it; it came from Maris's patched dress. Guessing as to its purpose, she took it as a washcloth and circled around the pond to put as much distance between her and the two others before sitting down to properly clean herself.

When she came back, her clothes clung to her dark skin, but she felt a thousand times cleaner. She had spread out her copper hair across her shoulders to let it dry before she would tie it back.

Ruben didn't look over his shoulder, but he spoke out as she walked up to them. "The preparation will be complete in one minute, seven seconds."

"Thank you," she said.

Maris cocked her head. She looked around and the silence filled the clearing. Then, Maris pointed to the pack that Kanéko stole. "What's in there? Ruben won't let me look. And I smell meat. And butts. And cheese. And I want to see inside it."

Not knowing herself, Kanéko opened up the bag. She saw clothes and realized that Maris had smelled someone's underwear but there was no food inside. With a grin, she pulled the bundle of fabric out. It was heavier than she expected, so she shook it twice. Three large hunks of cheese and salted meat rolled out, bouncing on the ground before stopping short of the water. She sighed with disappointment.

"The dalpre does possess an acute sense of smell."

Kanéko blushed, knowing that Ruben had read her thoughts.

"And I told you!" Maris grabbed the food and brushed it off. "Rub! Kan found food! And real food that doesn't taste like dirt!"

Ruben looked over his shoulder and smiled. When Maris showed him, he thought for a moment. "Bring it over here. We will combine it for breakfast."

"What about the next meal, Rub?" asked Maris. "Didn't think of that, did you?"

"Then we will store half for dinner."

Maris nodded happily, tossing the spoils over to Ruben who caught them without looking.

Kanéko watched him break off a chunk of cheese to add to the cooking vegetables, and then returned her attention to the clothes in her hands. Unfolding the bundle, she found a dark maroon uniform the mercenaries wore. On the right breast, a small patch said "Starisen." She frowned as she stared at the name. She had seen it before.

With a start, she realized the bag she had stolen belonged to Cobin, the man who had led the effort to kidnap her. She took a deep breath and felt a point of bitter joy that Cobin would suffer after everything he did to her. She set aside the uniform and pulled out two more sets of clothes, including trousers at least three sizes too large for her and five pairs of men's underwear. She made a face at the soiled underclothes and tossed them aside.

At the bottom of the bag, she found a number of travel rations—oil-wrapped packets of tasteless, dried vegetables and meats—and a thick leather envelope. Pulling it out, she spotted something on the bottom and let out a soft gasp of surprise.

A *kasói*, a curved dagger with a narrow point. She unsheathed it and looked for a name—her mother said every desert blade was named. To her surprise, she couldn't find one. She frowned. "Why would Cobin have a Mifúno blade?"

Ruben glanced at it. "It is a Kyōti weapon, not Mifúno. Mifúno is the name of the desert spirit, Kyōti is the region which includes the desert. If it is made in that area, then it has been blessed to take on the name of the first creature it kills."

"Okay, why does he have a desert weapon?"

When neither Ruben nor Maris had an answer, Kanéko shrugged. She strapped the dagger to her thigh. It felt better having a weapon next to her, even if knife fighting terrified her more than archery. She glanced over to the bow she had grabbed, a Kormar short bow. She wasn't comfortable shooting it, but she didn't have much of a choice. She only had a dozen arrows; it was enough for hunting... if she didn't miss. She worried her lip, remembering how many times she failed during Garèo's archery tests.

Ruben suddenly set food in front of her, and Kanéko jumped. She looked around and then did a double-take as Maris finished licking her plate clean. Kanéko hadn't noticed when Maris started eating, but it only took seconds for the dalpre to finish. She looked down at her meal, vegetables covered in cheese with a few strips of salted meat next to it. She thanked Ruben and started eating.

Maris bounced impatiently as Ruben and Kanéko ate. She toyed with the frayed ends of her dress, and then counted her fingers out loud. Eventually, she started to let out long sighs while looking forlornly at the other teenagers. When neither responded, she sighed even louder.

Kanéko felt it prickling on the edges of her annoyance. Between bites, she spoke up. "Why are you bouncing?"

"I'm done eating. And you are slow."

Ruben chuckled into his food, the same as Kanéko's but without meat. "At the mill, the consumption rate is six times faster than average. And pausing between bites is a foreign concept for the dalpre."

"It is not," Maris spat, "Ruben Habor!"

Ruben got a pained look on his face. "That was not mannerly."

Kanéko glanced over at Ruben. "Your name is Ruben Habor?"

Maris's tail wagged back and forth as she spoke, "No, his name is Ruben Habor Kalis Bomen Tater. And I remember that much. But there are seven more names I can't."

Kanéko cleared her throat. "That's a very long name."

Maris giggled. "Yeah, it is. But we use the short form because we don't think loudly. But Rub's daddy uses the long one. Because Rub's daddy has to."

Kanéko shot a questioning look over to Ruben who shook his head. When he didn't explain, she asked him, "Ruben? Why?"

He whispered angrily, "We do not need to go into details."

Maris spoke up, "It's because he ran away from Vo." She pointed one direction. "He ran away from home—"

"The Isle of Vo is in the opposite direction, to the west," snapped Ruben.

Maris pointed to the west and continued, "And he's not allowed to think loudly because something bad will happen. His daddy says so."

Ruben toyed with the last of his food, and then set down the rock he used as a plate. Standing up, he stormed off.

Kanéko bit her lower lip, thinking back to her nightmare and the scene where Stubbornness was consumed by the crack. She called out after him, "Is that why you woke Damagar up?"

Ruben froze in mid-step, and then continued walking.

Maris looked confused. "Ruben didn't wake him up. It was the rock falling. And it made a loud noise. And I screamed and that woke him up, right?"

Neither Kanéko nor Ruben answered her.

Maris whimpered and looked back and forth between them. "Right? Right?"

Kanéko watched his head bobbing in the grass. She stood up and yelled after him. "What is the Broken Thought?"

"Terminate discussion!" yelled Ruben in his deep voice.

"What is going on!?" Kanéko snapped.

Ruben spun around; his dark hair barely visible over the grass. Kanéko felt a tickle in her mind, and then he yelled out with his full volume, the surprisingly deep voice shocking her. "Cease. This. Discussion!"

It rumbled through the air and Kanéko heard it echoing in her thoughts. She screamed back. "Get out of my head, damn it!" Remembering how she broke the connection with Damagar, she imagined the wall of gears and pistons.

The details flowed across her mind and Ruben's echoes faded.

Kanéko stalked toward him. "Tell me."

"No!" yelled Ruben without the echoes inside Kanéko's head.

Ruben backed away but Kanéko covered the distance between them, shoving past the grasses to grab the small teenager. She picked him up with both hands and glared into his face. "Every time you yell, he hears you, doesn't he? Every time you yell, that crack thing happens, right? The blue fissure?"

He started to say something, and then closed his mouth with a snap. He whispered sadly, "Yes."

"Why?"

When Ruben said nothing, Kanéko set him down and pointed back to the fire.

Ruben hesitated then he stormed back to the fire. He stopped at Maris's pack and pulled out a ball. Maris gasped, bouncing to her feet as Ruben tossed it into his other hand. He threw the ball.

It flew a surprising distance as it arced across the field.

Maris squealed and ran after it.

When he turned around, Kanéko pointed to the ground. "Explain. I just had a nightmare where Damagar showed me the cliff collapsing. He asked for you. Now, why? What is the Void Child? Why does he see you as a crack? How did you destroy Stubbornness?"

With a sad expression, Ruben held up his hand. "I'm... damaged. My mind was sealed by my progenitors and Vo. If it opens fully, then every telepathic, psychic, and spirit within leagues will cease to exist. However, I suspect the seal is cracking with my proximity to Damagar and the stress of our current situation."

"Is that why Damagar is vulnerable? He has multiple personalities? A crowd working together?"

"Affirmative. I'm surprised you were able to perceive those details. Most titanic creatures have multiple personalities due to the complexity of coordinating their physical form. Those with high degrees of power also have additional fragments to handle each aspect of crafting magic. Fortunately, there is a cost to maintaining so many personalities, so many are left slumbering until they are needed. That means only a handful will be awake unless the creature anticipates danger."

"But why aren't you a danger to me and Maris? You recall my memories easily."

"You are not telepathic. You possess a large body of knowledge and memories, but more importantly, you have the analytical mind and creativity to form new thoughts. But, ultimately, you are seated in one body, one mind. You cannot project, only receive and interact."

The muscles in her back tightened. A small part of her hoped that her lack of magic was just a lie. She would have taken telepathy as something to show her father. She closed her eyes and fought back tears. When she calmed herself, she opened her eyes and said, "What happened to Stubbornness, that frog creature? Did you destroy it?"

Ruben sighed and frowned. "No, I can feel him in my head. He is a difficult thought to handle. He fights. He argues. He threatens."

"But, it will fade, right?"

Ruben shook his head. "No, not for me, not for a while. Stubbornness is a part of me. If I keep him separate, as Damagar did, the rest of my mind will fracture into a similar arrangement of personalities. If I accept him, he will merge into my thoughts, but I will retain a single consciousness."

"And it only happens when you yell?"

The voman pushed his rock away. "No, projecting is a reflex, like raising my volume. The more I project, the more it cracks. It will seal up over time, but if I crack it too often, the seal may shatter forever."

He sighed. "And many minds will die."

"Well," said Kanéko, "I guess we need to keep you silent, huh?"

Maris came running back with the ball. She held it out to Kanéko. "Please?"

Kanéko grabbed the ball and stood up. She spun around and threw it as hard as she could. It sailed over the grass and Maris chased after it. Kanéko saw the wind building up behind her as she sprinted, leaving a wide "V" in the grasses. She promised herself she would teach Maris at least something about magic as soon as they had a chance.

Sighing, she turned back to Ruben. "Teach me."

He looked surprised. "Instruct you in what field of study?"

"Teach me telepathy. Teach me to keep Damagar and you out of my head."

"You cannot. You do not have the ability to project."

"Look, I read the books. I know there are techniques I can learn to keep Damagar out. I also know there are things I can learn to make it easier to communicate with you. There is something beyond you pulling up memories. It takes too long and if you have another seizure, I need to know what is going on."

"Yes, but it requires working together. We have to share experiences to make—"

"Then teach me with what we've already done. You are teaching Maris Miwāfu so you can teach me telepathy."

Ruben stared at her with confusion, but she could see a bit of excitement in his gaze. "Why?"

"I'm tired of running. Everything is chasing me. There are ones I want to find me and others I don't. I can't do much about them, besides stay off the road, but if I can keep Damagar out of my head, maybe I can help you." Kanéko held out her hand, palm up. "Look, we have to help each other, otherwise we'll never get home."

He smiled and stood up to take her hand. She felt a tickling in the back of her mind as he smiled. "Deal."

Maris crashed back into the area around the fire, panting happily and her tail wagging. "Home? We're going home?"

Kanéko nodded confidently, feeling a bit more in control of her life. "Yes, we're going home."

---- **Chapter 28** ----

Life's Lessons

Experience is the best of instructors.

—Proverb

The rabbit scrambled over a fallen log, trying to reach a pile of greens heaped in the nook. Rain drizzled down, soaking the grass and leaves as a light breeze drifted through the trunks of trees.

Kanéko held her breath and pulled back the bow string. It cut into her fingers. Rain ran down her face. More water dripped from the arrow as she aimed for the rabbit.

Next to her, Maris crouched behind a trunk, her tail rocking back and forth as she wiggled her body. She kept her hands clamped over her mouth as if it could stop the whines escaping her throat. She looked excited despite her best attempts to remain still.

Kanéko hissed at her. "Maris, calm down."

The rabbit's ears perked up. It stood up on its back legs, and Kanéko swore under her breath.

The rabbit shot off in the opposite direction.

Kanéko swore even louder in Miwāfu and stepped away from the tree. The bowstring twanged as she launched the arrow at the rabbit. Knowing she missed, Kanéko fired a second. The two shafts whistled through the air. The first snapped on a rock, but the second caught the rabbit right in the back of the head, killing it instantly.

She stared in shock, and then screamed out with triumph. "I did it! Only a day with this bow and I did it!"

Maris cheered, hugging Kanéko before racing after the animal. Her tail bounced as she bounded over the stump and scooped up the kill.

Kanéko followed, beaming happily. She stopped and picked up the ruined arrow, sighing as she snapped the arrowhead off the ruined shaft and jammed the head into a loop of the fabric over the back of her hand.

Maris handed her the second arrow. "Here you go. Unless you want me to do it?"

"Do you know how to skin it?"

The dalpre nodded. "The womenfolk cook for the mill all the time."

"I've never done that, you go ahead."

Returning to the camp, Maris sat down heavily next to their fire. She reached over into Ruben's belt and pulled out his knife.

With a look of disgust, Ruben got up and walked away.

Kanéko motioned for him to follow. She led him to a spot a chain's distance from the fire and plopped down. "Now, teach me."

Ruben sat down in front of her. He pointed to his eyes and stared into Kanéko's. "Telepathy is about memories and concepts. To communicate, you bring up a shared memory. For example, say I want to transmit the idea of looking over a cliff, I will pull up these..."

In Kanéko's mind, she found herself recalling the cliff where Maris fell over as she was peering over the side. The memories were bright and sharp.

Ruben continued. "Now, you can read. So I can also bring up letters or words."

As he spoke, the words he used also appeared in Kanéko's head, but it took her more effort to focus on them. It felt like an obscure thought, one that she struggled with.

The vomen nodded. "You'll notice it is harder. Abstract ideas will always be more difficult to imagine than something personally experienced. So, what we do is we build up a set of images and memories that we both know to make it easier. The more we share experiences, the more I can project..."

A series of images, of Kanéko climbing the cliff, the fight in the inn where Kanéko dodged the men attacking her, and a picture of Damagar's eyes combined together into «climb the rock to avoid Damagar.»

Kanéko grew elated as she saw how he pieced it together, somehow combining parts of her memories and splicing them together. "How do I, um, respond?"

"The same way. Picture something in your head, and I will read it. You can't project, but if I am scanning your surface thoughts, I can pick up the visualization."

Kanéko thought for a moment before she brought up images of Boar Hunt Inn, their shared wagon ride, and the picture of Lurkuklan Tower. She found herself struggling with the tower, as if she couldn't remember the idea, and switched it to the Rock River village, which came clearly.

Ruben grinned, "Riding a wagon from the inn to the town?"

"Yes, but I tried the Lurkuklan Tower first."

"I've never been there, so I cannot remember it."

"Oh, that makes sense. But, I remembered things I've never seen when Damagar was in my head."

"Powerful telepaths project the needed memories. It is one of the most powerful magical and psychic beings in the world." His voice trailed off and he looked to the west.

Kanéko sat there, watching the sadness on his face. She reached out and rested one hand on top of his.

Ruben looked back with his eyes glittering.

Kanéko favored him with a smile. "Don't worry, I don't know what I can do, but you can trust me to help, however I can."

He smiled. *"Thank you, Great Kosobyo Kanéko."* Ruben had a flat, featureless accent, as if he learned from books.

Kanéko felt her heart fluttering. She never heard anyone speak in terms of respect for her, and she didn't know what to say.

Maris plopped down between them. "Hi!" She set a piece of bark on Kanéko's lap. The cooked remains of a rabbit steamed in the rain. Roasted tubers and some of the remaining cheese completed the meal.

Rain splattered her face, and she looked beyond Maris with surprise. The storm clouds that were on the horizon were now above her. Underneath her, a puddle of mud soaked her rear, despite the ground being dry when she sat down.

"Time is meaningless while learning."

Kanéko shook her head and sighed ruefully. "I'm used to it. I would lose a day trying to figure out a gear. Papa says I'm obsessed."

True to her word, Maris did know how to cook. The rabbit tasted like ambrosia, and Kanéko found herself polishing off her portion almost as fast as Maris. "Thank you, Maris, I don't think I ever ate so well."

The dalpre beamed. She licked her fingers and panted happily.

Kanéko nodded with her own pleasure. "I think I'll actually sleep well tonight."

Maris gestured to Ruben, who ate his own vegetables slowly, "Are you going to think at him again?"

Kanéko shook her head. "No, actually, I need to teach you something."

Maris's ears perked up. "Me?"

"Yes. I don't exactly know what I'm doing, but you need to have some basic training on your magic."

"You mean like when you stamped on my foot? And I got angry and hit people? That was scary and cool and fun, and it hurt." She paused. "And I like you again."

"Well," Kanéko blushed, "that was, um, let's say advanced training. My father used to tell me stories of how his master first taught him combat magic. What I did was close to those stories, as I remembered them."

"And that is how you learn magic?"

Kanéko giggled. "You are supposed to learn by moving a feather around. Then, learn how to pick up paper. You move to heavier and heavier items until anything you can pick up with your hands, you can do with magic. Once you do that for a few years, and then you learn how to do combat magic."

"But, it was easy to hit people."

Ruben spoke up. "Because you are a violent dalpre who strikes first and kicks second."

Maris glared at the teenage boy, and Kanéko choked on her laughter.

Maris pouted. "And I don't like you."

Kanéko reached over and grabbed Maris's tail to get her attention.

Maris tugged her tail free but turned around to put her back to Ruben. "And you'll teach me?"

"Yes, I will. We might have to skip a few lessons if we get into any fights. But, let's start with the basics: make some wind."

Maris tugged on her dress. "How? Besides eating a lot of cabbage?"

Kanéko stared in shock.

The dalpre smirked. "How?"

"Remember what it felt like when you were looking for the Jonahas flower? You sniffed in all directions? Could you do that again but think about the wind coming from the north."

Maris frowned, but she closed her eyes. A breeze rose up, tinged with ozone, and drifted through the camp from the south. It tugged at Kanéko's hair and fluttered Maris's skirt.

Ruben smirked. "The other north."

Maris cracked open one eye to glare at him. Then the wind rotated around to come from the north, blowing past Kanéko and Maris. It increased as it focused on Ruben. Dust and dirt kicked up, peppering Ruben. After a second, it died down.

Ruben casually plucked a leaf from his hair and tossed it aside.

Smiling, Kanéko pictured the lessons from her own books as she spoke encouragingly. "Okay, now slowly turn it to the right..."

A moment later, Ruben helpfully added, "... your other right."

Chapter 29

Change of Clothes

*The play continues even when you are not on stage. Your secrets may be
laid bare when you have no chance to distract or speak for yourself.*
— *The Invisible Blade* (Act 2, Scene 4)

Kanéko woke with Damagar's and Ruben's thoughts still in
her mind. They echoed repeatedly through her dreams, one
after the other, but never at the same time. They were quiet-
ing, but not fast enough to stave off a pulsating headache
that throbbed in the back of her head.

It was morning, too early for the sun to be up and too
late to pretend it was still night. She stared at the cloudy
sky and listened to the rain splashing on the ground next to
her. Their shelter, a makeshift canopy crafted from a few
trees, large leaves, and tied with one of Cobin's trousers,
had kept them mostly dry through the night, but the humidity had plastered her clothes to her body.

Kanéko yawned. She tried rolling over, but her bladder
and the moisture made it impossible to get comfortable
and sleep again. With a groan, she pushed herself up into a
sitting position.

The other two were still sleeping, wrapped around each other with Ruben's head buried between Maris's breasts. She had completely curled around his smaller body, her tail thumping lightly on his back.

Amused, Kanéko crawled out of the canopy and hurried down an animal path to relieve herself. She struggled with her stolen clothes—Cobin was large, and there was too much fabric in the way. She made it in time, but the effort to redress herself was just as difficult.

She took her time to return to their shelter. The water against her face felt good and helped clear the echoing thoughts from her head. By the time she returned, the rain had soaked into her clothes and bore down on her like fishing weights.

Kanéko stood near the canopy, water streaming down her face. She looked at her stained, ripped outfit and then to the bag she had stolen. Cobin was much larger than her, none of his clothes would fit unless she used his knife to cut them down. Reaching in, she grabbed the bag and walked a distance away to a relatively dry spot so she could adjust her clothes in privacy.

It took her a while to finish. She had never done it before, and her alterations were ragged. She would have been embarrassed to be seen in them, but she doubted that either Maris or Ruben would care if she had a ragged hem. Standing up, she dressed in her outfit and inspected the results.

His shirt still hung off her shoulders, the thin strip of fabric barely holding on after she hacked off the sleeves. It was the only way to remove the black band that identified Cobin as part of the mercenary group. She also cut the bottom of the shirt but accidentally cut too high and her outfit exposed her darker skin and her belly button. She considered trying again but she didn't have many other shirts to experiment with.

She had better luck with his pants, cutting the bottoms off them and cinching them with a rope. There was enough material to redo the bandages around her feet and give herself more padding for the long walk ahead.

Kanéko wished she had some color to add to the outfit but the only bright cloth in the bag was his underwear which she refused to touch. She didn't want to get rid of it either, just in case it became useful. She gathered up the larger remains of her attempts at alteration and jammed them back into the bag.

Her fingers brushed against the leather wallet inside the pack. She had forgotten about it. Pulling it out, she returned to the camp and sat underneath the shelter to avoid the rain. She glanced over to Ruben and Maris and then smirked; Maris was licking his ear in her sleep. Her tail and one leg twitched with her dreams. Kanéko shook her head with amusement and returned her attention to the wallet.

Unwrapping the string that held it together, she pulled it open. Papers of all colors greeted her. She found a thick, folded sheet and teased it out. Pulling it open, she flipped it over and read her own wanted poster. Fear rose inside her and she stared at a likeness of herself, except for a few streaks where water had soaked the image.

Kanéko still didn't know why they were trying to kidnap her. The power didn't give any information besides to take her to the *Burning Cloud Queen* for the reward.

Clenching her jaw, she flipped it over and spotted a sketched map on the back. With a grin, she tilted to get more light and inspected it. The Boar Hunt Inn had been hastily drawn, yet the sketch showed a surprising amount of details. Various villages and roads were all marked, with people's named written near them. There was distances between the places.

Remembering the trip approaching the inn, she recalled various villages they passed and guessed that mercenaries waited for her at every stopping place for thirty or forty miles in all directions but mostly focusing on the roads heading back to her father's keep.

She memorized as much as she could about the map before she folded it back up. While the poster terrified her, the map would be useful. She pulled out another piece of paper and whispered to herself as she read it. "To my cousin Cobin, how is darling Sinny? Is he taking care of himself? You know that he gets focused on being a captain and not sleeping enough. Please make sure he sleeps at least a little at night. And what about the Queen? Is my airship okay? You are taking care of both of them, right? I hope things are going well with your adventures and I wish I was with you and Sinny every day. Love, Las."

She could only guess that "Sinny" was Sinmak, the captain of the *Burning Cloud Queen*. He was the bastard whose name was written on the wanted poster, the man offering the reward. She pulled a face and wondered who "Las" was and what type of woman would fall for a bastard like Sinmak.

Kanéko carefully set aside the letter and pulled out the next. More letters from Cobin's cousin. Each one was signed "Las" instead of giving a more useful name. She found a card dividing the sections of the wallet and replaced the letters to move into the next section. She pulled the first one and read it. It was a report from Cobin, dry and tedious. It was addressed to Las, which surprised her. She would have thought Cobin would have been more formal, but he signed each report with "Cob" which implied a very familiar relationship. She put the report back and flipped through the remaining pages.

She spotted Pahim's name on one and stopped. Another report from Cobin on hiring Pahim only a few days earlier. It was mostly positive details about how well he handled orders and his willingness to obey even the more tedious commands. Kanéko snorted with disgust. Pahim might follow orders now, but she knew he would stab anyone in the back, if he could.

Below, there was a comment that interested her. "Sinmak plans on keeping Pahim's father's death a secret. Sooner or later, Pahim will find out that Sinmak killed his father. I mean, it was for a good cause since he was a spy, and Sinmak had to test that new sword he picked up in Panzir. Do you have suggestions to manage Pahim? You know how Sinmak is with his new toys."

Kanéko's anger for Pahim faded slightly as she read about Pahim's father. She crumpled the report, not wanting to ever forgive Pahim.

The rest of the reports were dry, just detailing Cobin's activities, so she skipped to the next section. To her surprise, it wasn't Lorban lettering that she read but correspondence in Miwāfu.

Her curiosity piqued, she shifted position and struggled through the sweeping letters and unusual symbols. She could read them; she just had to mouth out each word before she could understand it.

With every whispered word, her curiosity grew. They were letters from various members of the Tofugéru clan. Kanéko had never heard of them but that didn't surprise her.

If you are to encounter a poronēso named Waryoni Garèo, we would pay 500,000 pyābi for the unnamed blade that ended his life.

Kanéko sat up straight and read the sentence again. She knew *pyābi* was the currency of the desert but couldn't imagine how the brusque desert man could have done anything that would have justified that much.

The terms of his murder were also specific. She stared at the weapon at her leg and wondered why it was important that it had no name.

"Kan?" Kanéko jumped at Maris's voice. "What's that word?" Maris's breast pressed against Kanéko's shoulder as she pointed down at the letter.

Kanéko peered at it. "*Poronēso*? It means kin-killer. Someone who killed their own clan members. One of the worst of all crimes in the desert."

"But, it says Garèo is a *poronēso*. Did he kill his mommy and daddy?"

Kanéko worried her lip, realizing that Garèo's past was far darker than she could have ever imagined. "I don't know, Maris. If my mother knew, then she wouldn't have let him live. I remembered her telling stories about how killing your own clan was blasphemy before of all the spirits, how the desert herself demanded their death."

"And that word," Maris pointed further down, "that's the word for horse king, right? *Heru tonùfi*? It says he's one of them. But, Garèo isn't a horse king. Is he?"

Kanéko scanned down the page. She stopped on a familiar name and read the sentence. "No, they want the horse king's mount... Ojinkomàsu?"

A cold shiver ran down Kanéko's spine.

"That's Garèo's horse, right? He comes by the school some days. And Garèo always chases him off. And he likes carrots and sugar. And having his tail brushed."

"No," Kanéko said, her voice trailing off as she continued to read, "Ojinkomàsu is... it says here that Ojinkomàsu is Garèo's son's. Oh sun, I think Garèo's son was the horse king."

"What is a horse king?"

"Um, they are, well... I'm not entirely sure. According to what I was told, Mifúno, that's the desert, and the sun, Ta-chìra, bless the greatest of riders with the ability to talk to horses and with a divine companion, a horse born from the desert winds and rays of the sun."

Maris cocked her head and asked, "He can think to horses? Like Ruben?"

"I think so, but there are no *heru tonùfi* in the Waryōni clan. Garèo told me that when I was learning. But according to this..." She held up the page and pointed near the bottom. "Ojinkomàsu is one of the sun's horses, and Garèo's son is a horse king."

"And you know what? I'm going to ask him when we get home," announced Maris.

Kanéko looked up at the dalpre. "I'm not sure that is a good idea. Being a horse king, or even the father of one, would be a point of pride. But, he never talked about it. He doesn't talk about his family at all. He has to have a reason, right?"

"I guess..." She paused. "And I'm going to ask him anyways."

Kanéko didn't respond. She folded the paper and placed it back in the wallet. Closing it, she replaced the tie. A disturbed feeling bothered her as she flipped it over in her hand, and then jammed it into the pack.

"Come on, let's hunt some breakfast."

Chapter 30

Blindspot

Those who survived the flight from Vo created a small island of shared memories to stave off the approaching insanity.
—Balam Jidir, *The Escape From Vo*

Noon came, and Kanéko was lost in thought as she considered Cobin's letters and the revelation that Garèo was far more monstrous that she could ever imagine. But she couldn't picture the crass, self-centered man as a murderer, despite the contents of the letters. Her mother would have never let Garèo teach her if he killed his family.

She trudged behind Ruben as they followed an animal trail along the rolling hills. To the south, she could see the rocky hill curving out of sight.

Ruben walked in front of her, holding the map Kanéko found. He added information of his own, drawing in details from his memory. Hours of practicing telepathy with him had given her better insight into his thoughts. When he talked to her, she could tell the difference between the *votim's* stark recollections versus his own experiences. His personal experiences projected with a vibrancy so intense she almost imagined being there herself, the others felt dull and sterile. It reminded her of learning something from a book.

A thud drew her attention from Ruben to the side of the trail. Panting heavily, Maris bounded from one rock to another. Each leap carried her forward a chain. As she blasted by, the whirlwind assisting her jump battered Ruben and Kanéko, shoving them back. She landed on a tree branch, windmilling her arms until she regained her balance. The dalpre crouched down on the branch, her tail wagging, and then jumped across the trail to another tree.

Kanéko wiped the dust from her face and called out to Maris. "Don't cross the path! Stick to one side."

Maris stopped and spun around. She lost her balance. Falling off the limb, she plummeted to the ground. Kanéko covered her face as an explosion of air caught Maris inches from the ground, blasting dust and splinters in all direction. Maris's rear hit the ground a moment later.

"Owwie."

Kanéko uncovered her face. "Want to stop?"

Maris scrambled to her feet. She shook her head and jumped up. The wind blew up but died quickly, and Maris fell to the ground. This time, she landed on her feet. Whimpering, she pouted. "I got tired again."

Kanéko held out her hand for her. "Take a break. You need to regain your strength."

Maris skipped over to the trail. She took Kanéko's hand and trailed next to her. "I lasted longer this time, didn't I?"

Kanéko smiled warmly. "You did, but you still have a long way before you can fly again."

"But, I flew before. Why is it so hard now?"

"You have to build up your reserves. When you flew, days ago, you were unskilled, and you had no control. You used everything you had and drained yourself. It could be days, weeks, even months before you recover."

"But, I carried you. It was so easy." Maris pouted.

Ruben spoke up, "Fear is an excellent motivator."

"But, if I could fly us, we could go home sooner, right?"

Kanéko felt a pang in her chest. She smiled but didn't feel it. "Yes, which is why you are going to practice. If you get that strong, you can fly us the rest of the way."

Maris's tail began to wag happily. "Thank you."

"For what?" Kanéko asked.

"For teaching me. And not stepping on my foot again. And not being mean."

Kanéko stopped and turned to look at Maris. "I'm sorry I was a spoiled brat. It wasn't fair of me."

Maris's openness was rubbing off on her.

The dalpre said something, but Kanéko spotted movement over the dalpre's shoulder. She stepped to the side and peered at the plains behind her. A line of force rushed toward them. It was curved like the edge of a ripple spreading out in a pond. Her eyes sought the center, following the curve where it radiated from a single point, a dark blot far in the distance. She thought she saw red flickering in the darkness.

She felt an itch growing in the back of her mind. It was the familiar touch of a telepath, but it wasn't Ruben trying to connect to her. Instead, it felt like a dread gathering in her stomach. "*Sands!* It's Damagar!"

Ruben spun on his heels. His eyes were wide and sweat prickled his brow. He started to shake, looking around for a moment before he crouched on the ground and closed his eyes. He whispered tensely, "My earlier statement was incorrect. My defenses against Damagar will not be sufficient this time."

Kanéko dug into the wrappings on her hand and dug out the Jonahas root. She shoved one into Maris's hands and hurried to Ruben. "Take that and hold him. He's going to have another seizure."

Maris took the root and shoved it into her mouth. She stumbled forward to grab Ruben.

Turning around, Kanéko chewed on a bit of the root she had kept. As she did, she looked at the growing ripple of power. It moved faster as it drew closer and she felt her stomach clench with anticipation. Her eyes scanned along the grasses ahead of the wave, looking for something that would miraculously save them from Damagar. She knew that nothing would defend her, but she hated not being able to do anything.

She spotted a break in the rushing wave of invisible force. It was a widening gap in the ripple of power. Curious, Kanéko saw it spreading apart like the spokes of a gear. Her eyes trailed back but she couldn't see past the wall of wind that rushed toward them.

Then, the wave was upon her.

She brought up images of her designs, working through the mechanics when it hit her. She pictured them forming a shield—a wall of gears, pistons, and boilers. The force of Damagar's thoughts slammed into her chest, staggering her physically, but she could feel his questing probe crashing on her mental shield. Mental claws reached over her, but Kanéko brought up more images, combining the gears together and building it in her head with obsessive focus.

For a moment, she thought Damagar would still break through, but then the haze of the Jonahas root draped over her thoughts and the pressure subsided.

Kanéko found herself thinking about the pond they slept near two nights before. However, she could also picture Damagar standing in the pond, trying to track them down. She wasn't surprised when the image of the giant toad came through. It looked at her through her shield of gears. Dozens of personalities, all using the same crimson eyes, regarded her and something—the name Observation drifted through Kanéko's head—reached through the shield, pulling up memories of the land around her. No matter how hard Kanéko tried to obscure her thoughts with designs, she felt Damagar's Observation forcing her to recall the memories of her location: the path she had taken, the position of the sun, and even the route that they planned on taking.

The thoughts cut off sharply, but Damagar left Kanéko the impression he was coming for them.

She swore violently in Miwāfu and raced back to Maris and Ruben.

Maris held Ruben as the smaller teenager shook with a seizure. Tears ran down Maris's cheeks as she clutched Ruben tightly.

"Maris, are you all right?"

"I hate Damagar," came the whimper. "Hate, hate, hate it."

"Yes, but it's coming, and we have to run."

Maris unwrapped herself from around Ruben, who foamed at the mouth and shook violently. She looked up at Kanéko, refusing to let go of the Voman. "Where do we go?"

"I, um," Kanéko stood up and peered at the gap in the force. The force of Damagar's thoughts affected the world, but there was a wedge of untouched grasses leaning back toward a copse of trees a mile away. She pointed to the trees where the triangle converged. "There."

"What's there?"

"I don't know. If there is something that stopped its scan, there might be something that can shield us."

"Are you sure?"

"No, but I don't see another option right now. Damagar's wanted to know exactly where we were and I think he's coming for Ruben." She helped Maris scoop up Ruben and they raced for the spot she hoped would save her.

It felt like forever before they reached it. The last few chains were soaked by a squall of warm rain. By the time they crawled up the deceptively tall hill, both Kanéko and Maris panted for breath and were dripping wet. Kanéko's side ached and her legs trembled. Without pausing, they dove into the trees and out of sight of the plains.

"Kan? What are we looking for?"

Kan pushed the branches from her face. "I don't know. Something!"

"I can't—"

"Then just hold Ruben. I'll look for it!"

"What are you looking for?"

Kanéko's voice reached a high-pitched scream, "I don't know, damn it! Something! Anything!"

Crashing through the underbrush, Kanéko looked at every shadow and crevice, trying to find something that would stop Damagar's thoughts. The trees towered over her and rain dripped from the leaves, but she didn't see anything besides plants and rocks.

Frantic, she ripped out plants, scattering dirt everywhere. She pushed at the trees and dug into the ground with her feet, and then her hands. She had to find it, she had to protect them all from the creature.

"Kan? I see Damagar coming!"

The teenager's head snapped up, her copper hair flying across her vision. She stared through the trees at the dark shape hopping across the plains. The ground shook with each impact, and Kanéko felt her heart pounding painfully in her chest.

Swearing, she tore at the ground, flinging clods of dirt and rock in all directions. When she came up to a wind-blasted part of the trees, she stopped. Whatever prevented the wave of power had also protected a line in the trees. Standing up, she raced around a curve. At the far end, she smiled. Whatever it was, it should be near the center.

She grabbed rocks and flung them with all her might to where the curve would have been centered. It only took a few throws before one of the rocks rang out against something metallic.

Kanéko froze, listening to an unnatural noise fade. She spun around, not sure what set it off. She felt the ground shaking from the incoming behemoth. Picking up a handful of rocks, Kanéko systematically started throwing rocks as she approached.

One hit Maris's shoulder.

"Ow!" came the whimpering cry.

Kanéko ignored her as she kept throwing. Rocks bounced off the trunks of trees and scattered along the ground. She threw them faster, tossing handfuls of pebbles in a cloud and strained to hear anything ringing out. When she heard the pebbles hit metal, Kanéko stopped and tossed more rocks in the direction of the noise, and then sprinted toward it. She found the source after a few more tosses, a stump that looked too straight to be natural. She used rocks to scrape away lichen and revealed silvered metal beneath.

Kanéko raced around it, looking for some entrance or opening. She called out to Maris. "Come here, now!"

When Maris came rushing up, clutching Ruben to her chest, Kanéko pointed to the pipe. "Shove air in there!"

"Where?"

"Air! Now!"

Maris hastily dropped Ruben and ran over to the opening. She closed her eyes, no doubt working with the lessons Kanéko had taught her. Wind rose up around her, forming a vortex in her palm.

Kanéko wanted to scream at her to move faster, but she focused on crawling in a circle, digging at the ground. She felt her nails splinter on the ground, but desperation drove her to dig faster.

Wind howled and Kanéko looked up to see Maris feeding the tail end of a tornado into the pipe. It disappeared inside with a painful screaming noise. Underneath Kanéko's feet, the ground buckled. She spun around until she saw plumes of dust rising up from a scree of gravel.

"We need to dig there!" Kanéko rushed over. She dropped to her knees and scooped the gravel away as fast as she could. Her hands ached and her body trembled, but the fear of Damagar kept her digging.

Maris dragged Ruben down a few feet away, his tiny form shaking and jerking, before she joined Kanéko. As the dalpre dug her hands into the sharp rocks, a sudden wind slammed into Kanéko. It plucked the smaller rocks away from the scree and blew a cloud of rock dust high into the air and away from them.

Kanéko opened her mouth to order Maris to stop, and then closed it with a snap when she realized the wind blew away the dust and smaller rocks. She returned to digging through the gravel, trying to find whatever opening Maris's tornado had found. As the wind whipped past her, her nails scraped on something solid. "Here!"

Both girls dug into the gravel and the wind focused into a visible stream that blasted away at the rocks until they exposed a metal door set with a crystal mosaic.

Feeling the ground shake from Damagar's impact, Kanéko didn't have the time to look at the picture. She grabbed the handle on the door, planted one foot on the side, and hauled up with all her strength. The door creaked open and revealed a pitch black tunnel. It was short, only four feet high, but the edges were smoothed as if it was shaped with water or, Kanéko hoped, something magical.

"Maris, get Ruben!"

"Got him," barked Maris as the wind died down. She ran over to Ruben, picked him up and held him against her chest, before she dove into the darkness.

Kanéko followed, closing the door behind her and praying it would open up from the inside. As the heavy door slammed shut, the darkness swallowed them.

"Kan?"

Kanéko hissed sharply, "Quiet!"

The ground shook as Damagar landed close by. The ground buckled by its landing. A moment later, another impact sent dust streaming down on Kanéko's face. She clapped her hand over her mouth and sneezed into it.

Maris let out a high-pitched whine.

Her heart pounding in her chest, Kanéko tried to hold still. Something scraped the ground and she heard trunks cracking. The dull thump of timbers hitting the ground shook through the earth. She reached out in the darkness, and her fingers found a smooth stone wall. Trembling, she held her breath as more trees hit the ground.

A light cut through the darkness. Kanéko snapped her head around and looked at the light. Ruben's eyes glowed indigo as he stared out into nothing.

Maris gasped, "K-Kan?"

Kanéko turned to gape at Ruben. She whispered in a broken voice. "I-I see his eyes. I don't think Damgar can see it from outside—"

"But," interrupted Maris with a whisper. She pointed behind Kanéko. "What is that?" that?"

Kanéko followed the gesture with her eyes. They were in a short tunnel slightly over a rod in length. At the far end was another short door, sized for someone Ruben's height, but without the intricate crystal mosaic of the outer door leading into the tunnel.

The door glowed with another light. As she watched, the colors swam over the surface in blues, greens, and yellows. They rippled like the surface of a pond during a light breeze. Carved into the door were straight lines marked with a variety of slashes and crosses. They appeared to have some significance but Kanéko had no way of discerning them.

"It's... glowing," Kanéko said.

"I like Rub's glow more."

The blobs of color gathered together. Kanéko could make out shadows forming between the steady light from the door and the glow from Ruben's eyes. It appeared as if the door was forming droplets that reached out for the unconscious teenager.

Not trusting her own vision, Kanéko held her breath and reached out for the glowing door. The light painted on her palm made it easier to see that there were droplets forming on the surface. If it was a dripping roof, it would have been understandable, but the door was vertical and the droplets were stretching out toward Ruben.

The largest blob quivered and then broke free. It silently sailed away from the door and straight for Ruben.

Kanéko had seen the same effect before, in Damagar's memories when Ruben was nothing but a brilliant fissure and Stubbornness had been consumed. The energy in the door had to be related to psychic or telepathy and it was being consumed by Ruben's presence. She held out her hand but the energy passed through her palm with only a tingle. "Maris!"

Maris yanked him out of the way. "Mine!" she growled.

The droplet missed Ruben and splashed on the outer door of the chamber. It dissipated with the smell of burnt wood.

Whimpering, Maris whispered, "Is this Damagar?"

Kanéko crawled to her knees, the highest she could get in the tunnel. "N-No, I don't think so. Damagar is... loud, and he has red eyes."

She watched as another droplet fling from the door and raced toward her. She looked around for something to block it, but when she found none, she tried to catch it again.

It flew through her hand, leaving only a tingle.

Maris swung Ruben around again, his head hitting the side of the wall with a dull thump.

Kanéko snapped. "Be careful!"

Maris whined and clutched Ruben to her breasts. "I'm sorry! I'm sorry! Don't hate me, Rub!"

The energy bulged out and a dozen droplets of energy streamed down the tunnel. Kanéko stood in front of it, knowing it was a useless gesture by still hoping she could stop them. They splattered against her face and chest with the tiny prick of something passing through her, but she couldn't stop them.

Kanéko tasted burnt wood in her mouth. Then she was aware of an itch in her mind. It felt like when Ruben taught her telepathy, but less focused. Seeing more droplets heading toward her, Kanéko opened her mind and tried to project her mental shield.

To her surprise, the colored energy streaming through her began to peel around her. She caught a sense of personality, of a sentient mind, along her shields. A name seeped past her gears, Lopidir, but no thoughts were thrust into her mind or burned into her consciousness.

"What is this?" whined Maris.

"I-I don't know." Kanéko worried her lip. She decided to try relaxing her makeshift shields to get more information. "Something related to his telepathy... let me..."

Beyond her wall of gears and pistons, she could barely sense the howling void that Damgar had seen. Ruben's mind had been awakened and the blue fissure sucked everything in. Lopidir was just the next victim to the void.

The connection between Kanéko and the spirit snapped. Nausea slammed into her, and she slumped forward. Before she could stop it, her stomach heaved, and she felt acid burning her throat. Swallowing hard, she looked up to see more of the energy being pulled off the wall. It streamed down into Ruben and sank into his body.

"Kan... Kan, I can't avoid it. And I hurt Ruben."

Kanéko wiped her mouth and leaned back on the side of the tunnel. The energy had turned into a river as it poured into Ruben. Kanéko knew that the vomen was absorbing and destroying it, just as Damagar said he would. Sadness rocked her and she turned away. "L-Let it happen, Mar."

"Kan?"

"Ruben woke something and... and... we can't stop it."

A whine. "Is he going to be all right?"

Kanéko thought back to how Stubbornness had been swallowed by the fissure. If Damagar managed to rip open the outer door, Ruben would be a danger to the beast. In his state, he may be able to surprise and tear apart Damagar before the titan knew what would happen.

The only problem was the new spirit, Lopidir. She didn't know anything about it other than it had come from the door and was being consumed by Ruben's storm.

Fear one out. She sighed as she struggled with the answer. Finally, she forced herself to say "Yes."

When Maris relaxed, Kanéko felt guilty. She closed her eyes and let the tears flow. She wanted to swear, but she knew Maris would hear her no matter how quietly she muttered. Whatever Lopidir was, it would be destroyed before anyone would know.

She wasn't sure if she could face it, but the stream of light flowing from the door and into Ruben began to wane. Seconds later, the last droplet peeled off the now inert door and sailed through the air to splash against Ruben. It flickered once and then disappeared.

Ruben closed his eyes, the azure light fading with his closing eyelids.

Almost instantly, the tight quarters of their shelter grew dark.

Kanéko realized that she could feel the thump of Damagar, but it was faint and fading with every impact on the ground.

"Kan? I think Damagar is leaving. And Rub stopped shaking."

Another sigh of relief. Kanéko reached out for Maris and hugged her tightly. "I hate this trip."

Ruben's whisper filled the darkness. "I do not know about you, but I find the seizures to be quite pleasurable."

His sarcasm caused Kanéko to smile.

Maris snapped out. "They aren't fun, Rub!"

"Quiet," hissed Kanéko.

The three teenagers said nothing for a long moment.

Maris broke the silence with a soft whimper. "Where are we?"

Ruben rubbed his head. "In a *kotim*, a redoubt of Vomen who fled the Isle of Vo. It has food and water and shelter."

"How do you know?" asked Kanéko.

"I can feel it. Here, let me…"

A soft, green glow filled the tunnel. Kanéko looked directly at the door, expecting to see the rippling light on the surface again, but the shine came from crystals embedded around the door.

Maris asked, "Can we open that?"

"Probably…?" Ruben didn't sound sure.

Kanéko crawled past Ruben and reached the door. She held her hand over the surface for a moment, and then fumbled around for a handle. "How do I open it?"

"I'm trying, but the mechanisms are not functioning properly. I cannot project the command to open."

Kanéko watched him. "You project into it? How does it work?"

"Affirmative, but there is a counterweight that is jammed. Up to your right."

Kanéko crawled to her knees, the tunnel brushed the top of her head. She fumbled in the dim light until she felt a few ruptured pipes in the junction of the wall and the door.

"Can you make the light brighter?"

"No, this is the maximum illumination possible."

Kanéko ignored the rusted edges of the opening and stuck her fingers in the pipe. She felt around, trying to find the jam. When she couldn't, she gave a disgusted sigh. "Damn it! I can't reach it."

Ruben groaned and sat up. "It's about a foot above your hand. I cannot tell you how to release the jam."

Kanéko looked up and a smile crossed her face. "Can you describe it?"

"Yes. It is a pair of circular discs on a rode. The sand holds it down. When I activate the mechanism, a repulsion between the two discs cause them to rotate and line up a hole that allows the sand to pour through which releases the lock."

Kanéko tried to picture it. "Do you know how it works?"

"No, I just know what it is."

"Show me?"

"You may not have the knowledge."

Kanéko gave him a grim smile and held out her hand. "It's a machine. I can figure it out."

Ruben pressed his palm into hers. There was the familiar feeling of their minds touching. Kanéko looked for the remains of the spirit that had touched her thoughts, Lopidir, but she felt Ruben block her with a wave of embarrassment and humiliation.

Unwilling to press, Kanéko returned her attention to the tunnel. In her mind, she could picture it in incredible detail, from every whorl of stone, to how the crystals were placed in the door. She could see the reason for the slash marks and lines, a language, but she could find no shared meaning to understand it. She could, however, picture the door correctly. She brought up the image of the tube leading to the mechanism, but when she tried to picture it from the inside, the images faded.

«I'm sorry, Kanéko. This is as much as I can show you.»

Kanéko shook her head. She closed her eyes and tried to imagine it again. Like the tower before, the images refuse to form in her head. She tried different shapes and mechanics. Her mind spun as she flashed through the various gears, joints, and devices that she saw in *Emerging Wizardy*. Months of fantasizing over pictures of machines. She felt like she was flipping through the papers while admiring the pictures. Then, one image stuck, as if she was looking directly at it.

Shock and surprise radiated from Ruben. He sent a clear thought, «You are good.»

Elated, Kanéko tried to picture the next part that would logically attach to the first. She didn't have an image to remember but she could guess on its shape. It came in clearly. She continued to picture the image, rolling through the parts as the design came to life in her head. She could imagine how it worked, split it apart and put it back together. It was simple, once she figured it out.

She opened her eyes. "I got it."

Maris jumped with a start. "What!?"

Kanéko giggled at the line of drool that glistened on Maris's chin.

Wiping it, Maris glared back. "You've been holding hands for almost two bells. And I'm bored! And tired."

"No, no," Kanéko held out her hands, "It's all right. I need you now."

Maris's ears flattened on her head. "You do? And what did I do wrong?"

"Nothing. Just come here, please?" Kanéko lead Maris to the corner with the broken mechanism.

Kanéko motioned Maris into the corner. The dalpre crawled into it, reaching up into the hole. After a second, she announced, "I can't feel anything."

"No, close your eyes."

"Kan?"

"Go on, trust me. Close your eyes."

Maris obeyed.

Kanéko spoke softly. "Imagine your finger. I want you to think about reaching up into the pipe, just feeling around."

"I can't—"

"No, Maris, use magic. Use your air magic. Just reach up."

A breeze blew against Kanéko as Maris concentrated. A whistling sound rang out form the ruptured pipe, filling the tunnel with a high-pitched noise.

Kanéko smiled. "Now, reach up until you feel pressure. Just feel around."

"And... I... I feel something."

"Just explore it, try to picture it in your head. It should feel like a circle, right?"

Kanéko glanced to Ruben, who stared curiously back. She returned to whisper encouragingly to Maris. "Now, take a little wind and blow it around the disk. You are following a rod with a little screw, and then it takes an elbow turn."

The wind grew louder in the tiny cave-like opening. Maris frowned and screwed her face in concentration.

"You are doing great, Mar, now around there, I want you to try finding something jamming it. It will be a rock, little pebbles between the edge of a... block and the side."

"I... I can feel something between the circle and the edge. A few, they are big and jammed in tightly. I can't move them."

Kanéko smiled. She knew exactly where she needed Maris to concentrate her powers. "All right. Work on one of them. Just use your magic like you were pushing it aside. Find a direction that it can move and rock it back and forth."

Maris's tail dropped between her legs with concentration. She closed her mouth with the tip of her tongue peeking out from the side of her teeth. She worked at it for a long moment, and then she gasped. "It moved!"

"Great, now push it up until it is free. We need to get it moving again."

"And... I moved it."

"Now, focus on the next..."

It took almost another hour to release the mechanism. Kanéko spoke Maris through every step, using every trick she remembered from her books on the Crystal techniques, assisted by her understanding of the mechanism. But, when they heard the device shifting, she let out a gasp of joy. "By the Divine. Ruben, can you move it now?"

Something changed in the air, and they heard sand filling a canister. Metal scraped on metal, and the door swung open with an ear-piercing squeal.

Maris cheered, grabbing Ruben and Kanéko in a tight hug. Together, they entered. The door screeched as they shut it, but it didn't latch.

The redoubt looked like a cave about two chains in length and a pair of rods in width. Curved shelves lined one side while the other sparkled with crystals that glowed with an inner light. Papers and supplies were scattered everywhere, including a few floating on the surface of a steaming pool. The smell of ozone mixed with the heated humidity, almost choked Kanéko, but it felt safe and quiet.

Kanéko hurried over to the pond and plucked the papers from the surface. She shook the water off, and then looked at the strange lines and cross hatches that covered the surface. She held it out to Ruben who explained them.

"*Volis*, it's our language. It tells me what memories the *kotim* has."

"Oh, that might be useful." She hung it up to dry, "But, what about food?"

"Over here."

Ten minutes later, they found most of the shelter's supplies: travel rations, bottles of water, and clothes sized for Ruben's tiny frame. They also found papers, maps, and books in some of the shelves. More importantly, they found camping and travel supplies on other shelves. It was enough to supplement their supplies for at least a week of traveling.

Kanéko regarded the bounty, and then up to the pipe in the ceiling where sunlight filtered down through the opening. "Do you think we should wait a while, maybe a day or two, just in case Damagar is waiting?"

"An excellent proposal which would also enable Maris to recover energies and us to heal from our flight."

Maris perked up. "And we're staying?"

Kanéko looked over at Ruben who nodded. "Yes."

Maris squealed with joy. She raced to the water while stripping off her dress.

Blushing, Kanéko spun around moments before the dress came flying back to land on Ruben's head. Kanéko's blush grew hotter when Maris landed in the water. "Is she, um, naked?"

Ruben pulled his head from the dress and set it aside. "Privacy is a rather foreign concept at the mill. The high dalpre population density for eight acres means that—"

"Kan! The water's hot! Come on in."

Kanéko didn't dare peek. "I-I can't. It isn't right."

"Come on, it's water and a bath! And you need a bath. And you smell."

Ruben gave her a quizzical look. "Turning down a hot bath?"

"No, I, um, I—" Kanéko stammered, not sure how to explain the blush that burned her cheeks. She peeked over her shoulder at Maris splashing happily in the water. Her eyes were drawn to Maris's naked skin.

The dalpre swam through the surprisingly deep water to a shelf. Her tail jerked back and forth, sending droplets in all directions. The water slid off the dalpre's skin and Kanéko was reminded that Maris looked almost human except for her furry ears and tail. Maris squealed with surprise, "Soap! And I'm going to be clean!"

Kanéko moaned at the thought. She turned back to Ruben, worrying her bottom lip. It wasn't only Maris but Ruben. She had never been naked in front of strangers before, at least not in her later years.

Ruben smirked and handed her the dress. "I shall be in the entry hall. Please inform me when you are dressed once again. Have no fear from the dalpre, she does not bite unless you pull her tail."

Kanéko nodded and watched Ruben walk outside, closing the door behind him. Kanéko, feeling nervous, worked at the buttons of her stolen shirt as she walked toward the heated bath.

Chapter 31

Cabin Fever

Spirits cannot learn or evolve. They are only personifications of tales
and stories, unable to improve beyond the words repeated around fires.
—Tamis Glindour, *Finding the Spirit's Home*

Even after two days of recovery, Kanéko couldn't get clean
enough. She sat in the heated water of the cave, scrubbing
her skin with a rag. The scrapes she acquired from getting
into the redoubt were healing, but no matter how much she
scoured against her skin, she couldn't get rid of the Damagar nightmares, the fear of being chased, or the realization
they could be caught at any moment.

Dropping the cloth in the water, she grabbed some of the
hair conditioner—it was made from the oils of local plants
and stored in air-tight jars. Pouring a measure in her hand,
she reached down for the cloth. It fluttered on the bottom
of the water, moving with the waves of her movement and
the heat rising from the bottom. Kanéko's mind latched on
it and she poked it, ignoring the oil that dripped from her
fingers.

She had an idea. Delving into the water, she swirled the
cloth for a moment, and then used her fingers to hold the

ends, watching it billow out when she dragged it through the depths.

Kanéko recalled the pictures she grew up with. One stood out, a three-masted ship with massive square sails. She wanted to get to the ocean to see those boats and now it gave her an idea of how to get home. Then, she remembered that she didn't have her tools to build a boat. She filed the idea in the back of her head and finished her bath.

She dressed in a fresh set of clothes from Cobin's pack and wrapped cloth around her feet and hands. On the shelf near the door, she picked up the last of her Jonahas root and tucked it into the cloth on the back of her hand. Taking a deep breath, she headed outside.

She found Ruben first, sitting on a rock as he tended their cooking fire. Kanéko held a hand over her eyes to shield from the sun before she sat down heavily next to him.

Ruben whispered without looking up. "Ready to depart?"

"Yes. This is nice, but I'm getting a bit stir crazy."

Ruben pushed fried eggs, strips of rabbit, and some heated rations on a plate and handed the overflowing plate to Kanéko.

Kanéko took the tiny vomen plate, it looked like a saucer to her, and started to eat. "How is Maris doing? She wasn't in the shelter. Still sulking?"

"No," Ruben grinned. "She is being stubborn. She is trying to fling trees and branches around to build up her strength. But she can't carry much more than me. We tried six times to include a pack one-tenth your weight, but she can't handle the additional encumbrance. Maximum distance was fifty feet before critical failure."

A smile formed on Kanéko's lips. "She doesn't give up, does she? Where is she?"

Ruben gestured across the plains. Kanéko followed with her eyes, across the rolling hills covered with grass, to where Maris flew low to the ground, kicking up a plume of dust and grass as the dalpre followed a ridge leading to the north. The girl's dress snapped in the wind like a black cape, fluttering as Maris banked sharply and came into a large loop before reversing her direction and rocketing toward the south.

Behind the dalpre, the air flattened the grasses and left a trail behind her. When Maris rose from the ground, the trail ended but Kanéko could still see loose gravel, dust, and grass following Maris's wake. Maris dove back down and accelerated, moving faster than any horse Kanéko had ever seen, almost as fast as an arrow.

"I never saw an air mage before. I know from the books they can fly, but most air mages never have enough skill to do it that fast or that steadily. Hovering is the best most can do." Kanéko watched Maris banking straight up, rising into the air until she turned into a little dot. "That is part of the wind witch training, how to fly like that."

Kanéko felt Ruben's eyes on her, his mind tickling hers. She glanced over and stared into his blue eyes.

Ruben pressed forward with thoughts of his own and Kanéko let them drift through her consciousness. «Did you know Maris could fly? That night at the Boar Hunt Inn?»

Kanéko opened her mouth, and then decided to answer in kind. «Yes and no. Most mages experience their limits in the first days after manifesting. After that, their mind grows accustomed to the power and gives it focus, but also limits how much energy they can use at once. I couldn't think of anything else, so I was hoping she had the power to burn.»

«You improvised.»

The last word came spelled out since Ruben and she didn't share a common memory. Kanéko pulled up parts of her past, when she struggled to assemble the water screw with Jinmel, her father's blacksmith. She showed the endless attempts to get the water screw designs to work, puzzling out the ratios and rod lengths and moving away from the printed words into things that worked. It only took a moment, but when she finished, she and Ruben shared a new experience of her efforts.

«You are very adaptable, Kanéko. That is a talent even if you see yourself as being unable to use magic.»

Kanéko blushed and turned away, pushing Ruben from her mind with the shame of being mundane compared to Maris's and Ruben's abilities. She resumed eating, not looking at the vomen.

"Kanéko?" She tensed at Ruben's whisper, "I actually... have a favor to ask you."

Surprised, Kanéko peeked at Ruben. He turned to face her, his small arms and legs straining as he slipped off the rock and sat on the ground.

Ruben cleared his throat before he whispered, "The... *votim* and *kotim* don't really give me the ability to understand things. I know things but I can't put them together. They don't fit. I know the technique that Maris is using, though no vomen can use the Crystal Spheres methods. I have no ability to associate the individual skills that consist of an air witch, knight, or smith's abilities."

"It's easy. A knight just—"

"Kanéko Lurkuklan, that isn't it."

She closed her mouth, watching as he worried his hands together. He picked up a twig from the ground and started to shred it with his fingernails.

"When we connected, you thought about Lopidir."

Guilt rose up.

"He wasn't destroyed."

When she thought about it, she wasn't surprised. Ruben did the same with Stubbornness. "You absorbed the spirit, didn't you? He's in your head."

Ruben jumped, and then he chuckled dryly. "As I said, you're rather observant. His will makes him difficult to integrate into my mind, but I have no desire to fragment my personality to accommodate him or Stubborness."

Kanéko gave a hesitant smile, unsure what Ruben wanted.

The vomen tossed the twig into the fire and picked up another. "The problem is... he wants to help. He was guardian spirit of these lands, but the tribe that created and worshiped him has been dead for centuries. This is the first time any spirit I have consumed has responded this way."

"And, he wants to help?" She felt dizzy.

Ruben nodded. "I-I wasn't expecting that. When I absorbed Damagar's Stubbornness, all I felt was rage and anger. He rants at me from the back of my head. Then, he stops talking but I can feel him sulking. But, Lopidir didn't do that. He wants to help like he used too, but I don't know how."

"You know what he is, yes?"

A nod. "The *kotim* remembers him. Vomen would meet with the local spirits and other mental creatures before they moved in. Even with the crystals shielding the redoubt, there is too much risk not to become allies with the local entities. That was a long time ago, before Lopidir lost his tribe and the vomen... perished."

Ruben reached into the fire. Kanéko started to stop him, but the tiny hand didn't even blacken when Ruben picked up a handful of coals. Rolling it in his hand, he looked at Kanéko. "I know he can do this, but I don't know what else."

Kanéko let out a nervous giggle, staring wide-eyed as the coals poured from Ruben's palm. "Um, Ruben, could you take your hand out of the fire. It's kind of, um, nerve-wracking."

He pulled his hand back.

She reached out and took it, feeling heat coming off his tiny palm but no damage, not even a scorch. The only sign she saw was black marks from the ashes. "How did you figure this out?"

"Because I was cooking. It was a common memory, something that he could communicate with. But, we just have that one memory."

"Can't you just, um, spell to him?"

Ruben shook his head. "It doesn't work. He never learned how to read or write. He can bring up things we've seen since I absorbed him, but there isn't enough..." He sighed with frustration, "I can't talk to him without a commonality. I can feel him. I know he wants to help, but I can't figure out how."

Kanéko thought. Her eyes moved back and forth as she mentally walked through the cloudy scene, trying to find some way that she—as a non-telepath—could help. "C-Could you... no. Does he know his legends?"

Ruben frowned at her. "I don't understand."

"He can't write, but spirits are created by their people. Folk tales tell stories about their adventures and the spirits are shaped by those stories. That's how most spirits like these small gods are created, right?"

The vomen nodded slowly. "Affirmative."

"Can he tell you those legends?"

"I... not really."

Kanéko shifted into a different position, setting aside the tiny plate. She nibbled on her lip, and then brightened. "Can he show you what happened in a place? If you ask him?"

Ruben's eyes glazed over for a moment, and then he nodded. "Yes, but like the *kotim*, I have to ask for it." Another frustrated sigh. "He can't volunteer information. And I don't have the right identifiers."

"You said that the *kotim*, no, the *votim*, identifies things that you look at. Can he do the same thing? Say, that hill there," she pointed to a large hill, "does he know it?"

A nod.

"What happened there?"

"I-I can't."

"Fine, was there, um, ever, let's see, lightning that hit it?"

"No."

"A fire?"

Ruben looked surprised. "Yes! There were two prairie fires that came through here."

Kanéko grinned back. "He's about legends. The tribe must have had stories about him. Start with the first one. What did he, Lopidir, do?"

"I... he..." Ruben frowned, and then his eyes glazed over, "he saved a child there. It was a girl of six years, three months, and she got caught under a burning tree which was set on fire during a raid. Lopidir took the shape of a bear and walked through it. He used his claws to hack at the wood and picked it up."

"Okay, now how did he take the shape of the bear?"

Kanéko watched Ruben experiencing the crafted memories of the spirit, told a thousand times by an entire tribe. The voman's mouth would open, and he would describe scenes from some half-forgotten dream. Whenever the words trailed off, Kanéko asked a question, and then another, probing into Lopidir's past until Ruben started to tell stories again.

Chapter 32

Detour

Ancient trees from the Fasilmir Forest are cut and floated down the Fasil River, colloquially known as Logjam River. These are cut and shipped to Jinto Panzir for shipment to the rest of the country.
—Basmov Hilden, *Encyclopedia of Kormar* (3rd edition)

Kanéko listened to Ruben's whispered stories as she rested against a tree. The air was warm around her but the shade above her kept the direct heat off her face. It was the perfect spot to doze and she had trouble keeping her eyes open as Ruben's monotone voice droned on with remembered tales from Lopidir.

Movement out of the corner of her eye caught her attention. Looking up, she spotted Maris staggering back over a nearby hill. Grass and twigs stuck out of her black hair, and her dress had torn in the front.

Kanéko frowned and stood up.

Ruben's voice stopped mid-sentence as he looked expectantly at her. "She may require your attention."

Maris's ears flattened against the side of her head.

"Something wrong?" Kanéko stepped out of the shade.

"Maris Germudrir is learning how to use magic through trial and error. The chances of self-injury are high. She risks her safety if she continues to practice in this manner."

Kanéko shot a glare back at him. "Is there a better way to teach her?"

"I am unaware of any technique suited for learning in this environment. However, I'm not adept at utilizing my knowledge."

A prickle of frustration and annoyance plucked at Kanéko's temper. "I'm trying the best I can."

"There is no doubt of that, I was simply stating a fact. Maris has little self-control, and she is prone to excitement. Her injuries are rarely life-threatening, but frequent." Ruben stood up, his shorter frame barely reaching over her hip. "She will be in high spirits once she sees you."

Kanéko stared at him. "What?"

"Maris Germudrir is quite fond of you, Kanéko Lurkuklan."

A blush colored Kanéko's cheeks. She turned away to avoid looking into his blue eyes. She also began to think of gears and plans in her head.

Ruben chuckled once. "I don't probe into inner thoughts. That would require an intimacy that you have not granted me."

"Kan! Kan!"

Kanéko looked up. Maris looked completely different as she bounded down the hill. She had her arms open wide for a hug. Her ears were perked up and her tail wagging back and forth. Kanéko spotted wind gathering behind Maris and braced herself.

Maris launched herself forward in an explosion of grass, dirt, and flowers. She flew the last few feet to tackle into Kanéko, slamming her shoulder into the darker girl's belly and launching her into the shaded area.

Even expecting it, Kanéko could do nothing until they both landed among dry leaves and the soft ground. She let out a grunt.

Maris pulled back, her ears once again against the side of her head. "Are you okay?"

"Yes," Kanéko croaked, "but I'm having trouble breathing."

"And if you can talk, you'll live," said the dalpre playfully before hugging her again.

"Off! Off!"

When Maris knelt back, Kanéko pushed herself into a sitting position.

The dalpre squirmed, bouncing back and forth as her hips rocked to the side.

Kanéko giggled and plucked a leaf from the girl's dark hair. "What happened?"

Ears drooped and Maris looked sheepish. "I got excited. And I was flying really fast. And I fell. And I got wet, so I took a nap."

In the pause that followed, Maris hopped up and trotted over to the fire. Scraping the remains of lunch—Ruben made it while telling stories—from the pan, she dumped it on three small vomen plates and brought it back. Sitting down cross-legged, she set all three on her lap and began to eat ravenously.

Ruben gestured out in the fields. "Did you see Damagar again?"

"He's still heading west. And kind of south. Mostly in a big zigzag about... I don't know, forty leagues wide. He's doing that land, make a crater, and then thinks really hard."

"Forty leagues is excessive," said Ruben. "That is over one hundred miles which would—"

"But you measure distances all the time, Rub!"

"I do, by sight. Accurate to—"

"And then you can measure my kick when I knock—"

Kanéko sighed and held up her hands. When they quieted, she said, "He's still looking for us. Hold on." She walked back to the cave. Coming back with the map from Cobin's pack, she sat it down on the ground.

Maris reached over and used a finger sticky with food to smear out new points. "Here. And here. And here. And here."

When she finished, Kanéko peered at the map. She saw an obvious pattern to Damagar's movements. "Look, if we draw a line..." Kanéko used the end of a charred twig to draw a line through the spots Maris marked. Following it, it led straight to Rock River, the mill, and the tower. "He's heading on the same route we were thinking about."

Ruben nodded. "That seems reasonable. He could have picked up that you were heading home."

Kanéko shook her head. "I told Virsian we were heading home so Garèo would know. And we've been going this way for a while. This is the route we were taking, along the northern part of this ridge." Kanéko finished by pointing to the rough hills and ridges to the south, barely visible over the rolling hills.

Ruben sighed. "He is working with a systematic pattern to find us en route but most likely heading toward your destination, Lurkuklan Tower. If we remain here to hide, then the behemoth will arrive first."

Kanéko worried her lip. "I'm sure Mama and Papa can handle him, if Damagar beats us to the tower—"

"That is a high-risk gamble. Your parents are powerful but this is a titan," said Ruben but Kanéko ignored him.

"But, we need to warn them. How long do you think it would take for us to get there?"

Ruben said, "At best guess, we're four days, ten hours out."

With a sigh, Kanéko looked out toward home. "If Maris could fly both of us—"

Maris whimpered. "Sorry..."

Kanéko cleared her throat. "I have a different idea. Look, we can't take the main road because these marks are where Cobin and Sinmak have men waiting for us."

"And they have flying things going that way."

Kanéko paused, looking up at Maris. "What flying things?"

"There were these three yellow flying things. They looked like a wings about a rod across. And have little tubes on them that jetted air, but they had the same sign as Sinmak's boat on them. And I saw them and ran away."

Kanéko shook her head. "I-I don't know what you mean."

Maris opened her mouth, and then closed it. "I don't know how to explain it. They were floating in the air but moving really fast. They followed the road here," she pointed to the map.

She pointed to another spot some distance away. "I was over here."

"Did they see you?"

"I don't think so. They were going along the road and I was... picking branches out of my hair."

Taking a deep breath, Kanéko returned to the map. "Then we can't take that route. That follows the Icewalk River. We have Damagar searching south of that road and the river, right in the path straight home. So, why don't we," she trailed her finger down to a river south of the hills near them, "take the Logjam back home? Cobin doesn't have any men there and maybe we can circle around Damagar?"

"That route is unfeasible," announced Ruben.

"Why not?" asked Maris. "The mill is on the Logjam."

"We're down river from the mill and it goes through rough rocks. We'd be climbing the entire time. There isn't enough game or plants to feed us. The mill dalpre don't go upriver either, they have an alternative route along the road we originally planned on following."

"Yeah," added Maris, "we just make a barge out of the logs when we send it down, and then take it apart at Panzir before putting it on the train. And, when Bor and Rut deliver wood, they go with. And they take twelve days for a round trip, three down the river and nine back on foot."

Kanéko grinned. "Why not sail up it?"

"Sail?" Ruben shook his head, "even if we found a sailboat—"

"No, Ruben, I'm saying build a boat, at least a raft. We can use the blankets here from the cave and maybe get some wood. You found all that rope in the cabinet, we can use that. It doesn't have to be much, just enough to keep us floating."

"It won't work," insisted Ruben, "even if we built something, we'd spend most of our time fighting the current. We'd need a very strong, steady wind—"

Kanéko pointed to Maris who blinked curiously.

Ruben continued, "—blowing on us just to keep it moving... what?"

Kanéko gestured again to Maris.

"I fail to see how Maris could help us."

"Strong, steady wind? I bet it takes a lot less energy to push a sailboat than to fly around."

Maris's eyes widened and she let out a barking laugh. She jumped up and down, bouncing. Around her, wind swirled with her excitement. "I can blow it up the river!"

She paused, the wind dying down instantly. "What's a sailboat?"

The boy opened his mouth, and then closed it. Kanéko could see him trying to explain why it wouldn't work. She cleared her throat. "Ruben, trust me. There should be some trees in those rocks. We have cutting tools here in the cave. It may not be comfortable, but we don't have enemies on that river."

"I... I..." Ruben shook his head, a dejected look on his face. "I don't—"

Maris spoke up. "Rub?" She patted him on the head. "Kan is really smart. And you think good. And I can make wind. And I want to try. And I know the Logjam. And I've done it twice with Rut. And there are markers on the river to tell you where to avoid things."

"But—"

"Trust Kan, Rub. Kan can do it."

Kanéko couldn't help but blush again.

Chapter 33

New Plans

The *barichirōma* cannot hear their ancestral spirits. They cannot enjoy the gifts given by their clan and, therefore, are not productive members of desert society.

—*The Dangers of Kyōti* (Volume 3)

Kanéko shivered as she struggled to go back to sleep. She grabbed the fabric at her waist and pulled it up. Rolling over, she dragged the sewn vomen blankets over her skin, but the tiny shreds of cloth pulled up and exposed her backside to the air. Despite the heat and humidity, Kanéko felt cold and clammy. She whimpered as she flailed at the cloth, trying to pull it back over her shivering body.

She felt herself waking but she didn't want to face the world quite yet. Her fumbling hand brushed against someone's fingers and she froze, but the hand just pulled the fabric down over her rear.

Thankful, Kanéko tried to relax. But, her mind woke up fully and she felt the hundred little things prickling her senses. The humidity choked her, and she breathed in the dank smells of earth and water and grass. She could hear birds calling out in the distance and some creature barking.

Her eyes fluttered open and she stared at a thatch of leaves less than a link in front of her. A breeze blew past them, hot and humid, but she shivered with the sweat that prickled on her skin. She tried to push away the discomfort, but the more she thought about it, the colder she grew. Finally, Kanéko sat up with a groan.

Next to her, Maris watched her with concern. "Kan? Are you all right?"

"Yeah, why?"

Maris's ears drooped. "I heard you whimpering all night. And I was worried. And I couldn't sleep."

The dalpre gestured to her lap where she was sewing a pair of vomen blankets together. "I tried to work on the sail. And it looks like it works." The dalpre reached out toward Kanéko's blanket. She frowned for a moment, and then air grew tense around Kanéko. The air blew up under the blanket which floated a few inches off the ground.

The blanket started to slide away and Kanéko grabbed it to avoid uncovering herself. "Maris! That's amazing!"

Maris beamed. Her ears perked up with her emotions. "But it is a lot harder to do this then fly."

The wind stopped and fluttered down to the ground. Kanéko drew the blanket back over her body.

Kanéko stared with surprise. "Really? I would have thought it would be the other way."

Maris gestured up. "Up there, I can just let go and things move. And it just happens. But, here, I have to," she paused, "I have to be careful. Otherwise, it will blow everything everywhere. And then it won't work. And it will rip again."

"I didn't know that. Papa always said control took more effort. I thought endurance would be the hardest bit. I can't do magic, so I'll never know." She ended with a sigh.

Maris reached over, but Kanéko pulled back. "Kan? Are you sure? I mean, can't everyone do magic?"

A tear formed in Kanéko's eye. She sniffed and shook her head. "There is a test they can do. It costs a lot, about five thousand crowns for the basic test, twenty thousand for the full range. Papa paid for the headmaster of the Royal Academy himself to test me." She sighed, "I didn't respond to a single one."

"What is supposed to happen?"

"You hold a crystal jar in your hand. If you have the right talent, the globe starts to glow. The brighter the glow, the more power you can use. We went through the twenty-two common aspects of magic and forty-three rares."

"And nothing?"

Kanéko sniffed. "Not a single one. I have no magic. I never will."

"And I'm sorry, Kan."

Kanéko stared down at the blanket. She toyed with the seam and ran her fingers along the stitching. "W-When we got the letter, my father stormed out of the room. Mama, well, Mama does what she always does, she swore. I just kept crying, wishing it was a bad dream."

She looked up to see Maris watching her. The dalpre's ears were flat against her head and her tail unmoving. Kanéko gave her a sad smile. "My papa didn't talk to me for three months, I thought he was going to disown me. I-I just stopped being near him. I skipped meals and hid in my room as long as I could."

"What happened?"

"Mama is not a very patient person," Kanéko grinned, "she decided that I needed to have a new direction that didn't involve magic. Or me being a *barichirōma*. Five months ago, Garèo showed up and she hired him to teach me about the desert."

"I like Gar."

Kanéko chuckled. "He doesn't know how to teach any-one. He just threw me on a horse and told me to... to be amazing. We fought," she sighed, "so much. But... I guess he never gave up."

"And your daddy?"

"I think he still loves me. He got me my first Nash book. Bought it off one of the traveling merchants. I'd never read something that long, and it used strange words. It took me a month to finish it and as soon as I did, I bought myself the next book."

Maris reached over and took Kanéko's hand. She tried to pull away, but Maris held tightly. "But I learned something from the mill. We fight with each other. And we yell at each other. But when it comes down to it, I know that if anyone ever hurt my daddy, even Bor would drop everything to kill that person."

"Mar?"

"Yes?"

Kanéko bit her lower lip. "I'm sorry I called you an ani-mal."

The dalpre shrugged. "We're both puppies. What comes out of our mouths is as serious as what comes out the other end."

Staring at Maris for a long moment, Kanéko let the words sink in, and she smirked.

Maris grinned, and soon they were laughing.

As the laughter died down, Kanéko wiped the tears from her face.

Maris leaned into her. Kanéko jumped, but Maris pressed down and pinned her. "And I like you," she whis-pered.

Kanéko blushed. To distract herself, she cleared her throat. "Um, why don't we get going? If we hurry up, we'll make it to the river by nightfall."

"Yay!"

The dalpre spun. Crouching down, her tail shot back and forth before she jumped high into the air. Her body spun with a puff of air and she landed hard on Ruben's sleeping form.

He wasn't sleeping for long.

Chapter 34

Exhaustion

In this growing age of enlightenment, the antiquated survival skills once prized highly will become vestigial artifacts of a more brutal time.
—Palador Masrutab, *Education of Kormar's Youth*

Every part of Kanéko's body ached as she braced herself a-gainst the side of the cliff and hacked at the branches stick-ing out from the tree trunk. "Next time," she grunted, "we trim these before we drop them off the cliff. That way, they won't stick on every. single. rock!" She yanked back with each word. Her feet slid on the gravel underneath her and she had to forced herself tighter against the rough stone for balance and to avoid slipping.

"Affirmative," muttered Ruben. He held on the end of the branch she was cutting, pulling as Kanéko chopped at its base. He balanced on a log no wider than Kanéko's fist. Sweat dripped down his face, but he didn't even blink as it dripped from his dark eyelashes.

Kanéko sighed and got a fresh grip on the vomen ax. Grunting, she slammed down on the branch until the blade cut through the green wood.

Ruben tugged it free and tossed it on a pile of other branches.

"Kan!" Maris called out from a short distance away, "I'm running out of rope."

Maris had three logs braced between her legs as she wrapped the last of the rope between them. The raft wasn't anything like Kanéko pictured in her head. They only had eight logs bound together which barely gave enough space to sit down. Nine more logs were propped up against the cliff, ready to be joined together, but they were running out of ways to attach them.

Kanéko stepped over a branch at her feet and padded over to the raft. Her feet crunched on the gravel, and she felt moisture seeping through her foot wrappings. Up close, frustration grew as she inspected the large gaps between the tied logs. Her confidence of building the raft crumbled seeing their efforts so far.

She tried not to dwell on her mistake. In her head, it was over fifteen feet across and a solid platform without a single gap. However, the eight they started with were the straightest but still had bumps and parts sticking out that caused wide gaps in one place even when they were tied tightly together in another. The logs were also short. Anything over six feet was almost impossible to drag over the cliffs so their efforts for hours of work was a leaky square.

The dalpre finished tying the last of the rope and leaned back. "And I'm out of rope."

Kanéko looked around for something to bind the logs together. The river looked calm, but Maris insisted it was too strong to swim against. On the far side, a few ragged trees clung to steep cliffs. On the shore next to them, they had nothing but branches and gravel. Her eyes scanned up, along the bumpy cliff to the crumbling shelf at the top—

nothing besides stumps and rocks. She didn't want to climb it again. Ten times was enough for her.

She considered her options. "Use the clothes and the packs themselves? Tear them into strips and weave them into ropes. We can use these too..." She sat down heavily on the makeshift raft to unwrap the cloth around her hands and feet. The Jonahas petals fluttered to the ground and she bent over to pick them up.

When she straightened, she saw Maris watching her with a sad look on her face. "Kan, don't take those off."

"We need the rope, Mar," Kanéko tugged on her wrappings, "and these will work just as well."

"And we can use everything else, but not those. Please? Leave your wrappings on?"

"Why?" Kanéko looked into Maris's eyes and saw sadness in her brown gaze.

"You'll get hurt. You don't have shoes."

"I'll heal—"

"No!" Maris snapped and a wind rose up around them. "I don't care if you'll heal later. And you need to be safe now."

"It's just—"

"No!" Maris's voice increased in volume. The wind kicked up dust and water to pepper Kanéko's body.

Kanéko let go of her wrappings. She settled back, watching Maris warily. "I'll leave them on."

Maris stood up and stalked toward their packs. She sat down next to the packs and emptied their contents on the ground. Flipping the pack over, she chewed on the bottom seam to split it apart.

Ruben came up to Kanéko with a handful of thinner branches. "These have been used to bind logs together, but I am not able to understand the process to do so."

Kanéko took one of the branches and bent the green wood in her palms. She thought for a moment, and then used her fingernail to split the bark from the branch. The moist wood inside was flexible but she continued to peel it apart until she had a handful of thinner strands. She looked up to Ruben and smiled. "By itself, they won't work, but I think we can weave these with the cloth. We might get something sturdy enough to last a few days."

The sound of ripping interrupted them. Kanéko looked over to see Maris tearing long strips from one of her dresses and setting it down on the growing remains of their packs. Only one bag remained on the depressingly small pile of food and papers. Somehow, seeing the dalpre destroying her own outfit made Kanéko guilty.

She sighed and wiped the sweat from her brow. Her arm trembled from the effort and she felt exhaustion sapping her strength. With a groan, she slipped off the raft and sat down next to Ruben. Below her, the gravel was cooler, but she was thankful she wasn't sitting in the water. "Here, give me another one."

She started stripping wood and tried not to think about the sun baking down on them. She had never realized how hard it was to make something as simple as a raft. It looked easy in her book. "Next trip, I'm going to bring a chain's worth of rope."

Ruben grunted. "I recommend also a full travel pack, two stones worth of food, and a well-trained horse."

"And I want a ball!" added Maris from the cliff.

"You," Ruben muttered, "always want a ball."

Maris stuck her tongue out and Kanéko giggled. The dalpre got up and brought the strips over to Ruben and Kanéko. Sitting heavily on the ground, she dropped the fabric into her lap. Grabbing a pair of Ruben's pants, she looked at Kanéko. "I'm sorry, Kanéko, I'm just worried about you. And you keep hurting yourself."

"I'll be all right."

"And you will be because Ruben and me will be here for you."

Ruben cleared his throat. "Ruben and I."

"Ruben, me, and I will be here for you."

Kanéko rolled her eyes and stifled another giggle. "Come on, the sooner we can get this thing built, the faster we can get on the river."

Maris nodded. She finished tearing a strip of cloth from Ruben's dark trousers.

Kanéko realized something. "Think you could get us a little wind?"

A breeze kicked up, cooling them as they worked to build the raft.

--------- Chapter 35 ---------

Setting Sail

Rarely does reality match the beauty of the imagination.
—Tsukarefu Mabúza, Tears of the Stone Raven

By the time the sun kissed the horizon, Kanéko was tugging the final rope into place. Her fingertips were rubbed
raw as she let it scrape along her hand. The fabric and
wood looked like it wouldn't work, but they managed to
bind it together into something that held in place. Grunting, she forced it down and let it go; she hovered her hand
over it in case it broke free. When it didn't, she let out a sigh
of relief.

"And we have the sail!" announced Maris. The dalpre
brought the billowing fabric over to Kanéko. She had sewed
it from the vomen blankets and other supplies while they
were traveling to the river. As Ruben and Kanéko tied the
logs, Maris finished attaching the blankets to a crossbeam
of Kanéko's bow and a sturdy stick. She held it up and Kanéko admired the neat stitching that combined the thin
fabric into a single sail.

Kanéko smiled as she fought the urge to crawl on the raft
and go to sleep. "Looks wonderful, Mar."

Maris beamed happily. Her entire body jiggled with her energetic wagging. "Is it ready to put in on the raft?"

Kanéko shook her head. "We still have to get the mast on." She pointed to a hole she had cut in the middle of the raft.

"And where is the mast?"

Kanéko padded to the cliff.

Ruben sat on the mast, the vomen ax dangling from his hand, and watched with mute amusement. As Kanéko approached, he stood up.

She paused in front of the log and stared at it with trepidation. Her back and arms hurt from dragging logs over the gravel. The idea of one more, even the last one, didn't appeal to her. The only thing that got her to kneel down and grab the end was the hope that she would finally be heading home in a few short minutes.

The wood bore down on her, and she staggered backwards toward the raft. The end dragged through the pebbles, scraping loudly.

Maris rushed over and lifted the other end. Groaning, she hefted it on her shoulder. The dalpre took the bulk of the weight, but Kanéko didn't have the energy to insist on taking more. Inching back, they carried the mast over to the raft to set it in the hole.

It didn't fit.

Kanéko frowned. She strained to hold the mast in place as she twisted it around. The ragged hole refused to accept the end of the mast. She swore under her breath, and then said, "Mar, can you get it?"

Maris grunted and reached down, but the wood began to tilt. She caught it with both hands, and then inched down to kneel on the raft. She tried to twist it around, but it threatened to fall as soon as she let it go. After a few seconds, Maris's ears flatted against her head. "Sowwie."

"Um, Ruben?"

"Repositioning," whispered Ruben as he knelt down between them. He carried the vomen ax, but when he tried to chop out an opening, he couldn't get the angle to cut. "Please raise the mast three links."

Kanéko and Maris strained to lift it, but their flagging strength couldn't raise it more than a few inches. It dropped back down with a thud that shook the raft.

"Sorry," gasped Kanéko.

Ruben glanced up. "That makes it difficult to widen the opening."

Kanéko glared down and threatened to kick him. "I know that, but we're trying."

"Fine," Ruben said, "attempt to lift it as high as you can for seventeen seconds."

Kanéko looked at Maris who nodded. Taking a deep breath, she wrapped her arms around the rough wood and hauled up. Her muscles screamed in pain as she shook with the effort to hold the log.

Maris did the same.

Out of sight, she heard Ruben scraping at the hole. The smell of freshly cut wood drifted up and the raft shook beneath him.

The mast slipped from her hands and plummeted down. It hit the gravel with a thud. Gasping, Kanéko backed away and looked at it. It fit inside the hole perfectly. She grinned, and then caught sight of the ax to the side.

Ruben looked up from next to the mast. He held out a glowing blue hand with five spectral claws sticking out of his fingers. He said, "Lopidir," as if it would explain everything.

Kanéko stared in shock.

"We had a legend you helped us remember. This is him helping."

She grinned nervously.

Maris bounded next to her and stopped. "Great, and now we just drag it to the river? And why do you have blue fingers? Do you have blueberries? You were hiding berries from me?"

Kanéko's grin froze on her face, and she blanched. She looked at the raft where they built it on the rocks for easy access. Half a rod away was the shore of the river and, by her best estimate, they had to drag it a rod from its position just to find out if it floated in the shallow waters. "*Sands.*"

Maris giggled. "Don't worry, we'll just push it into the water. Come on!"

She padded around the raft. Kanéko and Ruben joined her. Kneeling down, all three pushed at the raft, but it didn't budge.

Kanéko felt frustration rising as she tried again, straining with her might but she managed to push it only an inch. The weight of the wood against the gravel kept it firmly in place. Her feet dug into the pebbles, skittering uselessly. Her knuckles turned white with her effort. She felt her muscles burning with the effort, but she didn't want to tear apart the raft just to move it. She slumped against the raft and dropped her head to the rough wood. "*Sands, sands, sands!*"

Maris and Ruben stopped pushing the raft. Maris rested a hand on Kanéko's shoulder. "Don't worry, Kan. We can move it."

"But," Maris said with her tail against her leg, "we have to take it apart to move it. And that will take all night."

"No!" cried Kanéko. She dug her feet into the ground and tried again. She screamed out with the effort to shove the raft. It shifted a few more inches, but then she lost her balance as her feet slipped and she hit the raft with her chin.

Her back and arms screamed out with pain, and she felt the tears threatening to break her resolve.

"Damn it!" She turned around and sat down hard on the gravel. "I just wanted to go home." Her hopes were shattered. For all her imagination, she made an obvious mistake that would cost them a night or even a day to recover.

But even in her sorrow, she was planning to take apart the raft. She learned from her mistakes in building the first one, the second would be closer to the raft in her head.

Maris rested her hand on Kanéko's shoulder. "It's all right."

Kanéko took a breath and let it out with a shuddering sigh. She stared up at the cliff, trying to remember if there were more supplies that she missed. "I know, I'm just..."

Maris patted her on the head. Kanéko waved her hand at Maris to stop her, but the dalpre just patted her again. Then, Maris paused. "Um... Kan?"

"What?"

"Ruben is pushing the raft into the water."

Looking around with bleary eyes, Kanéko stared as Ruben shoved the raft across the gravel. His eyes were lit with an intense glow, the same blue that surrounded his body. The edges of his form blurred, and a frog-like creature had superimposed itself over his body. It was Stubbornness, Kanéko recognized it from Damagar's memory. The raft left a path through the gravel as Ruben drove it through the rocks. Water welled up from the shallow gouge behind him.

She could only stare in shock as the tiny teenager moved the heavy logs by himself. When he reached the river, he gave it a final shove and it slid across the surface. Before it could move far, Ruben lifted one foot and stomped down on the corner. Despite his small stature, the corner sunk to the bottom of the river as the far end stuck up out of the water.

"Are you," his voice rumbled with an angry croak, "going to just give up? Just like that, you pathetic little girl? I thought you were supposed to be someone interesting. Instead, you are just walking away because of a little—"

"Ruben!" Maris stood, her hands balled into fists.

Ruben and the ghostly image of Stubbornness turned to Maris. Large eyes narrowed and the frog creature reached out to his side. Energy crackled and a spear began to form in his webbed hand.

Wide-eyed, Kanéko surged to her feet. "No!"

Three sets of eyes stared at her. Kanéko blushed at the attention, and then took deep breath. "No, I was giving up. Thank you, um, Stubbornness."

The frog-like creature grunted without amusement. Along with it, Ruben's eyes ceased to glow, but the croaking voice hovered in the air for a moment. "I refuse to let the Broken Thought stop here, Kosobyo Kanéko. Not until Damagar takes his revenge for this... thing," he gestured down at Ruben, "killing me."

Ruben closed and then opened his eyes. They were no longer glowing. Resting one palm against his forehead, he sighed before he spoke in his normal voice. "He is very angry."

"Is he serious?"

"Yes, but he can't hurt us."

Maris rushed over and smacked Ruben on the head. "Don't you dare talk to Kan like that!"

Ruben looked up at Maris, a hurt look on his face. "I did not do that."

"You were rude, Ruben Habor Kalis! And I don't care if you are pretending to be a giant frog!"

Kanéko turned away to avoid either of them seeing her smile.

Chapter 36

Being Alpha

In a pack, there are always Alphas, one male and one female. They are the leaders, the arbitrators, and judges.
—Salamos Kerimudir, *Pack Mentality*

Kanéko was cold and miserable. She looked off the back of the raft to the rolling river behind her. White ridges of foam rolled in the gray waters and the raft left a ragged wake. She lifted her head to feel the wind buffeting her face.

Yawning, she rubbed her eyes. The sky was bright but gray, it looked like early morning. Lowering her gaze, she took in her surroundings. On the other side, Maris leaned on the mast, staring ahead without moving. Next to her, Ruben slumped forward, mumbling as he tried to remain sitting up.

"Maris? Ruben?"

Maris's ears perked up and the dalpre rolled to her hands and knees. "Kanéko! You're up!"

Ruben grumbled and slumped forward before jerking back into a sitting position. "Keep her up... we need to keep moving."

Kanéko frowned, confused, but Maris hugged her tightly. Burying her face in Kanéko's shoulder, the other teenage girl whimpered. "You yell at me whenever I pass out, but then you fainted on us." The wind died down. Kanéko watched the sail grow slack, and then patted Maris on the shoulder.

"Wind, Maris."

"Oh, sorry!" exclaimed Maris. The wind rose up again, filling the sail and the raft lurched forward.

Water welled through the gaps of the raft and soaked Kanéko's rear. She lifted one hand and watched the river water dripping from her fingers.

Maris was exhausted, with dark-rimmed eyes and puffs of air fluttering her black ears. Her tail slapped weakly on the wooden raft, splashing on the water welling between the gaps.

Kanéko frowned. She leaned over to look at the drowsing vomen.

Ruben slumped forward, nodding off and starting with the effort to stay up. His tiny body rolled to the side before curling into a ball.

"What happened?"

Maris whimpered. "We've been going all night."

"Couldn't you find some place to moor?"

"Moor?"

"Stop. Tie off."

Maris shook her head. She reached back and grabbed Ruben. Pulling him into her lap, she pointed down river. "We tried twice. The rope snapped the first time, and then Ruben fell off."

"Oh," Kanéko yawned again, "How did I sleep through that? Why didn't you wake me?"

"You needed sleep more than I did. And I could keep going. And Ruben kept me company, but then he got tired."

Maris giggled, and then yawned widely. Her long tongue flipped at the end before she closed her mouth with a snap. "And now I'm tired."

Kanéko reached out and stroked Maris's head. Maris leaned against her palm, her body trembling softly. The wind sputtered. Kanéko shook her head sadly. "Look, I'm sorry I'm pushing you so hard."

Maris clutched Ruben in her lap and held him tightly. "You're in trouble. And you are..." She stroked Ruben's head like she was petting a dog. "You're my alpha."

"I, um, I don't know what that means."

Maris tugged on Ruben's ear. The vomen groaned and flailed at her hand, but Maris just rested her wrist on his arm to hold him down. "With dog dalpre, we always know where we are compared to others. You are either above me or below me. The elders are usually above me and my daddy is the alpha at the mill, the one in charge. And if he says do something, I do it." She took a deep breath. "And now, your daddy is my daddy's alpha. And so... I guess you are in charge of me," she looked up at Kanéko with an anxious smile, "you're my alpha."

Ruben lifted his head. "Technically, alphas don't exist. There is only... breeding pairs..." He slumped back.

Kanéko felt guilty. "But, I never asked you to stay up, just to get me home."

Maris stroked Ruben's head. "You would have stayed up for me. You keep pushing yourself, trying to get home. And if my alpha does that, then that is what I do. And I can't do anything else."

"I don't want you to hurt yourself, Maris. I don't want you or Ruben to get hurt."

"I fell off a cliff. And I got hurt. But not badly. And we are so close, and I-I just want to go home, Kan. And I want you to be home."

"I know," Kanéko smiled and patted Maris, "but I can wait another half day if I have to. You need to sleep."

"But—"

"Now," commanded Kanéko.

The wind shifted, and Kanéko crawled up on her knees to turn the mast, bringing the raft up to the edge of the ravine. Moving slower, they found a shallow beach of gravel and rocks. She jumped off the raft and used the remaining rope to tie their makeshift vessel to some sturdy branches, testing each knot before moving to the next.

"Maris, I think you can…" Kanéko's voice faded in her throat as she saw Maris lying down on the raft, her eyes already closed. Maris reached out and grabbed Ruben, pulling him close and curling her body around him.

Finding a small trail, she decided to give Maris and Ruben a chance to sleep. She crawled up the ragged rocks and dirt until she found a knot of short trees and leafy plants. Remembering the gaps in the raft, she gathered up materials to reinforce their vessel and returned.

Seeing her two friends sleeping, Kanéko felt a strange sense of protectiveness for them. She set the branches and leaves on the end of the raft and began to repair and reinforce it as the two slept.

Distant Threats

Kanéko dozed on shore, her feet propped up on the raft and a pile of leaves underneath her head. A rope tied to the raft draped along her thighs and rested in her palm, just in case the raft broke free. She could feel the leaves and sticks packed between the logs on the back of her shins. The hot summer sun baked down on her skin and she let a soft smile cross her lips.

For a moment, she could forget all the pains and suffering of her trip. As long as she kept her eyes closed, she could pretend she slept next to the stream by the tower or even on the boulder at the milestone of her father's land.

Thinking of home, her mind drifted back to the water screw that preceded her journey. She brought up the plans in her head. The hours of telepathy with Ruben combined with using the designs to shield herself from Damagar gave the images unusual clarity. She picked up the gears mentally and explored them, flipping them over and rearranging the patterns. She easily changed the gears in size and teeth and set them back down, assembling the water screw with her imagination. With a mental push, she set the gears in motion, feeling how one gear blocked another. A frown furrowed her brow. She plucked a gear away, and then shrunk it. Setting it down, she followed through the mechanics, making changes from one central point until everything moved in perfect harmony.

A sense of elation filled her as she finished correcting the design. It worked perfectly and she memorized the alterations she needed to fix it for when she got home. That was, assuming her father didn't tear down the entire horse stable.

Homesickness gnawed at her heart. She sighed and cracked her eyes open. Above her, clouds rolled across the bright blue sky.

"This isn't so bad," she whispered.

She closed her eyes and let the dreams take her again. She thought about returning home and standing on top of the tower, looking across the fields. She remembered her father trying to explain why there were fields, but as a little girl, she was dreaming of flying not farming.

A ripple coursed through her dreams.

In the lands surrounding her parent's tower, a darkness blotted out the fields and the leaves rotted away. She gasped, clutching the imaginary edge of the tower, and tried to open her eyes. She couldn't, and she let out a soft whimper.

The darkness grew, and men rose out of the ash of the fields, dark men with sharp swords and shadowed expressions. Between two trees, an obsidian shadow pushed up over the leaves and stood up in the distance. Two eyes, crimson and terrifying, opened and bathed the entire tower in the ruby glow.

«We are Damagar.»

Kanéko's heart skipped a beat. She raised the now comfortable shield against his intruding thoughts. Clockwork and gears rose from the ground, forming a shield of memories and obsession against his intrusion, but Damagar didn't attack her. Instead, he hopped completely into view, his pitch-black skin shimmering in the light of some unseen sun. When he hit the ground, there was no rumble of impact.

She was dreaming again.

«Kanéko Lurkuklan, Kosòbyo Kanéko, we are looking for you.»

The rumbling voice of Damagar echoed across the fields of her mind, cracking at the tower.

Kanéko could feel his presence beating on her, pressing down on her skin. "What do you want?" she snapped.

«We need the Broken Thought destroyed. You must kill R.u.b.e.n.» Kanéko could feel Damagar's inability to visualize Ruben. The letters burned in the air and in her thoughts for a moment before fading. She found Damagar's blind spot interesting but couldn't see any way to take advantage of it.

"I won't let you have him," she declared.

Damagar's emotions boiled up like a storm cloud behind him. She could see the dark clouds rushing toward her with the echo of a dozen voices in the thunder. «We offer you a trade, Kanéko Lurkuklan, Kosòbyo Kanéko. Your parent's lives for the Broken Thought's.»

A new image slammed into her, carving into her imagination with terrifying clarity. Damagar's mind plucked her from the top of the tower and held her above it. The dark figures brightened into Sinmak's and Cobin's mercenaries. They charged with a deafening roar as her mother and father rushed out of the castle gate.

Her mother yanked up her ancestral bow and drew back the string. Light pooled between her fingers, forming an arrow of sunlight. She fired a single arrow which shot in a straight line before punching through the line of attackers. For every man who fell, three more charged forward. As she drew back another arrow and fired, Mioráshi's dark skin reflected the sunlight. The arrow joined the first and together, the two arrows slaughtered men in a long line.

Ronamar stopped a rod in front of Mioráshi. He reached up between one arrow shot and another and clasped his hands together. Bringing them down, he punched the ground with incredible force. Magic burst from inside his fingers and chain-wide fissures ripped open from the earth. Dozens of men fell to their doom, but a hundred more replaced them.

Her nightmare froze, paused by Damagar's terrible imagination. She felt his presence growing, a pressure that squeezed her chest. She shuddered at the feeling and whimpered as she tried to dredge up her shields.

Damagar reached out for her, his dark claws raking the gears that floated between them. «A trade.»

Her nightmare resumed, and the hordes of men swarmed toward her parents.

Her father pulled a massive stone sword from the ground, the blade easily two yards long. It glinted with crystals in the stone surface. He attacked. It sheared through man after man, but then one man got a lucky blow and jammed his knife into her father's side.

"Papa!"

The nightmare froze again. Kanéko felt Damagar inspecting her, seeing how rage and frustration boiled inside her. She knew it was Strategy and Observation that watched her every thought and reaction.

She lifted her shields again, blocking the creature from her innermost thoughts.

Damgar withdrew his thoughts, one last image fading behind him. «A trade. The body of the Broken Thought for you parent's lives. Choose well, Kanéko Lurkuklan, Kosòbyo Kanéko. My thoughts will return in one day. We have made the arrangements, only a trade can stop our plans.»

Chapter 38

Enthusiasm

On every journey, there are paths a person must walk alone.
—Mifúno proverb

"Daddy!" Maris's scream startled Kanéko. She scrambled to her feet, heart pounding and looking wildly in all directions as she tried to get the nightmare of Damagar out of her own head.

Maris stumbled back. One foot reached out over the logs. Kanéko was too dazed to reach out.

The dalpre fell back and plunged into the river. Water splashed in all directions, soaking Kanéko and Ruben.

Unperturbed, Ruben stood up. "Careful, you are near the edge," he called out.

The dalpre bobbed to the surface. Her ears and hair were plastered against her head as she flailed at the edge of the raft before grabbing one of the thicker logs. Her grasp shook the wooden frame and Kanéko grabbed her edge for balance.

Maris sputtered. "They're going to kill daddy! And mommy! And the puppies! And I saw them! And I don't like you, Rub!"

She tried to pull herself on the raft but slipped off, splashing again and shaking the logs. With a whine, she attempted again but only managed to pull the corner under the water and force water to seep through the gaps.

Ruben pointed to the side. "We are at the shore, just walk around."

Maris continued to paw at the raft, either not hearing Ruben, or too panicked to listen.

Knowing that Maris wouldn't stop until she either got on the raft or destroyed it, Kanéko got on her knees and crawled over while reaching out with her hand. Her feet remained on the rocky shore.

The water-logged platform tilted precariously until Ruben stepped on the edge.

The shorter teenager grabbed Kanéko and held her tight. "Please, Kan! My parents are in trouble. And Cobin is going to hurt them!"

"It's okay, just get up. One foot... one foot, there you go. Now put your foot down on the bottom and step up." Kanéko helped Maris up on the raft.

"Sure, it wasn't a hallucination due to stress?" asked Ruben, his face dripping wet.

Maris spun around, whacking Kanéko with her tail. "It wasn't a dream! I saw it! They burned down the mill. I... oh." Her ears flattened. "I dreamed it? It was so real."

Kanéko flipped her damp hair over her shoulder and wiped her face. "It wasn't a dream. I think it was Damagar. I felt his thoughts in my head just now. He threatened my papa and mama."

"But, it was so real. I saw the barn and the path and even Bor and Daddy and Mommy."

Ruben sighed. "Damagar would be able to pull those identities from your memories. He would be able to identify the people you treasured the most."

"Could he negotiate without us meeting him?"

"Yes. If he left a programmed personality in both of your heads, it could be triggered by your perception of time passing, a failure for certain actions to happen. For example, if I'm still alive at this point, your dreams would include his next demand."

"But," whimpered the girl, "he said that if we don't hurt you." She looked at Ruben with tearful eyes. "He would burn down the mill. It was…" She tugged on her ear. "…so real."

"Creatures with such a complex mind are capable of predicting probable actions and therefore have contingencies in place to manage those threats."

Kanéko started. "It can plan that far ahead?"

Ruben shrugged. "Most intelligent creatures are rather predictable, given enough information."

Maris sat down heavily on the raft, her tail smacking Kanéko's foot. She folded her arms across her chest and ruined dress. "I don't like Damagar. And he's mean! And he wants to hurt my pack. And he has nasty red eyes." A pause. "And I think he has rabies."

"R-Rabies?" Kanéko stared incredulously at Maris.

Maris's ears flattened as she looked away. "Or something like that," she muttered.

In the silence that followed, Ruben yawned and wiped his face. He looked around. "Where are we? I don't have a reference point to locate us."

Kanéko shrugged, but Maris spoke sullenly, "Sixty-one miles from the mill."

Ruben cocked his head with a silent question.

Maris gestured up the river, about a quarter mile ahead of them where someone had attached a bright green sign to the side of a tree. The lettering was large, almost a meter tall, and even from the distance Kanéko could read "494 mi".

"Five hundred miles from where? What is that?"

"A mile marker. There is one every…"

"Mile," supplied Ruben.

Maris glared at him. "And they start at Ice Point Fortress. And that is where the Logjam starts. The mill is at mile 433. We have a surveyor's spike right underneath the sign on the road. And the sign is on the dock."

Kanéko breathed out a sigh. "Sixty miles from home. It seems so close, but so far away. I wish we were going downstream; we'd be back by tomorrow."

Ruben spoke up, "Sixty one miles, four chains." When Kanéko looked at him sharply, he shrugged. "I found a reference point."

Maris whimpered. "Kanéko? What about my family? Is Cobin going to hurt them?"

"I don't know. I don't know if Damagar lied, but he threatened my family too. He showed me Sinmak's men attacking the tower."

"Is it real?"

Kanéko turned toward Ruben. "Is it?"

Ruben shrugged. "Natural telepaths can lie just as well as you and me. However, with a sufficient mental scan, it could identify probable plans, even before we make them."

Maris said, "I want to go home. And now."

Kanéko scrambled to her feet. She let out a long sigh. "That's what we've been doing for days. We are going as fast as we can."

"I want to be home." Maris glared and folded her arms over her chest. "Now."

A breeze flutter around them with the dalpre's impatience.

Kanéko reached down and grabbed her stolen pack. She had been using it for a pillow while she slept but a few of the pages were scattered around from when she woke up. She rescued them and filed them back into place before returning everything to Cobin's canvas pack. "Come on, we need to leave now."

Maris hopped on the raft. She shoved the other packs near the mast, and then spun around to look at the other teenagers. "Let's leave now?"

Ruben groaned and hopped off. He headed in the opposite direction.

"Rub? Where are you going?"

"I must defecate. I will be one minute, thirty-six seconds."

"I... I..." a whine rose up, "Please hurry."

Ruben disappeared up the trail.

Kanéko reached out to drop her pack on the raft, but Maris snatched it from her hand. The dalpre jammed Kanéko's stolen possessions near the mast and looked back. Kanéko felt a small prickle of annoyance as she stepped out on the raft. She had to reach out with her hand for balance because of Maris's pacing.

Maris grabbed the sail and tugged it smooth, spreading it out. A breeze rose up behind her, billowing out the fabric as she inspected it.

Kanéko watched Maris in silence, trying to stay out of her way as the dalpre paced back and forth.

"Where is Ruben?"

"Still going the bathroom, give him a second."

"I am, but I want to go home now."

"We all do, Maris," Kanéko snapped. "We are going as fast as we can."

"I know, but—"

"At least sit down."

Maris glared at Kanéko, but she sat down heavily on the raft, splashing water in all directions. Folding her arms over her chest, she looked away from Kanéko and growled softly.

Ruben crawled down the path, his short arms and legs struggling with the slope. Kanéko wondered why he was having trouble now when he didn't earlier. "I have returned," he said in a deadpanned voice.

Kanéko released the ropes. Ruben helped her push the wooden craft into the river, and they hopped on. The raft swung out, floating back down the river.

"Maris, your turn."

Maris crawled up on her knees and held out her hands. The smell of ozone floated off her body as ripples of water stretched out across the surface. Kanéko felt the air growing tense around her, a pressure that beat on her skin and made it hard to breath.

Despite the pressure around them, the raft continued to drift toward the currents and away from their destination.

It took a moment for Kanéko to realize there was no wind filling the sail but the pressure continued to build. Her ears popped. "Um, Maris?"

The dalpre said nothing, her brow furrowed in concentration and her tail perfectly still.

A rumble rolled through the air. Kanéko looked around and then up. Dark storm clouds rushed toward her, coming from an almost perfect circle that appears to be five miles across. Beyond it, the mid-morning sky was a brilliant blue. It was a stark contrast to the boiling darkness surrounding them.

The rustle of winds grew louder as the first eddies of moisture-ladened hair tugged at Kanéko's copper hair.

"Maris? This doesn't feel right." She couldn't take her eyes away from the gathering storm. She remembered something about air mages being able to affect the weather, but it was rare because of the raw power to affect anything thirty feet away much less thousands.

The wind increased, blowing harder. It filled the sail with a snap. The raft shuddered violently, slowing down in the center of the river. As the wind speed increased, the wooden craft pushed up the river. Water welled over the front of the trunks, rolling down the cracks and soaking Kanéko's rear.

"Great, that is just the right—"

Another rumble coursed through the clouds. Lightning flashed. The first splatters of rain struck Kanéko's face. She cringed at the sudden wind that buffeted her body. Wiping the water from her face, she said, "Maris, slow down."

Maris frowned as she held up her hands. Shimmers of energy rose off the dalpre and more wind buffeted the sail. The raft surged forward.

Kanéko glanced down and saw a wake forming behind them. She held out her hand, "Slow down. The sail and the mast, the raft, can't take this."

"No," the dalpre growled, "it's all right. I can get us home."

"Maris, trust me, go slow." Kanéko reached out and the wind blasted her hand back. Blood welled out from a sudden cut. She frowned and shoved her hand back, trying to grab Maris but the wind howled shrilly and deflected her grip.

"Maris!" She yelled as loudly as she could, but Maris ignored her.

Kanéko balled up her fist and tried to punch Maris, but her hand couldn't pierce the rushing air. She grunted and tried again, somehow bruising her knuckles on the wind that almost threw her off the raft. Rubbing her hand, she looked over at Ruben for help.

Ruben reached for Maris. His hand wavered as he pushed through the wind. His blue eyes started to glow, his form blurring along the edges and the shape of Stubbornness wavered on the edge of her vision.

Before he could touch Maris, Kanéko heard cloth rip. Her eyes widened as she stared at their hand-sewn sail. A large rent formed along one of the seams, snapping threads spreading open as it tore wide open.

Swearing, Kanéko grabbed the mast with one hand and tried to stop the tear with her other. Her fingers slipped on the rain-soaked fabric.

"Stop her, Ruben! She's going to ruin everything!"

She wasn't even sure if her voice reached him. She tried to shield the sail with her body, but it was too late. Another blast of wind slammed into her, throwing her against the wooden beam. The impact along her spine drove the air from her lungs before lifting her and tossing her through the sail. Fabric tore loudly around her as she fell down on the far side, hitting the boards with enough impact that water splashed on her.

Kanéko opened her eyes in time to see the snapped-off end of the mast plummet toward her. She rolled to the side, losing a chunk of hair to a rough-hewn log, and managed to dodge as the mast slammed into the raft edge.

Everything tilted for a moment before the carved wooden pole rolled into the river, yanking the remains of the sail with it.

She scrambled to her feet. Splinters tore at her hands, but she ignored them. "Okay, you damn *bitch*, I told you... to... stop!"

She swung with all her might but aimed upwind from the dalpre. The wind caught her hand and started to push her away, but Kanéko threw her entire body into her punch. It cut her face, throwing her to the side, but she managed to slam her shoulder into Maris's chest.

Her momentum carried her over the edge of the raft. Letting out a shriek, Kanéko spun around in time to see Maris flying off the opposite side.

She plunged into the water. It flooded her nostrils and open mouth. She swam for the surface, flailing for fresh air as she choked on the water rushing into her lungs. As soon as she surfaced, she sputtered and coughed.

It took a moment for her to regain her wits. When she pulled her soaked, copper hair from her face, she didn't see the raft. Treading, she turned around to see it and Ruben had floated down the river. Maris wasn't on it as the raft slowly moved toward the center of the river and the faster currents. In its wake, the heavy rain planted circular ripples along the surface of the river.

Muttering to herself, Kanéko swam after it. "R-Rub... Ruben!"

"I do not have control over this."

When she reached the raft, she flailed to catch it. As soon as she could, she took a deep breath and coughed to clear her lungs. "I-I got it."

Kanéko tried to pull herself onto the raft but her makeshift clothes weighed her down too much. She gave up after the second attempt and just pushed it toward the edge.

Ahead of her, Maris reached the shore. She crawled out of the water dripping wet. Her dress hung down off her shoulders. The fabric had torn to reveal most of her other shoulder and parts of her thigh. Her ears were down as was her tail. She didn't look back as she stomped toward a large rock a few feet away.

As soon as Kanéko's feet touched the bottom, she shoved the raft toward the shore and stormed out of the water. Her vision was blurred by the rain and wind that continued to blow against her. She stopped in front of Maris trying to tug her dress back into place. "Why are you being a *sun-bleached idiot!*?"

Maris shivered, her dress sticking to her soaked fur and water rolling down her face. "I'm sorry, Kan, I just—"

"You just wanted to dump us in the river!?"

"No," Maris whimpered, "I just wanted to go home." Water running down her face made it look like she was crying.

"I told you to stop blowing. We would have made it if you were patient."

"But I—"

"No, buts!" screamed Kanéko, "I want to go home too! That isn't an airship or a fancy boat. I told you it couldn't handle it. It just would have taken us a few days, but we would have made it!"

"I'm sorry." Maris stood there, her ears against her head and her chin pointed down.

"Damn you. Now we have—"

"Kanéko, please desist," said Ruben as he hopped off the raft.

The wooden craft bobbed in the water, falling back from the shore. It already began to break apart, the ropes holding the logs trailed in the water behind it as it separated into pieces. Kanéko started after it, but then she saw that Ruben had tossed their supplies on the shore. She spun on the balls of her feet to glare at Maris again.

Ruben stopped in front of her, standing between Maris and Kanéko. "Kanéko, she is sorry."

"I-I," Kanéko tried to calm herself, but the anger continued to fill her. "Damn it! I wanted to go home! And that stupid, idiotic, and unthinking little—"

Maris jumped to her feet. "I said I was sorry!"

As if to respond, the wind rose up around them. Raindrops splattered against Kanéko's face.

"It's too late! We could have been home in two days. Now, it's going to take another damn week! We—!"

Ruben raised his hands. "Kanéko. Please stop."

"Shut up!"

Ruben's eyes flashed blue, glowing brightly. He spoke with a deep, rumbling voice. "I will not shut up!"

"Drown in sands!" Kanéko balled up her hands to strike.

"STOP!" The bellowing croak stunned Kanéko from her tirade. Ruben's eyes glowed an intense blue. Over his body, a shimmering shape of Stubbornness loomed over her. The frog-like creature glared down at her with the same blue eyes. The command echoed though her mind, repeating endlessly.

She staggered back, reeling from the force of his words and projection. Forcing her hands to relax, she looked pointedly at Maris. "Go ahead then."

Maris whimpered.

Kanéko waved at both of them. "Get out! Just go. Fly away and go rescue your damn family. I don't care!" Tears burned her eyes.

"Kan, I can't—"

"I said leave! You can't wait, so don't!" Kanéko grabbed a rock from the shore and whipped it at Maris. It stopped in mid-air as the wind plucked it from its flight. It spun twice and shot out over the river, away from the three teenagers. Droplets of rain flew after it.

Kanéko grabbed another rock.

Ruben stepped back, his eyes still glowing. He turned toward Maris. "Let's go." He still spoke with Stubbornness's croak.

"W-We can't leave Kan, Rub."

"Now," said the croaking voice.

"Are you sure?"

Kanéko nodded sharply.

"O-Okay," whimpered Maris. She rushed over and grabbed Ruben's and her pack. Coming back, she looked at Kanéko. "A-Are you sure, Kan? I didn't mean to break—"

"Go away, you *stupid fucking, rotted cesspool of a bitch!*" screamed Kanéko.

Sniffing, Maris reached down and picked Ruben up. She shifted her position slightly, and then rocketed up in the air. Wind shoved Kanéko back from the force of the takeoff. Her blast faltered and Kanéko watched as Maris strained a-gainst Ruben's weight. After a few seconds and a stubborn look on the dalpre's face, she managed to regain her flight.

Kanéko blinked at the dust that stung her eyes and she wiped the tears from them.

Maris hovered a few hundred feet above her, and then shot out to the east, disappearing in a heartbeat.

Kanéko stared at the bright blue sky. In the back of her mind, she could imagine Damagar laughing at her. One moment of anger, and she was utterly alone.

The rain stopped instantly. One moment it slammed a-gainst her face and the next, there was nothing. Looking up, she could see the disc of dark storm clouds breaking apart as fast as it formed. The morning light peeked through the clouds and soon bathed her in sunlight once a-gain.

The anger drained away in an instant, leaving only a sick feeling behind.

She sat down heavily.

"Damn the shitty sands."

Chapter 39

Regret

Tachìra sees everywhere the sunlight touches, be it on his lover Mifúno or in the dead lands surrounding the oceans.
—Wamyudeso Tsúba, *The Clans of Sun and Night*

An hour later, Kanéko sat on the shore, glaring out over the rolling river and the sheer cliffs on the opposite side. The water lapped at the rounded pebbles at her feet and she considered throwing another one into the water. Her hands grabbed the nearest rock, digging into the sandy soil with her fingernails. She sighed as she rolled it in her palm. It left a smear of wetness from the brief rain.

"I just damned myself, didn't I?"

With a lurch, she flung the rock as far as she could. It sailed into a low arc to plop into the water. Kanéko watched the ripples that spread out from the impact until they quickly disappeared from sight.

She sighed again and thought about her options: she could wait for Maris to return, wait for a boat to come down river, wait for one of the mercenaries to kidnap her, or she could start walking. At least the route along the river wasn't on Cobin's map. She hoped there wouldn't be any posted rewards at any of the villages along the shore.

"Better get going..." She grumbled. "*Just keep moving.*"

Standing up, she brushed leaves from her hair and pulled it into a ponytail. Using her bit of wire that survived her entire trip, she tied it back. Grabbing the bow Ruben rescued from the river and Cobin's bag, she looked over the shore one last time. Turning away from the river, she inspected the steep sides.

She mapped out a way to climb before she moved. Taking a running start, she jumped and grabbed a ledge. Pulling herself up, she leaped to the next. She swung over and landed on the edge of a bulge before jumping up to the next one. It only took her a few minutes to reach the top and she smiled at the realization that she would have never been able to climb that easily before her trip. She found a tiny joy in her ability to move quickly along the rocks.

At the top, she shielded her eyes from the midday sun and scanned the rocky terrain to the east. The rolling hills were broken by sharp ridges and tufts of grasses. Most of the ridges followed the river, which gave her at least some relief from climbing. In the distance, to the east, she saw a flash of light.

A moment later, an itch tickled the back of her mind, like Damagar or Ruben trying to communicate. Holding her breath, she looked across the sky for Maris and Ruben, but didn't see the signs of either of them. She lowered her gaze to the surrounding lands, looking for Damagar hopping toward her, but there was nothing for dozens of leagues in all directions.

The itch became a pulsating headache. Clutching her head, she concentrated on the pain. It felt like telepathy to her, but it was raw and unfocused. She remembered how she thought of Ruben when he was looking for her and pictured him, but the image wouldn't stick. She hesitated, then imagined Damagar, but the headache only grew worse. She guessed it wasn't Damagar looking for her, but she couldn't imagine anyone else scanning for her presence.

She guessed that picturing the person searching for her would help identify the source and tell her if she needed to get ready for rescue or defense. With a bit of concentration, she let her mind grow unfocused and then began to dredge through her memories, picturing man after woman in rapid succession. None of them stuck or remained in her mind.

Until she pictured Garèo fighting with Ojinkomàsu. Instantly, the image solidified into startling sharpness and the headache faded instantly.

Kanéko froze. Garèo wasn't a telepath. She shook her head and tried more images but there was nothing left, the pulsating discomfort had faded away. After a few more seconds of trying, she gave up and repeated to herself, *"Just keep walking."*

Chapter 40

Gallop

The eight horses of the sun ride to serve Tachìra, their hooves beating a tattoo against the sand with a speed that touches two horizons in the same day.

—Wamyudeso Tsúba, *The Clans of Sun and Night*

After another hour of trudging, Kanéko was sick and tired of rocks. Along the side of the river she followed, the water had carved out many deep ravines around ribbons of sturdier rocks. It left her only a choice of walking along the bottoms, occasionally through waist-deep fetid waters or up on the top where a few short trees struggled to find a perch. She spent much of her time either following mossy trails or hopping across the narrow spots between the sides of ravines. Her feet ached, her legs hurt, and she wished she could find something to ease the gnawing in her stomach.

When she first saw smoke on the horizon a half hour before, she had hoped for a warm meal and maybe a wagon. But, as she approached, she thought about the last time she entered a village—Lassidin—and how poorly it went. The idea of risking herself, even though it was an isolated village, sickened her and she turned away from the twin columns of smoke before she even spotted any buildings.

Bypassing the village ate away precious time. Soon, she was sweating from the effort to climb the wall of a ravine that she couldn't jump. Her fingers and toes ached from the effort. She looked worriedly at the sun, there was only a few hand's widths from the horizon and nothing around her looked safe enough to sleep for the night. She had five hours at most until sundown, but the concern hung in the back of her thoughts.

Moving away from the east-west ridges meant she had to climb. She hopped down and crawled up the other side. There would be many more before she got out of the area.

Twenty minutes later, Kanéko wiped the sweat from her brow. She ached from head to toe and the bow and pack weighed her down, but she didn't dare leave either behind. Her mother's lessons made a lot more sense now, pack light but ready for anything.

A whinny drifted through the air. Kanéko stopped and shielded her hand over her face. She scanned the horizon until she spotted a horse running across the top of a ridge. As she watched, the horse easily jumped across a ravine. It appeared to not carry a rider, but it was moving too fast not to be driven by something or someone.

It took a heart-stopping second to realize it ran toward her. Gasping, Kanéko spun around frantically trying to find a place to hide. On the far side of a narrow ravine, she spotted a small alcove just underneath the top. It looked large enough for her to hide from sight. Without a second thought, she jumped off her trail and landed on the far side. It took her a moment to slide down on her belly and swing underneath the outcropping. Her bare toes caught the ledge and she inched herself into it until she was safely balanced on the narrow rock while holding on to some thick roots.

The painful beating of her heart measured out the time with agonizing slowness. Kanéko forced herself to take longer breaths, covering her mouth with her hand as she prayed whatever ran toward her would pass by.

She didn't know how long she cowered in the shadow, but it felt like forever before she heard the horse's hooves. It beat with a rapid four stroke, and her heart matched the staccato. Dust trickled down her face, tickling her nose. The drumming grew louder, and then stopped. A heartbeat later, she heard it hit the bottom of the valley; dust streamed down from the rocks above her.

Hooves tapped loudly on the rocky ground. Kanéko's heart slammed into her ribs as she heard the equine walking down the top edge of the ravine opposite to her. It was the path she was just on.

She shivered and held the roots tighter, ducking her head. Slowly, she inched her free hand toward Cobin's dagger. In her mind, she suddenly thought of Garèo's horse, Ojinkomàsu. The image was incredibly clear but completely unexpected; she imagined Garèo when she had the headache before. The thought disappeared just as the riderless roan horse walked past her alcove.

She gasped. "O-Ojinkomàsu!?"

Ojinkomàsu stopped and turned his head to look at her.

Kanéko swung out of her alcove, blinded by the light as she examined Garèo's horse.

The roan looked at her, the same golden eyes she remembered from when Garèo first showed up.

"Thank the sun, Ojinkomàsu! It is you!" Stuttering, Kanéko crawled up the side of the ravine and then hopped over. Her hand stroked along the hot side of the horse but his

skin was dry as a bone. *"It's really you,"* she sobbed as she clutched on to him, breathing in the familiar scent.

Ojinkomàsu rested his nose on her shoulder and exhaled loudly.

Kanéko leaned back to look into his eyes. She spoke in Miwāfu because it seemed the right way to speak with a desert horse. *"Ojinkomàsu, why are you... How are you here?"*

The horse shook his mane and stepped back.

Kanéko nibbled on her bottom lip. Both Garèo and her mother were adamant that she never consider riding Ojinkomàsu. They never told her the reason, but Kanéko was desperate to get home. She decided to beg for forgiveness later. *"Mama told me to never ride you, but do you think, maybe I could?"*

The horse bumped his head against her shoulder.

Kanéko took a deep breath. She reached out and grabbed Ojinkomàsu's mane; it was hot in her fingers, and she grasped it tightly. The powerful horse tensed, and she hesitated, worried he would kick. When he didn't move, she hopped onto him.

The desert folk rarely wore a saddle on their horses, but she didn't have the normal blanket either. She was surprised by the heat rolling off Ojinkomàsu's body. She settled down on his muscular back. A soft gasp escaped her lips, she was on top of Ojinkomàsu.

Kanéko opened her mouth, and then she felt a tickle of a presence in her mind. It was light and delicate, just like Ruben when he reached for her surface thoughts. She looked around sharply, looking for her friends or the waves of force that represented Damagar, but she couldn't see either. She didn't know if she should shield her thoughts or open up.

The tickle faded after a moment without another image.

Heart beating faster, Kanéko leaned over to Ojinkomàsu to speak in his ear, *"Ojinkomàsu, please, by Tachìra's blessing, take me home?"* She never had a need to call on the sun spirit, but she remembered Cobin's letter.

Ojinkomàsu burst into movement. His hoofs slammed into the ground as he galloped back down the valley. He found a steep incline on the side of the valley and shot up it. He left an avalanche of rocks behind him as he reached the top of the ridge and accelerated into a gallop.

Kanéko grabbed tightly, but Ojinkomàsu moved with such grace she never risked losing her balance. She concentrated on the connections of their bodies, the way they moved together. She never felt such an intimate bond with a horse. She anticipated every leap and gallop as if she had been riding her entire life.

Once on top of the ridge, Ojinkomàsu accelerated in the sunlight. He raced along the rock and the ground blurred beneath him.

She pressed her body tight to his, sweating from the heat that rolled off his body and the sun beating down on her.

Before she knew it, Ojinkomàsu galloped out of the ravines and into a wide valley. He aimed for a road straight down the middle. She knew the route; it was one of the many ones on Cobin's map. Kanéko pulled at his mane, trying to pull him off, but she couldn't deter the horse. *"Ojinkomàsu! Stay off the road, there are people looking for me! They can't find me!"*

The horse continued to gallop, his hooves accelerating along the smoother road. He was running too fast; the world was blurring around her as he continued to race.

She tugged harder but she couldn't pull Ojinkomàsu away from his path. He swung to the east and she saw a caravan far up ahead. Whimpering, she tried one more time to pull him away, but the powerful horse continued to ignore her.

Sunlight flashed as they raced along. The wagons rushed up, faster than Kanéko expected, and blew past. Kanéko stared over her shoulder in shock. One of the wagons teetered on two wheels before it came crashing back into place. Papers and fabric blossomed around the caravan before floating down. Arcs of magenta lighting traced the ground where they passed.

No horse could move that fast, she knew that much. No living creature could cause a wagon to tilt on its side or force the world to become nothing more than a blur of green and brown.

She blinked. When her eyes opened, the caravan was too far away to focus on. She frowned as she turned around and pressed her body tight to Ojinkomàsu. Cobin's letters about Ojinkomàsu being one of the sun spirit's own mounts seemed more probable with every beat of his hooves.

For a brief moment, she wondered if she could become the horse king. She had never demonstrated any powers but there was a chance. No, she decided after a moment of hope and fantasy. She had been tested for other cultural magic. She had nothing, not even the basic ability to gain power from the sunlight like most desert folks.

Kanéko sighed and closed her eyes against the sudden tears. She pressed her body tight against Ojinkomàsu to avoid the wind ripping at her face and tried not to dream of a world where she had all the powers.

--------- Chapter 41 ---------

The Germudrir Pack

The future is fluid, changing with every action and thought. It is also difficult to guide and lead. Only by being aware, can the future be altered.

—Saraboin Klum, *The Predestination of Man*

As the sun approached the horizon, Ojinkomàsu galloped along the road with Kanéko crouched down against his body. Her slender form shook from exhaustion, but Damagar's threat continued to burn in her mind. Her hands tightened on her mount's mane as she whispered into the wind. *"Please hurry, I need to get to Mama and Papa."*

They came up the sweeping road that led to her father's lands. She was startled with how fast he could race. They had covered a day's travel in an hour. The horse's hooves drummed on the ground, and Kanéko's eyes scanned the horizon looking for Damagar. They raced past a sign for the Germudrir Mill. Memories of her first visit, when she met Maris, washed past her and she closed her eyes tightly, pressing her cheek to Ojinkomàsu's neck to avoid crying.

She caught the scent of freshly burning wood. Frowning, she opened her eyes and looked around. Smoke rose up above the trees in the direction of the mill, but instead of four small plumes as she expected, she saw a thick column of dark smoke billowing up.

Kanéko sat up on Ojinkomàsu and pulled back on his mane. The horse resisted and yanked his head from her fingers. She grabbed him again and hauled back with all her strength.

He shook his head and tore his mane free of her hands. His hooves continued to drum against the ground as he galloped toward the tower.

In the distance, a rumble rolled through the tree trunks. Ojinkomàsu's ears perked up, but he didn't slow down.

Kanéko thought she heard a different noise right before the rumble. She held her breath and strained to listen.

The strange sound came again, a sharp crack of noise followed by a second rumble that rolled through the woods. Birds burst out of the trees as the ground shook from the impact. A moment later, the breeze kicked up eddies of dust as it blew past Kanéko and Ojinkomàsu.

A few seconds later, it happened again. It was a bark followed by a roll of thunder.

Kanéko tensed as she listened carefully. It sounded distant but loud. Only one dalpre could bark that loud: Mamgum. And if Mamgum was in trouble, so was Maris and Ruben. *"Sands!* That's the pack!"

A deep, powerful rumble rolled through the trees, the leaves fluttering as a wind rose up. Kanéko looked up as a tornado formed from the dark smoke rising from the mill. The narrow funnel plunged out of sight as the air pressure around her increased. A moment later, the wind blew past Kanéko and tugged at her hair.

She tugged at Ojinkomàsu's mane toward the mill. He resisted, but Kanéko grabbed his mane with both hands and yanked him around. At the same time, she pictured exactly what she wanted him to do, in case the tickling her mind was somehow the horse reading her thoughts.

He finally relented and headed down the side road in a trot.

Kanéko tapped on the side of his neck, trying to get him to accelerate but Ojinkomàsu sullenly remained at the slower pace instead of flying across the countryside as he had before. When she jabbed him in the flanks with her heels, he accelerated into a gallop but no faster.

They came up to a haze drifting through the trees. The stench of burning wood quickly became overwhelming.

Kanéko's eyes teared up from the pain until she pulled on Cobin's goggles. The shadowed lenses shielded her from the sting of smoke and the wind from Ojinkomàsu's speed. She wondered why she hadn't put them on earlier.

As they drew closer, Kanéko slung her bow.

They passed a dalpre sitting in front of a tree. His head was resting on his chest and he sat in a puddle of blood. Kanéko felt horror rise in her throat as Ojinkomàsu passed. She turned to look at the fallen dog man, wishing he would move, but the body slumped to the side and didn't get up.

Ojinkomàsu reached the mill in only fifteen minutes. As they came up to the last curve, Kanéko spotted a mercenary from the *Burning Cloud Queen* threatening a female dalpre with a large spiked hammer. Kanéko lifted the bow and tensed up, worried that she would miss and strike the woman.

Ojinkomàsu's strides grew longer, and he sailed over the ground. Kanéko discovered a rhythm to his movements, a way of predicting when his gallop would not interfere with her bow shots. She didn't know how she was aware of it, but she focused her attention on shooting first. She timed his bounds and fired at the apex of Ojinkomàsu's gallop.

The arrow flew true and plunged into the man's back. He let out a bellow of pain and collapsed.

The dalpre gasped as the man fell, and then promptly grabbed the mercenary's hammer and attacked him with it.

Kanéko turned away at the violence, a sick feeling in her stomach.

In front of her, the tornado faded away in tiny eddies of dark wind. The world grew quieter, and she could pick out whines and whimpers over Ojinkomàsu's galloping. As they approached the mill, he slowed down.

The barn was burning. The closest wall slumped to the side and the splintered remains of the building spread out across the entire field. On the far side of it, the barracks were engulfed in flames. Embers rose in the shimmering air, and the smoke choked her.

Mercenaries surrounded a large knot of dalpre. Each one brandished their weapons toward the captured workers.

From her quick look, she could only see women and children. The older dalpre were standing between the armed men surrounding them and the younger ones, snarling as they shielded the children with their bodies. Mamgum was in the center, cradling Ruben's tiny, limp form.

When she saw Ruben slack in the older woman's arms, Kanéko let out a soft whimper of her own. She clutched her bow and aimed her arrow at the back of the mercenary standing in front of Mamgum. Ojinkomàsu's stride grew longer and smoother, giving her the chance to fire.

The arrow flew true, slamming into the back of the man's skull. A shower of blood splattered across the prisoners.

Before the body hit the ground, the side of the house exploded. Howling winds blasted fragments of wood and splinters into the yard. It knocked down a pair of mercenaries but narrowly avoided the captured dalpre.

Kanéko let out a gasp and almost fell off the horse, but Ojinkomàsu sidestepped and she remained firmly on his back.

A man jumped out of the house as the roof collapsed. He hit the ground and rolled twice before hopping to his feet. When he spun around, a sword and some mechanical device hung from his belt. He had a reddish beard streaked with white that ended with a wispy braid. He looked well into his fourth decade. The wind blew a large, floppy hat across the ground and it came to a halt at his feet. With a chuckle, he picked it up and jammed it back on his head.

Maris flew out of the house, her hair billowing in all directions. Fragments of the ruined house circled around her in a miniature tornado. There were roof tiles, pieces of clothing, and even some plates Kanéko recognized from lunch. Her torn dress barely hung on her shoulder and Kanéko could see multiple sword cuts bleeding through the ruined fabric. Maris lashed out with her hand and a burst of air shaped like a fist flew toward the man.

He drew his sword and parried. The blade sparkled magenta and the wind split in half around it. Spinning the sword, he brought it into a ready position and laughed. "Come on, girl! I can do this all day!"

"Rot in the ground, Sinmak!"

Maris surged forward, the air blasting out behind her. She accelerated with her fist drawn back. The wind gathered around her, the sound of the screaming wind deafening. The suction tore out the ground around her as the debris shot forward in a stream to slam into Sinmak.

It took a moment for Kanéko to respond to the surprise at finally seeing Sinmak. This man had been chasing her for days, all across the country, and she had never crossed him. She expected someone big and hulking, not a man with a ragged beard and an ill-fitting jacket.

Ojinkomàsu hit the ground hard, jolting her.

Shaking her head, she rejoined the fight. She shifted the aim of her arrow and fired at Sinmak. The arrow shot across the mill yard, but before it hit, he ducked below it without even looking.

Sinmak turned to look at her. She could see the reddish, evil glint to his eyes. "I was looking for you, Kanéko Lurkuklan." He spat out her name and a frown flickered across his face but faded quickly.

Rising into the air, Maris threw blasts of air at Sinmak.

He dodged between them as the dust and dirt rose up in a cloud around him. When he couldn't jump out of the way, Sinmak brought the glowing blade to parry the nearly invisible burst of wind. There was a flash of sparks on the impact but the blade managed to block Maris's magic from passing.

Ojinkomàsu circled around the yard and Kanéko used the opportunity to fire at Sinmak again.

The mercenary dodged easily, leaning to the side as the arrow snapped past him. His movement was precise with only an inch of clearance from her attack.

She frowned and shot again, firing arrows as fast as she could.

Maris join in, throwing more blasts from her fists. The air howled around her as she floated in the air, the winds ripping at her body as she twisted back and forth to fire faster.

He continued to dodge both of them without appearing to take any effort. His sword glowed brightly with every movement, and Kanéko didn't see a single blow land.

She stopped firing, but Maris continued. The wind pressure grew, and tiny vortexes of power curled into existence. Maris lifted her hands up as a tornado formed above her.

The tornado shot down, tearing up the ground, raising a cloud of dust and dirt.

Sinmak parried it with his sword. Magenta sparks popped away from the blade as he kept the tip of the miniature tornado against his weapon and the impact of metal on air somehow was negated. He stepped back quickly, moving toward the barn as the wind howled.

Kanéko glanced at Ruben's prone form, and then set her jaw. *"We need to stop him, Ojinkomàsu."*

He accelerated into a gallop.

She tossed her bow aside, something Garèo would rebuke her for, and drew Cobin's blade.

As they rushed in, Sinmak's face clenched. He hopped back and turned to face them. Kanéko swung her dagger down but he caught it with his own blade. He staggered back from the force of her attack and Ojinkomàsu's charge.

Before he could regain his balance, a blast of wind slammed into him, ripping half a foot of dirt out from underneath him. The winds screamed as Maris held out her hands in front of her, her clothes ripping from the force of elemental power she directed.

Ojinkomàsu charged past, and Kanéko had to grab his mane to avoid being yanked off by the force of the gale. As soon as they were out of the blast area, the air went still, and she settled back into place. He raced in a tight curve to bring them around.

Kanéko groaned at the pressure of the horse's speed. She struggled to turn herself so she could look at where Sinmak had been.

To her surprise, Sinmak still stood. He had stepped to the side and narrowly avoided the trench formed by Maris's magic. He bowed to Maris. "You are going to have to—"

Wind picked him up and threw him back. He made no noise as he flew backwards into the barn. A crack rocketed through the mill yard and the barn collapsed in on itself.

Kanéko slid off Ojinkomàsu and stormed toward the yard. The unnamed blade in her hand shone in the firelight.

The mercenaries watched her warily, a few of them turning to keep their swords between Kanéko and themselves, but others stepped closer to the dalpre and lifted their blades as if to strike the helpless prisoners.

Kanéko stopped in her tracks.

"Kan!" Maris slammed into her and nearly knocked Kanéko off her feet. "You came back!"

Kanéko jammed her weapon into her makeshift sheath and hugged Maris tightly. As they embraced, she inspected the cuts and scrapes visible through Maris's shredded dress. She didn't see anything life-threatening and let out a sigh of relief. She sighed and said, "I'm sorry. I should have never told you to leave."

"And I like you!" Maris panted heavily with a smile.

With a gesture to the mercenaries and dalpre, Kanéko asked, "What about them?"

Maris frowned and a whimper rose in her throat. "I can't get close to them. And every time I do, they threaten to kill Mommy. And the others. And they were going to kill the puppies. A-And I can't let them do that."

Kanéko patted Maris on the back. "Do you know what he wants?"

"Rub. And Sinmak tried to stab him, but then Mommy stopped him. And she got hurt and pulled him into the pack. And then all the assholes penned up the women and puppies. But then the mean man," she pointed to the barn, "told them not to kill the puppies unless someone fought back. So no one is moving."

"Why?"

"Because if you hurt the puppies, the mommies would kill them. And if any got away, the daddies would hunt them down and strip their bones clean." Maris growled, "And no one hurts our puppies."

"What about you?"

Maris leaned against Kanéko and panted. "I'm so tired. I took off and tried to hurt Sinmak. He's the alpha asshole. And if he goes down, and then his pack will run away. But he's good at fighting. And he makes fun of me. And I can't hit him. And that sword of his can block my magic."

Kanéko rested her hand on Maris. She could feel heat radiating off her sweat-slicked skin. "Maris, how much energy do you have?"

A whimper. "I'm tired, Kanéko. I keep missing. And I almost fell." Maris's body trembled with exhaustion underneath Kanéko's hands.

Realization dawned and Kanéko slumped. "He's running you to exhaustion. If he can get you, he will use you to trade for Ruben for some deal he made with Damagar. I'm guessing I'm the price for the titan's help."

"Mommy won't ever give up Ruben."

"Even if he threatens to kill you?"

Maris looked up, a hurt look in her eyes. Kanéko could see that Maris's mother would have a hard time choosing between her daughter and Ruben. Maris whimpered pitifully. "Why? Why would he do that?"

The dalpre's face grew violent and angry as she glared toward the barn. "And I hate him so much."

"I know, I know," Kanéko turned to follow her gaze. "But, that means—"

The air blasted around her as Maris took off.

Surprised, Kanéko lost her balance. By the time she scrambled up, she could only see a trail of dust leading directly into the barn. She gripped her sword and charged after Maris. *"That means don't go charging at him!"* Swearing violently, she raced into the collapsed building.

Inside, she could see Maris hovering near the core-driven saw. The dalpre threw blasts of air toward the ground. "I hate you! I hate you! I hate you!"

Sawdust rose up in great plumes of choking clouds. Thankful for the goggles protecting her, Kanéko weaved through the broken roof and shattered remains of the saws. She drew the layout of the barn in her head, filling in the details as she made her way to the far end.

Sinmak parried Maris's blasts. His sword glowed brighter with every stroke as the rapid bombardment rained down on him. He was on the near side of the mill's massive blade. On the other side was the aisle leading directly to fire core chamber. Her memories filled in a gap, there was nothing besides the blade besides Sinmak and the core.

A grim smile stretched across her face. She peeked up and whistled once. Maris slowed down and grew quiet. The dog ears perked up as she threw another blast down.

"Maris! Line him up with the big blade!"

Maris frowned and looked over.

Kanéko peeked over at Sinmak. When she couldn't see his eyes, she pointed where she wanted Sinmak to stand.

Maris nodded, and then turned back to Sinmak. "Die!" Sherained blasts against Sinmak. The impact shook the ground and sent sawdust flying everywhere. But, for all the strength Maris had left, a few blasts sputtered inches from her fingers. The dalpre's body jerked down before she regained her flight.

"Sands!" Kanéko hurried through the dust, moving from memory. She found the fire core. The iron chamber continued to burn with a steady heat. She grabbed a hook and pried open the door.

Kanéko had never seen the inside of a core chamber before, only read about them. Standing in front of one, looking at the two foot wide rune producing a column of pure, unrelenting flames, she felt awe and fear. This was magic that she could use, something to save Maris and the mill.

She tore her thoughts away and propped the door open with a heavy brick. She looked down the aisle. At the end, behind the spinning blade, Sinmak and Maris fought. She gripped her dagger tighter and raced back around so Sinmak was between her and the core.

When Sinmak saw her, he smiled. "Give me a few seconds, girl. Your friend is almost done."

Kanéko glanced up at Maris, who floated lower. The wind didn't cut nearly as tightly as Maris panted for breath. Her entire body shook and the aura of power around her flickered in and out.

"Drown in sands," muttered Kanéko under her breath, *"she really is running out."*

Sinmak parried another air blast. Kanéko charged in after Maris's attack, slashing with the knife. Like before, Sinmak parried both Maris's and her attack. Kanéko accidentally left an opening, but Sinmak didn't take advantage of it. The sly smile on his lips gave her the impression that neither of them were a threat to the mercenary.

Annoyed, she remembered Garèo's training. He insisted she never use the same attack two times in a row, because it was too easy to remember. She changed her attacks, going from slashes to pierces and mixing in the occasional punch and kick.

Sinmak parried her blows, but the sly smile faded from his lips. As she picked a random attack, she saw a tic on his cheek spasming. The wilder her attacks and the less she planned her maneuvers, the more he strained to defend against her. Every time she lashed out with her feet or swung her fist, the tic on his cheek would jump before he managed to dodge out of the way. Soon, sweat glistened on his forehead, and he panted with effort.

Kanéko pressed her attack, trying to push him back toward the saw.

Sinmak grunted and wiped the sawdust clinging to his head. "Going to throw me into the blade? Seriously?"

"*Yes, that's—*" Kanéko blanched as she realize she almost told him her plans in the heat of battle. She had never fought so hard before and it was hard to keep her thoughts and her mouth separate.

"Please. The blade doesn't move. I'm not going to make such a stupid mistake as to impale myself on it."

Between one parry and a strike, Kanéko noticed that he hadn't reacted to her accidental declaration. Curious, she wondered if he could speak Miwāfu. Keeping her face a mask of rage, she yelled, "*You're a fluffy bunny!*"

He didn't respond. He didn't smile. He only parried her blow.

Kanéko felt elated. "*Maris, he doesn't know Miwāfu! As soon as he goes to duck under the blade, do you think you can charge him and throw him into the core?*"

"*Yes, Great Kosobyo Kanéko!*" Maris swooped down to hover behind Kanéko. Streamers of air howled past Kanéko, yanking at her hair.

The smell of ozone choked Kanéko, but she continued to assault Sinmak.

Sinmak backed up further. The saw blade caught his hat and yanked it from his head. He sighed and smirked. "Brave plan. But, I can just do this…" He ducked underneath the saw blade, still parrying with his own weapon.

"*Now!*" screamed Kanéko as she dove to the side.

Maris exploded into movement and flashed past Kanéko. The wind threw Kanéko into a wooden beam as the dalpre rocketed underneath the saw blade catching Sinmak in the stomach with her fists. He flew back with a look of surprise on his face, losing his blade in the air.

Sinmak's blade twirled in the air before the saw caught it, launching it out the door of the mill. Kanéko ducked to avoid it, but it was already past her before she could respond. She turned toward the fire core, but the wind pummeled her body and she started to slide away.

Bracing herself against a nearby pipe, Kanéko forced her head off the ground and looked down the aisle. The cloud of sawdust blew past her as Maris's wind cleared everything loose from the ground. She had a clear view of Maris struggling with Sinmak right at the entrance to the core.

Despite Maris's surprise attack, Sinmak managed to brace himself a few feet away from the core. One boot wedged between the joints holding the pipes, and he held on to a wooden brace with one hand. His other was free as he tried to pry Maris away from him.

Maris was holding his chest, her arms wrapped around him and her legs straight out as wind howled around her. The flames from the core were being pulled around them in streamers, sucked past the two by the force of Maris's attempt to drive Sinmak forward.

Kanéko concentrated on forcing her dagger through the pressure that pummeled her and crawled underneath the saw blade. She tried to stand up, but the intensity of the wind forced her back to the ground. She was thankful for her goggles, otherwise she wouldn't be able to see with the winds tearing at her face.

Sinmak pounded on Maris's back with his elbow. But, even his most powerful blow didn't budge the dalpre. He gave up after a few seconds and his hand dropped to his side.

Kanéko felt a fierce joy as his other hand began to slip from the pipe, but it faded when Sinmak brought his hand back up. This time, he had the mechanical device from his belt. With a start, Kanéko realized it was a gun of some sort. It had a long muzzle and a large canister attached to it. She had read about them, but never imagined she would see one in person.

Sinmak struggled with his weapon, trying to aim the muzzle at Maris's back. The tip wavered violently, bouncing around without pattern. He fired a shot but missed Maris completely. It hit a pipe and a gout of steam roared out.

Kanéko tried to call out to Maris, to encourage her, but her voice didn't carry over the force that pummeled her.

To Kanéko's horror, Maris's energy sputtered, and the wind died.

Sinmak's foot hit the ground and he used his momentum to slam his elbow into the back of Maris's head.

In the sudden silence, Maris groaned as she slumped, but it ended with a growl that shook the rafters. She surged back up and slammed her head against Sinmak's chin. At the same time, the air cracked as the wind burst back to life, but in the opposite direction, into the core. It tore pipes free from the moorings and dragged Kanéko back along the ground until she found a fallen beam to brace her feet.

The wind surged into the fire core and the column of fire deformed from the force rushing past it. Pressure gauges climbed into dangerous levels. Kanéko saw, but couldn't hear over the wind, joints cracking from the pressure. Steam burst out in plumes only to be sucked back into the core.

Sinmak's eyes grew wide as his hand slipped off the pipe. Maris's magic surged and both of them flew toward the door to the core chamber. His hand flashed out and he caught the edge of the opening, holding on as his feet dangled in the howling flames inside the chamber. Straining, he brought his gun up, but the weapon shook and wavered from the winds buffeting him. He couldn't even tilt the gun to aim at Maris's tail.

Suddenly, Sinmak smirked.

A sick feeling filled Kanéko. She didn't know what he had in mind, but he stopped trying to shoot Maris and instead aimed directly away from her.

He fired.

A shot burst out of the gun and raced down the aisle. It slowed down in mid-air, its forward momentum arrested by the force sucking everything toward the core. The shot itself was crystal, a sphere with some liquid inside it. Kanéko took a double-take as she realized it was an alchemical shot. The liquid would be enchanted to burn, freeze, or explode when cracked.

Agonizingly slow, the shot reversed its course and shot back down the aisle. Its course became clear, and Kanéko saw how it would strike a building support right behind Maris.

"Look out!" Kanéko screamed out frantically.

The alchemical shot slammed into the support beam and exploded into green flames. The blast picked Kanéko up and threw her into the spinning blade. The serrated edge tore the pack from her shoulder, leaving a deep cut.

She hit the ground with her ears ringing. Desperate, she scrambled to her feet and swayed as a wave of vertigo crashed into her. Her eyes came into painful focus, just in time to see Sinmak kicking the door of the fire core closed.

"You know," panted Sinmak, "that was almost a mistake... on my part."

The saw blade was no longer between them. Kanéko glanced to the side to see it bouncing off into the woods, toward the river. She scanned the mill in the sudden silence, looking for Maris.

When she didn't find Maris, she said, "W-Where is she?"

Sinmak gestured to the core with one shaking hand. He panted for a moment and took a deep breath. "In there."

"In the core?" A whimper rose from Kanéko's throat. There was no way Maris could survive in there, not with the relentless heat. "She's in there? Let her out before she's—!"

"Is killed? Do you really think she could survive that?" Sinmak said in a cold voice. He gave her a hard look with his reddish eyes. "I thought you were supposed to be—"

"You bastard!" Kanéko charged, her dagger high.

The end of Sinmak's gun snapped up, and she skidded to a halt. She couldn't stop herself fast enough, and the muzzle jabbed into her throat, shooting a bolt of pain into her. She stood in front of him, shaking with anger and fear.

Tears ran down her cheeks as she looked up at the core. She couldn't find the words for the growing devastation that threatened to consume her sanity. Maris was gone in an instant. "Gods no. Why?"

"Because, I was hired to kidnap you, girl." Sinmak had a voice like gravel and she had to strain to hear it over her panting. "I might have made a deal with that fr... Damagar for the boy, but that was only to get you."

He groaned and rubbed his cheek. "Though, I was hoping that I could take my men and run but apparently that is a bad idea for everyone here."

Sinmak sighed. "Still, no one wanted the bitch and you'll be a lot easier to manage without her protecting you." He jammed her with the muzzle of his gun. "Now, move."

She stared past his shoulder at the fire core door, trying to figure out some way of getting past Sinmak.

"Now, Kan... Kanéko Lurkuklan." He stumbled over her name, skipping the last vowel, but then said her name in a mechanical voice. Muttering, he turned his head slightly to the side. He tapped the muzzle lightly against her throat before shifting it down to her collar. "I think we need to discuss your future."

"You killed her."

He rolled his eyes. "Yes, but she left me no choice." He stepped forward and forced Kanéko back. "That is now in the past. I need you to pay attention to your present. Your present is that someone will pay me a lot of money to deliver you to Jinto Panzir within a week. I don't care why. I don't know what he has in mind. I don't even know if he is a he. However, what I do care about is getting my men out of this forsaken area and get paid lots of money."

Fresh tears blurred Kanéko's vision. She never tore her eyes away from the core. "No... no... I can't leave her. Not now."

Sinmak continued to push her back, working her toward the barn entrance. "Death is a part of life. Pay attention to what you have left, for that is more important. I need you to move."

"I won't."

"Then I will start killing everyone until you do. I will start with that friend of yours, the dwarf."

She finally glared at him. "Then I'll kill you."

"No, you won't." He sounded confident.

Sinmak's face spasmed just as one of the beams above them cracked.

Kanéko flinched from the sound.

He reached out and grabbed her. She let out a shriek as he shoved her away from the core. He took a step himself just as the timber came crashing down less than a foot behind him. He didn't flinch as it rolled back away from him. Strolling forward, he jammed the muzzle against Kanéko's throat, bruising it again.

She stepped back. "The poster said unhurt."

He shrugged, and then gave her an evil grin. She shivered at the sight of it. "I can afford a healer. Now, head up to the front. I need to deal with the vomen for that damn frog..." His voice cracked. "Damagar! Damn it!"

Kanéko looked confused.

Sinmak shook his head and groaned again. "That damn be... Damagar burned your names into my head and now I have to use the entire thing. Do you know how annoying it being forced to say Waryoni Garèo or Kanéko Lurkuklan every single time?"

She gave him a mock smile and shrug.

"No matter. I'll get rid of Damagar as soon as I deal with the vomen. Then I'm getting out of here before your parents or Waryoni Garèo... gets involved."

"What does Garèo have to do with this?"

"Don't care. Cobin has a problem with him and I like my employees to be happy. Happy employees give their all and don't betray you in the middle of a heist." He jammed the gun into Kanéko again. "Now, move or someone gets shot."

Tears running down her cheeks, Kanéko obeyed. She kept her eyes on his gun, waiting for a chance to lash out. She didn't understand it, but her imagination slowly began to work through the mechanical device.

They stopped long enough for Sinmak to grab his sword from the grass outside the barn. Then he prodded her into the yard. He stopped Kanéko a chain away from the dalpre and looked over her shoulder at the captured workers. "Now, old lady, give me the boy."

"Never," growled Mamgum. An answering choir of growls, from children and adults alike, rose up, but when the mercenaries stepped forward, everyone but Mamgum flinched back and whimpered.

"Do it, or I'll do the same I did to your—" His face spasmed and Sinmak clamped his mouth shut. He cleared his throat. "Do it, or I'll kill Kanéko Lurkuklan."

Mamgum snarled. "You touch her, and then I will end you."

Kanéko barely heard the words. Her mind replayed Sinmak's actions. His facial spasm, a tic, came back. The same tic was there right before he threw her aside to avoid the timber. She also saw it when she charged him. Every time he was attacked or he was in danger, the muscle spasm preceded his action to avoid being hurt. She mentally ran through the magical powers she read about, trying to recall something she could use against him.

Sinmak gestured for one of the mercenaries. "Get a rope and tie up this girl. Then get ready to sail out. Now, Bitch," he pointed at Mamgum, "Give me the damn boy before I count to three."

Kanéko identified his powers with a flash. Sinmak had prescience like Falkin. To test it, she reached down for her dagger. Sinmak's gun rose up to her forehead, and he looked at her, a muscle jumping below his eye. A brief frown crossed his face as he considered some response.

Kanéko recalled the sentence he had almost said before his tic. Seizing an opportunity, Kanéko knew she had another weapon to use. She glared at him. "Or you'll do what? Kill her like you just killed Maris?"

"Yes, just—" His face spasmed, and Sinmak inhaled sharply. He shook his head minutely.

The sound of whimpering and cries from the dalpre silenced instantly.

Kanéko turned to see that they all staring at him with looks of surprise and shock. Then, the expressions turned to anger as the knot of dalpre shifted. Children were set down and crowded into the center. The adults, male and female, drew back their lips into snarls as a growl rose up from all of them.

Mamgum let Ruben slip to the ground. Right before he dropped out of sight, she could see his blue eyes watching impassively. He looked still weak and injured but he was alive.

Sinmak held up his hand. "I said I wouldn't hurt your children."

"You... killed my Mar?" Mamgum's voice was a deep growl that shook the air.

He gulped and his cheek twitched. "I won't kill any... look..." It looked like he was struggling with words. Then he suddenly turned on her, reaching out for her.

Kanéko spoke quickly. "He did! He threw her in the core! He burned her!"

Sinmak grabbed her, his fingers digging into her shoulder as he struggled to clamp his hand over her mouth. "Gag her!"

The air changed. It was a subtle pressure but the hairs on Kanéko's neck stood on end.

She turned to see that the dalpre were all staring at Sinmak, murderous intent in their eyes. Even the children had joined in, with hairs sticking up like hackles and ears pulled back. Bared teeth shone in the haze of smoke and dust.

Sinmak glanced back, his eyes widening.

The mercenaries backed away, their faces growing pale.

With a grunt, Sinmak released Kanéko to grab his weapons. He started with his sword, but then switched to pulling his gun up to aim toward Mamgum.

Kanéko surged forward to spoil his attack.

He jerked out of the way and struggled to frantically aim at Mamgum.

Mamgum stepped forward. "You..." She took a deep breath.

Around her, the pack suddenly crouched down and covered their ears.

Kanéko started to cover her ears, but knew that if she did, Sinmak would fire his gun. She steeled herself against the incoming pain and grabbed his arm, pulling down with all her might.

The mercenaries surged forward, but the dalpre weren't cowering from them.

Mamgum stepped around them as she inhaled. "Will..."

Kanéko felt the air crackling with power. She winced as she remembered the pain the last time Mamgum yelled.

"DIE!" The sound of Mamgum's scream became meaningless with volume, a deafening blast that crushed Kanéko against the ground. It roared around her, bouncing off every surface and echoing back endlessly.

The agony in her ears was overwhelming. She blacked out for the briefest of moments but came to before she hit the ground.

Dazed, Kanéko managed to catch herself on one knee. She tried to look around, but the deafening noise left her vision blurry and she couldn't see through her tears. She scrambled to her feet and backed away, trying to clear the ringing in her ears. She hit something solid and hot behind her and spun around, flailing. Her hands caught Ojinkomàsu's mane. Gasping for breath, Kanéko leaned into him until her vision cleared.

Half of the mercenaries were on the ground clutching their bleeding ears. The other half fought for their lives as the dalpre swarmed over them. Sticks, rocks, and teeth were used with brutal efficiency. Blood splashed everywhere. More than a few mercenaries were staggering helplessly, but there was no mercy from the pack as they were pulled down. No quarter was given as man after man fell with a gurgling scream.

Her hearing came back quickly, but a high-pitched whine made it hard to make out words beyond the screams.

Near the house, Mamgum attacked Sinmak with a timber as thick as Kanéko's thigh and as tall as Kanéko. The enraged mother wielded it like a two-handed sword, slamming it repeatedly against Sinmak's blade. He tried to parry, but the metal of the weapon was already bent from the brutal and ceaseless attacks from the enraged mother.

A mercenary stalked toward Kanéko. His knuckles were white around his sword and she could see the muscles in his arms tensing. He bellowed and charged forward.

Kanéko grabbed at her dagger but missed it. Frantic, she fumbled for the hilt but her fingers refused to wrap around the weapon.

Something powerful shoved her aside from behind.

She stumbled. With a rush, she could hear more clearly.

Ojinkomàsu spun around on his front hooves. His back feet kicked out, catching the mercenary in the chest. A burst of light and flames exploded from the hooves and the man flew back across the yard before he hit a tree with a sickening crunch. His smoking body didn't get up.

She stared up at horse with shock and surprise. "Ojinkomàsu?"

A gunshot rang out over the yard and through the ringing in her ears.

Kanéko snapped her head around. Sinmak was on the ground, his body beaten almost to a pulp. Blood ran from a bruised eye. One hand hung limply on his side, but his other held his gun. Steam rose from the tip of the gun.

Shaking, Kanéko followed the line of the gun. It pierced Mamgum's stomach, right above her navel. The heavy timber dropped to the ground as Mamgum pressed both hands to her belly. Blood soaked through her shirt and spread out across the fabric. She let out a whimper and crumpled to the ground.

Sinmak groaned as he crawled to his feet. He rocked the gun back and the next shot clicked into place. He held it out toward the crowds. Around him, the battle died down as people watched in shock.

"Now, that was a mistake... on her part. Things are getting messy." He panted. "Time to leave! Someone get the bartim's daughter! Then kill the boy and all these fucking dogs!"

The barn exploded. A pillar of flame shot up, a mile high column of intense flames that beat against Kanéko. The air around the ruins were sucked up into it. The pillar blossomed into a mushroom-shaped cloud above them. The blast threw Kanéko, Ruben, and Sinmak into the air. It flattened the main house and blew apart the barracks.

She tumbled along the hard-packed ground. Her body came to a stop in a tangle of arms and legs among the dalpre. Frantic, she pulled herself out and forced herself to stand.

Flames roared from the remains of the barn. The large, heavy timbers were on fire, the heavy wood burning brightly. Heat surrounded Kanéko, sucking the moisture from the air and she had trouble breathing. She stepped out from the dalpre and looked around for Sinmak and Mamgum.

Silhouetted by the flame, Sinmak picked up his bent sword and made a show of jamming it into the sheath. It stuck, and he forced it in; the tip of the sword ripped through the side and stuck out at an angle. He picked up his gun and held it in his good hand. He turned to Kanéko, a shadow against the intense light and heat from the barn. "This has gone on long enough. Either you come with me, child, or I will kill every single person in this mill."

Behind Sinmak, someone walked toward him through the fire. Kanéko's mouth gaped open as she recognized Maris striding through the flames. The girl's body was on fire, her black fur like pitch in the light. Around her, the fires grew more intense and wood burned away in heartbeats. Above, the clouds began to rotate into a tornado flickering with lightning in the dark, violent clouds. Maris's eyes were two points of white flame and her teeth glittered from her snarl.

Sinmak started to turn, following Kanéko's gaze.

Kanéko panicked and yelled out. "I'll surrender!"

He turned back. A slow smile crossed his lips. "Then, just let me—" He stopped as his tic jumped. "I'll—" Another tic. He closed his mouth, but his cheek continued to jump. Slowly, his eyes widened. Even over the roar of the flames, Kanéko heard him speak in a voice of horror, "Why is everything a mistake?"

The roar of the flames died and left a stunned silence in the yard. Around Maris, the fires gathered, sucking away from the burning wood and debris and formed into a sphere of energy between Maris's hands. As the heat warped the air around her, the remains of Maris's dress burned away in a shower of embers.

Kanéko started to look away in embarrassment but peeked back as jealousy reared its head. Maris was using air and fire magic at the same time, fusing them together into a single spell. It was the epic fight Kanéko always dreamed of, but it wasn't her in the flames saving the day. It was Maris using magic that only one in a million could use. Kanéko knew she would have been jealous but she was too relieved to see Maris alive to care anymore.

Sinmak caught her expression. He turned around. When he saw Maris, he stepped back with shock. His hand shook as he jammed the gun into the holster and fumbled with his sword.

"You—" gasped Maris, her voice rough from the heat that raged around her.

Sinmak yanked the sword from the sheath. He cut his palm with the effort and the flash of blood vaporized in the air before it hit the ground.

"—hurt—" She pulled back her hands. The sphere grew brighter and hotter, expanding until it covered half of Maris's body.

"—my mommy!" Maris threw her hands forward. The sphere of flame shot from her fingers.

Sinmak parried with his sword, which flared into a blade of magenta waves. The sphere of flame split in half and the two halves bounced across the yard, igniting the ground as they blew past Kanéko.

Maris crouched down and kicked off the ground. The remains of the barn exploded behind her, sending embers shooting into the forest beyond the yard. She shot forward and slammed into Sinmak's stomach. He folded in half over her burning body, his eyes bugging out from the impact. She rocketed ahead, leaving burning air behind her, as they flew up over the trees.

Sinmak's sword exploded into brilliance. Magenta lightning bolts shot out in all directions, sparking and popping as it formed a sphere of feedback that matched the white-hot flames that surrounded Maris.

They arced up into the sky, rising in a star of white and magenta flames. The air rippled around the two as they dwindled to a point of blinding light.

Kanéko, protected by her goggles, could see it as clear as day. Around her, the dalpre and Ruben shielded their eyes. She held her breath, watching as the light reached its apex. It flashed out and then exploded into a blossom of raw magic. The power tore apart the clouds and the crest of energy came rushing back toward the mill.

Straining to see, Kanéko searched the skies. She spotted a dark shape arcing out into the distance. She didn't know if it was Maris or Sinmak, but she hoped with all her might Maris had survived the explosion.

"Maris!" Kanéko ran forward. She wouldn't make it. "Ojinkomàsu!"

She stumbled toward the burning trees. She heard him running up to her, and she grabbed him as he passed. He moved in perfect harmony with her desire, slowing down just enough for her to settle on his back and then accelerated toward Maris's falling body.

They hit the concussion wave without slowing. Energy crackled along the trees and ground. Lightning bolts arced between Ojinkomàsu and the earth as the horse sailed through it. The roar of the explosion followed right behind the crest. Kanéko winced from the deafening sound of it, but then he passed through it. He accelerated into a gallop as he raced through the forest. The halo of light around him intensified until the brilliance surrounded the horse as he tore through the woods.

Chapter 42

Sinmak's Fate

Sacrifice for king and queen and country. That is the greatest honor that
any Kormar citizen can perform.

—The Puzzle King

When Kanéko reached the smoking crater, she fell off Ojinkomàsu and hit the ground hard. The rocky surface dug
into her knees, but she got up and forced herself to limp
forward. At the edge, she peered down the steep incline. At
the bottom was Maris, face down in the ground surrounding by radial marks. Scorch marks, cuts, and bruises covered her naked body but otherwise she appeared unhurt.
Her tail was limp against her thigh.

Ozone burned Kanéko's throat as she slid down the incline. She knelt down next to the dalpre. "Maris?"

She touched Maris, and then snatched back her hand
from the intense heat that radiated from the dalpre's body.
Shucking off her jacket, she wrapped it around Maris and
used it to insulate her as she pulled Maris to her chest.
"Come on, don't die on me."

Tears ran down Kanéko's cheeks. They dripped from her
chin and hit Maris's skin. The droplets danced for a second

and sizzled before evaporating. She clutched Maris tight to her body and ignored the heat that choked her.

"Please, I need you. Y-You..." Kanéko choked on the words, "You're my friend. You and Ruben are my friends."

Maris groaned but didn't move. Her ears twitched.

Kanéko sobbed. "Please, just wake up."

A hand rested on Kanéko's shoulder. She looked up to see a tiny hand and felt the mental tickle of telepathy. At first, she thought it was Ruben, but when she lifted her gaze, it wasn't the teenager she saw. It was an older figure, a male voman about a foot taller than Ruben. He had thick dark beard and a lighter color of blue eyes. There was a sad smile on his lips.

Behind him, a black wolf with bright blue eyes sniffed the ground.

She latched on the tickle of her mind, and then felt surprise as the voman's mind connected with hers. «Who are you?» She asked by picturing the voman's image.

He spoke in a powerful, deep voice, "I am Tagon Pavir." At the same time, he projected a series of symbols that represented his name in Volis, the language of Vo. "And this," he said before an image of the wolf blossomed in her mind, "is my companion, Jason Magol."

«You are—» She tried to picture Ruben, but the image of Tagon's own son refused to focus in their thoughts. Kanéko switched to spoken words, "Ruben's father?"

Tagon nodded, a wry smile on his face. "You had no previous skill with telepathic communication before you departed. A recent occurrence?"

"Yes, because of Ruben."

"That would be obvious. The adorable Maris Germudrir has many talents, but telepathy is not among them." He gestured to Maris. "May I inspect her for injuries?"

Kanéko nodded and twisted her body to present Maris. She wondered if she should cover the dalpre's naked breasts or close her thighs, but it was hard enough to move the curvy girl in her position. Somehow, she felt embarrassed for Maris.

Tagon pulled off his own jacket and folded it into a pillow. He guided the dalpre to the ground. He hummed quietly to himself as he inspected her.

Kanéko couldn't bear to see Maris helpless. She turned away and crawled out of the crater. Standing up on the edge, she scanned the surrounding forest. She wanted to run home, to check on her parents, but Maris needed her more.

A glint caught her attention. She spotted other places where debris smoked among the trees and underbrush. She padded to the closest one and squatted down to inspect a piece of metal. It was the sword blade, heavily cracked. The heat fused the metal together, twisting it into a useless hunk with cracks webbed across the pitted surface.

She looked up to see more of them: pieces of Sinmak's sword, a burning belt, a smoldering boot. In the distance, about a quarter mile away, she saw a thick plume of smoke rising above the trees. Curious, she stopped herself and looked down. "Tagon, could I check something?"

Tagon looked up, his eyes not blinking. "Keep safe and keep in the relative vicinity, please. Your father's influence is strong in this area, but there are many mercenaries still in these woods. I would rather not have you kidnapped at this point."

He smiled wryly. "That would be embarrassing to both of us."

Wondering what her father knew, Kanéko headed toward the smoke. The black wolf followed a few paces behind her. She got a few chains before she realized she had no weapon. She turned back with second thoughts but stopped when the wolf sat down behind her. The wolf blinked once and Kanéko was reminded of when Ruben really paid attention. She turned back and continued along her way, knowing that somehow Tagon was watching her through Jason.

She came around a tree and saw a smoking corpse. She gasped and stepped back. Her hand rose to her mouth, and she cringed. Sinmak was charred to the bone. She felt sick to her stomach. His half-burned hat rested on the ground, inches from his fingertips. The smell was rank, of burnt flesh and hair, and her stomach rolled with nausea.

Standing in front of death, Kanéko felt a pang of sadness. Her kidnapper, or the man who tried to kidnap her, was dead at her feet. She tried to dredge up anger for him, but all she felt was sick to her stomach at his destruction.

She looked away and spotted a glint of metal nearby. She padded over a pair of boulders to find Sinmak's gun lodged in the crook of a tree. The wooden handle was charred, and the wisps of smoke rose up from the wood. It took her a few minutes to climb up and grab it. It was hot in her hand, but it hurt less than grabbing a steam pipe.

Dismissing her pain, she flipped it over and inspected the gauge. It had a needle on a dial of numbers going from zero to five thousand. The glass over the dial was cracked, but she could see where someone scratched five marks on the brass fitting. The needle hovered just over the middle of the scratches. There were two tubes on the gun. One was a long brass muzzle that lead to a spherical canister attached to the gauge. The other appeared to be a feeding tube of some sort. There was a single lead ball in it; it rattled loudly as she rocked it forward, but when she tilted the gun up, it snapped into place.

She searched the area, spreading out until she found seven more shots. She used her shirt to hold them and carried everything back to Maris and Tagon.

As she approached, she heard a new voice she never expected: Virsian. She ran the last few steps and looked down in the crater. "Vir!"

Virsian bent over Maris, breathing hard as she rested her hands on Maris's stomach and forehead. Yellow-green energies rose from both of their bodies as Virsian worked her healing magic. She didn't look up at Kanéko's outburst.

Kanéko stepped away when she realized the healer didn't need a distraction.

Tagon joined her at the edge of the crater.

She looked over at him, and then reached down to grab his hand. As soon as she felt the itch of his telepathy, she brought up the image of the gun. It came quickly, like with Ruben's knowledge. She focused on it. Images flashed through her head and she continued to pull the construction of the weapon, how to use it, and what it could do. The images burned through her thoughts and she used it to explode it into parts and reassemble it in her mind.

«Kanéko Lurkuklan, we need to discuss your manners with telepaths,» came the amused thought from Tagon.

She projected a burst of an apology but continued to draw out knowledge from him. She focused on the gauge to determine its purpose. When it welled up in her mind, she smiled. The design of the gun would allow five shots, but it was made by hand. That meant tiny imperfections changed how it fired the shots. The scratches on the dial must have been Sinmak's attempt to identify the charge left in the weapon.

Tagon didn't stop her but she could feel his amusement fill her as she finished investigating the weapon. When she learned what she could, she started to pull away, but Tagon stopped her. «Tell me what happened on your trip?»

Kanéko looked at him, not sure where to start. She began her tale with an image of the stables, right before Jinmel came back. Unlike Ruben, Tagon knew the tower as intimately as her and the images formed clearly. She found it easy to relive the last few weeks of her life, images racing one after the other. She could feel his listening to the tale, experiencing her trials, but his mind was picking through her thoughts for specific memories: Ruben.

When she realized that, she continued her tale but gave more detail with Ruben. The first time she remembered Ruben's thoughts inside her own, Tagon closed his eyes and smiled. The bittersweet mixture of sadness and joy crashed into her.

Tagon smiled and his hand tightened on hers. «I missed touching his heart.»

Kanéko tried to understand how two telepaths couldn't communicate with their minds. «For how long?»

He shook his head. «For...» A calendar flashed through his mind. «...eighteen years, five months.»

She remembered Ruben saying something similar, but the date didn't seem right. «What happened? Was that when he was born?»

An image flashed up, of a much younger Tagon watching a female voman holding a child. The memory began to play forward in slow motion. The little one starting to crack open his eyes, and then the memory ended sharply. The thoughts flew back in time until the point much earlier of Tagon resting his hand on the female voman's belly. «The day his mind woke up. With his consciousness outside of his mother's natal shields, he became a danger to us all.»

She could feel Tagon's sadness. She respectfully slipped her hand away. She looked down at Virsian and Maris.

Virsian groaned as she pushed herself up but slumped back on her knees before she could straighten. Her tail rested slackly on the ground and Kanéko could see the feline dalpre's ears droop.

"Vir?"

Virsian looked up and gave her a tired smile. "Kanéko, you're safe."

"What about Maris?"

"She will live, but there will be scars on her mind and body. Her resonance," Virsian held up her arm where the hairs stood on end. Crackles of static electricity ran along her fur. "is much worse for me. I can feel her energies burning my insides and itching the back of my throat. She got powerful quickly."

She stood up with a groan and stepped back. When she reached the edge of the crater, she started to crawl out. Kanéko helped her, and together, they stepped away. Even a rod away, the hair still stood up on Virsian's body.

Virsian gave Kanéko a tight hug. "I'm glad you are safe." She looked over Kanéko's body, at the scratches and bruises, and then sighed. "Even if I could help you, your body has too much feedback from prior healing. You need time to recover."

"W-Why are you here, Vir?"

"Garèo."

"He's here?"

"Yes, after this creature named Damagar destroyed the inn, I followed him to Rock River. We were ambushed, but then Tagon called me and I came as fast as I could. Garèo said he was being called to your father's place."

Kanéko pushed her away. "I-I have to go home. I need to be there too. Mama... and Papa, they need me."

Tagon came up and rested his small hand on her wrist. «Damagar is there. I can feel his mental presence from here. He is calling for the death of my son.»

Kanéko tensed, and she felt sick to her stomach. She could still hear the creature's demands in her mind, the shadow of a creature that still resided in her thoughts. She pushed Damagar away and looked down at Tagon. "What can I do?"

He looked up with his unblinking blue eyes. "My initial response is to keep you here—"

Kanéko scowled.

He continued, "—but you are not inclined to do that. I recommend you go to your parents and do whatever your skills are best suited for."

She worried her lower lip. She didn't know how an inert girl could help her father and mother against the most powerful magical creature she knew. "What is that?"

He smiled. "Adaptability, intelligence, leadership, and strategy. I will join you as soon as I make sure Mamgum is stable and my son is safe. Ruben..." He paused for a moment. "...will want to watch over Maris."

Ojinkomàsu trotted up and stopped next to Kanéko as if he knew she was about to leave. His body radiated heat like Maris, but it was the heat of the hottest summer day and not the searing flames of an inferno.

Kanéko looked up at him and felt hope. She had no magic, but she could do something. She looked around for somewhere to put the shots for the gun. She noticed Virsian had a leather satchel on her. She requested it and Virsian handed it over. Emptying the contents, Kanéko loaded the bag with the lead shot and used the handle to form a makeshift holster around her waist.

Grabbing Ojinkomàsu's mane, she pulled herself up and settled into place. Looking down at Maris, she spoke to Tagon and Virsian. "Please, keep her safe and bring her to the mill. She has family there and they need her as much as both of you."

Chapter 43

The Fall of Lurkuklan

For their remarkable ability to tap into the incredible records of the Vo, the vomen lack the ability to craft new ideas or plans. Infinite stores of knowledge no doubt hampers creativity.

—Jamlatu Rasmifor, *Vo, The Silence of Evil*

Ojinkomàsu flew more than galloped along the road from the mill. His unshod hooves struck the ground with dizzying speed, a drum beat too fast for any human to match. The wind tore at Kanéko's face; the only reason she could see was because she still wore her stolen goggles. Ojinkomàsu's mane snapped at her face like tiny whips, cracking as the world blurred around her.

She saw a horse ahead of her galloping toward the keep. Even from a quarter mile back, she recognized the rider. "Garèo!" she yelled out.

When she woke up in the river, Kanéko thought Garèo would come to save her. However, he never came rushing to her side. Instead, the most unlikely of friends had come to her rescue. And with their help, they did the remarkable. She didn't need Garèo, her mother, or anyone to protect her. She only needed herself and her friends. A smile crossed her lips with the realization she was far more capable than when she left home.

But, she was still happy to see Garèo safe. She had some questions to ask.

He turned his head but didn't slow down his strawberry roan. Ojinkomàsu sprinted forward to catch up, and then matched the pace. Together, they raced along the dirt road toward the tower.

Kanéko peered over at him, and then called out over the drum of hooves. *"Great Waryoni Garèo, well met."*

"Kosobyo Kanéko, I must thank Tachìra for keeping you safe."

She smiled, but he continued.

"But, from what I heard..." His eyes twinkled. *"...you haven't needed my help for quite some time... Great Kosobyo Kanéko."*

Kanéko blushed at the compliment; Garèo rarely used her full name like that, it was a sign of respect in Miwāfu.

He gestured back the way she came. *"I felt Ojinkomàsu fighting at the mill. Is everyone safe?"*

She shook her head. *"Maris was hurt, and Virsian is healing her. Tagon is—"* she pictured a startling clear image of Tagon rising up in a caricature of a knight standing over both of them, *"Tagon is protecting them. The mercenaries are all dead, I think."*

He nodded once. *"Your Miwāfu is considerably surer."*

"It's easier to fight one's enemies when they can't hear the words you say."

Garèo cocked his head as he looked at her, an unreadable expression on his face. Then he nodded. *"Close. I'll teach you the proper song someday."*

She shivered at the thought. She looked away, and then stopped. Turning her gaze back to Garèo, she inspected him closer. She saw scars of battle that she didn't remember before. His dark skin was shadowed under his eyes, and fresh blood and cuts traced his skin. She could see someone, probably Virsian, had healed injuries, but the blood was too fresh to be more than a few hours old.

"What happened?" She gestured to his arm where a slash cut through his shirt and the ragged edges of a freshly healed wound puckered in a line.

Garèo's eyes darkened. *"My past and my mistakes. An enemy named Cobin attacked Rock River in an attempt to draw me into a fight. He almost killed me."*

He tightened his jaw and gripped his mount's mane tightly.

She thought about the letters she found in Cobin's pack. There would be another time to ask for more details, but she was curious about the rumors that Garèo had killed his family. She looked into his eyes and saw a challenge for her to ask him. She shook her head, and then said, *"Is Cobin...?"*

"Dead." He grinned suddenly. *"And you'll be glad to know that Pahim was arrested with the others. He is awaiting a trial and sentencing from your father. I hope he isn't fair."*

Kanéko felt a surge of fierce joy at hearing about Pahim, but then shame and guilt crashed into her as she remembered the way the dalpre attacked the mercenary in the woods. She had felt sick when Sinmak's body smoldered in front of her and she didn't think she could wish the same fate on Pahim. Even with his betrayal, she couldn't stomach the idea of her father's punishment. She turned her eyes away from Garèo, not wanting to see her doubt, and focused on his horse.

The strawberry stallion looked like Ojinkomàsu in lines and in the chest, but where Ojinkomàsu was the image of a perfect horse, Garèo's was more like the horses she saw in the pictures. A desert equine with a strong body and just a hint of golden eyes. She thought it might be a descendant of Ojinkomàsu, but it wasn't the time to ask.

She turned her attention back to the road and watched as the trees blurred past them. She let her mind wander for a second, alternating between the worry she felt for her parents and reliving the fight with Sinmak.

"Kanéko? What is at the keep? Ojinkomàsu has been pulling me there since this morning."

She turned back to him. *"This morning? He was... I was riding him then. We were miles away."*

Garèo held out a hand in apology but didn't explain. He pointed ahead. *"What's at the tower?"*

"Damagar. A giant toad with magical powers."

"Why?" Garèo's face darkened. *"Why is that creature there?"*

Somehow, Kanéko wasn't surprised that Garèo had encountered Damagar. *"Ruben. He wants someone to kill Ruben."*

Garèo stared at her incredulously. *"Why Ruben?"*

She ran her hands through Ojinkomàsu's mane to gather her thoughts. *"Ruben can kill Damagar. When Ruben thought Maris was in trouble, he yelled loudly and... something cracked. Part of Damagar's mind, Stubbornness, was torn away and swallowed up by Ruben. Damagar is afraid of what will happen when Ruben... um, matures, I guess. Cracks out of his shell."*

"Ruben!? Ruben can do that?"

Kanéko gave a tired smile. *"You said you got the special cases. You have a dalpre that can do fire and wind magic. A vomen who can tear apart the minds of other telepaths. And... me."*

He opened his mouth with surprise, but Damagar's roar beat across the air. Miles away, flocks of birds burst out of the treetops and flew away in a cloud. When the rumbling faded, silence filled the forest.

Kanéko gulped and looked sadly at Garèo. *"Damagar's Self-Preservation is willing to do anything to make sure Ruben dies. And he won't stop until we are dead."*

Garèo stared at the rapidly approaching rise to the tower. He turned back to talk to her. *"Damagar is a behemoth, a ti-*

tan. One of the most powerful magical beings in existence. Armies have failed to kill behemoths. Why do you think you and I have a chance?"

"He isn't fully awake yet."

He looked confused until she tried to explain. *"When he was in my mind, I felt his thoughts. There isn't one personality in there, but many. Most are sleeping and Damagar can't access their powers. He is as weak as he can be right now, which means we have the greatest chance of driving him away. If Mama and you can do enough damage, I'm thinking—"*

"Girl, there aren't enough knights in this country to defeat Damagar, no matter how hard we try. There aren't enough warriors of the desert either. The last one to do so was the Puzzle King, and he had a sands-damned army with him!"

Kanéko felt a surge of anger fill her. "I have to try, damn it! I have to do something, and I won't sit on the edge of a fight, just because I'm a sand-damned *barichirōma* and can't use magic!"

He pulled back. He opened his mouth to speak, but then a second roar shook the forest. It echoed loudly across the trees and shocked both of them into silence. The sound of it faded after a few seconds, and Garèo's horse came to a stumbling halt; Ojinkomàsu stopped neatly next to him.

"You know," said Garèo, *"running away is an option. Toyomìsu..."* He patted the horse he rode. *"...can outrun Damagar. He is Ojinkomàsu's get."*

Ojinkomàsu snorted and bumped his head against Toyomìsu's neck.

Kanéko shook her head curtly. *"No, no it isn't. I can't run. I refuse to run."* She tapped Ojinkomàsu who took off.

Toyomìsu followed suit, and soon they were galloping again.

Garèo sighed. *"You're right."* He reached back to the empty sheath on his back. *"Father, I'm sorry but I need you again."*

Sunlight exploded in his fingertips, spears of it stretching out from beneath his palm.

Kanéko was glad for her darkened goggles as she saw a dagger materialize in his hand. She stared in shock at a weapon she never knew he had. She had also not missed that Garèo had called it "father."

He unsheathed the weapon and held it tight.

They passed the boulder that marked the edge of her father's private lands and came to a stop as they looked down past the fields to Lurkuklan Keep.

Damagar, the massive black and crimson toad, crawled up the side of the tower. One foot braced on the surrounding keep wall; his front legs wrapped around the base. His mouth opened and his tongue snapped out to rip hunks of rock in a rapid-fire pounding. His eyes looked in all directions, rolling in his skull, but one always remained focused on the woman on top of the tower.

Mioráshi could be seen from a mile away as she perched on the side of the tower and leaned over the edge. Her entire body bathed in a spear of sunlight that reached up into the sky and pierced the clouds. The column of sunlight brightened every time she fired her bow, a brilliant arrow of solidified light streaking out from her weapon and slamming into Damagar's face and eyes. The air rumbled with the sounds of her bow shots; a beat of pressure followed by a crack of noise. It looked just like the dream Damagar threatened her with.

"Mama?" whispered Kanéko. She had never seen her mother shoot so fast or with anything besides normal arrows, but she could see how her mother spun sunlight into an arrow and fired is less than a second.

"The Kosobyo hóri, your clan's bow magic."

"I-I've never seen it before."

"When Kosòbyo rejected you, your mother decided not to break your heart by showing magic you could never use. She probably didn't realize she would sacrifice her own well-being when she decided being your mother was more important." There was something in his tone that indicated that he had more opinions about her mother.

Kanéko watched as her mother stepped back from the attacking tongue. She leaned back and fired half a dozen arrows straight into the air. As the arrows shot up, Mioráshi pulled back her bowstring for a seventh shot. Sunlight gathered into a broad-headed arrow already nocked on the bow string. The six arrows reached their apex and then rained down in a hail of light. Just as they struck Damagar's head, Mioráshi fired with a massive bolt directly into his left eye.

He fell, smoke rising off his body. His front claws gouged the side of the tower, and he slammed inside the courtyard.

Kanéko saw her father charge out of the tower, a massive sword in his hand. The blade was longer than him, but he swung it easily and slashed into Damagar's foot.

The behemoth roared loudly and grabbed the tower, pulling himself up. His eyes flashed with magic, and large stone claws burst out of the ground to attack Ronamar.

Her father swung his sword, and the stone shattered into a thousand pieces. The resonance between Damagar's and her father's earth magic crackled the air, and dust plumed out between them. Ronamar flung his hand up and the shards he just broke fired up into Damagar's belly, peppering the creature with a thousand sharp edges.

Kanéko gasped. "That's Papa!" She yanked on Ojinkomàsu's mane and dug in her heels. "I have to get down there!"

Ojinkomàsu reared and bucked once. She let out a scream as her grip slipped and she fell back, slamming hard into the ground. Pain radiated up through her rear as she stared up, open mouthed.

"Ojinkomàsu—?"

The horse stepped to the side and slammed into Toyomìsu. It wasn't a mild bump.

Toyomìsu responded with a slam back as he bared his teeth.

Ojinkomàsu took another step then drove into Toyomìsu again.

Garèo yanked his foot up as the two horses crashed into each other.

Toyomìsu lost his footing and squealed as he fell.

Garèo jumped off his back to avoid being crushed and landed heavily on the ground next to Ojinkomàsu.

Ojinkomàsu pushed against Garèo, who shoved back.

"I can't ride you!"

The horse tried again and Garèo punched him with a right cross, his lips pulled back in a snarl. *"You aren't my horse and you never will be!"*

Kanéko looked back and forth between Garèo and Ojinkomàsu, but neither moved. She focused on Damagar and stood up sharply. With an exasperated sigh, she stormed over to Ojinkomàsu. "I'll ride him if you—"

Ojinkomàsu spun into her and threw her into Toyomìsu just as the younger horse managed to regain his footing. She ducked and rolled over, but Toyomìsu clipped her shoulder and she hissed as she stumbled to the ground. Regaining her feet, she stepped back unsteadily. *"Ojinkomàsu? What are you doing?"*

Garèo growled. *"He wants me to ride him. He always wants me to ride him. Ever since that night in the desert."*

"Why won't you!? You said he's Tachìra's and there is a giant toad trying to kill my parents!"

"No! Tachìra gave him to Hebòmu, not me. I won't ruin Tachìra's or Waryōni's reputation by riding Ojinkomàsu. Stop asking me, you damn horse!" He balled his hand into a fist and punched Ojinkomàsu again.

The horse reared back, squealing. Shoving forward, he butted Garèo in the chest.

"Garèo, who is Hebòmu?"

"My son! He was the horse king, not me." Tears ran down Garèo's check. *"I don't deserve Ojinkomàsu. I killed my father... and my grandfather. I'm a poronēso. I shouldn't have the greatest horse in the desert. I should be... Ojinkomàsu shouldn't be with me."* The dark skinned man sighed and leaned against Ojinkomàsu as a sob ripped through. *"Just go with Kanéko, Great Tachira Ojinkomàsu."*

Frowning, Kanéko struggled with a response. Her eyes flickered over to the tower.

Rocks rained down on Damagar as the creature slammed into the stone building. He pushed on the keep wall with his back feet. Blocks the size of Kanéko's head fell from the other side and the entire tower bent in the middle. Her hand flew to her mouth as she watched the tower starting to tumble, more blocks falling every second.

"Garèo, look!" she screamed, unable to tear her eyes away from the falling tower. Her mother jumped to the highest edge of the tower, balancing on the top and still firing arrows with inhuman speed. She didn't seem to notice the tower leaning dangerously except for the controlled hops she made to remain on top and in sight of the attacking behemoth.

Garèo's voice shot through her senses. *"Drown in the moon-cursed sands!"* The vehemence of his swearing caught Kanéko's attention.

Kanéko rushed over. "Garèo! Just ride him!"

He turned to her, his eyes flashing. *"I will never!"*

Seeing his hands still in fists, Kanéko let out a hiss of annoyance. She reached out for Ojinkomàsu who reared away. With a growl, she stormed over to Toyomìsu and leaped on him. Kicking her heels into his side, she set off toward the leaning tower with no idea how to save her mother.

Kanéko couldn't take her eyes off the tower.

Damagar slammed into the crumbling tower repeatedly, each blow knocking tons of rock from the crumbling structure. Her bedroom window shattered, papers and dust poured out of the widening gaps in the rock. Crenelations tumbled off, plummeting with incredible clarity as the world slowed down, her heart beating a thousand times for every jerk of Toyomìsu's body. Moments later, the top of the tower sheared off and Kanéko's heart lurched as she watched her mother finally succumb to gravity.

Painful seconds later, she heard a horse racing behind her. She held her breath, knowing that Ojinkomàsu would catch up. Nothing prepared her for when the sunlight beating down grew incredibly hot and bright. The air choked her as Ojinkomàsu rushed past in a blur of sunlight. Blinded briefly even with her goggles, she shielded her face with Toyomìsu's neck, blinking at the spots. When her eyes cleared, Ojinkomàsu had covered half the remaining distance between her and the tower.

Garèo was riding the magical horse, his curses rising with every heartbeat.

Ojinkomàsu moved faster than ever before, his feet not even visible on the ground. The sunlight formed a wave around him, spreading out across the fields and kicking up a wall of dust, dirt, and crops. It rose with every rod Ojinkomàsu covered in a blink of the eye. It obscured Kanéko's view of the tower as the stones started to hit the ground, shaking the earth, and her heart lurched when her mother's bow fired one last time and went dark.

She tried to scream, but her voice froze in her throat.

Before her, Ojinkomàsu and Garèo ignited in golden flames. They surged forward, piercing the dust cloud rushing at them. Ojinkomàsu's impact cracked the air and sent out a shock-wave that kicked up boulders the size of houses out across the field behind the tower. The horse burst through the rubble and out the other side, carrying rock and dust after him in a giant vortex.

Kanéko gasped and slowed Toyomìsu near a charred scarecrow, lifting up in hopes of seeing her mother and Garèo on the back of the burning horse.

Ojinkomàsu curved to the left, his speed carrying him a quarter mile past the tower before he could fully turn around.

She couldn't breathe as she held onto Toyomìsu and followed Ojinkomàsu's movement with her eyes.

When the first golden arrow fired from the back of Ojinkomàsu, Kanéko slumped forward with relief. Somehow, Garèo and Ojinkomàsu had rescued her mother.

Mioráshi's arrows shot across the fields, piercing Damagar's skin in a precise line leading up to his eyes.

The obsidian behemoth roared and turned around. Crouching down, he ignored Kanéko's father who just slashed into his back leg and jumped after Ojinkomàsu. He missed the spirit horse and spun around in pursuit. His eyes flashed crimson and stone claws burst out of the ground, narrowly missing the glowing horse.

Kanéko panted and sent Toyomìsu toward the tower. She could feel Damagar's thoughts pounding against her shields, but she kept him at bay as she rode into the courtyard.

The tower was ruined, rubble everywhere. Her eyes went first to the stables in the back, where she spent nights working on the water screw. Underneath a light layer of rocks and dust, she spotted the boiler still leaning drunkenly toward the back of the keep. No one had cleared the timber from the mouth of the tank since she left for the trip. Then again, it had only been a few weeks—it seemed like so much longer.

The rest of the keep fared far worse. The tower smoked from the still burning stoves from the first floor and the magic that had felled it. Dust rose up and billowed over the courtyard of the keep. When she slipped off Toyomìsu, she felt it tickling the back of her throat. She coughed and looked around for her father. Not seeing him, she called out. "Papa?"

From near the tower, she heard her father's surprised but distracted voice. "Kané? Is that you?"

She hurried through the dust, picking her way over the shattered stones. She saw her father crouched over the rubble, his sword balancing on one knee as he peered over his shoulder at her. She stumbled as she ran over, excited to see him.

"Go away!"

She came to a shuddering halt at Ronamar's icy voice. "P-Papa?"

Ronamar stood up and swung his sword over his shoulder. It landed with a dull thud and his body jerked slightly from the impact. He strode over to her, the ground rippling beneath him. A wall of liquid stone formed between him and the fight.

"Kanéko," he said with a low growl, "leave. You aren't safe here."

She felt the ground boiling underneath her and a swell of something rising up underneath her feet. She stepped back and the bulge followed her, pushing her back. "Papa? What are you doing?"

He let out a low sigh and turned his back. "I don't have time for this."

Kanéko stepped on the ridge, reaching out for him.

Ronamar flung his hand at her.

She flinched, expecting him to hit her, but the blow came from below as the ground surged forward. It threw her back as the earth crested in a berm. She hit the ground with a thud, but after all of her climbing and falling, she continued into a roll that brought her back to her feet.

She glared at his back, feeling more shut off than ever from him. Her jaw tightened into a hard line. A thousand things flashed through her mind; Damagar's thoughts reached out for her and she raised her mental shield. She felt him withdraw, and she redoubled her mental shields by increasing the complexity of her mental designs.

Then, between one heartbeat and another, Damagar slammed down between Kanéko and her father. One crimson eye focused on her as the immense frog leaned over.

«We are Damagar!»

As her father dropped to one knee clutching his head, Kanéko stood strong. She snarled. "I know."

«Where is the Broken Thought? Where is his body!?» The force of his mind slammed into her, cracking the designs she used to protect herself. She felt his claws digging into her mind, trying to pluck the memories from her head.

In a flash of insight, Kanéko decided to give it memories. Drawing on her ability to picture things, she built up an image of Ruben sneaking around the far side of her father's lands. She poured all of her concentration in it, carefully letting flashes of images leak out through her mental shields.

Damagar's mouth opened, and she felt its fury rise. The pressure of his mind nearly crushed her, but she bore back, standing against the incredible strength threatening to destroy her sanity.

Then, Damagar closed its mouth with a snap and yanked one leg from the ground. Black blood sprayed from his leg and splashed across her face. A growl shook the ground.

Underneath the creature, Ronamar finished stepping through his swing. Blood soaked his weapon as he spun.

Kanéko stood there, the creature's blood soaking her clothes.

Her father did a double-take. "What are you doing here!? Get out! You can't be here. I said it isn't safe!"

Damagar roared above them as it hopped to the side to aim a kick toward them.

Ronamar rushed forward, bringing the massive sword into a powerful blow.

Kanéko's heart skipped a beat when she saw the pitch black claws and her father's sword coming toward her. Her body froze, the world slowing down. She saw the blade, picturing how it would strike into Damagar's foot just a moment too late. She saw a way to avoid both and took it.

The world snapped into real-time once again. Kanéko took a step to the left. Her father's sword cut the air above her head, slicing through a few copper strands before crashing to Damagar's foot that missed her by an inch.

Kanéko caught a look of horror on her father's face as he stared at the blade. His eyes focused on her, and he let out a sigh of relief. She pulled the gun from her belt. She never took her eyes off her father as she aimed it point-blank at the joint of Damagar's foot and then pulled the trigger.

Compressed air exploded from the muzzle, firing the lead shot into the thick hide of the behemoth. Flesh and blood exploded in all directions and she heard the shot bouncing off the ground on the other side.

Above her, Damagar lurched forward, shadowing her world in darkness.

Then light and heat crashed into her.

Damagar let out a bellowing roar as he jumped backwards. Fire dripped from his face and chest, raining down on Kanéko.

She let out an inarticulate shriek and rolled away. She caught a ridge of rock flowing underneath her and used it to jump to her feet. By the time she looked again, Damagar was hopping toward the far edge of the fields. She noticed that he aimed directly for where she pictured Ruben sneaking around and a smile crossed her lips.

Turning around, she looked up to see a flaming streak cross the sky, rocketing over her toward Damagar. Without a doubt, it was Maris using both wind and fire magic. Continuing her movement, she spun around and watched Maris circle Damagar with a burning trail behind her.

Maris hovered for a moment and raised her hands high above her head. A vortex of wind energy dropped from the clouds above, igniting into bright white flames. It shot down and splashed into Damagar.

The giant frog slumped to the ground from the force of the blow.

Ojinkomàsu circled Damagar with Mioráshi shooting from his back.

The behemoth roared, spinning away from Maris to take the arrows on his side.

Light burst around the sun horse and his body disappeared with acceleration as the Ojinkomàsu charged Damagar. The horse slammed into the unsteady Damagar and the behemoth staggered back, barely keeping his balance.

Damagar jumped at the last minute to retain its footing. Its eyes flashed brightly, and the yellow-green glow radiated around its wounds. They sealed back up as the healing magic spread out across its body. Its crimson eyes flashed a-gain, and the ground buckled, firing spears of earth into the air at Maris and along the ground near Ojinkomàsu.

Maris dodged them, leaving a trail of flames behind her, while Ojinkomàsu charged through them. The magical horse wove around the remaining spears of stone and quickly distanced himself from the attack.

Kanéko felt something looming over her. She turned just as her father grabbed her shoulder and spun her around. His hand came down across her face, the crack of his palm deafening her. She blinked back tears and staggered back.

Ronamar grabbed her shoulders with both hands. His fi-ngers dug painfully into the flesh. He pulled her close and yelled at her face-to-face. "I said leave!"

Kanéko's tears ran down her cheeks. "I can help, Papa!"

"No, you can't. You can't do anything."

His fingers continued to dig into her skin, and she felt her joints creaking. She fought back the tears when he shook her.

Her father shoved her back, away from Damagar. "You can't do anything," he repeated with a growl.

He turned his back on her and grabbed the sword from the ground. Pulling it out, he shook the pebbles from the blade and walked over the rubble to the remains of the keep wall. Ronamar didn't even look back at her.

Kanéko sniffled as she stared at her father. Tears ran down her cheeks as she prayed for him to turn around, to treat her as anything besides just an inert and helpless girl.

He didn't.

She sulked as she stormed back to Toyomìsu. The straw-berry roan looked nervous, tapping on the ground as his eyes followed Ojinkomàsu's brilliant form. Kanéko sighed and grabbed his reins. She pulled herself up and settled into place, taking one last look at her father.

Ronamar was reshaping the wall into defenses.

After everything she survived, even Damagar's attack, she wished he would see that she could help. Kanéko's hands gripped tightly around the reins until her knuckles hurt. She stared at the combat beyond, with Maris and her mother and everyone with incredible powers. Jealousy and despair strummed inside her heart, reminding her of one inescapable fact.

She couldn't fight like the others.

No powers.

No magic.

Nothing.

Kanéko yanked at the reins. Toyomìsu turned around and Kanéko took one last look at the ruined courtyard of her father's keep. Her eyes focused on the boiler and the water screw, still standing in the ruins of the old stables.

An idea flickered through her thoughts.

Unwittingly, she brought up the plans for the water screw, the designs coming clearly after hours of using it to defend against Damagar. Hours of thinking, planning, and preparing. And now she saw something different in the brass and iron ruins. She yanked on Toyomìsu's reins to stop him. The idea grew in her mind and she saw the boiler as a weapon. A cannon, much like Sinmak's gun, but on a much larger scale. Something she could use to hurt Damagar.

A smile crossed her lips. Kanéko slid off Toyomìsu and hit the ground lightly. She circled around the keep toward the boiler. The designs already formed in her head, pulling apart the components of the boiler and the water screw and assembling into a weapon. At the same time, she could still feel Damagar's mind pounding against her thoughts. She projected her ideas on her mental shield, using it as a drawing board while shielding herself from him with the opposite side.

Damagar's mental claws skittered against the designs, but the creature gave no hint that he saw them as anything other than random images to keep him out.

Grinning, she dove into the rubble around the boiler, pulling rocks and shattered timbers away as she looked for damage to the tank.

It didn't take long before the sweat rolled down her back and her muscles ached. But every time she heard the scream of her mother's arrows or the boom of Maris's attack, she realized she couldn't give up. Her fingers bled as she tossed aside rocks. She found her old magic book, her precious childhood primer, and tossed it aside. Underneath, she found a rent in the copper shell and she inspected the damage.

Hissing with annoyance, she set part of her mind aside trying to figure out how to repair it as she continued to inspect the boiler for more damage. A large timber blocked her way and she found a heavy pipe to use as a lever. Grabbing it with both hands, Kanéko strained to pull it out of the way.

As she struggled, she heard someone walking behind her. Rocks scattered down through the rubble, and she tensed up, waiting for her father to stop her. She felt the presence, and then a tickle in the back of her mind as Ruben settled into place.

He grinned at her, and his eyes started to glow their bright blue. A ghostly image of Lopidir settled around him as he reached under the timber and lifted.

Kanéko bore down on her lever and together they pushed it aside.

The timber had covered up another hole. She sat down with an angry sigh. *"Drown in sands."*

Ruben rested a hand on her shoulder. «What are you trying to do?»

Kanéko looked up, and then over to her father. Her eyes returned back to the boiler.

«I don't know, but I think I can make a weapon out of this. If we repair all the holes, and then increase the pressure, we can fire that,» she pictured the timber still inside the mouth of the boiler, «toward Damagar.»

«It would be hard to aim that. You have a high probability of missing.» Ruben's thoughts came with images of Damagar, the surrounding terrain, and a slew of angles and projections. Kanéko plucked them from his mind, adding them to a growing idea.

Tagon crouched down next to her, not touching either Ruben or Kanéko. "I was unable to prevent my offspring and the relentless dalpre from helping you."

Kanéko grinned. She reached out for Tagon.

He yanked his hand back, but Kanéko grabbed it. She felt his mind touching her own, filled with fear and terror. On the other side of her thoughts, Ruben's own mind mirrored the fear. But, in the endless seconds that followed, nothing happened.

«You are magically inert,» came the relieved thoughts of Tagon. «You are also an insulator for us.»

«Father?» Ruben sounded surprised and hopeful.

An intense joy filled Kanéko as father and son finally heard each other in their heads for the first time in over eighteen years.

«Approximately eighteen years, five months,» project Ruben.

Kanéko drew their attention to her plan. «We can do this. Can Damagar read your thoughts?»

Ruben shook his head. «Not us, as telepaths we are adept at shielding. But he can read everyone else. I feel his personalities scanning their thoughts, using it to anticipate their attacks. And we, even with Lopidir, don't have the strength or time to repair Kanéko's boiler.»

She thought about Damagar. She could feel one of the countless fragments of his personality assaulting her, claws scratching at her mental shields. The more she concentrated on it, the more she could feel Damagar cracking through it, its mind reaching for her own. She closed her eyes and explored the pattern; it grew like a flower with useless pipes and pistons, mechanics that did nothing. It reminded her of the plans she bought for the water screw—overly complicated and incapable of working. Damagar's presence faded from her mind.

Her eyes came back into focus to the short voman in front of her.

«What if we build two weapons? Say one that is impressive and scary and then this,» she started to gesture toward the boiler, but aborted her action to picture it in her mind, «If we don't tell people how it works, Damagar won't be able to see it, right? If they don't understand, he won't.»

Ruben cocked his head for a moment, looking at his father, and then both vomen shook their head as one. Tagon's thoughts drifted through her mind. «It won't work. Damagar is centuries old and far more intelligent. Even with a few functional persona fragments, it will figure it out.»

«But, he doesn't—»

Tagon projected, «A collective like Damagar must have hundreds of fragments inside its head. We don't have the time to determine which ones have been awakened and their capabilities. You don't know what memories each one has. It just takes one mistake for it to unravel your plans.»

Frustration filled Kanéko. «We can't win? There is no chance? I will not give up.» Images of their fight slammed into her and she felt a sob rising in her throat.

Tagon rested his hand on her knee. «No, we can, but you need to be smarter than Damagar, all of Damagar's personalities.»

«How?»

Tagon sent a wave of helplessness.

She fought her annoyance. Her mind spun furiously, and then she got an idea. «What if we include everyone?» She pictured everyone fighting Damagar but excluded her father. «And not just build a single thing. Create as many alchemical and mechanical devices as we can imagine. Make everyone else believe they are creating the real weapon. If we spread out the tasks to everyone, Damagar will have to pluck the components from everyone else and puzzle it together. He can't just put things together, right? Just like you two can't. All the knowledge but unable to understand it? Hopefully, by the time we finish, he will be defending against the wrong one.»

Tagon's hand tightened on her knee. «That won't be enough. That timber,» he pictured the timber in the boiler, «would just stun him.»

«If Ruben used that distraction to let himself loose—»

Tagon inhaled sharply and withdrew his mind at the thought of his son cracking his shell. «You can't release him! It will kill him, me, the kotim!» Fear poured out of Tagon. It choked Kanéko and she felt years of pain pouring into her heart.

She formed a shield between them, cutting Tagon off from her mind as she focused on Ruben.

The tiny teenager stared back at her; his face blank but his mind spinning as furiously as her own. He nodded without a single thought.

Kanéko felt Tagon intruding so she thought furiously. «Ruben, he will try to kill you. You know how much he fears you. I need you to be a threat. When I, we, the weapon fires, you must attack his mind with everything you've got.»

Ruben looked nervous and the emotion colored his response, «I trust you, Kanéko Lurkuklan. You'll do it. You'll stop Damagar.»

Tagon's mind cut into them. «I will not let you—»

A crack of intense thought shot across Kanéko's consciousness. She looked up to see Ruben's eyes glowing and focused on his father.

Tagon stumbled back, fear naked on his face, but his hand didn't leave Kanéko's skin.

«Tagon, I trust her.»

He sighed. «I register my disapproval, but I will allow myself to be vetoed,» the memory of Tagon telling Kanéko to use her strengths came up. «What do you need?»

The speed with which he changed his mind was staggering, but she didn't have time to marvel at it. Kanéko held on to both telepaths and began to build. She yanked knowledge from both men, pulling it into separate designs and patterns. Weapons pulled up from the recesses of their minds and assembled in her head. She built up the plans for catapults and alchemical bombs, objects of destruction that could be crafted by everyone fighting Damagar. All of them were missing critical components, but she gave as detailed instructions as she could.

Then, she split the plans apart, assigning tasks to everyone, including herself. Plan after plan layered on top of each other, with contingencies if Damagar responded in a certain way. She mixed in the lies and misinformation she planned on giving, dredging up every fantastic article she ever read in *Emerging Wizardry*. A headache pounded in her head from the effort; it was impossible to keep track of so many things, but Tagon and Ruben took on that task and let her focus on just planning their attack.

Finally, she determined who could perform each duty and what order to give them. Each element had to come from different people, at random times. She took advantage of Tagon's and Ruben's ability to memorize the exact order. She left herself the critical task of retrofitting the boiler into a weapon. For all their abilities, neither Tagon nor Ruben understood how to adapt to the unexpected. But, they could memorize instructions with a clarity that she could never match.

She finished and looked back at her plan. Hundreds upon hundreds of directions and tasks, each one interleaved with each other. It was filled with lies, deceptions, and would tax all of their abilities to keep it coordinated.

In a flash, Ruben and Tagon filtered out their assignments, both to catch the others in the field to assign duties and to perform actions of their own. They knew which ones were real and which ones were faked, but only Kanéko could understand how they fit together.

It was a good plan.

Well, it was a plan.

Chapter 44

Combat Leadership

Stress and exhaustion bring out other battles still waiting to be re-
solved.
—Gepaul Proverb

Kanéko wiped the sweat from her brow with the hand
holding her hammer. She peered over the edge of the boiler. Ojinkomàsu and Maris circled Damagar as they peppered him with fire and arrows. Tagon joined them, riding
his massive wolf between the legs of the obsidian behemoth and slashing out with knife and bow.

A furlong away, Ruben worked hard to trench out a pattern that Kanéko gave him, seeding it with flowers as he
worked. The flowers, in a more perfect situation would
have a disrupting effect on magic. Since they weren't near
the Tastolian Sea, they were useless.

Damagar hopped toward Ruben, but Ojinkomàsu
slammed into him from behind. The creature roared and
lashed out at the sun horse. Garèo brought Ojinkomàsu underneath the claws and neatly avoided the killing blow. Mioráshi fired directly into Damagar's belly and left behind arrows that looked like quills before they faded.

Kanéko turned her attention back to the boiler and the last hole she struggled with sealing. She tried to find a plate of metal, but she had picked the entire area clean trying to repair the other holes. She looked at the last one, still steaming from the heat Maris used to seal it into place.

Her father's voice interrupted her. "What are you still doing here?"

"Go away, Papa."

"I told you that," came his growl, "but you're still here."

Kanéko glared at him. "And now I'm telling you the same. I don't have time to explain it."

"You have everyone running around doing things. Stupid things instead of fighting that... that thing. What are you doing?" His boots crunched on the rocks as he stared at the boiler. He frowned and gestured at it. "And why are you bothering with this? We're in a battle, girl. There isn't time for one of your foolish plans."

She threw her hammer down. "Listen!" she screamed, "You've been telling me I've been useless since I failed those tests!"

Ronamar stepped back, a surprised look on his face, but Kanéko wasn't done. "I know I can't do magic. I'm a *barichi-rōma*! But, I refuse," she screamed loudly, "to give up because of that."

"But, you can't—"

"I can do whatever I want! And right now, I'm going to kill Damagar because he threatened my friends and family. Even you, you *egotistical bastard!*"

He stood there like she gutted him. His massive sword slipped off his shoulders and slammed into the ground.

Kanéko let out a frustrated sigh, and then turned away to find something to repair the last hole.

"Kané?"

"Go away."

Her father hesitated, and then spoke in a soft growl. "How can I help?"

She turned on her heels to look at him incredulously.

Ronamar slammed his sword into the ground. He gestured to her repairs. "How can I help?"

"Really?" she asked.

He nodded.

She stared at him for a long moment, thinking about her father's abilities and what she needed. She pointed to the hole. "Bury this in rock."

"What?"

"The boiler. I can't find any metal to fix it, but solid rock would do the job. I want you to bury it. I need a layer at least a yard thick and completely surrounding it. It needs to be heavy and air-tight as possible. But I need the top clear."

He looked up and Kanéko followed his gaze. In the mouth of the boiler, a large timber continued to stick out. The far end had a ragged end, like a spear.

"You need that out?"

"No, that's my," she thought of a good lie, "distraction. I need it to look like a spear."

Ronamar snarled. "I don't have time—"

"Then, go away."

He stepped back, and then stopped. "This is what... a test?"

"Yes," Kanéko snapped, "to see if you can take orders from your powerless daughter. And if you cram that ego of yours into your throat and do what you are told, maybe I'll let you work on the real weapon to kill Damagar."

Chapter 45

Improvised Plans

No matter how perfect a plan. No matter how well it is executed. Even if every contingency is considered, no plan will ever survive misinterpreta tion by your allies.

—Xristor Namfun

The sun baked down on Kanéko, and she wondered how long she could keep up the frantic pace. For over a half hour, she struggled to retrofit the boiler, give orders, and run from Damagar when he drew close. She wiped the sweat from her brow and looked to where Damagar was currently pinned down by Garèo, her mother, and Maris.

The fields surrounding the keep were ruined. Large gouges of land were torn up from where Ojinkomàsu accelerated. Both Damagar and her father used earth magic and large sinkholes had formed from the use of stone in their attacks. The home that she had grown up in had been almost completely destroyed. She didn't have time to mourn it though, not with the battle going on. Much of the earth smoldered from Maris's fire blasts. Kanéko felt a surge of jealousy that her friends and family could manifest such powerful magic, but then she remembered that she had an important role in the fight.

She braced herself with one foot on the spear-like timber and the other on the copper edge of the boiler. She hefted a pair of iron bars stolen from Jinmel's forge, and then struck the two together with all her might. The vibration ran through her arms and she almost lost both bars. After hitting them together twice more, she dropped one into the boiler. It disappeared from sight with a splash and a clang. Kanéko tossed the second into a pile of tools at the base of the copper tank. The action, she remembered, was used in sympathetic magic. She only hoped Maris would be able to use it.

The tank itself was hidden from sight. Her father's magic had brought solid stone from below the tower and melted it over the entire surface, creating a shell two yards thick. Kanéko stepped out on the smooth surface and slid down. Her cloth-wrapped feet smacked on the stone.

"Kané," her father spoke with an exhausted voice as he walked over the remains of the wall of the keep, "I finished creating the tunnels under those trenches your vomen made. And I filled it with all our oil. You had better be right because you just used up our winter heat for the next five years. After this, we may have to move to Rock River."

"Is it weak enough to collapse if Damagar lands on them?"

"Yes, but I don't understand—" his voice cut off when Kanéko glared at him. He closed his mouth with a snap, "No more questions. Fine," he grumbled, "what's next?"

Kanéko pointed up to the timber, slowing as she saw a flicker of pain crossing his face.

"Papa?"

"That creature is in my head again. I can feel him," he groaned and clutched his head, "like claws in my eyes."

"Just a little longer."

"Why?" he moaned, but Kanéko heard a different timbre to his voice, Damagar was using her father to ask questions. The creature had done it twice before, both times with Maris, but Kanéko refused to answer any question asked of her. Inwardly, she winced and felt Damagar's mind pounding on her shields, trying to crack the designs that filled her thoughts.

She thought about her plan quickly. "Because I need fifteen more minutes before it's ready to kill Damagar. Just focus on this thing and not what we're doing out there."

He looked angry, upset that she wouldn't tell him anything more. His jaw tightened into a line. His voice lost the sound of Damagar's possession. "What next?"

She pointed up to the timber. "I need you to seal the opening there."

His brow creased deeply when he looked up. "Another pointless task?"

"Papa..." she started.

"Fine, how tight?"

"Very, but don't dig into the metal or the wood."

He rolled his eyes but walked over to the stone shell and then up it as if it was flat ground. Kanéko watched him, unsure how much to tell him. She let out a hiss of annoyance at herself and stared out over the field at the other remaining parts of her plan; Damagar figured out how to neutralize most of her other designs in a surprisingly short time.

As the behemoth tore apart her plans, Ruben had created a circular trench in a rough circle. Maris scorched everything inside the ring before her father used his magic to hollow out a pit, a hundred feet deep and filled with supernaturally sharp rocks, stones, and crystals. She didn't know how much oil he brought up, but she hoped it would be enough for Damagar to consider it a threat.

Hooves beat the ground and she spun around. Ojinko-màsu came galloping into the courtyard, radiating heat and flames. Her mother's dark form leaped off the horse before Garèo reared him to a stop.

Kanéko gasped and held out her hand but her mother swept her up, hugging her tightly. Her mother's body smell of ash, blood, and sweat. As she hugged her mother back, she forgot about the fight and the pain in this one moment of happiness.

"*I knew you would come out on the bloody top,*" whispered her mother, squeezing her tightly.

She saw Garèo try to get off Ojinkomàsu, but the horse stepped sideways to keep Garèo on his back. She smiled at his frustrated look.

Mioráshi tightened her grip. "I'm so proud of you, *my beautiful daughter.*"

Tears burned in Kanéko eyes. She held her mother tightly and tried not to think about her exhaustion or pain.

Mioráshi broke the hug after a moment to kiss her on the cheek. "*Your dalpre tells me that you have something in mind. We only have seventeen minutes before I run out of sunlight.*"

"*What happens then?*"

"*No more arrows, so if you are going to kill him, do it soon.*"

Kanéko's mind spun, integrating the new information. "*Mama, do you have any powerful attacks with the hóri?*"

Mioráshi growled. "*Many, but that sand-damned, dickless creature keeps anticipating me. I'm stuck with these pathetic arrows that only pierce the hide, but they are fast enough he can't dodge. Garèo has the same problem, the craven shit-eating, sand-choked kin-killer. Ojinkomàsu and Waryōni needs space and time to charge and that bloated corpse of a rotted toad refuses to stop long enough to die.*"

An idea hit Kanéko and she adjusted her plans. "If I could get him to hold still, could you hit him harder?"

"If you give me... say ten seconds for a shot, he won't live to see nightfall. But, I can't get—"

Kanéko interrupted her mother. *"I'll stop him. I'm going to hurt him bad, and then we need to hit him with everything we got."*

Mioráshi kissed her again. *"I'll be waiting, Great Kosobyo Kanéko. We'll kill the shit-fucking bastard. The minature boy told me the signals. You use it and I'll erase that moon-fucked creature off the ground the sun shits on."*

She stared in shock. She didn't expect to hear the words of respect and honor ever coming from her mother's lips.

Her mother spun on her heels and ran back to Ojinko-màsu. With a jump, she leaped onto the horse, then burst into motion. In a blink, they were gone in a flash of heat and light.

"I heard swearing. Your mother?" Ronamar's voice drifted down.

Kanéko looked up where he stood at the mouth of the boiler. Liquefied marble dripped from the opening, hardening into solid rock. She didn't know what to say, so she just nodded.

"What's next?" came the rumbling voice.

"Can you put crystal on the tip? Like an arrowhead?"

"Yeah—"

"Oh, and that timber," she pointed to another ceiling joist, "attach it to the top like a cross."

"Let me guess, put a crystal edge on it?" came a frustrated growl.

She almost blurted out something when he guessed her next step. She cleared her throat and waved as casually as she could, "Sure, why not? Make it look threatening."

Kanéko stopped and stared at her plans. She looked up at the setting sun, and then down to the battlefield.

Ojinkomàsu already joined Maris, circling around Dama-gar as the obsidian frog fired a wave of sharp rocks after Ta-gon's black wolf.

Kanéko winced when it almost caught them. She took a deep breath and whistled three short blasts and one long. It was the "come" sound that Maris told her about.

The dalpre responded immediately, peeling away from the fight and shooting back. Wind tore up the ground be-hind her.

Kanéko braced herself for the blast of air that struck her face when Maris landed.

"Kan!"

"Maris! I need you now. First, recharge my gun." She po-inted to Sinmak's gun resting on the tools.

The dalpre bounced over to the weapon. She had recharged the gun once before during a frantic, whispered lesson. Now, she held it above her head and screwed her face into concentration. Wind drew toward her, shimme-ring the air like waves of heat. It sucked down the muzzle of the gun, a whistling noise filling the air, as the needle on the gauge slowly rose up. The whistling grew higher pitched and Maris growled as the last third of the gun re-sisted the increased pressure. She finished with a gasp.

Kanéko noticed Maris's new outfit, another dress, was al-ready ruined with fire and blood. She favored her left arm but the brown eyes that focused on Kanéko remained clear.

"I can hurt later," whispered Maris, "and I'm getting tired, Kan. Really tired. Are we almost done?"

"Yes, just a few more minutes."

She nodded, her tail snapping back and forth. The mo-tion sent flecks of sweat and blood in all directions.

Kanéko gestured for her to follow and took her to the tools. Picking up the iron bar, she held it out for Maris.

The dalpre took the bar, staggering under the weight and looked up with confusion at Kanéko.

Kanéko wrapped Maris's hands around it. "Right now, I need you to concentrate on this bar."

"Why?"

"Because you need to know it. Really know it. Look at the scratches and the dings, feel its weight..." An exhausted joke bubbled up. "Know how it tastes."

Maris's ears perked up. "This is magic? Licking metal?"

"It will be."

With a smile, the dalpre sat heavily on the ground and focused on the bar.

Kanéko patted her on the head.

Maris looked up and beamed happily, her tail thumping against the ground.

Kanéko returned to the boiler and inspected her father's work. In a few short moments, he had pulled up quartz from the ground below. It flowed like water up the side of the shell and formed into a long, sharp blade along the timber.

"I used most of this stuff to form spikes in the pit."

"All right, Papa, just a little more."

Ronamar held his hand out and the last of the quartz formed a long point at the tip of the timber. The end sparkled in the sunlight. He sighed and slid down. He looked exhausted and stumbled when he hit the ground.

Kanéko rushed up to grab him and felt his weight crushing her. She dragged her father next to Maris.

Maris's ears shook as Ronamar walked closer. At the same time, Kanéko heard her father's labored breath and worried. The air between her father and Maris crackled and the dust trembled in an unseen breeze. It was feedback between two powerful mages, but subtle and threatening at the same time.

Her father dropped to the ground. He sat up and stared at Maris with a look of wonderment and confusion. He raised his eyes to Kanéko when his daughter leaned over him. "She's a dog. Why is she so powerful?"

"I need you to teach her sympathetic magic."

Maris's head snapped up. "What?"

"There is another iron bar, just like that one, somewhere safe. I need you to heat it up and add as much air and fire a-round it as you can. She has the power, I know it."

"Where is it?"

"It doesn't matter. Just use the bar."

Maris whimpered. "I don't know how."

Kanéko spoke to her father. "Papa?"

Ronamar shook his head. "I can't teach a dalpre magic. Not in the middle of a battle. She can't possibly—"

Kanéko snatched the iron bar from Maris's hands. Swinging it around, she shoved it into her father's chest. He grabbed it, surprised. She leaned over and spoke in a hard, angry voice. "Papa, she is smarter than she looks, and you are dumber than you speak. Now, by the Divine Couple, shut up and just do what you are told. I need her," she pointed to Maris, "to heat this up as fast as she can."

Realization dawned on his face. She saw him glance over to the pit in the fields, obviously thinking that the other bar was in the pit. She made no effort to correct him, but his eyes were the one place she needed to be to trick Damagar into getting in line for the boiler's shot.

It was time.

"I-I have to go," she said in a broken voice. Standing up, she grabbed Sinmak's gun from the pile of tools. The heavy weapon reminded her how tired she felt. Wiping the sweat and grease from her face, she looked over at her father and friend.

Ronamar whispered into Maris's ears. Power curled around both of them. Magenta motes swirled around them as their energies conflicted with each other. Her father grimaced as the energies arced along his skin. With sweat dripping down his pale face, he continued to speak in her ear.

Damagar fought with everyone at the far end of the fields. Blood coursed off his obsidian hide, but he still lashed out with endless magic. His body glowed with healing magic as he formed stone claws to grab at both Tagon and Ruben who rode Jason.

Ruben jumped from Jason just as Ojinkomàsu flashed by. By the time Kanéko's eyes focused on the burning form of the horse, the vomen was already crawling up Garèo's arm.

A groaning sound echoed from inside the boiler, dragging Kanéko's thoughts back to her plans. She held the pneumatic gun with both hands and took a deep breath. One step, and then a next, and then finally she sprinted for the pit. She could feel Damagar's attention focusing on her. The creature finally saw her as a threat.

It would only be seconds.

Her heart pounded in her chest as she focused on running. The sunbaked ground tore at her feet. She strained to hear Damagar as she ran as fast as she could.

The world grew dark, and Kanéko felt wind rushing toward her. With a gasp, she lunged to the ground and rolled as Damagar slammed a foot into the ground, barely missing her. Her world shook and buckled from the impact and she felt his mind focusing on her. Gasping, she scrambled away from the pool of darkness, holding onto the gun with all her might.

Damagar's thoughts slammed into her, clawing at her shields.

She staggered and continued to crawl toward the edge of the darkness.

Suddenly, a second mind joined the first, two inhuman personalities tearing at her mind. She felt her mental shields cracking under their efforts. Its assault increased, adding more minds and personalities into cracking her. She felt the force squeezing her skull and tearing into her. It hurt, hurt more than she could imagine. A sharp pain blossomed in her nose, and she wiped it to find blood on her palm.

Just a few more seconds.

Damagar broke into her mind with one powerful surge of mental force. Her shields shattered under its blow, and she felt alien thoughts pour into her skull. A powerful personality—Recall—tore through her memories. She remembered her trip with terrifying clarity, every pain and agony being forced back on her. Damagar forced her to experience everything in the heartbeat it took to read her thoughts.

Kanéko sobbed, feeling her muscles spasm as she struggled to retain the very idea of herself. She tried to bring up the shields, to think about anything else, but Damagar commanded her mind absolutely. It shredded through emotions and thoughts. When it reached the core of her being, she felt dread fill her as it used her own intelligence to understand her plans.

"Get away from my daughter!" roared Ronamar. Two fists came down on the ground right in front of her. The earth rose up into one massive spear and slammed into Damagar's gut.

Her father grabbed her from the ground and ran for the light. Damagar's roar deafened her, and she couldn't orient herself as her father sprinted out from underneath the behemoth.

«You must be destroyed!» came the powerful thought and Ronamar fell to the ground clutching his head.

Kanéko rolled across the ragged ground and came to her feet.

Before her, her father bellowed out in pain when one of Damagar's claws pinned him. The weight of the creature bore down on her father and the rocks cracked from the pressure.

Blood dribbling out from her ears and nose. She swung her gun around and fired it twice into Damagar's throat. The two large bullets punched through his hide and the creature roared. When Damagar didn't lift his claws, Kanéko aimed for the creature's ankle and fired again.

The bullet slammed into the joint and bones cracked.

Damagar staggered back with another roar. Black blood splashed across her face.

Kanéko didn't wait for a second chance. She grabbed her father and pulled with all her might. Ronamar scrambled to his feet and they ran from Damagar. He tried to guide her away from the pit, but she slipped from his arms and sprinted toward the trench.

Damagar's claws slashed down, narrowly missing Kanéko. She dove to the side. Spears of rocks burst out of the ground right in front of her. She accelerated and ran up the newly unearthed stones. Spotting another rising a few feet away, she jumped off one to land on the other. It was remarkably easy when the heat of battle fueled her actions.

She hit the ground running, knowing that Damagar would catch her but hoping to get a few more precious seconds for Maris to finish heating the tank.

Damagar's form sailed over and landed heavily on the ground less than a chain from the edge of the pit. A crack formed in the surface, spreading out in all directions.

Kanéko slid to a halt. Gasping for breath, she tried to avoid looking up into Damagar's crimson eyes. No matter how much she tried, she couldn't help when her eyes caught Damagar's.

«Your mind is difficult to read, but not impossible. You are only human.»

Recall and Observation projected as one, and she felt another half dozen concentrating on the rest of the battle. She couldn't form a shield against its intrusions. Damagar delved its mental claws into her mind, and she let out a sob as it pulled the final parts of the plan from her memories.

Kanéko cried out as Damagar took a small hop backwards to get out of the line of fire of the boiler. She saw all her plans, her hopes, shattering as Damagar took another step away.

Damagar's thoughts pounded into her. «The Broken Thought is alive. We told you to kill him. You failed.» He replayed the threat he gave before—it came with the same clarity that the powerful telepathic could force into her mind. «And now we must destroy all of you.»

Kanéko tried to prevent him from getting inside her head. She lashed out with her emotions, but Damagar didn't even flinch. Barely able to control her body, she crawled away from it, trying to escape. "I can't kill him. He's my friend."

Damagar opened its mouth. It leaned forward, its tongue snapping out. It punched Kanéko in the chest and splattered her with sticky fluid. Before she could even twitch, the tongue yanked her forward and she fell. It dragged her closer.

She screamed and grabbed for the ground with one hand. Her fingers dug into the earth trying to prevent it from dragging her, but it continued to haul her closer. She focused on keeping a grip on her gun, she didn't want to be unarmed.

Something slammed into Damagar's tongue and she was driven face-first on the ground. The wet muscle slurped as it wrapped around her. Groaning, she tried to free her hand, but it kept her limbs pinned to her body. She managed to roll on her back and free one hand from the muscular tongue.

Ruben held Damagar's limb with both hands. Images of Lopidir and Stubbornness overlaid his edges, blurring his body with a blue haze. His glowing eyes were blinding as Ruben held Damagar to the ground.

Strong hands grabbed Kanéko and pried her loose. Her father grunted as he tore the fleshy limb from Kanéko. She looked up to see her father, the side of his face bloody and bruised. She looked around to orient herself to find the firing line for the boiler. "Papa! Ruben! Pull him this way."

"No," Ronamar grunted, "I have to get you free."

"Papa, get him in line!"

"What line!?" bellowed her father.

"Between the tower and the pit. Now!"

Ronamar didn't appear to understand, but when Ruben started to pull, the bartim followed. He chanted as he yanked, casting a spell as he pulled. The pressure around them increased as Ronamar's magic fought against Ruben and Damagar. Arcs of bright energies and dust crackled between the three powerful beings. Black scorches formed as the magenta arched along every surface.

Behind Damagar, the ground boiled up and swelled up into a crest that rose over the behemoth. The slope shoved it closer to the firing line.

Damagar planted its feet to jump.

Animated claws burst out of the ground and clutched at Damagar. The stone hardened as it pulled Damagar down.

The giant creature pulled one paw free but as soon as it set it down, more stone reached up to pin it.

Ronamar gasped. "I can't... do this... for long."

The images around Ruben swelled in size and power. Lopidir became a transparent blue giant, reaching up to grab Damagar's jaw and yanking it forward.

Kanéko jammed the gun into the holster and grabbed the sticky tongue. She pulled with all her strength. She dug her feet into the ground and screaming with every inch it took to pull the behemoth. Her strength was insignificant compared to her father's power and Ruben's might, but she knew that even the smallest effort might get Damagar in the right position. In the distance, she could hear the high-pitched whistle of a cracked boiler and it fueled her desperation.

The behemoth lashed out with magic, forcing the earth to rise up. A sharp point rose underneath her, and she pushed away as it speared between her feet. It slashed at her hands and feet. Getting an idea, she leaned into it.

When the sharp stones cut into her side, she screamed. She twisted until the edge cut into Damagar's tongue. Blood splattered her face as the stone cut almost through the tongue.

A blast of pain radiated from Damagar. Its spears of stone crumbled into dust.

Ronamar and Ruben took advantage of his pain to drag him another foot closer.

Kanéko looked toward the boiler and saw a wave of fire and sun coming at her. Her mother stood on the back of Ojinkomàsu, the bow pulled back as far as it would go. Energy roared around her, forming into a spectral shape of a serpent coiled around Ojinkomàsu.

The sun horse glowed with brilliant flames, surrounded by a herd of translucent gray horses spread out chains in both directions. She didn't know where the other horses came from, but they were ghostly and wavering in a light. They rode as a single herd, as though a single mind controlled them. It looked like a wave of liquid fire and sunlight burning up her father's fields.

"Not yet, not yet," whimpered Kanéko. She spun around and called out to her father and Ruben. "Harder!"

"We are!" bellowed Ronamar.

They pulled Damagar another foot.

Kanéko continued to struggle. The high-pitched whine of the boiler grew to a piercing scream and she knew she had no more time. "Now!" she screamed and pulled with all her might.

Damagar stumbled forward. It planted its claws into the ground and stopped itself.

Kanéko saw that he was a few feet away from the line, but despite her efforts, the behemoth refused to move.

A deafening bang shot through the air. Kanéko sobbed as the crystal-tipped spear launched out in a blur of wood and crystal. She turned her head, trying to follow it as it shot above her head.

When it hit Damagar in his chest, right below his jaw, she gaped with surprise. The timber, moving too fast to focus on, punched into the behemoth and lodged itself inside its throat. She traced a line from the timber to the boiler and realized she made a mistake in aiming it. It was only a lucky chance they were in the right place.

Damagar staggered to the side and fell back. Geyser of black blood poured out from the its wound. Its immense form bounced on the ground and rolled away from the oil-filled pit. Wisps of yellow-green energy rose up as it resumed healing itself.

"*Sands! Damn the sands!*" She screamed, tears in her eyes. The exhaustion sapped the strength in her limbs. The failure, her failure to execute the plan, devastated her. She failed them. Her mother, her father, her friends. All because she had no powers.

A crimson eye focused on her and the powerful mind tore into her mind, it was a distinct mental voice, the one called Strategy. «You have become a liability.»

As Damagar rolled over, his tongue shot out and wrapped around her chest, squeezing until she screamed out from the pain. She felt ribs cracking from the pressure. Damagar surged forward, yanking her off the ground and throwing her up. In her mind, she knew what he planned: to bring her down on the other side and crush her into oblivion.

Frantic and dizzy from being thrown up, Kanéko grabbed the gun in the holster. The tongue pinned it to her body, but she forced the tip of the muzzle toward the sticky limb. She yanked the trigger. The shot punched through the thick tongue. She fired again, but the gun hissed loudly, and the shot slid uselessly out.

With the wind whipping past her, she felt her body being brought up and over Damagar. She looked down to see one crimson eye following her arc. She lost the grip on the now useless gun and tried not to think about her imminent death.

Light shot across her vision as Mioráshi's arrows followed after Damagar. A dozen arrows pierced its tongue in a line right up to the spot where Kanéko cut Damagar's tongue. Then a large bolt slammed into it and severed Damagar's tongue with a wet ripping noise. Kanéko's body jerked as she was thrown into the air, the tip of Damagar's tongue trailing behind her and nothing anchoring her to the ground.

The world blurred underneath her as she flew high across the fields. Spinning around, she was consumed by the terrifying realization she had no control over her body. She would hit the ground with fatal speed, and there was nothing she could do. She sobbed and prayed that Damagar would be defeated. She closed her eyes and held her breath against the wind that whipped past her.

The impact cracked bone and she felt her neck straining from the blow. The wind continued to howl around her, and she felt a flash of pain consuming her body. But, she was alive. She couldn't breathe without pain, but she was breathing.

Cracking open one eye, she looked into the eyes of an inferno. Maris held her tightly, arms wrapped around Kanéko's chest as a fireball surround their bodies. The flames seared Kanéko's lungs until she choked.

Then there was no flame. Maris's eyes rolled into the back of her head and they started to plummet to the ground.

Kanéko screamed. "Maris! Wake up!"

They hit the ground in a deafening explosion. Kanéko felt the air rush up underneath them, cushioning them before the impact with the hard earth. She landed on her arm and the snapping bone shot a wave of agony through her body. When she looked down, two sheared ends stuck out of her skin. Blood gathered in her wound and dripped down her brown skin.

She sobbed, alive but in agony. She looked at the bright blue sky and gave a prayer to Kosòbyo and the Divine Couple.

Maris groaned and sat up. "I lost my power again."

Kanéko tried to push herself up but grinding bones stopped her instantly. She looked down at the compound fracture of her arm and let out another sob of fear. "I failed. I couldn't do it."

The dalpre scrambled to her feet, bruised by her impact. Her outfit was in tatters, barely covering her body as she panted heavily. "Are you all right?"

Kanéko whimpered and shook her head. She held out her hand for Maris. As Maris pulled her to her feet, Kanéko cried out.

Maris peered over, and then gasped. "Your arm! You're hurt!"

Kanéko blinked back the tears and staggered forward. They were just inside the woods outside of the lands, a full mile away from the ruins of the keep. She leaned her shoulder on the tree and looked out at the battle. Her family and friends still attacked Damagar but now it was a losing fight.

"No," whispered Kanéko, "not yet. Think, damn it."

She gasped as she remembered some of the contingency plans they came up with. She pulled them up and scavenged something new out of it. She turned to Maris. "Mar, do you have anything left?"

Maris, her face pale and dripping with sweat, looked at her. She nodded and pulled on a determined face. "You are my alpha and my friend; I will always have enough."

"Can you get close to Damagar?"

Maris's ears and tail drooped. "Yes, but he keeps blocking me. I think he can read my mind."

Kanéko thought for a moment. "I have a new plan. I need you to fly out as far as you can, as long as you can get back in... fifteen seconds or so. When you see a signal, I need you to fly back as fast as you can and burn Damagar from the inside."

Maris panted as she looked out at Damagar. "How, Kan? He doesn't have any holes."

Kanéko sobbed from the pain shooting up her leg. She couldn't wipe the tears. Instead, she rested her cheek on the ragged wood of the tree trunk. "I'm working on it. But if you can't do this, I'll come up with something else."

Maris looked at her, a whimper in her throat. Then, she took a deep breath. "You are my pack leader. If I have to die to do what's right, and then I will."

Kanéko smiled. "Don't die on me, but you... you might burn out if you do this. Lose your magic, maybe forever. It..." She couldn't explain the repercussions of over-using magic in such a short period of time.

The wind rose up around Maris, pushing back at Kanéko. "It isn't worth it if I can't defend the pack."

Tears fogging her goggles, Kanéko braced herself for Maris's takeoff. "One last thing, when you get up, send a flare, a burst of light up?" At Maris's nod, Kanéko continued. "Two signals. The first is one short, two long, one short. That will ask Mama to use her strongest attack and the others to pin down Damagar to give her time. The second is two long, two short. That's the sign for Garèo to charge."

Wind whipping around her, Maris said, "I need room to go faster. I need to get further out."

"Accelerate?"

"Yes," the tail began to wag back and forth. "Don't worry, Kan. You are smart, and I like you. And we will win."

Maris shot into the air, blasting Kanéko with wind and dust. Pebbles bounced off Kanéko's goggles.

She looked up at Maris, hovering in the air, wind sputtering. She spun around twice, and then launched huge gouts of flame out over the fire. They were the same signals that Kanéko had asked for. Before the last burst of fire faded from the air, Maris flew away from the fight.

In the battle, everything changed. Mioráshi stopped firing her arrows as Ojinkomàsu raced for the edge of the fields. Tagon turned his wolf on his heels and sprinted for the opposite direction. Ronamar and Ruben charged for Damagar.

Ruben's body glowed brightly as his eyes ignited into azure flames, visible even from a mile away. The world around him shimmered and cracked. She had only seen the psionic storm in Damagar's memories, but the sight of rents tearing through reality sent a shiver of fear along her spine. Psychic winds, terribly silent and untouched by the physical world, pulled at Damagar.

The titan roared. Ghostly figures rose up to the surface of his skin, clawing at Damagar's physical form as if it could keep them from Ruben's singularity. Damagar's eyes flared red with power and the ground underneath Ruben boiled.

Ronamar rushed in and jumped forward. He brought his fists down on the ground and the earth beneath Damagar and Ruben liquefied. Ruben sank down to his knees, but Damagar's weight sucked the creature into the earth to its chest.

Crimson eyes flashed and the earth solidified. Damagar bellowed as he yanked his feet free of the rock, but Ronamar was already finishing a second spell. Blades, each one a chain in length, burst out of the ground and speared into Damagar.

The creature lashed out at him, but his claws passed too close to Ruben. A ghostly form, some feathered creature, was sucked out of Damagar and fell into Ruben's storm with a silent scream.

A golden flicker caught Kanéko's attention. She looked at Ojinkomàsu who raced around the outer rim of the battlefield. The brightness came from Mioráshi's bow, which left behind a golden stream. The stream blossomed and expanded, forming a snake's tail. As the spirit horse accelerated, the snake continued to grow and expand. Power crackled in the air and the world grew dark as sunlight gathered into the glowing snake.

The sun faded to a pale light as Mioráshi summoned the power. Shadow crossed over the lands as Ojinkomàsu finished circling the league around the keep in less than a minute. As they reached the end of their circuit, where the sunlight snake's tail rattled above them, they curved in and started to charge toward Damagar.

A head formed behind Ojinkomàsu; a massive feathered snake's head gaping open with fangs dripping with sparkling poison. Kanéko gasped with recognition. It was Kosòbyo, her mother's clan spirit. The bow string snapped and Kosòbyo shot forward like an arrow. He punched into Damagar's side, right where the timber cross cut into him. The shape of Kosòbyo's head bulged out from the obsidian skin, the fangs clearly visible as they tried to rip out of the obsidian toad.

Damagar staggered to the side, hopping to avoid falling over. Miles of the spirit snake disappeared into his body. It shoved out from the inside as cracks of sunlight burst through Damagar's tearing skin. But, it wasn't until the last of Kosòbyo's tail disappeared into Damagar's body that the snake burst out in a shower of sunlight.

In the pale light of the sun, Ojinkomàsu flared into life. The herd surrounding him charged forward, leading Ojinkomàsu as they raced toward Damagar. In the front, a gray horse led the charge. The ground rumbled with a hundred hooves as the horses punched into Damagar through the opening left by Kosòbyo. A fraction of a second later, they came out the other side, tearing an equally large hole into the behemoth. Ojinkomàsu, coming up the rear, was as bright as the summer sun as he blew through Damagar and left behind only a smoking crater.

Damagar, wounds gaping on both sides of his body, roared out in pain. His body glowed with a crimson light as flickers of yellow-green energy welled up inside him.

Kanéko prayed that Maris would see the sign. But, unsure, she blew three short whistles and then a long one. She waited a heartbeat and did it again. And again, trying to summon the dalpre with the desperate hope that it would be enough.

Ruben and Ronamar still fought at the feet of Damagar, tearing at his mind and soul. Ronamar fought with his massive blade, but then he stopped in mid-strike to clutch his head.

The wind shifted rapidly, pushing her toward Damagar and the fight. It buffeted her body. Her broken bones scraped against each other and more blood poured down her arm. She clutched to the tree and braced herself, still whistling for Maris.

Wind formed on the opposite side of Damagar. It blew through him, toward Kanéko. Flecks of blood, dust, and rocks shot through his body. She hoped Maris knew what she was doing, otherwise, she was blowing air in the wrong direction.

The air ignited into flames. Heat and fire blossomed across the sky, turning the faded light of the sun into an inferno that burned away the clouds. The trees above her were incinerated by the blast as a living sun appeared in the center of Damagar. Afterimages of the star streaked across the sky above Kanéko. The wind blowing toward Kanéko were canceled by Maris's forward movement and Kanéko realize that Maris used the winds to slow down.

The air cracked into a rumbling boom. It punched Kanéko in the chest and pinned her to the tree. Around her, the limbs tore from trees and flew into the fields. Kanéko let out a scream as her broken arm ground into itself and her chest grew wet with blood.

Inside Damagar, Maris turned the air molten, sucking in wind as she burned with white-hot heat.

Despite being half-dazed in pain, Kanéko couldn't help but think that Maris was duplicating the effects of Jinmel's smithy. She realized she was losing focus to concentrate on the mechanics. With a groan, she brought her attention back to the battle.

Ruben stood in front of Damagar, his psychic winds tearing at Damagar as the behemoth's insides were ravaged by fire and wind.

Damagar's body bulged before a pillar of flame burst out of his back. It rocketed high into the air, a chain across and miles high. The sun disappeared in the glare of the flame's brilliance.

The creature exploded.

Kanéko saw the final shock wave coming, but she couldn't move in time. She clenched herself, ready for one more agony.

A shadow blocked her vision. She gasped and fell back as her father punched the ground to yank a pillar of earth from the stone. Throwing apart his hands, it blossomed into a protective shell. It was the same spell he cast to protect her from the exploding stable, all those days ago.

Ronamar turned a half step and brought the shell down around them as the inferno crashed into his shield. The air burned in her lungs before darkness surrounded them in suffocating protection.

He wrapped his arm around her, holding her tight. "Good job," he whispered into her ear.

In the darkness, she felt Damagar die, the last agonizing scream of the titan crashing into her ruined mental shields and burning into her dreams forever.

Chapter 46

Celebrations

There is a peace right after that final blow, a moment of indescribable
joy brought on by survival, luck, and fulfilled hope.
—Balador Virs, *The Snow Queen's Betrayal* (Act 2, Scene 1)

Even at midnight, Rock River celebrated. Confined to one
of the borrowed bedrooms in the mayor's house, Kanéko
could hear cheers rise up from the street.

While she was fighting at the mill, Cobin and the mercenaries attacked the village to lure Garèo away from her and
into a trap. They fought across the city, eventually ending
with Cobin's death on the *Burning Cloud Queen*.

It wasn't until later that the villagers knew about the
fight at the Lurkuklan Tower and Damagar's defeat.

She lifted her body to peer out the window at the airship
grounded in the center of the town square. Lanterns hung
from every hook and rope and the *Queen* sat in a pool of
light. Children climbed over the ship as the adults sat on
the deck and drank to the defeat of Sinmak's troops.

On the ground next to the *Queen*, the mayor of Rock River and her father were making a proclamation. She couldn't

hear the words, but when the mayor lifted his hands, the crowds cheered loudly enough to rattle the windows.

Her father started a speech, but she lost herself as she remembered the words he said at the end of the fight.

"Good job."

Those two words echoed in her head, the first she had heard them in a long time. She didn't know if her father trusted her yet but there was no question he had finally acknowledged her abilities.

Kanéko sat back down on the bed and winced. Her cracked ribs were bound tight, and the cloth bandages dug into her side. The town healer had wrapped her broken arm because Virsian couldn't heal Kanéko for another month. The feline dalpre offered to stay in Rock River until the feedback faded and she could finish the healing process with magic.

It was going to be a long wait for Kanéko. She scowled at the book next to her. She had found it as they were leaving the ruins of her home. It was the first Nash novel, but the excitement had faded with reality. The book never talked about climbing cliffs, shitting in the wilds, or the itch of bones taking their time to heal.

"Tomorrow, Maris gets all my books," she croaked.

She returned her gaze to the *Burning Cloud Queen* and wondered if she could convince her father to give it to her. No one in town considered mechanical devices to be interesting, but Kanéko knew she could learn from the flying ship. She sighed, not sure if her father would ever let her continue working with machines, even after Damagar's death.

Kanéko settled back down on the bed and let her mind drift into a daydream of commanding the airship. After a few seconds, the ache of her ribs forced her to roll over. A moment after that, the pressure of her broken arm against her side encouraged her to shift positions again. She flopped on her back and let out a groan.

After a few minutes of shifting around, she gave up and decided to force herself out of bed. She only had her bag of Cobin's stolen clothes and a hastily packed sack from the rubble of the tower. The first shirt she pulled out of the latter came with a handful of rock dust and debris. She sighed and shook it clean. Dressing with a broken arm and wrapped ribs was one more thing she never read about in her novels. It was much harder than she thought possible, and by the time Kanéko finished pulling her boots on, she was sweating.

She swayed for a moment, and then headed down the stairs. The steps creaked under her, and she clutched the railing for balance. The house was empty around her, but she could see flashes of lanterns outside the door. She hesitated with her hand over the handle before opening it and stepping outside.

A wall of sound greeted her, but as she stood in the door, the people closest to her grew quiet. They looked at her, but she didn't see joy in their faces. Instead, she found distrust and anger in them. The silence rippled out down the street. She could feel their eyes on her.

She had seen a few posters with her image pasted to fences when they arrived. Their looks told her that they somehow blamed her.

Kanéko said softly, "I'm sorry."

When they didn't respond, she said it louder. Then a third time as loud as she could.

The villagers turned their back on her and walked away to join other parts of the celebration. As they drifted apart, one person remained behind.

Ruben watched her with intense blue eyes. He wore a brown bowler with a matching vest, trousers, and tie. His cream shirt contrasted with his hat and his eyes. "Kanéko Lurkuklan."

Kanéko's tears burned in her eyes as she watched the retreating backs. She turned back to Ruben. "Why are they upset at me? The attack on town wasn't my fault."

Ruben shrugged and stepped forward, his small feet tapping on the cobblestones. He shoved his hands into his pockets as he stopped at the foot of the stairs leading up to the mayor's home. "They blame you anyways. The same behavior was exhibited in the two years, seven months following the destruction of the first Lurkuklan Village."

She sighed. "It wasn't my fault."

"It will pass."

"Just like that?" Kanéko stepped down, holding the railing as she came down the stairs.

"Yes. Nature of society. People are hurt, frightened, and confused. They need a focal point, an anchor to remain together. You are that anchor right now and the focus of their distrust and blame. Time will fade those emotions."

She stopped at the bottom of the stairs, right next to Ruben. She sniffed and wiped the tear from her eye with the back of her good arm. "I don't think I can do that."

Ruben reached out for her. "You can do anything, Kanéko Lurkuklan. You possess no magical powers ..."

Kanéko tensed, and her hand froze inches away from Ruben's.

The vomen continued, "...but you still are the most capable of us all."

She took his hand. The familiar caress of telepathy filled her. He sent an image of Maris in a nearby house. His mind traveled upstairs and faded with the lack of shared memory. He projected that the dalpre was awake and eating slowly, a difficult concept to communicate to Kanéko since neither had seen Maris take her time eating anything.

She smiled. "She's looking for me?"

He smiled and pointed to a house three down from the mayor's. "Affirmative."

Kanéko followed him into the house and up to Maris's room.

Maris whimpered as she tried to eat. The dalpre had a stubborn look on her face as she kept on chewing. Most of her body was covered in bandages. Where the cloth didn't cover skin, dark bruises covered every inch. Maris looked up with blood-filled eyes. Her left had swollen shut, leaving her with one good eye.

"Kan?" The dalpre's voice was ragged and hoarse, like gravel encased in flesh.

Kanéko gingerly sat down on the edge of the bed. "You look horrible."

"I got hurt." Maris coughed. "And I burned out. And I can't do magic right now. And I stopped moving too fast and things broke." Another cough. "And I hurt inside."

"Of course, you silly dalpre, but you are amazing. Even with that wind thing you did to stop yourself, which I never thought of," Maris smiled at the compliment, "But, you need to stop doing this. You just—" Kanéko felt tears in her eyes again. "You just won't give up, will you?"

"You are... my friend. For pack or family, I don't know how to do anything less than everything."

Kanéko smiled and smoothed out the blanket next to her. "You know what?"

Maris coughed. "What?"

"I like you."

The dalpre's ears perked up. She surged forward and grabbed Kanéko around the waist. A whimper escaped from Maris's throat as she hugged Kanéko tight.

Kanéko squeezed Maris back with her one good arm.

Maris reached out and grabbed Ruben by the neck, yanking him into the embrace. He gasped for breath as she ground him into her breast.

"Mar-Maris?" gasped Kanéko.

Maris whimpered, "Yes?"

"Doesn't this hurt?"

"Yes, but I love you," sobbed the dalpre. "And love hurts. A lot."

About D. Moonfire

D. Moonfire is the remarkable intersection of a computer nerd and a scientist. He inherited a desire for learning, endless curiosity, and a talent for being a polymath from both of his parents. Instead of focusing on a single genre, he writes stories and novels in many different settings ranging from fantasy to science fiction. He also throws in the occasional romance or forensics murder mystery to mix things up.

In addition to having a borderline unhealthy obsession with the written word, he is also a developer who loves to code as much as he loves writing.

He lives near Cedar Rapids, Iowa with his wife, numerous pet computers, and a pair of highly mobile things of the male variety.

You can see more work by D. Moonfire at his website at https://d.moonfire.us/. His fantasy world, Fedran, can be found at https://fedran.com/.

Fedran

Fedran is a world caught on the cusp of two great ages.

For centuries, the Crystal Age shaped society through the exploration of magic. Every creature had the ability to affect the world using talents and spells. The only limitation was imagination, will, and the inescapable rules of resonance. But as society grew more civilized, magic became less reliable and weaker.

When an unexpected epiphany seemingly breaks the laws of resonance, everything changed. Artifacts no longer exploded when exposed to spells, but only if they were wrapped in cocoons of steel and brass. The humble fire rune becomes the fuel for new devices, ones powered by steam and pressure. These machines herald the birth of a new age, the Industrial Age.

Now, the powers of the old age struggle against the onslaught of new technologies and an alien way of approaching magic. Either the world will adapt or it will be washed away in the relentless march of innovation.

To explore the world of Fedran, check out https://fedran.com/. There you'll find stories, novels, character write-ups and more.

License

505

but not in any way that suggests the licensor endorses you or your use.

- NonCommercial — You may not use the material for commercial purposes.
- ShareAlike — If you remix, transform, or build upon the material, you must distribute your contributions under the same license as the original.

No additional restrictions — You may not apply legal terms or technological measures that legally restrict others from doing anything the license permits.

Preferred Attribution

The preferred attribution for this novel is:

"Flight of the Scions" by D. Moonfire is licensed under CC BY-NC-SA 4.0

In the above attribution, use the following links:

- Flight of the Scions: https://fedran.com/flight-of-the-scions/
- D. Moonfire: https://d.moonfire.us/
- CC BY-NC-SA 4.0: https://creativecommons.org/licenses/by-nc-sa/4.0/

Credits

This is a book I've been working on for over twenty years. It has gone through so many iterations and readers that I've been unable to document them all to give them proper credit. For all those people, credits and not, thank you for helping me see this book to fruition.

Alpha Readers

Aimee K.	bil J.	Bill H.	Brent M.
Cassie M.	Ciuin	Dylan B.	Evelyn C.
George D.	Greg H.	Greg T.	Kelsey L.
Kris P.	Laura W.	Mark H.	Mary J.
Nathan S.	Nick T.	Phyllis R.	Riley O.
Shannon R.	Stacie S.	Stacy	Steve W.
Tony M.	Tyree C.	Uriah	

Editors

Shannon Ryan   Sarah Chorn

Beta Readers

Marta B.   Mike K.   Randy R.   Kenneth E.

Sensitivity Readers

Teri C.

Colophon

Each chapter of this book was written as plain text files formatted with Markdown and include a YAML header at the top of each one. These files are managed in a Git repository located on https://src.mfgames.com/fedran/flight-of-the-scions/. Emacs and Atom were used as the primary environment for writing.

These individual chapters were combined together using a TypeScript-based publication framework called MfGames Writing, a set of tools for converting those files into PDF (via WeasyPrint), EPUB, and MOBI.

The cover was created using Inkscape and TypeScript. The color scheme uses eight shades of a single color and an another eight of the color's complementary. These colors are shared among all of the Kanéko novels. Likewise, the "0047-00" along the spine indicates this is the first published book ("00") with Kanéko as the main character ("0047").

The font used on the cover and interior is Source Serif Pro and Source Sans Pro in various weights and styles.